RECLAIMING
karma

ESSEX HOUSE

KHUSHI T. SAHA

To all of the oldest siblings out there:
Don't be afraid to choose your own adventure (if it involves
multiple O's, even better).

Shout out to my editor. This book only happened because you
are a rockstar.

TRIGGER WARNINGS

This book contains mentions of drug/substance abuse, overdose, alcohol use, tobacco smoking, attempted suicide (not a main character), death of a spouse, and divorce. Mental health, body positivity, and neurodiversity are represented.

EM-dashes are used at the sole discretion of the author (who can't write without them). No AI was used to write this authentic story.

Caution: This story includes a cute, funny roly-poly French bulldog who might convert you into a dog person if you aren't already.

Note: the words in *italics* are in Bangla, the language of West Bengal in India and Bangladesh in South Asia, unless otherwise noted within the story. And the terms 'Indian' and 'South Asian' are used interchangeably.

PRESENT DAY

teterboro airport, new jersey

CHAPTER 1

ᔭ

*L*ies.

Everyone told them; it's just that most people don't admit to them. And quite frankly, they could run the gamut from all-out colorful deceptions to little white fibs that stretch the truth by only a fraction.

Zayn Stavros would know. He'd told many untruths in his past, mainly as an unruly teenager trying to get out of trouble. But currently, at thirty-seven years old, he was a full-grown man entrenched in a whopper of a lie. A lie so enormous it might be more than he bargained for. Sure, he'd get what was owed to him (he'd been banking on his inheritance since he could remember), but was it worth dredging up the past—something he believed he'd buried into nonexistence? Because, here was the thing: keeping up a charade of this magnitude might require the average man to expend more energy than normal; however, for Zayn, it was becoming easier by the day. Being his former high school sweetheart's fake fiancé felt more real than anything he'd experienced in the relationship department. It felt … right. And this worried him; it shook him to his very core. This was a woman who'd surprised him by boldly initiating the farce, true. However, their history was marked by heartbreak, also of her instigation, as she'd always conducted her life according to a certain set of rules and boundaries that he could never be a part of.

Sure, that heartbreak had happened almost two decades ago, and Zayn should be over it by now, right? Frustratingly, he faced the truth; no, he wasn't over her.

"Eye on the prize."

There was a reason he chanted this whenever they had to cross a line that involved physical touch, or they shared information that only an engaged couple would and should know about each other. Whatever lines they were crossing were justified—but really, he was saying this more to himself. When all this was over ... when he had his inheritance safely in his hands, and she could focus on her life back in New York, he would know he'd protected himself from any emotional damage. This woman had a way of making him drop his defenses. It wasn't her fault directly. Their attraction rose thickly between them whenever they were so much as in the same room.

Zayn didn't do relationships for one good reason. In fact, the object of that reasoning was currently coming into view and scattering his thoughts into fragments he'd need to put back together later. But she was also the co-conspirator in his crazy scheme, so he was in a bind—a shitty, fucked-up bind—that left him hornier than a teenager out at his first strip club. But also feeling like a love-sick boy with his first major crush, who knew the feelings were unrequited.

Fuck me.

Kareena Sharma walked toward him, having left to take a

2

phone call with her daughter before they took off. They were in the private jet terminal lounge of New Jersey's Teterboro Airport. Her shoulders were back and her face forward, her deep brown eyes only on him. Her look of determination did nothing to mar her pretty face, and he was stupidly entranced.

For what it was worth, the fortitude she held was valid. His relatives also sat in the private lounge; those who remained in the New York City area after his *pappous'* (grandfather in Greek) will reading four weeks ago. There were about half a dozen of them, all waiting to board the Stavros private jet to Athens, Greece. From there, they'd take the Stavros yacht to the multi-acre estate on Naxos Island that had been in their family for generations. Though most of them had no clue he and Kareena were pretending, believing wholeheartedly in their last-minute whirlwind romance, they were curious about her. It'd all happened so suddenly—a stroke of cupid's arrow making the two former high school sweethearts meet again, falling head over heels for one another. So deeply that marriage was the only answer.

He kept his eyes fixed on her as she made her way to the seat next to him, not entirely sure he could look away. She was undoubtedly going for casual comfort in her travel wear, especially compared to some of the others in the lounge who were dressed up to the nines for the flight. Her outfit was anything but. Her body-hugging, mandarin-orange tank top-style sweater dress reached her mid-calf and was paired with thick-soled white tennis shoes. The way she wore that dress, with the fabric clinging to her rounded hips, thighs, full breasts, and plump backside, left little to the imagination. It was way sexier than it ought to be. His gaze traced the sway of the knit pattern running vertically along the material, moving in a loose

'S' shape back and forth along her body, caused by the side-to-side jut of her hips. Her brown skin had a golden sheen from the deep orange color, as if she had already soaked up the sun from the beaches they were traveling to.

She grabbed her thick, wavy black hair, pulling it forward over one shoulder, running her fingers through the locks as she sat down in the seat next to him. It was a small gesture he knew well. It spoke volumes about how nervous she was to get their story straight so as not to tip anyone off. Too much was at stake.

"I'm dressed too casually," her husky voice whispered as she leaned into him. He did his best not to lean in too close in return, just enough to keep their charade going if anyone happened to look their way, but still far enough not to get pulled in by her sensual, musky sweet scent.

"Why would you say that?" he asked in surprise, doing his best to hide the fact that he'd inhaled her fragrance and that it was like a lightning strike straight to his crotch.

"Oh my God, Zayn, you really are used to the life of luxury," she scoffed, but a teasing smile curled her pouty pink lips. "There's a separate sitting area outside the bathroom. It's super sleek, with gorgeous fresh peonies—those are my favorite." He knew this, remembering that fact from high school when he'd had a large bouquet sent to her house after she'd lost a big tennis match.

She continued, and he tried to concentrate on what she was saying. "The sweet attendant in there asked me if I needed anything. She offered to touch up my nails for me." She looked at her naked, medium-length, oval-shaped nails thoughtfully. "There's also iced mineral water available on tap with freshly sliced key lime—key lime for Pete's sake—and kiwi to flavor it with." She shook her head in amazement, and her eyes landed

4

on something across the room. "Plus, I didn't even think to pack my Louboutin stilettos for a beach wedding."

He followed her gaze across the private lounge to where his cousin, Penelope Stavros, sat with her fiancé. Pen's slim, nymph-like form was encased in a short frilly cream-colored dress, and cream red-bottomed stilettos. She giggled as she practically sat in her fiancé's lap. Brutus Henson (of the wealthy Australian mining family, not the notable American puppeteer family, though they were distant relatives), chuckled happily as the two canoodled like the young lovebirds they were.

Zayn had no idea what Louboutins were. He could only guess she referred to footwear. She'd mentioned 'stilettos' and those were recognizable, even to him, a man who didn't pay much attention to fashion. No, he was more about discussing the pros and cons of Japanese versus German excellence regarding high-quality, high-functioning kitchen knives.

"You look great," he said, speaking the truth, his eyes roving over her with approval. In fact, all eyes in the lounge were on her. She was the only Indian person amongst his Greek relatives (his Indian father was in the middle of a merger deal for the pharmaceutical company he worked for and couldn't get away for a few more days), and she was quite striking with her quiet beauty. He felt proud to call her his, even though it was a lie.

"You have to say that because you're my fiancé—fake fiancé," she said hurriedly, correcting herself quietly.

"You don't have to keep mentioning that," he teased.

Her hands clasped in her lap and fidgeted, picking at the knit material of her dress. He grabbed the hand closest to him to still her movements and placed it on his thigh, hoping to calm her. He heard her make a small noise in the back of her throat, and she inhaled loudly, more nervous than before. And shit, if he

5

wasn't enjoying the sensation of her warm hand on his thigh. It'd be so easy to move that hand a few inches toward his crotch and alleviate some of the tension that continued to grow between them since they'd begun this entire thing; hell, even before they started this charade.

She settled back in her chair and sighed, but her hand remained in his and squeezed lightly.

"What? You don't get the finest mineral water and the option for a manicure while in the restrooms at LaGuardia Airport?" he drawled, teasing her.

She chuckled, her nervousness seeming to have waned a bit. "I don't know if there'll be *toilet paper* in the stall I'm in when I'm traveling like a regular person at LaGuardia."

"That's an utter shame," he said sympathetically. "The men's room here is fully stocked with toilet paper. There's also an entire assortment of condoms on the counter; in case anyone wants to join the Mile High Club. Should I grab a few?"

She swatted his thigh, her hand still in his. "You did *not* just say that."

But she giggled, a deep snigger that ended in a snort. He chuckled in return. Snorts were her 'tell.' He'd known that since the first time he met her as a teenager. It meant she was comfortable and found the situation entirely hilarious.

"What are you two laughing about so secretly?" his cousin Pen said, having left her fiancé to come and speak with them. He'd noticed that ever since the young woman had been introduced to Kareena, she'd seemed fascinated by her.

Kareena batted her eyes at him, turning on a charm that he knew existed, but made more of an appearance lately since they'd started their fake engagement. He liked it.

6

"My fiancé said we should stock up on condoms. Apparently, there's an entire buffet of them in the men's room."

Penelope's jaw dropped before she began to laugh. Kareena laughed with her, and Zayn grinned, winking.

"Zayn, you are terrible," Pen said. "But…" She stood up, walking back to her fiancé as she said over her shoulder, "Let me make sure Brutus is fully stocked up."

"Who's going to tell her that you're joking?" Kareena's shoulders shook in giggles.

"Who says I am joking?"

Brutus's guffaw echoed across the lounge, confirming that Zayn had indeed been teasing, and Pen shot him a dirty look.

"Great. Now I'm in trouble with the bride-to-be."

"Serves you right," she said, tossing her head. She stared out the window as the rain splattered the tarmac, making it shiny black. "Do you think we'll get out on time with this rain?"

"I do. Theo is a wonder. A little November rain is nothing for him."

"Theo?"

"The captain of the Stavros private jet."

She sighed, leaning back again. "I can't believe all of this, Z. I mean, I knew you guys were stinking rich, but this is all so new to me. It's hard not to seem so wide-eyed and innocent about it all."

"Here's my advice," he said, leaning close to her again, staring into the depths of her deep brown gaze. "Enjoy it. Pretend, at least for the time being, that this is your way of life going forward." The thought of their fake engagement ending gave him a sudden sour taste in his mouth. He knew it would have to end at some point, so why did the idea make him so bitter?

Focus.

He had one goal, and he needed to remember that. She was his fiancée until the claims period for his grandfather's will ended. Then he could collect his inheritance; they could have a very loud, very public argument; and they would go their separate ways, ending the Zayn and Kareena saga for good.

He let go of her hand and stood up, shoving his hands in his pockets, suddenly irritable. He needed to move.

"I'm going for coffee. Want any?"

HIS SUDDEN MOOD changes took a little getting used to ... again. She remembered he could jump from one emotion to the next or hop from one subject to another in the blink of an eye. She'd always felt like she couldn't keep up back when they were teenagers. But now she knew the signs and symptoms; she knew he suffered from some form of ADHD, though she wasn't entirely sure if he'd been formally diagnosed or not. Her seven-year-old daughter was diagnosed as being on the spectrum, too.

She nodded up at him. Caffeine would be good right about now so she gave him her order.

He jerked his head in acquiescence, but suddenly leaned down, his warm, minty breath hovering momentarily on her cheek before he placed a kiss there. Heat spread down her neck and through her limbs, as though she'd been covered with an electric blanket. He lingered a little longer than expected and whispered, "Eye on the prize, Karma," before standing up fully and clearing his throat, saying he'd be right back.

And now the heat spread even further—heck, to the tips of

her hair—in reaction to that special nickname he'd given her in high school. He winked, and a grin tugged at his thick lips. That grin, combined with his sexy auburn beard, made her want to smile goofily and doodle hearts in her notebook. That silly little mantra was just that—silly. But it justified two virtual strangers pretending at something very intimate. It also put them in cahoots, like they were on a secret covert mission. It made her feel like a giddy teenager again, back when they had to sneak around in their secret high school relationship. She knew they had to play their parts now. They were adults, mature, and could keep their faculties. But man, it was getting harder each day, especially when he looked at her like she was indeed the object of his every desire, making his cinnamon brown eyes burn bright.

A tall shadow cast over her, and she realized why Zayn's demeanor had gone from irritated to heated so quickly. His eldest cousin—the new patriarch of the family, CEO of Stavros Titans International, and manager of the Naxos estate since their grandfather's will reading—was standing over her, a smarmy look on his hawk-like face.

She shivered, and not in a good way.

This man happened to be the only one skeptical about their sudden engagement—and to their dismay, rightly so. There was a reason he was now the head of the family. Though not the friendliest of the loud bunch, she'd heard he was cunning and sharp, with an innate ability to sniff out lies before they were even told. So, to say that she and Zayn needed to stay on the ball was an understatement. But her giddiness deflated, nonetheless, knowing that Zayn was only looking at her like that because of his cousin.

"Silas," Zayn said coolly while walking in the opposite

direction. "I'll be back. Just grabbing coffee." He gave Kareena a wary glance, but she waved him off. "Try to behave," he grumbled to his cousin before leaving.

She watched him leave, the muscles in his broad back rippling under the fitted pastel sage green waffle knit polo he wore as he ran a hand through his thick hair. The lightning bolt tattoo that went from his wrist up his forearm and circled his large bicep in sinewy veins before disappearing under his sleeve, jumped at the movement. It was difficult to take her eyes off his retreating figure, especially when his ass looked so taut and firm in his dark tan pants.

She was forced to, however, when Silas sat down in the chair Zayn had just vacated.

She took a deep breath, willing her nerves to stay calm. This was easy, she told herself. She and Zayn were helping each other out. Silas was their opposition, and she was reminded of that fact when he stared at her with a guarded look.

"Yes?" she asked.

"I'm still wondering about you two."

"How so?"

"Seems pretty convenient how the fates brought you together, right when Zayn needed an engagement to secure his inheritance."

He leaned back and crossed one leg over the other, getting comfortable. Apparently, he was going to stay there until she addressed his comment.

"Interesting to hear you speak about fate."

"Don't you believe in it?" he asked curiously. "If not, you've signed up to be a part of the wrong family. We Greeks are staunch believers in fate and destiny, at least when it's convenient for us." His laughter had no humor to it.

"I didn't say that. But the way Zayn and I recently met again —well, I couldn't plan it even if I tried. I've been thinking that it was something akin to fate, too."

That was partially true. She didn't believe in fate, or karma, or anything of that nature, though it absolutely was a human mind's last-ditch effort to understand why things happened seemingly without reason. As an MD, she had to be pragmatic when it came to finding answers, and sometimes, there just wasn't anything concrete, which was infuriating to her rational thinking. But, even she, Ms. Practical as she'd been dubbed by so many close to her, couldn't deny that the way she and Zayn had run into each other weeks ago, in the middle of Manhattan, had been complete fate. It really was as if an outside force decided it was time for them to face each other again. Why?

"Zayn is the golden child of the Stavros bunch," he said harshly.

Kareena tilted her head. "Why would you say that? He's had more than his fair share of struggles to get where he is."

She knew Zayn had denied working for the family business. He couldn't handle the monotony of an office job, numbers, or running a business he had no interest in. He was too creative, too emotional, and too inflammatory in nature to be boxed in like that.

"It seems that even though he tries to shun his Stavros side, he still gets celebrated for it, unlike the rest of us."

"Did you want to become something other than the CEO of Stavros Titans Shipping International?"

Silas scoffed. "Absolutely not. I've always known I'd be the head of this family. You can't be the oldest without knowing your place."

Kareena nodded in agreement. She, too, was the oldest, but

within her nuclear family, and had always been expected to do what she was told and watch out for her younger sister.

"But Zayn was grandfather's favorite, and I'm still confused as to why. My cousin isn't even fully Greek. Did old *Pappous* find Zayn special because of it? It seems rather odd to me."

"You can never understand the relationship between two people. They'll always share unspoken words or emotions that only the two of them can be privy to."

"Spoken like a true psychiatrist," Silas said, nodding with admiration, crossing his arms over his chest. He didn't need to know that she was on forced sabbatical for the time being, so she merely smiled cordially. "So, tell me, why would someone like you—someone attractive and intelligent, with undoubtedly a good head on her shoulders—want to be married to a wild card like my cousin? He can be difficult."

"Don't fall all over yourself with compliments for me," Zayn said sharply from behind them, neither one of them having heard him approach with two steaming cups of coffee. "You don't need to answer that, Kareena. Silas is trying to rile you up."

She took the cup he handed her while he sat in the chair on the other side of her. "No, I want to," she said and took a deep breath as the two men stared at her. "When life gives you a second chance, wouldn't it be senseless not to take it?"

She couldn't look at Zayn when she said this, worried her emotions would bleed through. Her goal when they'd first come up with this scheme was to help him in any way she could. It was the least she could do after the way she broke up with him years ago and the heartache she'd caused for both of them. But now, she wasn't so sure if the second chance was her way to make amends, or something entirely different altogether.

If anyone had told her last month that she'd keep running into her former high school sweetheart and that they would both agree to this enormous falsehood too, she'd go so far as to say she was being punked. It was like that ridiculous show of the same name on MTV that she used to watch back in high school (with Zayn, in fact), and later in college with her sorority sisters.

And now, her hotter-than-hot fake fiancé answered, his deep voice gravelly, "I agree. It was meant to be."

"Well, isn't this all just too sweet?" Silas sneered.

"Silas, what crawled up your ass? Can't you, for once, crack a smile? Your baby sister is getting married, for Christ's sake."

"I'll smile when I figure out what you two are up to. Mark my words—I'm not fooled like the rest of them."

"Spoken like a true Scooby Doo villain," Zayn drawled, sitting back in his seat and crossing an ankle over a knee. He pulled off the lid to his coffee and blew on it. And Kareena, though she knew the weight of what Silas said would destroy their plan if he uncovered a hint of their lie, couldn't help giggling at Zayn's comment. Silas was indeed being a jack-assed crank, and she was glad he got up and walked away, albeit grumbling.

She could finally relax, for the moment. She leaned back, sipping her coffee, thinking back to when and where this all started. If she hadn't been in the middle of arguing a losing conversation with a family member hellbent on getting her married off again, she might not have collided with Zayn that day in Manhattan.

But she did, and now all she had to do was protect her heart. Because the one thing she was certain of despite how much time had passed since their young, intense romance; she knew their connection was unbreakable. Frayed with age, yes, but the link was still there. He was the one person who could make her throw caution and rules to the wind in a screw you salute, not caring about anybody's opinions. But when all of this was done, when he got his inheritance and she returned to New York to her daughter and picked up her life again, she did have to care about others' opinions. And rules were absolutely non-negotiable.

4 WEEKS AGO
new york city, new york

CHAPTER 2

ר

*H*e was hallucinating.

He blinked once, then twice, rubbing his eyes with the heels of his hands. He'd just stepped off an eleven-hour flight, so he might be seeing things. Because what were the odds that on his first day back in New York in months, in a city that boasted eight million people, he'd see *her?* A vision so unexpected that it left him standing motionless while people scurried around him. A person he'd avoided for two decades.

His pulse quickened, though she was about half a block away, walking in his direction amongst teeming pedestrians, a phone pressed to her ear. She juggled an armful of … what was that, an animal? It was a bundle of tan and brown fur as she elbowed people distractedly, almost tripping over an uneven portion of the pavement.

Was it her?

She held herself with a self-assurance, even while inundated and preoccupied, which he didn't quite remember from long ago. He recalled a young woman poised on the outside but worried about what others (namely her family) would think about her true emotions, and thus her confidence always felt a little off (at least to him). But that was what he liked about her. She was strong *and* vulnerable.

This woman in question resembled her; there was no doubt. Same thick, black hair, but shorter, reaching a few inches past her shoulders, gleaming bluish black in the late fall light. Same curvy stature, though she seemed a little more filled out than before, accentuated by the snug, rosy mauve peacoat she wore with the belt cinched closely around her waist. A gust of wind flipped the hem open, and he caught a hint of skin ... smooth and brown like his favorite childhood Indian dessert, *Gulab jamun* (who was he kidding, it was still his favorite).

She passed by without noticing him, still ensconced in what seemed like a heated conversation. She shifted the fur bundle from one arm to the other, the phone now clutched between her shoulder and ear, and he turned to stare at her backside. It was plump and shapely, made even more so by that form-fitting coat. She practically strutted away in her brown heeled knee-high boots, making her cheeks jut side to side ever so slightly. His innards went fizzy, reminding him of a time when he had all sorts of access to a perfect behind like that.

A part of him wanted to race after her, but he crushed that impulse. There was no way that woman could be her, and even if she was, it was a long time ago. He'd had many years to make peace with what had happened.

She's the past. Let her stay there.

His future was why he was in New York; everything he'd been working toward was only moments away. Beating the odds in what his family believed he was capable of, despite hardships thrown at him, he'd succeeded and then some. His career as a renowned chef was nothing to sneeze at, cooking for some of the richest, most famous people around the globe, and even advising some on the restaurateur business. It carried his busy social life, with acquaintances from all walks of life meeting his needs, but not getting too close. In his personal life, he had a great best friend who always had his back, supportive parents (though he'd fought hard for that support from his dad), and a love life that lacked the love, which was how he preferred it. Beautiful women, great sex, and occasionally friendship and companionship were all he craved in the relationship department, and cooking was a gateway to that kind of non-committal connection. He'd learned early on that working with his hands in a hot kitchen, creating sensory-exploding food, made women of all ages and sizes come looking for him in another kind of sensory-exploding experience. It was a gratifying way for him to remedy the incredible stress that came with the culinary world. And it beat the chemically toxic, fucked up ways that were so easily available for that stress. He would know. He'd been an on and off user for a long time, taking energy-boosting, focus-inducing 'uppers.' Ironically, they were the same kind of drugs that would've most likely been prescribed to him if he'd had his attention issues diagnosed. But it was so much easier to get them under the table in his line of work. And the habit had only grown as his fame and career did.

He'd wised up when his best friend watched him crash, having taken tablets laced with something more than the Adderall he was used to. He'd kicked the pill-popping habit with some difficulty, but it was worth not seeing the constant worry on his close family and friends' faces. He substituted tobacco now when the stress threatened to overtake him; not the fruity vape pens, but real, old-school cigarettes. That and putting his sexual prowess to use. Was he a player? Not quite.

But he had a physical appetite that could hinder his creativity if left unsatisfied, and he had no problem getting women into bed. The culinary world was glittery and jagged; fast and hard, but beautifully creative, and he thrived in it. Things were good— better than good, he had to admit. And within the next hour, things were only going to get better.

He'd returned just that morning after an incredible summer at sea cooking for a Greek tycoon. It'd been more like vacationing on the Mediterranean than work, where he was treated like the celebrity chef he was, cooking luxurious food and socializing openly with the guests on the enormous yacht. Getting paid to party *and* cook no-expenses-spared meals, all while enjoying the scenery and the waters of a place he'd always called home? Fuck, yes. And it was much needed. He'd craved the break after the aforementioned life-threatening pill disaster and been asked to distance himself from the trendy new restaurant he'd been moonlighting as head chef. Bad press was never a good thing for an establishment vying for its first Michelin star. So he'd been extremely fortunate to hear through the rumor mill that the Greek was hiring a chef for his boat.

Now, he was ready to get back into the culinary world, but on his own terms. No more working for people, making someone else's dreams come true. His time had finally come. The family meeting at the Stavros Titans Shipping International offices in Manhattan would be a turning point for him and the next generation. After months stalled in probate, his grandfather's will had been settled. Everyone was coming from everywhere to hear what old *pappous*, the helm of the empire for more than fifty years, had left for them. But Zayn already knew what his grandfather had in mind for him. He practically danced on a cloud made of the finest spun sugar knowing that the old taverna on their family estate in Greece would finally be his. A place he could reopen with more fanfare than the dusty old bar it'd become. It had all the bones for a modern, charming eatery, and the location tucked in a cliffside on a beach on Naxos couldn't be beat. It was accessible from both the water and town, making it perfect for locals and tourists alike.

His cousins might have sneered at the thought of reviving the place. They were only concerned about the shipping empire portion of the family business; the one that put the Stavros name on the map back when Napoleon ruled with his tiny iron fist. But to Zayn, the taverna was all he cared about. He'd never been like his other cousins. They'd treated him like their own, sure, but there were hints of derision. He was half Greek after all— and thus never fully one of them. On top of that, he'd been the only grandchild who still found it fascinating to visit the taverna and explore the adjacent olive grove with their deteriorating grandfather well into manhood. Learning about what the soil could produce, and the people who'd worked on it for generations, riveted him. And it wasn't just to "humor his *pappous*" as everyone else mocked. Zayn had never been great at school; he'd always known university wasn't for him, and thus, held no interest in Stavros Titans Shipping International. But this part of the family empire, the tiny portion that didn't even make a dent in the family wealth, was what held his interest. All of the other nineteen cousins had grown out of what they described as childlike mischief, fun, and games, having also explored the lands with their grandfather when smaller. But, as soon as they held their freshly signed university diplomas, they were ushered into the global shipping behemoth, as so many others had before them. But that wasn't Zayn's destiny.

Zayn took what should've been one last look at the woman's retreating figure and experienced a longing that tugged at him. He swore angrily under his breath. What was wrong with him? She was nobody to him. But instead of continuing in the opposite direction, something in his gut told him to follow her, and good thing, too. She walked rapidly, even in her heels, and wasn't paying attention to the crosswalk signal, which now blinked a bright orange hand-shaped signal.

He sped up, taking longer strides, which wasn't the problem. He was tall, well over six feet, and could catch up to her in no time. It was just that there were so many damn people out on this blustery October day, and he found himself dodging and sidling bodies.

He'd also noticed in alarm that a huge truck was barreling down the avenue, just as she stepped into the street. It blared out its angry, deep horn that should've resonated with everyone, but no one noticed. New York City in the morning rush hour was its own urgent beast, as throngs of people hurried to beat the clock, hitting the pavement with speed and agility. The truck he noticed, as he waded through pedestrians, wasn't slowing down either; it didn't have time to, and it was headed straight for her.

Zayn shoved his way through the crowd, garnering heated words and annoyed looks as he bumped shoulders and flailing limbs.

"Sorry," he said impatiently, "Excuse me!"

He slid past a nanny pushing an expensive stroller with a wailing toddler in hand, narrowly missing a spilled hot chocolate mess underfoot. He burst through a group of slower-than-sea-turtles-nesting-on-the-beach tourists and knocked into their tour guide, walking backwards in front of them with an open umbrella in hand, shouting "to me" repeatedly.

"Apologies," he grumbled, now close enough to yell a warning at the woman.

"Kareena!" he shouted, cupping his hands around his mouth, now sprinting to the intersection. *"Kareena Sharma!"*

She didn't hear him, or maybe he really was mistaken and it wasn't her. Infuriatingly, he wondered why no one waiting on the curb she had just stepped off of was doing anything. But of course, everyone's eyes were glued to their own devices. Zayn hated being attached to his phone, but admittedly, social media had been lucrative lately when he needed it the most, so he couldn't blame people's behavior. Though a modicum of self-awareness in a bustling, over-crowded city never hurt anyone, did it? In this situation, it could be life-saving.

He jostled past those on the edge of the curb and raced straight to the woman heading obliviously into danger. With a force that took his breath away, he moved her forward a few feet. A low "oof" emanated from her, but all he felt was her soft, warm body mold to his as they careened together, flying and finally hitting the ground with a thud.

They rolled and came to a halt as they reached the curb on the other side just as the Stavros Titans Shipping International truck charged loudly past them, gears changing in an awful groan.

Oh, the fucking irony.

The guy in the passenger seat hung out of the rolled-down window and yelled, "Watch where you're going!"

"What the *hell*!?" The woman's shocked yelp was muffled by thick black hair blanketing most of her face as she lay in his arms.

And fuck, it *was* her, and she felt familiar … good-familiar.

Dammit!

It had been a shock to his system to see her again, but now, being inches away from her face, her mouth, her body under his, the rush of forgotten emotions collided inside him like a wild bird rattling inside a cage. The smell of her herbal sweetness, once a distant memory, was now dragged into the present. The strength of it was almost foreign, but it was as if he breathed the sweetest, purest form of oxygen known to man.

Fucking hell.

He jerkily pulled away, rising quickly to his feet, as he brushed the dirt off his grey slacks. His grey suit jacket was streaked with grime. But he only had concern for her, though a part of him didn't want to. He watched her get her bearings, a tangle of limbs, whatever the hell the fur bundle was (it wasn't alive, was it?), and a work bag, while she pushed the hair from her face.

God, she was a sight for sore eyes, even in her rumpled state.

Her deep-rose peacoat, a silky blend of wool and possibly cashmere by the looks of it (and the momentary buttery soft feel of it under his palms), was now ripped at the hem and smeared with dirt, too.

"Oh, my God!" she said in disbelief, as she finally looked up at him with those familiar, expressive dark brown eyes; the ones that had haunted his dreams regularly so long ago, until he'd finally gotten over her.

He didn't utter a word. But he reached a hand down to help her stand as she continued to struggle, picking up wayward items that had flown from her bag, still clutching whatever mongrel was in her arms.

The air caught in his throat as their fingers touched. Why did it feel like he was suffocating in her presence?

He pulled away swiftly while she fumbled to close and smooth down the bottom half of her coat over her thighs. She shouldered her bag and juggled the fur while her eyes darted around the pavement, clearly looking for something.

"Here, let me," he offered, taking the bulky fur ball from her.

Thankfully, it wasn't alive and appeared to be a sort of outfit or costume.

"There it is," she said in irritation, bending down to scoop up her phone, which now had a crack going down the screen. The person on the other end was talking a mile a minute, loudly, as if they hadn't even noticed their listener had survived a near-death experience.

She put a finger up to him and the phone to her ear. She stepped onto the curb, and he followed, bundle in hand, watching her.

"I said no. Why can't you understand? Let me—" She listened for a few seconds. "But, just let me—" She paused, listening again. "I—"

Her face paled, and her countenance turned placid, while her eyes squeezed shut. She turned away from him with hunched shoulders.

Zayn remembered that expression. He couldn't help the chuckle that escaped him, making her glance over her shoulder with a glare. Now, he outright laughed. She'd never changed. Whoever was on the other end was asking her to do something she didn't want to do, but she'd do it because she'd always been that person—the one who bent to others' wishes (back in high school, it was her parents), sacrificing her own wants.

Same old Kareena Sharma. He shook his head in disbelief.

She hung up and turned to him, a frown on her face before it transformed into a bemused grin. He smiled back, because that's what this girl could always do to him—this woman. She was now a full-grown woman, exceptionally striking with a heart-shaped face that had matured, yet still retained the youthful roundness in her cheeks. Her lips were the same dusky pink, full and plump, and still reminded him of the soft, powdery skin of the sugar figs that grew all over his family's estate in Greece.

"Z, is it *really* you?" she uttered in that husky voice of hers.

He laughed, realizing that had been his exact reaction to her apparition only moments before.

She took a hesitant step forward, a hand outstretched as if to test his realness. Her fingers met his abs, and instinctively, his muscles flexed under them. The warmth penetrated the fine cotton of his white button-down shirt, through his undershirt to his skin, and he unconsciously leaned in.

Their eyes locked, and he heard an almost inaudible "whoa" emanate from under her breath. He nearly wrapped his arms around her. Thank goodness he caught himself. Instead, he stepped back, breaking the connection.

Here was the thing: one could get past teenage angst. It'd been almost twenty years, for fuck's sake. So how the hell, after all this time, did the reminder of what she did—dumping him unceremoniously before leaving to pursue her life without him at Columbia University—still have the capacity to rear its ugly head? Immediately his mood sobered; the fizzy, heady sensation from before fell flat. That feeling of never being good enough after it all went down, something he hadn't felt in ages, something he'd combatted for years after they parted, penetrated him.

"Yeah," he finally murmured more harshly than he expected, standing up taller and looking down at her coolly. "In the flesh."

CHAPTER 3

❧

"*I* ... uh," Kareena stuttered, her heart flipping over inside her chest.

She couldn't believe she was staring up at Zayn Stavros, her high school sweetheart. The boy she'd regretfully had to break up with the summer before freshman year at college. The boy she'd pined for her entire first year at Columbia University, and then some.

He looked ... amazing.

But the person standing in front of her wasn't the teen she remembered. Here was a full-grown man, tall like she recalled, with the same dark copper curls, laced with burnished highlights, and beautiful, deeply tanned skin. She noticed slight freckles smattering his nose and a light growth of beard on his sculpted face. She'd never loved facial hair, but on him, good golly, it only complemented his handsomeness and ignited a nervousness that felt all at once new, but familiar, because she hadn't experienced it in forever.

She gulped, staring up into his cinnamon brown eyes, now with slight creases around them, trying to assess his mood. It wasn't lost on her that he'd pulled away so that she couldn't continue to feel that real warmth of his. She was in the business of human behavior; she'd know. But her hand itched to feel his solidness under her palm anyway.

He wore a simple long-sleeved white button-down with grey slacks and a matching suit jacket, which was rumpled now. A large dark stain smeared the front and onto part of his white shirt, and yet, she felt faint. Her heart beat rapidly, like a moth transfixed, its wings fluttering to a flame, and possibly its own demise.

Get a hold of yourself, Kara.

She smoothed her hair as she took a deep breath. He'd been upset with her the last time they'd seen each other. She'd been upset then, too, but she knew it was the right thing for both of them. They'd been in two different places, with her Pre-Med track and his uncertainty about his future. Plus, her parents would've never in a million years approved of her dating a guy like him. And she'd been right, because when they found out, she'd been forced to end things with him.

But here and there, she'd caught a few tidbits about his successes, glad to know he was doing well. The gossip grapevine in their Indian community was long and extensive, and a lot of times, truths were accompanied by overelaborations. But if she listened closely, she could pick out the facts.

She'd learned about his culinary accolades from one aunty, known as the community matchmaker, a legit 'auntypreuner' who made it her business (literally) to know the happenings of everyone. Thus, Kareena could believe there was some truth to those tidbits about Zayn. This had partially relieved her. He'd always been talented in the kitchen, even as a teenager, and she was proud he'd found his way.

He'd travelled the globe, she'd overheard, while visiting her parents for *cha* (tea) and snacks one afternoon out in Connecticut. She'd brought her daughter, Tamannah, with her, just a toddler then, who'd recently learned to walk, which kept her distracted. But when his name came up in casual conversation, Kareena had been all ears. They said he'd been cooking for a huge American star and his famous attorney wife at their Italian villa in Lake Como. Everyone loved Zayn's food, and the star's attorney wife raved that he was an unconventional gastronomic genius.

At a high school reunion for Greenwich Preparatory Academy, the private school they'd both attended and graduated from, she learned more from his former swim teammates. He'd rubbed shoulders with one of India's wealthiest families and had a hand in curating their award-winning menu in Mumbai. The conversation veered toward his half-Greek lineage and how his hobnobbing with the rich and famous made sense since he came from a well-known shipping family. She'd walked away from that discussion after they tapped into his love life and who he was sleeping with, because apparently, it was titillating as hell, turning the grown men into the stupid, horny high school boys she remembered.

Was all of it the *real* truth? She had no idea. She did her best to never look him up. She didn't want to know. But she believed the good stuff and tried to ignore everything else.

What she knew now, though, was that the man himself stood in front of her, in the real, live flesh, after being absent from her life for over a decade. What had it been, seventeen or eighteen years now? Looking at him only made it feel like seventeen or eighteen minutes. The nearly tangible pull to him, the profound attraction she felt for him, and ALL the bottled-up emotions came rushing back, as if they were teenagers again. Her cheeks heated up, and she knew they were as pink as her coat.

She cleared her throat. "Zayn. My God, it's been forever," she finally said, shaking her head in disbelief, after telling herself to get real. They'd been kids, and that was ages ago.

"Eighteen years and..." He paused, looking up at the pale, silvery sky. "Three months. But who's counting?" he said with that smooth, deep baritone of his, staring coolly down at her. And yet, even with the biting tone, his voice reminded her of a happier, simpler time; a warm, comforting blanket that could keep her worries at bay.

But wait a minute, he was keeping track?

All of a sudden, a yearning so deep it almost put a chokehold on her materialized and she had to yank herself back to reality.

"Your dad, huh?" he asked curiously, gesturing to the phone in her hand with a raised brow.

She shook her head.

"My dad's oldest brother. The 'patriarch' of our family." She air-quoted, doing her best not to roll her eyes. Her father was on bed rest—a recent development—and had passed on the responsibility of his eldest daughter to his brother. Now, her uncle was happily butting in, trying to make family decisions where he could, *and* he didn't even live in the US.

He snorted and said with scorn, "Only your family can get you to make *that* face, and hold your undivided attention, even when a truck is coming straight at you."

She flinched at his tone more than at his words. Was he ... was he still mad about everything? Impossible. He was just different now, more mature, less relaxed, judging by his solid stance and the stiffness of his wide shoulders. She watched a muscle tick very slightly along his cheekbone, wondering what he was thinking. She couldn't read him like she used to, but that made sense; she didn't know him anymore.

But hold up, *what freaking face was he talking about?*

"Thank you for ... pushing me out of the way. You basically saved me," she squeaked in embarrassment before clearing her throat. "Zayn, I owe you—"

"You don't owe me anything, Kareena." His tone was clipped.

Did he have to sound so sexy even when he was being anything but friendly?

And she didn't know why, but the words tumbled out of her anyway. "Well, I'm totally out of it, hence walking into oncoming traffic." She waved a hand behind her at the street. At his bored expression, instead of shutting up, the words continued to spill out. "Everyone is trying to marry me off again. But, guess what? I'm not having it a second time. The list of biodatas they sent me is enough to drive anyone insane, and the candidates, just ... no." She shook her head vehemently and couldn't help the disgust in her tone.

Why did she feel like she had to explain all of this to him? He obviously couldn't care less, based on his bland expression.

"Right," he finally said skeptically, as his biceps tensed and bulged under the smooth fabric of his suit jacket. She noticed that he still held the now completely crumpled bundle of fur that was to be part of her daughter's Halloween costume.

"Here, let me take that from you," she said, feeling silly.

He nodded, handing it over, and she couldn't take her eyes off the breadth of his chest and the thick muscles of his arms. His biceps curled, stretching the fine twill of his jacket sleeves.

"What exactly is that?" he asked.

When had he bulked up so much? She remembered a tall, solid, and extremely good-looking teen, but with a leaner swimmer's physique. He was hot then, but now he was in full-on hunk territory.

"What?" she asked, now staring at the hint of curly auburn chest hair that the first undone button of his shirt revealed. Her eyes caught the flash of a thick gold chain around his neck, distracting her. It was like she couldn't get enough of every detail of him, as if he would disappear all over again.

"The hairball. What is it?" he asked, a smirk curling those thick lips of his.

"This?" She shook out the jumble of fabric for him to see. "It's half of my kid's Halloween costume."

Technically, it was half of a lion's costume, the one that was used in last year's *Wizard of Oz* play, where Tamannah had been a munchkin. She'd borrowed it from the school. Kareena's idea was to pair it with cute dog ears she'd found at a pop-up Halloween shop and paint her daughter's face to achieve the look of a French bulldog—specifically, their pet Frenchy's mama.

The silence that spread between them was so loud she forgot they were standing on a busy street corner. She glanced up at him, but his eyes were only on the costume in her hands, and if she wasn't mistaken, she saw a thoughtfulness pass across his features, making him frown.

"So ... what's going on with your father?"

It took her a minute to register the change in topic. He's always been like that, his mind shifting from one subject to the next quickly, making her feel like a slowpoke.

"Heart trouble. He just had a stent put in."

Zayn's eyes widened in surprise. "The good Dr. Sanjay

Sharma, leading cardiologist at Greenwich General, had a heart attack?"

She huffed, stupid tears coming to her eyes. She would not let them fall; she chanted to herself. The whole thing with her father was aggravating. Her *abba* knew what he was supposed to do to ensure he didn't end up like one of his patients. But ... stress was a key factor that he didn't have a handle on yet, and genetics were impossible to change. He'd finally succumbed to seeking a nutritionist's help along with the daily power walk he and her *amma* took after dinner. But getting him to give up his beloved *mishti* (Indian sweets) and anything fried had been harder than anyone expected. Her next goal was to get him to seek therapy. Not that he had oodles of problems in their cushy Greenwich community, but he could always seek someone outside his family to talk to and find ways to manage stress and anxiety—and maybe not push some of that stress and anxiety onto her.

"It wasn't a full-on heart attack. They found a blockage, that's all." She sniffed back her tears and shrugged as though it was all tidy and taken care of, but inside, she was terrified. The thought of losing her beloved father, one of her biggest supporters in life, was something she wasn't sure she could handle, not after already losing her husband.

Somehow, Zayn seemed to sense her fear and nodded, continuing with a softness that belied his tense stature. "I'm sure he'll be fine." He paused. "And, I'm so sorry about your husband."

"Thank you," she said quietly. Of course, he would know about that. Though he wasn't an active part of their South Asian community anymore, his father and her father still spoke, having grown up together in India.

It'd been two years since her husband, Arjun, had died in a sudden car crash, but her heart was still tender. They'd eventually found something akin to love in their arranged marriage, but it had veered more toward a really good partnership. He'd turned out to be the best friend she could ever have, one who saw her struggles within her nuclear family dynamics and understood the older child pressures (he was the oldest in his family, too). And he'd been an incredible father to their daughter.

"Listen," he continued. "Are you injured in any way?" He inspected her closely from head to toe, and she flushed even hotter under his scrutiny.

"I'm fine. Just a little banged up, but nothing I won't survive."

They both glanced down at her coat, the ripped hem, and the dark grease smudges. She noticed a bloody gash that had already stopped bleeding right above her knee. "Sheesh, Z, every time we meet, I get some kind of leg injury. Do I need to send you a doctor's bill?" She chuckled as she thought of how they'd first met eons ago. He'd been after a wayward volleyball that had smacked her hard in the thigh.

He cleared his throat. "Yeah, well, consider me saving you my duty and restitution. It was a Stavros moving truck." He shook his head in disbelief, and she laughed.

"You're kidding!"

"I wish I were," he said wryly. "Good thing I was around … even if you might've deserved it, just a little."

Her gaze flew up to his, and though he wasn't smiling, his eyes danced with humor.

Something inside her eased, and she relaxed just a little. This was what she remembered about their relationship as teenagers. It could be easy. They got each other, and she could be herself around him. She felt a slight inkling of that now, and she realized she wanted to talk more with him. Considering the last two years she'd had, it might be nice to catch up with someone from her past.

"Hey, listen." She shifted the costume awkwardly in her arms, finally resting her chin into the rough material. "I have to drop this off first. But … do you want to grab coffee and catch up? It's been so long—"

He shook his head, stopping her. "I'm late for a meeting as is." He looked at his watch before running a big hand through his thick curls, pushing them back from his wide forehead.

And now she felt like an idiot. It was only she who felt the hint of old camaraderie between them, as if they were still innocent teens. For a woman in her thirties, married, a mother, and now a widow, she might have foolishly held onto girlish ideals about them, she realized. Man, she needed to grow up.

"It was great seeing you, Kareena." He nodded, giving her another once-over with those beautiful cinnamon-colored eyes, now making something flutter in her belly which she couldn't remember the last time she'd felt. "I hope the second marriage thing doesn't work out, for your sake." He smirked with that devilish charm she remembered.

"Same." She laughed self-consciously, looking anywhere but at him. Why was this the story of her life whenever she was around him? "I'm dodging family members, uncles, and aunties left and right. It's exhausting." She shifted back and forth on her feet under his watchful gaze. "I wish I could just bury myself in a hole and disappear sometimes. But … I can't. Duty calls."

He remained silent, and she finally met his gaze again. And

now she saw that his countenance had softened, before it went back to expressionless.

"Speaking of duty ..." He partially turned in the direction she'd just come from. "I have to go. Good luck with everything, Kareena."

He walked back across the street, the little white figure of the crosswalk sign indicating it was safe to go. He was taller than everyone else, his back broad, his stride confident, his ass—

Stop it, Kara.

She looked away and sighed. This was surprising, but also a good thing. Seeing him after so many years was like seeing a ghost, but now she didn't have to secretly wonder anymore about her lost teenage sweetheart—the angry young man she'd had to abandon so long ago. She'd seen for herself that he looked better than great and seemed to be doing fine, more than fine. She could release whatever angst she'd been hanging onto and all those hidden girlish dreams.

So, why did it feel like she'd lose a part of herself if she did?

CHAPTER 4

8

*T*he skyscraper loomed overhead, a shiny, haloed beacon of hope for a future he was eager to begin. Stavros Titans Shipping International took up two entire floors of the massive building on Sixth Avenue, and the rumor was they'd be expanding to another.

But a deep brown gaze, like big wounded doe eyes, kept appearing before him, dimming what momentum he had to get to the will reading. He couldn't stop seeing Kareena, rumpled and disheveled in her torn coat, juggling her belongings, her near-death experience still a thick moment hovering between them, while she casually mentioned a second arranged marriage.

An uncomfortable feeling, a fiery one, seared through him at the thought of her being married again to someone else. He'd thought he'd extinguished any form of that feeling long ago.

He had to admit, married life and having a kid hadn't put a dent in her appearance. She was as pretty as he recalled—except if he was being honest with himself, she was even more beautiful—and just as sweet and a little sassy; all attributes that had disarmed him the first time. She *was* the same old Kareena Sharma, and the good parts still remained, too.

Eighteen years and three months should've been enough time for him to forget most things about her. But no, his traitorous memory had carved her into his brain. Her expressive eyes, ones he could read like a book, shifted from shock to confusion, then nervousness, and settled on openness. He wasn't prepared for that, and yet, it felt right. When she'd mentioned the first time they met so long ago, he'd experienced the same comfortable camaraderie they'd shared before they started dating senior year of high school. And as much as he tried to keep it under lock and key, the echoes of long-ago pains had resurfaced in his chest. She was the one who got away—or more accurately, walked away.

The mention of a possible second arranged marriage had stunned him, and the idea of her being a mother perplexed him. Begrudgingly, he experienced a moment of pity that she was being pushed to look into another arranged marriage, which was ridiculous. He shouldn't care what path she led. She was the one who chose gratifying others above herself, though interestingly, she seemed less malleable by her family than before. He truly hoped she did get out of it, *if* she was being serious.

But he'd be completely lying to himself if he said it didn't pain him to know that she'd had a child with another man. Was it a boy or a girl? Did they look like her or like her deceased other half?

But why the hell was he wasting time on speculations? She'd ripped his young heart out and tossed it in a blender. Yes, he'd been pissed early on, depressed, restless even for years after her. They'd made plans for a future together, and nineteen-year-old Zayn believed them. She'd been like a lifeline at a time when he had no idea what his future would hold, and he'd felt close to hopeless without her calming presence in his life.

"Teenage love never lasts."

He'd heard that more times than he could count from anyone who thought he wanted to hear it, until he finally believed it, and moved on. Thankfully so, or he wouldn't be where he was today. And though he'd had to struggle with his parents (namely, his father) for what he wanted, he'd used his anger and frustration at not getting what he thought his tender nineteen-year-old heart wanted as fuel to prove to everyone that he could succeed.

In the beginning, his father, Kiran Roy, didn't understand Zayn's career choice. Why would his son, a teen who'd had trouble focusing in school to the point where he'd had to repeat his senior year, decide to pursue something as difficult as the culinary arts? There was no clear-cut career path, like so many other occupations the older man was familiar with. He'd even argued that since his son had such a temper at times, maybe he might go into law like his best friend and channel that passion into becoming a beast in the courtroom.

What Kiran didn't understand was that Zayn needed to carve out his future, not ride on the coattails of others. He needed that struggle to prove to himself that he was not only good enough, but better than others might perceive him to be.

But Kiran was just as stubborn as his son. As the Chief Negotiating Officer for Sun Pharma, an Indian-based global pharmaceutical company, he'd thrown his weight around, landing Zayn an internship with his company.

That both started and ended terribly.

Zayn went in begrudgingly on the first day, took one look at the small cubicle he'd been assigned, and stormed out of the building. There was no way he was going to spend his time crunching numbers, filing contracts, or whatever the hell he was being required to do that summer, all while wearing a monkey suit and tie. It just wasn't him.

His mother, Sofia Stavros-Roy, was the one who noticed his interest in food, as she was home more than her husband, who travelled incessantly on business. She understood that her son's interests needed to be something his brain could handle; something that could channel his restless energy. He'd been a great swimmer in high school, leading his team to victory at state competitions. But Zayn had lost his drive for competitive swimming once school ended.

Her keen eye noticed the tinkering around he did in their home kitchen, coming up with all sorts of food combinations, like the unexpectedly delicious chocolate hazelnut spread on toast with a dollop of bright lemon curd he'd made himself. And sometimes major fails, like his first attempt at eggplant curry on dough for a pizza-like snack. It wasn't so much the flavors that impressed her, but his continuous fiddling with ingredients to get the tastes right. She urged him to assist their home chef in the kitchen, whether in their vegetable garden or with meal prepping. Lo-and-behold, his demeanor went from restless to focused. Sudden outbursts stopped, indicating he'd been frustrated with a lack of direction.

As a young man himself, Zayn's father had defied his own arranged marriage, disappointing his family by marrying Zayn's mother—the fiery flight attendant he kept meeting on his international flights. His parent's had their own challenges along the way ... like when *her* family found out about their shotgun wedding and her pregnancy. Shocked and upset as they'd had plans for Sofia, they'd punished them. Their child would only be allowed access to the Stavros' wealth if they dropped the "Roy" portion of his last name. Kiran argued but acquiesced after understanding the weight the Stavros name carried. What mattered more to him was making a family with the person he loved.

So, with much convincing, namely using their love marriage as the basis of her argument, Zayn's mother convinced Kiran that Zayn's love of cooking was something he needed to nurture. Though the comparison was not exactly apples to apples, Kiran understood. Deep down, though challenges would arise, he knew his son could do this if he wanted it enough. Yes, it was a fast-paced, pressure-cooker of an environment and it seemed counterintuitive to their son's overactive mind, but even he had to admit their son was good at it.

After receiving his father's approval and successfully graduating from the International Culinary Institute of Switzerland, Zayn took any job he could pack into his schedule. From washing dishes and taking out garbage, to working as a line cook. No task was too menial to prove himself worthy of the vocation. From Paris to Mexico City, he took opportunities that gave him both experience and exposure, accepting low-paying positions or ones that didn't pay at all in exchange for room and board. The opportunities to work with influential culinary geniuses had him honing his skills and talent further, only opening more doors for him. He was known as the bright new talent to watch for, with a knack for flavors that pushed the boundaries.

Now, with an endless list of experiences under his belt, he was at that point in his career where he was ready to make a go of it himself. He didn't care what people thought about him anymore. The notion that just one little run-in with Kareena

Sharma could bring back even a fraction of his old "I'm not good enough" self-doubt had him laughably irritated.

"Scared to go in?"

The familiar dry tone of his best friend, Aariv Abbas, corporate lawyer extraordinaire, snapped him out of his reverie. His good mood returned.

"Well, aren't you a sight for sore eyes, *Cuz*?" he drawled, pushing thoughts of big brown eyes out of his mind. He turned to take a good look at his friend. Though Aariv wasn't his true-blood cousin, they were close enough to be related.

He wanted his best friend there to hear the will reading, and then they could go grab lunch and celebrate. He hadn't seen him in months.

He looked the other man up and down, surprised that in the middle of the work week, he wasn't in his usual stiff suit. Instead, he was casual in a relaxed blue button-down, no tie, and simple khaki chinos, with a brown leather bomber jacket.

"Thanks for finally showing up," Zayn joked.

"Fuck off," Aariv grunted, as they shook hands before they met in a bro hug, patting each other heartily on the back. "You look good." His friend assessed him closely, a hint of concern making him frown. "And more importantly, you're not dead."

Zayn could only be humbled by this comment. This man had saved his life, having found him half unconscious in a pool of his own vomit, foaming at the mouth. Fortunately, Aariv had come in search of him when he missed their usual Sunday pick-up game. Zayn had popped a few pills that morning (the same ones they later learned were laced with something more lethal than just an energy boost) in preparation for a long hustle later that day. Thank God for doling out spare keys to friends and family—a running joke they'd had before, but completely necessary.

"Just inside," Zayn said sardonically. At Aariv's raised brow, he started laughing. "A joke, *Cuz*. You remember jokes, right?"

"Not something to joke about, Man." Aariv adjusted his glasses. "You're not using anymore, are you?"

Zayn took a deep breath, understanding that his best friend needed to grill him like this to feel reassured. It was the lawyer in him, but also the 'good son' responsibility that was ingrained to make sure those around him were all right.

"Clean as a whistle, unless you count these." He pulled out a crumpled pack of cigarettes from his pants pocket, holding them up for his friend to see.

"An improvement, but still not good for you."

"One step at a time, *amigo*," he said, trying not to sound annoyed. His friend meant well.

"How was it cooking for the tycoon on his boat?" Aariv asked, thankfully changing the subject.

"Exactly what I needed. Excellent food, access to unlimited fresh seafood and ingredients, fuck ton of top shelf alcohol, and the ladies ... there was this one estranged from her husband and ready for anything—"

Aariv put a hand up, stopping him.

"I don't need the details of your sex life, but glad you had a good time. How will this help your career going forward?"

"Have you been talking to my father, Aari? What, no friends your own age?"

At this, his friend cracked a small smile. "Just curious, and trying to help."

"Listen, the rich Greek knows people, just like my family

43

does. This new restaurant is going to launch itself," he said confidently.

Aariv nodded, grinning. "Excellent. I can't wait to see what you do."

"Now it's my turn for the third degree. What's going on here?" He waved a hand at his friend's non-formal workwear. "Where's your attorney's get-up?"

Aariv cupped the back of his neck, grinning. "I took a personal day. The partners insisted. I have so many unused."

Was that a sheepish look on his friend's usual serious face?

Then it dawned on him, and he couldn't be more thrilled for Aariv. And per usual, he couldn't resist teasing, "So, what did you do with the big *lathi* (stick) she got you to pull out of your ass?"

"Jesus! Could you be any more juvenile?" The other man half-snarled, but the loopy smile spreading across his bearded face overshadowed his usual grumpiness.

"You know I can," Zayn quipped. He was the polar opposite of his best friend—had been since secondary school back in India. But it was why they worked.

"I knew I liked Chrissy. She's the best thing to happen to you. And look at you, finally putting work on the back burner. She's a fucking saint."

Aariv looked away, cracking a wicked smile and rubbing his chin. "She's hardly that."

Zayn's jaw dropped. Had the world gone mad? First, he ran into Kareena Sharma, a person he thought he'd never encounter again, and one whom he refused to admit he had any curiosity about. Now, Aariv was cracking jokes about what sounded like a fuck-tastic sex life when usually he was more discreet.

"I'm going to ask her to marry me," his friend stated seriously.

And if the day couldn't get any weirder, Zayn might be convinced he'd stepped off the plane into an alternate universe.

"Seriously? That's fucking great!" He gave his friend another hug, one so big and tight that he lifted the other man off the ground with zeal. "I'm so happy for you, Cuz."

His best friend had struggled with his parents about marriage and their expectations. However, Aariv had *reluctantly* fallen in love with a Russian-American who was sunnier than the workaholic, cloudy grump Aariv.

"I guess miracles *do* happen," he said, dropping his friend back onto the sidewalk.

"Okay, Z. Enough." Aariv smoothed his shirt, shutting down any further conversation about his personal life. Nothing new to Zayn. He'd get more details as Aariv became more comfortable with his decision.

The other man finally noticed Zayn's dirt-smudged clothes. "That hardly seems appropriate for a will reading. What the hell happened? Did you get run down by a truck?"

"Something like that. You'll never believe it." He shook his head, not ready to go into that territory just yet. Then he'd have to admit to himself how much seeing Kareena again had affected him. "A truck *was* involved—but more later. We should go inside." He gestured toward the building.

His friend nodded curtly. "What exactly do you need me here for, by the way? Worried, your grandfather cut you out of his will? Or that a grubby cousin might fight you for your dusty bar?"

"Taverna," he corrected. "No, nothing like that. No one wants that tired, old place but me. Your offices were nearby, and

I thought you'd want to say hello to my mother and sit in on the will reading. You know, make sure everything is right and tight." It never hurt to have a high-powered attorney as a friend when legal matters were involved. "Then we can grab lunch and celebrate my inheritance, and your impending engagement."

"I haven't asked her yet." Aariv reminded him. "And I do enjoy a good will reading," he said cynically.

"I didn't say you got a boner from them, but yeah, Aari. You're a sucker for this kind of shit. Petty family members, possibly duking it out over pennies. Loads of money siphoned down to the next generation."

"Bring on the drama."

Zayn wasn't sure if Aariv was joking or not. The man seemed more lighthearted. Not that he was complaining, but something, or someone more like it, had changed him.

"It should be straightforward, but you never know with the Stavros side of my family." He waved a hand in the air, as if to shoo some of the family's dramatics from the vicinity. With a family as old as his and wealth that most people couldn't even dream of, it wasn't surprising that internal squabbles occurred, especially when there was a "changing of the guard."

"And *then* we can go eat," Zayn continued. "I could inhale two dozen fresh oysters and a rare, juicy steak with plump shrimp and crispy salty fries. Oh, and that famous garlic aioli they have at the Grand Central Oyster Bar—we need tons of that shit." He clapped his hands and rubbed them together in anticipation, almost tasting the chilled, briny, sweet meat and salty, pungent sauce.

"You make food sound like porn."

"It can be. Food porn is my thing."

"Are we talking about your secret sexy chef identity, or

actual food?" Aariv asked wryly as they made their way to the attendant and showed their IDs.

Aariv was the only one, outside of his hired Social Media Manager, Shelly, who knew about his online alter ego. *Sinful in the Kitchen* was a side gig, a complete fluke, but it helped rake in money when he was in between jobs. It was surprisingly enjoyable and edgy, allowing him to display skillful knife tricks while making food, shirtless. He never spoke, so there was no script. And it was completely stress-free in that he just had to show himself preparing a midnight snack maybe once a week, if that. Without his deep voice giving himself away, and the fact that he hid his face behind a black, leather-studded executioner's mask, he kept himself anonymous, separate from his professional chef side.

Who knew that coming home late one night after a long day, needing a midnight snack to soak up the countless beers he'd had while helping the kitchen staff clean up (he never thought he was too good to help the junior staff—he'd been there once), would take off? He didn't even remember recording and uploading the first video to his barely used social media account, which was already handled as *Sinful in the Kitchen.*

That first video partially showed the bottom of his chin—he had no idea what he was doing with filming. He'd made some kind of amalgamation of Greek nachos, with tortilla chips, melted mozzarella, diced cucumbers and tomatoes, and crumbled feta, with fresh herbs. He'd chopped up a good can of tinned anchovies in olive oil and thrown that on top, too. He never once imagined he would go viral.

It was days after, and completely forgotten, when a certain SheldonHot1 messaged him about his video hitting a million views. When he didn't respond, because who the hell cared (what were view counts, and why did they matter so much?), SheldonHot1 bombarded him with more messages wanting a meeting to discuss legitimate branding partnerships.

Zayn wasn't an idiot. He refused to work with his family's shipping business, sure. But he had a pretty clear understanding of professional opportunities. He had Aariv do a little poking around and found out that SheldonHot1 was actually Sheldon Hinsdale who worked for a legitimate consumer branding company in Manhattan. He'd acquired pretty successful side projects (a few B-list reality stars in the New York area worked with him). That's when Zayn took the in-person meeting with Shelly, and he walked out realizing he had another avenue of cashing in his talents. Had he heard throughout his career that he was too hot to work in a kitchen? Yes, countless times. The culinary world had its own level of inappropriate behavior that was overlooked. Did he let those accolades go to his head as a young chef and exploit them to get women into bed when he could? Absolutely. But he'd never thought to capitalize on it in a legitimate way. He understood nothing about engagement rates, call to action, or analytics, but he trusted Shelly's enthusiasm for a good-looking guy, doing what he loved—cooking—and shirtless in the kitchen, getting paid to promote kitchen brands.

Aside from filming himself, he didn't have to do a thing. Shelly managed it all—the branding, the partnerships, the editing, and commenting as Sinful himself. Zayn raked in the paycheck, with a cut to his manager.

"Both," he finally said to Aariv as they got into the elevator and he pressed the button for the fourteenth floor. "My alter ego is absolutely about sex, but so is my food. That's kind of my thing. Take oysters, for example—a food aphrodisiac. And I can do so much with that ingredient. Make it sexier than it looks, make it taste as good as a woman's pussy if I needed to."

Aariv grunted. "Nothing is *that* good."

Zayn considered this and grunted in agreement.

"I'll pass on the oysters at lunch if it's just you and me."

"Ha!" Zayn hooted, cracking up. "Fair enough."

"Aren't you sick of seafood at this point?" Aariv asked curiously.

"Never. I'm half fish. The ocean is in my blood."

Aariv snorted. "Maybe you could be a merman in your next video. Or put on an Aquaman costume."

Zayn shook his head, disgusted. "Hard pass."

Aquaman was child's play. His content was edgy for a reason. His audience, he was told, consisted of horny young women, horny *and* bored older women, and anyone in between who had a fetish for danger, sex, and good food content.

They got out of the elevator and checked in with the front desk admin. They made their way down a long hallway to the largest conference room, where they were told the reading was being held.

"Let's get this shit over with," he commented before opening the door, and they went in.

CHAPTER 5

☾

A WEEK LATER

*H*ad it only been a week since Kareena ran into Zayn—or more accurately, since he'd saved her life?

The brief moment stayed with her, as if she'd caught a feverish, unshakeable ailment. Seeing him had awakened something inside her, something she hadn't known she'd hit snooze on.

What did that say about her?

She was a full-grown woman left breathless by a teenage flame. It wouldn't be the first time she'd admitted her considerable inexperience in the sex department. But it was the first time she felt a keen sense of urgency, a rushing sensation in her belly, and below, telling her she was a woman with very sexual needs that couldn't be ignored any longer.

Again, what did that say about her? How had she become an old maid? Was revirginizing yourself a thing?

Admittedly, her marriage to Arjun had its moments. Nice, at times, but purely a necessity for procreation when the timing felt right. But when was the last time she'd orgasmed—like lost all control without having to do any of her own ... ministrations?

"It's called masturbation, dummy," she said to her reflection as she stood in just her bra and panties in front of the bathroom mirror. She was a medical professional. Why was she such a ninny all the time?

Because it'd been in high school ... with Zayn. That was the last time she'd actually orgasmed without masturbating. It'd felt like a roller coaster ride that wouldn't end; truthfully, she hadn't wanted it to. She remembered, in particular, a time he'd snuck into her bedroom when her parents were out. She'd straddled him while his long, thick fingers inched and reached deeper and deeper inside her, driving her insane to orgasmic bliss. The precariousness of the situation only fueled the heady sensation.

God, their young romance had been like every popular teen television drama series at that time. They were *that* couple, finally surrendering to their attraction during their senior class trip to Los Angeles. They'd already been hanging out together outside of school, but she was his math tutor. Their parents knew one another, and more importantly, *her* parents had approved of the activity. But nothing was set in stone vis-à-vis "them," though their attraction was mounting and was becoming harder to ignore with teenage hormones raging.

The end of Senior year and the summer before college were nothing short of magical, though they had to sneak around. There were many more kisses, and other titillation experiences, as well as trading dreams for the future. He knew she was going to Columbia University in the fall, but his plans weren't concrete. His enthusiasm for cooking was growing, though, and she encouraged him with that, breaking down the large goal of his future into smaller, manageable wins for him to tackle—a strategy she'd used when tutoring him. It had been mind-boggling to her that someone her age knew so much about flavors and gastronomy (a word she'd heard but never fully understood until they met).

The one thing she regretted was that she'd never given him the courtesy of recognizing him as her boyfriend. Oh, all of her friends knew, her younger sister, Reyana, too. She had a feeling his mother might've known; Sofia Aunty always doted on her when she came around. But no one within the South Asian community, a social group they spent half their time with knew. Some of the kids (outside of her best girlfriends, who were also Indian) might've suspected, but not the adults. That was just how things were done—anything considered unacceptable behavior was kept a secret—not so different from normal teenage behavior. For Kareena, though, a South Asian American daughter who was the ultimate 'good girl,' it was like committing an illicit crime.

If she let herself overthink it, she'd tell herself there was a reason her own arranged marriage turned out passionless. She was undeserving because of how she treated Zayn—never recognizing him as her boyfriend, and ending it with him, which felt abrupt and too fast for both of them to process.

But how could she have told her parents about them? They'd never understand. All they saw was a boy who was bad on paper. He was a terrible student, with quite possibly a learning disability (which she knew now to be behavior indicative of the ADHD spectrum, similar to her daughter).

When they'd found out about them (the culprit was still a mystery to her), she discovered she hadn't been wrong. It was as if she'd dragged their family name through the mud. More disappointed than angered (at least on her *abba's* part), her parents couldn't understand how their *shona meh* (golden girl) could've deceived them. She'd been forced to break up with him, and it'd taken all of freshman year at university, and more, to get over him.

The sound of feet padding quickly down the hall toward her bathroom pulled Kareena out of her memories. She needed to get a hold of herself, she thought, smoothing her hair, trying to quell the recollections of young love that lit up her body like a house lit up for *Diwali.*

"What're you doing?"

A smaller version of herself stood next to her, observing her curiously, breaking the brief but vivid walk down Memory Lane she'd let herself tread.

Tamannah looked her mother up and down in just her underwear, while she clutched one of her stuffies to her. The black and white panda, aptly named Pandy, was floppy and worn.

Her daughter's big, dark brown eyes, so like her own, boldly held her stare in the mirror as she combed her small fingers through her puffy, long locks, more brown than black, like her father's. She had beautiful, tight curls like his, but insisted on brushing her hair every morning, completely obsessed with self-care at the moment. Unsure where a seven-year-old had gotten the idea of self-care, Kareena let her, suspecting her sister (a self-proclaimed fashionista and beauty guru) had something to do with it. The brushed-out curls resulted in a poufy fro-like wonder, but what could Kareena do but foster her daughter's independence? Since Arjun's death, everything was a battle. Combining the trauma of his death with the new routine of going from preschool to 'big kid' school had only made things worse. Every morning for the first year without him was filled with crying fits, full-body tantrums, and refusing to eat. It was as if Kareena had lived an entire exhausting day by the time she'd dropped Tamannah off for school at 8:45 am. So, she'd take anything her daughter gave her now, because her behavior had improved considerably over the past two years.

Kareena looked away from her daughter's probing gaze. How did a seven-year-old see through her, like a wizened old swami? But she knew why. Ever since seeing Zayn, she'd had random moments of losing her train of thought or forgetting what she was doing. Her daughter was noticing because Tama never missed the details.

"Want to try some of Mommy's makeup, *Beta*?" she asked, trying to gather her wits about her.

Tamannah shrugged her shoulders. "Okay. But only a little bit. I'm doing the clean beauty hack."

Kareena stuttered. "You are? Where did you hear about that? Was it Reya *Khala* (aunt)?"

She shook her head. "Marigold's mom."

"Ah." Kareena should've known. Marigold was the girl in the brownstone two doors down from them who also lived with her mother. But unlike Tamannah, Marigold's parents were divorced. Kareena liked Abby, Marigold's mom, just fine, but didn't love her outspoken tendency toward women's grooming habits. Recently, Tama had come home talking about getting her arm hair waxed. She was seven.

"Well, I don't plan to go wild with my make-up either. Just a little of this blue eye-shadow." She dipped her finger into the pot of shimmery pale aqua cream and swiped it onto her lids.

Tama clapped at the look, oohing and aahing.

"You look like a mermaid! I want some, Mommy," Tama said, completely forgetting her clean beauty mantra.

"Of course, Baby. Come here."

She leaned down and put a little bit on her daughter's eyelids

The little girl inspected herself. "I'm as pretty as you, Mommy."

And just like that, Kareena's eyes welled up. She was so emotional lately. What with her forced sabbatical from work, the challenges of raising her daughter by herself, and her parents taking it upon themselves to get her married again—because every Indian woman should be married, especially one with a young child. Now her father's health was keeping her up at nights more than was probably necessary. He seemed to be doing fine from his last cardiovascular procedure. But, it felt as if she was being pulled in so many directions that she didn't know which way was up, down, sideways, or backwards.

She leaned down and hugged her daughter tightly. Tamannah tried to pull away, and Kareena murmured into her hair, "Not done yet." She held her a little longer before letting go.

When she released her to stand up, she felt her daughter's fingers trailing her abdomen, exploring the faded silvery stretch marks left from pregnancy.

"I see your tiger stripes," she said before gently pinching Kareena's skin. "I think they look like silver fire tattoos. Or, kind of like demon marks, like in the new K-pop movie."

"Well," she said as she ran a brush through her wavy mane, thinking about this random statement. "I like to think of them as more like battle scars. I loved being pregnant with you, but it was hard, and we got through it." She spritzed her hair with hairspray before grabbing her eyeliner and applying the black kohl carefully to her lids.

"You and Daddy?" her daughter prodded, as Kareena finished with eyeliner and pulled her mascara out, giving a light brush over her already thick lashes.

"Mm hm," she murmured.

She'd truly loved Arjun, though they were more 'best friends' than passionate lovers. She'd known from the get-go that there'd be no shivers with him, no I'll-die-if-I-don't-have-you kind of hunger. She'd experienced that already, and it wasn't with Arjun. But he was an understanding man, a little more reserved with his feelings than she would've liked, but gentle, and passionate about his job as an ER doctor. Considering some of the crappy arranged marriages she'd witnessed second hand (one of her childhood best friends had come out of a verbally abusive situation, divorcing her husband to her family's chagrin), Kareena considered herself lucky.

Arjun had died in a car accident, on his way back from a medical conference in Pittsburgh. A truck driver pulling an all-nighter nodded off and swerved his semi into the opposite lanes, pushing through the metal guardrails. He hit three cars total, including Arjun's Audi Q8, which was the first car on impact. He'd died immediately, and infuriatingly, the truck driver hobbled away with only a broken collarbone and a few fractures.

Kareena received a large settlement from the trucking company, part of which she donated to a well-known ADHD research organization. She invested the other half in a 'rainy day fund,' not even sure what she'd do with that lump sum. No doubt it would go toward continuing education for Tamannah. But the settlement did nothing to fill her loss.

After that, Kareena's life continued to derail. A year after her husband's death, a patient of hers attempted to take their own life. Luckily, they'd mistaken an entire bottle of laxatives for sleeping pills, resulting in major stomach cramping and diarrhea, rather than un-aliving themselves. Relieved, but worried she'd missed the destructive signs in her patient, the practice's administration recommended she take time off. Her sabbatical would give her time to focus on her daughter and her personal life, which she hadn't done after Arjun's death.

Truthfully, after a few months off, she finally felt a little better. But she had a feeling that had more to do with the Desi American podcast her sister practically forced her to guest host as the professional MD advising South Asian Americans on life, love, and everything in between. Never did she think she would enjoy something so … out there, at least for her. Podcasting sounded more like her sister—someone who never followed conventional rules—not rule-following Kareena.

Just then, a tan blur barreled into the bathroom. It knocked her daughter over and licked the little girl's face.

"Aloo! Stop!" Tamannah shrieked, giggling. "You're eating my makeup!"

Aloo, their two-year-old pup, only licked more, his entire body wriggling excitedly, his butt moving independently in the opposite direction as the rest of him.

"Okay, little man. Sit," Kareena said sternly. Aloo looked up at her and proceeded to take a comfortable position on top of her daughter's chest. "Oh, boy. We still have a ton of work to do with you."

She picked him up and kissed his head before releasing him. He ran out of the bathroom on another mission, and Tamannah chased him happily.

Kareena took a look at her finished makeup and hair. Sexy and simple, that's what she was going for, only swiping on a little blush and applying a shimmery nude gloss. She wanted the aqua shimmer on her eyes to stand out because it perfectly matched the beautifully dreamy, sea-foamy turquoise color of the *lehenga* she'd picked to wear for that evening's *Diwali* festivities.

She knew people would be decked out in their fashionably best for this particular party. *Diwali* was a huge week-long celebration, one that kicked off the entire holiday season for Kareena and many Indians alike in the States. It was a celebration of light over darkness; good over evil. This year, following the Lunar calendar, it happened to fall before Halloween, and Kareena always found it a little disconcerting that the two holidays were so close to each other, though opposite in nature. One was all about the light, and the other all about the dark. In a way, there were similarities, as Halloween marked a time between the living and the dead, and people lit lights all over to ward off the spirits of the deceased—hence jack-o'-lanterns. At least that was what Tama had recently schooled her about after deep-diving into the history of All Hallows' Eve because Kareena had no idea what the origins of the holiday were when asked. Foolishly, she had believed her daughter, like any other seven-year-old, would only be excited to dress up and get candy.

She was wrong, of course. Tamannah wasn't like most seven-year-olds.

Kareena walked into her bedroom where she'd laid the three-piece sumptuous outfit on the bed. She hoped it was fancy enough to meet New York's finest South Asian professionals, including artists, actors, and activists alike.

She skimmed her hand lightly over the *choli* (crop top blouse), the voluminous ankle-length skirt, and the matching *dupatta* scarf, anticipation rippling through her. She'd never worn it, though she'd received it years ago from a relation on Arjun's side for their daughter's traditional Hindu naming ceremony. It hadn't fit because Kareena was still carrying baby weight, and even over the years, she found it impossible to drop the extra pounds. More recently, she'd been determined with pilates and yoga. Most of the weight slowly and steadily came off, which was a feat in and of itself, considering her obsession with anything resembling a slice of New York-style pizza—the greasier the better, topped with grated parmesan and hot pepper flakes.

Tamannah came skipping back in, now in a flannel, banana-print nightgown, announcing the babysitter's arrival. Bananas were *all* the rage at the moment with her second-grade class.

"Mommy, why can't I go with you? I celebrate *Diwali* too, you know."

Her daughter plopped onto the thick ivory rug, on her back, splaying her arms and legs wide like a starfish.

"I know, Tama. But we've been over this. It's an adults-only party at a fancy place here in the city. I'm pretty sure it'll be boring, but I have to go." She sighed, telling herself that sometimes it was okay to fib to one's kid.

A night out without the possibility of a Tamannah meltdown

made Kareena feel a little light-hearted. The girl was extremely sensitive, especially in social settings. Kareena hated the judgmental looks she got from some people and the dismayed whispers about her daughter's *kharap* (ill-behaved) temperament. She wanted to protect her daughter while simultaneously showing her mini-me how to be strong in the face of mean-minded folks. But she also needed just one childless evening. She hadn't had one since her daughter's school year began, having thrown herself into school volunteering, which she'd never had the time to do before.

"And we're celebrating in Connecticut with *Nana* (grandfather), *Nani (*grandmother), Reya *Khala,* and all of our friends in the community this Sunday, remember? *That's* the official *Diwali* celebration and way more fun than this one, with sparklers, and lighting all the *diyas* (small lanterns), and the *puja* (worship ritual) to Goddess Lakshmi. We want all the good fortune this year, remember?"

Kareena could use a little good fortune this year, and she really hoped Goddess Lakshmi was on the same page.

Tamannah's face crumpled up, anyway, and Kareena held her breath. Was a meltdown on the horizon?

"Tamannah, where are you? What are we ordering for dinner?!" a voice called from downstairs.

Whew! Saved by the babysitter, Kareena thought as Tama scrambled off the floor, shouting as she ran down the stairs to look at the food calendar she'd made over the summer (an activity her therapist had her do as a way to feel empowered, and organized, but also helpful to her mother).

Kareena continued getting dressed, shrugging on the blouse with all-over silver and gold floral and fauna embroidery work on top of the delicate georgette material. It had a sweetheart neckline, showing off a hint of her ample bosom's cleavage. The long sleeves were sheer chiffon in the same blue-green color.

She began closing the hooks from the bottom of the front opening, going slowly so as not to snag the material with her nails. As she got to the last two hooks, it was as though the blouse was just shy of a few inches. The hooks barely closed, leaving a big gaping hole between where they were sewn, revealing very smooshed boobs, and the tight cleft in between.

She could hear her mother's outrage that Kareena hadn't taken the blouse to her favorite tailor in Jackson Heights to get it fixed before the party. This was a practice her mother had instilled in her ever since Kareena filled out in high school, when all of her Indian clothes and school uniforms had to be taken out. Her mother did all of the seamstress work, excellent with a sewing machine, needle, and thread, even with her full-time job as a hospital pharmacist. But when Kareena was on her own in college, her mother found a trusted tailor in Jackson Heights, Queens, for her to go to for all of her Indian clothes, well into adulthood. And usually, she did.

Unfortunately, she wasn't living that version of always-on-the-ball-with-life Kareena. That version was somewhere in hiding until she could get her shit together. No, living-by-the-seat-of-her-pants Kareena was the version she was inhabiting currently, and this was her reward—an ill-fitting outfit on the evening she intended to wear it.

She grabbed her boobs and tried to flatten them, maneuvering them so that, magically, she could create extra space and pull the blouse closed. But sadly, she was no magician.

She'd always been self-conscious about her chest. When she'd hit puberty, her mother told her she was as beautiful as the goddess Lakshmi herself. But that never made Kareena feel great about her figure, because her mother would suck her teeth in frustration and shake her head while staying up late into the night to take out her daughter's clothes. If anything, Kareena felt a little ashamed.

Pregnancy, birth, and nursing didn't help matters. Her breasts hadn't returned to their pre-pregnancy size, shape, and bounce. They probably never would.

Kareena stared at the gaping hole, beads of moisture casting a sheen on her skin from the struggle to make her breasts fit. She didn't have a backup plan, and not going wasn't an option. She'd been anticipating this party for weeks. No one would inquire about marriage or work, and she could be free for just one night, unlike what she experienced in her familiar South Asian community in Connecticut.

She ran to her bathroom, opened drawers, and rummaged around. Underneath an unused sewing kit (ironic), and bobby pins she didn't know she had, she found safety pins.

"Not today, you piece of shit," she grumbled under her breath in case little ears were listening, as she scooped up a handful.

After successfully sticking herself a bunch of times, both in her thumb and her boobs, and miraculously not getting blood on the fabric, she closed the gaping hole. Tenuous, yes, but if she didn't make any sudden moves (like going too buck wild on the dance floor), she could pull it off for a few hours without her top busting open.

She held her breath as she stepped into the skirt and fiddled with the hook. Thankfully, it closed with ease.

When she looked at herself in the mirror, she gasped. She didn't hate what she saw. But when she turned to view her profile, her hands immediately went to smooth down the back flesh that rolled out where the blouse met her ribcage. Of course, it didn't budge; it wasn't like she was working with kids' modeling clay. It'd have to do. She noticed her faded silvery stretch marks—the ones that made her feel like a strong tigress—partially peeping out from the skirt's waistband, around her torso. Now she felt like a meek, embarrassed kitten. Did she want to step out with all of her physical flaws on view for everyone to see?

"You're totally beautiful, Kara. Own that shit." She heard her sister proclaim every time Kareena shot herself down.

She'd tried, but feeling self-conscious about her body on and off was her norm. Tonight, though, she vowed to be nicer to herself because, damn it, she did look pretty good. She twirled around, lifting the skirt. The chiffon and georgette floated up and around her like an embrace.

She finished her look by putting on large dangly earrings and a matching necklace in heavy silver and turquoise gems. Then she slipped on thick stacks of skinny silver and gold glittered bangles on each wrist.

The final piece was the cheer chiffon *dupatta*, with silver beads stitched on the entire two and a half meters of fabric. She tucked one corner in the waist and wrapped it artfully so that the material draped over her shoulder and down her back in a pretty waterfall.

She stepped into silver heels and grabbed her silver clutch, throwing her essentials in. She fluffed her hair, taking one last look in the mirror. Elation set in her bones as she gave herself a nod of approval.

She went downstairs to the living room. Tamannah and the babysitter, Tara, were settling down to work on one of her daughter's large three-hundred-piece puzzles. The small pieces were spread out messily on the glass coffee table. She knew it'd be complete by the time she got home. Puzzles were one of Tama's specialties.

"Wow. Dr. S., you look ... *smokin'*! No lie," the teenage girl said in awe, nodding.

Tara lived in their neighborhood and loved to babysit when she wasn't busy studying or playing tennis. She kind of reminded Kareena a little bit of herself when she was that age.

"Uh, thank you," Kareena said, trying for confident, but inwardly experiencing a bit of awkward teen-getting-ready-for-the-prom-angst. Her hand went to her chest, making sure the pin was still there.

As Kareena made sure Tara was all set for dinner and knew where the emergency numbers were and what time bedtime was, Tamannah got up and hurled herself at Kareena, hugging her hard. Aloo, feeling left out, scrambled from his dog bed by the window, snuggling into Kareena's legs with a SpongeBob squeaky toy clamped between his jaws.

"You two be good for Tara. I know you always are." She kissed Tamannah on the head and booped Aloo on the nose, making him sneeze.

She left with a smile, jumping into her Uber, which was already waiting outside. She liked to make a quick getaway if she could. Goodbyes were hit or miss with her daughter.

For the first time in months, Kareena was adamant about letting loose (even if it was just a little). She planned on having an unforgettable time.

CHAPTER 6

ᕌ

"*C*hef? Excuse me, Chef? What do you think?"

Zayn turned away from the little porthole window on the kitchen's large swinging door that separated them from the party space. He'd been watching guests arrive for the *Diwali* party for some time now, wondering why he'd taken this gig in the first place. But then he remembered his plans for his future had fallen through. His inheritance, it turned out, was way out of his reach.

But, before he let himself go down *that* rabbit hole of fuckery, he needed to address the issues at present.

He turned to the staff who stood waiting in their stiff chef whites. Zayn wished he could say something to the effect of, "At ease, soldiers." But this wasn't his staff, and he needed to run things the way their executive chef did.

He inspected the platter put before him, as though he were a king himself, with everyone hushed and holding their breath. Plump, pan-seared scallops were individually placed in large seashells. A pineapple-pomegranate curry sauce was artistically drizzled over each one and topped with a smattering of pink pomegranate seeds.

The other dish consisted of thick cubes of grilled paneer, marinated in a yogurt, ponzu sauce, skewered with grilled mango slices, and drizzled with a vibrant mint chutney. A sprinkle of pink sea salt finished off the small bite.

"It all looks great, Maria. Finish plating and send everything out."

"Yes, Chef," everyone said in unison, a collective sigh passing through them, before jumping into action.

And this was exactly why Zayn had begun to detest working for establishments that were on the Michelin Star journey. Not all, but many, were militant, even going so far as to use verbal abuse to manage their staff. Effective, sure, but talented staff members were pushed to limits, finding other ways to enhance their performance (his reasoning for taking 'uppers' in the first place), or complete burnout.

He couldn't be too picky at the moment, though. After the complete 180 his inheritance had taken, he needed work to keep himself occupied before he figured out his next move. A colleague he'd known since culinary school luckily approached him with the catering job. His restaurant, an up-and-coming Manhattan global cuisine sensation, was double-booked that night. The chef who was to execute one of the two jobs had come down with the flu, and he needed a fast replacement. He'd heard Zayn was back in town and had called him immediately.

Zayn agreed on the spot. What else did he have going on? He needed to keep himself busy—that was his nature when it felt like his sky was falling. The party itself was nothing to ignore either. The annual Light It Up on the Hudson party was thrown by *Desi Ignites*, a social networking group that seemed to be on everyone's lips lately. Even his father had mentioned it, hearing that it was a notable networking group for young professionals. He'd thought maybe Zayn could connect and meet more South Asians his age there. Zayn took Kiran's advice in stride, though laughable for a grown old man who was successful in his own right. It was the Indian way, or at least Kiran Roy's way. No matter how old he got or even how great his career went, his father would always aim to advise and help his son. Why? Because Kiran shared Zayn's goal-oriented way of pushing his career and wanted to encourage him in any way he knew how, even though he was still unsure of what his son did.

To his father's credit, the event *was* pretty high-profile, indicating that *Desi Ignites* was doing something right. Indian actors who'd made careers in the US and the West, along with popular DJs, musicians, fashion designers, even comedians and writers, were going to be there. Zayn was already acquainted with a few through his social circles and work. It was impressive, and he knew the opportunity was a big one. Only someone with his expertise could fill the vacant role last minute.

When he scanned the menu a few days in advance, he recognized the flavor profiles. He'd been emailing with this same colleague back and forth all summer to help get the flavors just right for a South Asian style buffet that was upscale but still encompassed the familiar tastes Indians craved and expected at any party. The final menu included leveled up versions of the classics like tender tandoori goat with crunchy green peppers, spatchcocked game hens marinated in yogurt and lime with a delicate balance of spices, tamarind glazed short ribs, vegetable curry in fragrant coconut milk and saffron, jackfruit and potato in a lightly spiced stew, saffron and pistachio studded beautifully long-grained basmati rice, and all sorts of breads for dipping and carrying the delicious sauces (hot buttered naan, flaky paratha, perfectly chewy chapatti).

The cocktail hour was another story, and quite clearly a last-minute addition. *Desi Ignites* wanted to host a 'VIP social hour' for VIP ticket holders to have access to some of the A-listers before the big party began. He'd already been notified that the cocktail menu was a placeholder and had been asked to find a way to tweak things.

His phone pinged, and he dug it out of his pocket. He grumbled at the text from his assistant.

"Sinful in the Kitchen hasn't put out a new video in weeks. His fans want to know what happened to their sinfully hot chef…???"

For fuck's sake. **"I'll get on it this weekend."** He texted back.

He needed to keep his fans happy for now and roll with the branding partnerships. Either that, or find a wife, stat.

A WEEK AGO

"So, let me get this straight, you only get your inheritance—this taverna—*if* you're engaged by the time the claims period for the will is up, or the new year? Whichever one comes first?"

"And the olive grove," Zayn muttered, throwing a dart a little too hard. It bounced off the board and clattered to the floor near his feet. He kicked it away.

They were *not* having the extravagant lunch at the Grand Central Oyster. After the will reading, a dazed Zayn needed somewhere nearby that had some form of alcohol to soothe the migraine beginning to thump his temple. They ended up down the street at an old pub that was pretty much empty except for them.

They were in the back, where Zayn aimlessly threw darts, first having downed two tequila shots in a row as soon as they entered the gloomy bar. He was now on his third beer; the alcohol had taken the edge off of his fury.

Aariv was in a booth and had invited his girlfriend, Chrissy, to join them. It was a crisis, sure, but Chrissy had called last minute to see what Aariv was doing for lunch, and Zayn at that point couldn't care less who knew about his dire situation. He just needed help figuring it out.

The pretty and petite redhead sat on Aariv's lap, munching thoughtfully on a basket of mozzarella sticks, while Aariv picked at his grilled club sandwich.

"And you knew nothing about this?" she asked, pointing a soggy cheese stick at him.

"Obviously not, or we wouldn't be here," he said with annoyance. "No offense, Chrissy."

"None taken." She pulled Aariv's plate to her, inspecting it. She opened his sandwich and took the bacon out, breaking it into bite-sized pieces before popping them into her mouth.

"This is so nuts that I'm not even considering the marriage portion of my grandfather's request. Me? Get married in a year and receive a huge lump sum to fund my restaurant? No thanks. I'll make a go of it without the extra burden of putting an official ring on it."

Aariv snagged a mozzarella stick from her basket and asked, "Might I make a suggestion?"

"Knock yourself out," Zayn said.

"I think … a pretend engagement is the way to go—"

Zayn tilted his head back and laughed; a big belly-aching laugh that had the other two looking at him like he'd lost his mind. With the turn his life had taken, he might just be.

He wiped the tears from his eyes as he said, "You have to be joking. What woman in their right mind would agree to a fake engagement?"

"To you?" Aariv answered. "You're not *that* bad-looking, and if the return was more than adequate, you might be surprised."

"Thanks," Zayn snapped.

"Who was the last woman you dated—and not just slept with—but dated, spent time with, maybe took to a nice dinner, took a walk in the park with…"

His friend was being serious, and Zayn sobered up enough to ruminate over the question. Who was the last woman he'd dated?

"Really? No one?" Chrissy asked incredulously.

"I'm thinking," Zayn grumbled as the server finally dropped off his double order of fish and chips. He doused everything in vinegar. "Honestly, no one I can think of can help me with this —if that's where you're going. Unless the woman I had a thing with on the yacht this past summer lent a hand."

"Yeah, why not ask her?" Chrissy asked, continuing to pick at Aariv's sandwich.

"She's not technically available. Her situation is complicated. She's separated from her oil baron husband. But I highly doubt she'll go through with the divorce, seeing as being

72

separated with kids gets her all the perks of marriage, without having to sleep with the old man. And from the looks of it, he's probably shriveled all over." Zayn shivered dramatically.

"Her husband was on the boat, too?" Chrissy asked wide-eyed.

When he nodded, Aariv shot him a disgusted look. "You're a real piece of work, you know that?"

"I do. Jealous?"

"Well, who else?" Chrissy urged, not one bit of disgust in her expression. It seemed she was just focused on figuring out how to help, not willing to make any judgment calls. He liked her even more for Aariv, now. "Does this woman have friends who'd pretend?"

"Oodles, I'm sure. But I'm not willing to get tied up with women who are just desperate and money-hungry enough to do anything in exchange for a life of champagne and caviar dreams for the rest of their lives."

"What's that supposed to mean?" Chrissy asked, a little miffed. "You don't think some of these women would help out of the goodness of their hearts?"

"Hell no. They'll expect more than I can give them in return. Trust me on this."

As they mulled this over, Zayn wolfed down the rest of his food and ordered another beer. Chrissy and Aariv chatted for a bit, trading snuggles and kisses, while he did his best to ignore them. Then she took off, as her lunch break was over, but told him she hoped things worked out.

Aariv gave Zayn a look, shaking his head.

"Hey, don't stare down your nose at me, Aari. I'm not a relationship guy, especially not lately. My job makes it impossible."

Aariv snorted. "You just don't want to get caught up in one. It's too hard for you."

"Not hard, too complicated when my life is already complicated enough." He corrected, though Aariv wasn't that far off the truth. It was too chaotic from what he'd witnessed in other people's relationships—the two who'd been sitting squashed together only moments ago, even though there was room for at least eight others in the booth, were a prime example.

"You just haven't met the right woman," Aariv said, sipping his water.

And just like that, those brown eyes from earlier that day, from a moment that felt like eons ago, reappeared before him. He could argue that he'd met the right woman a long time ago. He just wasn't the right man for her. But again, he didn't want to bring her up. He needed to forget her.

"Maybe you need to put an ad out on some of the dating sites. Not Dil Mil, or any of the South Asian sites. That'll only throw you into hot water. Those women are serious about finding husbands…" Aariv talked to himself, trying to find a solution—and thank God for friends like him. Zayn wasn't so sure he could help him, but the fact that he was here, on his day off, coming up with schemes that could only best be described as cockamamie, spoke volumes about what a great friend Aariv had always been.

"What would I even say on any of these sites, Aari? 'Man seeking woman for short-term relationship; must be willing to pretend to be his fiancé, and agree with ending engagement with no consequences.'" He scoffed.

"Don't forget 'a monetary return for services.' And make it

clear that it's completely above board, no funny business, or sexual favors."

Zayn wiped his greasy hands on the paper napkin and picked up a dart, aiming it at the dartboard. "This is too fucking wild. Posting an ad like that will only *encourage* the psychos. No, thank you. There's a reason why I don't do dating apps."

"What else do you have, Z?" his friend asked seriously.

"I'm not *that* desperate."

"Aren't you?" Aariv asked. "You've been planning for this almost your entire life. What the hell are you going to do if you don't open your dream restaurant? Don't let this one thing deter your goals."

He'd already thought about that, but had no answer yet. One thing was for certain: he couldn't see himself doing anything other than working his own eatery. It was his time.

And all he could see was the smirk on his oldest cousin, Silas' when the lawyers came to the stipulation of Zayn's inheritance. *Pappous* had dictated a note to him, and they read it aloud.

"Zayn, it's no secret that you are my favorite, so I do this for you with love and kindness in my heart. You must marry and settle down to fully receive your inheritance. Be engaged by either the new year or by the end of the will's claims period (whichever comes first), and you'll receive the taverna and the olive grove. Be married in a year, and you'll receive financing to support your endeavors and the family you will create. Why do I do this, you might ask? You have so much to offer in life. You were meant to share it with someone who deserves it all, and you. If she's not already in your life now, go find her. I know she's out there."

Silas had snickered loudly. "Never thought *Pappous* was so sentimental."

It was true. Their grandfather had rarely shown any kind of warm sentiment, except toward a handful of his grandchildren. Silas wasn't one of them, having received only firm guidance once he stepped fresh-faced as a college graduate into the Stavros Titans' finance department.

"Yeah, well, you didn't know him like some of us did," Zayn had said through his teeth.

"I didn't need to. I knew where I stood from the beginning. And now I have what I worked hard for," he said smugly, now the appointed CEO of the company, along with executor of the family estate. "So, what do you plan to do, Cousin? Do you have a fiancé hidden somewhere, or a girlfriend none of us know about?"

"Maybe, maybe not," he answered elusively, not giving Silas a hint of his thoughts.

The room erupted with conversations about what he should do. But Zayn remained speechless as the conditions sank in. Aariv, sitting beside him, murmured that he could look over the documents, but it seemed binding, which meant he couldn't do a thing about it. His mother, sitting on the other side of him, just shook her head. Had she known what her father was thinking at the end?

"So," Zayn had nearly shouted, speaking over everyone and addressing the lawyers, "what happens if I don't get engaged?"

Murmurs and whispers abounded around him. He ignored them.

One of the attorneys studied the documents in front of him, finally stating, "You forfeit all and everything gets folded back into the estate."

"This is bullshit!" he growled.

The smirk Silas gave him warranted a punch to mar the unbridled arrogance, and Zayn's right fist itched to do so. But his mother's hand on his arm stayed him.

"Look, this is simple, Zayn. Why not give up your inheritance—"

Jeers came from some of the cousins who, like Zayn, weren't fans of Silas. Grown-ups now, yes, except for some of the youngest who were still finishing college, but everyone knew the older cousin's bullying tactics. From playing unfairly as kids, to pushing his way to the top, even throwing his sister under the bus recently for an unclear financial error, Silas had always been built to be a tyrant. Too bad he was so good at managing the business; otherwise, *Pappous* might've picked someone more compassionate for the job.

The older man stood up, smoothing his black button-down shirt and tie. His wiry body stood tall, like every other Stavros, his flat red hair peppered with silver. He raised his hands in a calming gesture, quieting the room. "Let me finish. I've had investors approach me about the land—hotel developers. It's worth a lot of money. If I brokered the sale, I'd hand off fifty percent of the profit to you, Zayn." He broke off with a chuckle of self-importance, casting a steely gaze at him. "It's a lot of money, more than even old *pappous* left you, I'm sure."

"Only fifty percent, Silas? That land is rightfully mine." Zayn seethed.

Silas thought about it with a humorous expression. "Sixty percent, forty percent then."

"No," Zayn said automatically, struggling to keep his composure.

"Don't be so hasty, Cousin. What other option do you have?

This way, you get something out of all of this. The land is rightfully yours *if* you are engaged by New Year's or before the claims time is up. With the old man's penchant for tying up loose ends on anything and everything with his name on it, I'd say you have weeks to make that happen, because we won't see any claims. *Weeks,* Zayn—maybe four or five tops. Think about it. Or, again, I ask you, is there someone in your life who you've been eager to get on bended knee for?"

When Zayn didn't answer, Silas continued, *"Pias to avgo kai kourefto* (common Greek phrase meaning impossible; literal meaning: grab an egg and shave it). You can go back to your life. You don't need to stay in one place. Go party, get your women, travel the world; do the things that make you happy."

"You have no clue what makes me happy," Zayn snapped.

"True. But is there really more for you?" Silas looked from face to face in the room, searching for agreement from the others. His gaze landed back on Zayn smugly. "Ah, you're talking about your cooking." He clasped his hands behind his back. "Zayn, be serious. You can open a restaurant anywhere. You don't need to do it on Naxos. If you're such a great and famous chef, shouldn't your food speak for itself, anyway?"

True, Zayn could open a restaurant anywhere, and people would come because that's how good he was, despite his cousin's mockery. But what he wanted was to do so on Naxos, a place that had always felt like a part of him. It was his way of showing an allegiance to his grandfather and his mother—those who understood him and his disinterest in the shipping empire. This was his version of giving back to the Stavros name and contributing to the family. Naxos had always been home to him.

"Silas, you underestimate me." Zayn stood up. His body felt

taut, like a rubber band ready to spring. "You will never have that land. You will never see one penny from those developers."

"Is that so, Cousin?" Silas stepped closer to him. "Let me tell you this. I don't back down from a challenge, and right now, you don't stand a chance." He shook his head, that haughty look crossing his face again. "You have very little time to find some poor, unsuspecting woman to fall for you. When you fail, that land comes back to the estate, and only *I* have the deciding power on what to do with it."

Zayn had felt like thrashing the wiry man, but he held on firmly to his emotions. It never worked to show a bully one's feelings, and quite frankly, Zayn had the weight and strength advantage if it came to physical blows.

"We'll see," he'd said curtly, turning on his heel and leaving the room. Had he stomped out? Most likely. But it was better than losing control while everyone watched.

He sighed as his mind came back to the dim bar. He finished his beer.

"A matchmaker might be able to broker a situation that could benefit both you and a willing candidate—and them, of course. They're all sharks dressed up in expensive Banarasi silk saris after all. You might be looking at a hefty fee.

Zayn almost choked on the last of his beer. He shot Aariv a dirty look above the rim of his pint glass.

"Never in a million years. I hate the whole idea of matchmakers."

Aariv shrugged. "I'm just giving you options."

Zayn absorbed this new idea. What choice did he have? He could refuse the inheritance and agree to let Silas sell the land, making some serious money in the process. That kind of capital would be more than adequate to start his own venture. But the idea didn't sit well with him, though it was by far the easiest. What would that say about him if everything he'd hoped and dreamt for, the plans he'd discussed with his grandfather before he passed away, could all be bought off with a big chunk of change? By doing so, Silas would have his hands in everything on the Naxos estate, something Zayn couldn't abide. Silas didn't care for the locals. What would happen to them if developers came in and gutted the olive grove, the working olive oil mill, and the taverna, along with the attached cliffside property? These were people of the land, who'd been there for generations. Where would they go? There was no way he was going to give Silas the satisfaction of winning.

The matchmaker option made him nauseous. He'd always hated the idea of someone controlling two people's destinies, like a puppet master who would only work for a steep sum. It revolted him.

The only option was the fake engagement. That was the only way he could secure his inheritance and ensure the security of the families who'd been working hand in hand with the Stavros family for hundreds of years. But who the hell could he find to make this all come to fruition? And more importantly, who would be desperate enough to play this game, and what would he have to give in return?

CHAPTER 7

९

PRESENT DAY *DESI IGNITES DIWALI* PARTY

*K*areena stood at the edge of the party, having no idea who most people were, but undoubtedly recognizing a few famous faces. She tried not to gawk as a well-known TV personality (THE fashion expert on a famous reality show) arrived—no fanfare, just smiles and genuine hugs to others he knew in the room. She smiled blandly, trying not to look uncomfortable. She wasn't much of a talker in social gatherings where she didn't know anyone. But the point was to come early and meet some of the big-name guests, including the founder of *Desi Ignites*, who wanted to collaborate with the podcast on an event right before the holidays. So, where the hell was her sister?

A server passed by offering her a specialty cocktail, notably named the Lakshmi-tini. She took it gratefully, asking what was in it and was told it was a chef-prepared recipe created specifically for the party, consisting of mango puree, rum, citrus syrup, and a dash of buttermilk and yogurt.

"So, basically a boozy mango lassi," she remarked skeptically.

The server shrugged and said there was also cinnamon in it, referring to the delicate sprinkling of brown powder on top. Cinnamon was a sign of wealth and fortune, as was the goddess Lakshmi, who was prevalent during this time of year, so she supposed the drink was appropriate for *Diwali*. She thanked him, taking a sip, surprised that the cinnamon's warmth came through, as the hint of spice balanced out the sweet mango—it could also be the rum, she thought, trying not to drink the tasty drink too quickly.

She glanced around the spacious venue, noticing the pretty, amber colored orbs holding flickering tea candles as centerpieces on each of the twelve top round tables. They were on one side of the room, where a buffet was set up; the silver chaffing dishes were empty at the moment. The same orbs hung all over the room from the rafters, held by thick, colorful ribbons in pink, orange, red, and yellow. Fluffy blooms in bold mustard and deep burgundy were braided into garlands that encircled the orbs on the tables and looped around the back of each black lacquered chair.

Toward the main entrance, past the dance floor, she'd passed a long wall covered completely with frothy marigolds in blood red, blinding fuchsia, deep gold, and pristine ivory. Along with the creamy sandalwood incense burning around the room, she was reminded of all the *Diwali* celebrations she'd attended in the past. Though this one was by far the most stylized, some things remained the same and gave her a bit of ease.

She hadn't been able to make out the design created on the wall until she stood where she was now, across the room. It was a thick blanket of the ivory marigolds, with the other multi-colored blooms embedded within, reading 'Happy Diwali.' Shiny golden unlit *diya*s dotted the walls, nestled within the petals. It took her a minute, but she realized the panel was the backdrop for a sort of red-carpet moment where the guests could walk down and get photo ops.

Suddenly, arms grabbed her from behind and twirled her around.

"Hey, Sis! You look gorg! A perfect Princess Jasmine!"

She looked up into the eyes of her younger sister, Reyana, who always color-coordinated every detail of her look, wore purple contact lenses to match her gold and purple *lehenga*. And, of course, though she was already a good few inches taller than Kareena, she still wore towering heels, making Kareena have to crank her neck to have a conversation. But she looked amazing, like a model. She always did.

"Aww, thanks," Kareena said. "You look amazing as usual." She placed a hand self-consciously on her chest, checking that the safety pin hadn't moved. "You have no idea how much I wrestled with this blouse."

"Well, when you got 'em, flaunt 'em, that's what I always say."

Kareena sighed. "Of course you do. But you've never struggled to get in and out of clothes. It's embarrassing. You'll be on boob patrol, won't you?"

"You know it," her sister said distractedly, her eyes shifty. Suddenly, she grabbed Kareena's wrists tightly. In hushed tones, she said, "Okay, I have to warn you—I am so sorry. I didn't mean for this to happen."

Goosebumps prickled almost painfully up her arms. What was Reyana talking about?

"I don't even know how they got tickets," her sister continued nervously, her gaze darting around.

"Calm down." Kareena glanced around, too, now just as shifty, Reyana's nervousness contagious. "What are you even talking about?"

"No, we don't have time—" And she stopped abruptly, looking over Kareena's head.

"There you are. You just left us, *Beta*. How impolite." A hoity-toity voice whined behind her. It was a voice no one could ever mistake. With a mixture of Indian and British accents, it commanded authority, with more than a hint of superiority wherever she went.

"*No!*" Kareena mouthed, now wide-eyed, before her sister forcefully turned her around. She barely had time to wipe the horrified expression off her face. "Well, what a surprise!" she squeaked tightly, looking down at the elegantly dressed older woman. "Pinky Aunty. *Namaste*." She put her palms together and bowed her head slightly in greeting. "What brings you here?"

There could be only one answer, Kareena thought, waiting for the woman to unload a combination of her importance.

"Well, of course I'm here." She sniffed, bobbling her head, making her perfectly coifed silver bob glisten. She looked interestedly around at the VIP guests mingling with celebrities. Kareena couldn't quite tell if it was disgust, admiration, or a combination of both that crossed her face. Her eyes landed on a famed social media star who'd recently transitioned. The smaller woman's nostrils flared while her mouth tightened into a tiny 'o.'

"But, I'm so *glad* I found you, Kareena." The snooty woman continued. "Look," she pulled the man who'd been following her toward them. "See who I have with me."

She held the arm of an uninterested, but not bad-looking, Indian man. He was taller than Kareena, and wore a nice-looking tan suit, but had paired it was the loudest, ugliest burgundy and gold tie she'd ever seen. Pinky ushered him forward; her smile was toothy, and her eyebrows waggled.

Kareena was confused. Should she know who this man was?

She held out her hand anyway and slapped a pleasant smile on her face. "And you are…?"

Pinky giggled and blushed. What was going on here? "*Beta,* this is Sameer Sarkar, my oldest sister's son, and my youngest nephew." She spoke proudly, the man clearly the apple of her eye, as she pinched his cheek, making him turn red. "He's been to a few of my parties," Pinky Aunty added. She hosted most of their community events as she had the biggest house to entertain in—a seaside mansion on the Jersey shore. Her eyes shifted back and forth between the two of them. Her smile faded slightly as they stared at each other awkwardly. "But, of course, you wouldn't remember each other. You met a long time ago when you were still in high school."

He still didn't ring a bell.

"You did a Bollywood dance for *Holi* one year; he was your dance partner?"

"*Right!*" Now it made sense. She remembered a geeky guy with thick glasses and major brace face. This guy looked nothing like that scrawny teen, who couldn't hold a beat if his life depended on it. She'd teased him about not really being a *Desi* because he had zero rhythm. He had not found that funny.

This guy wasn't bad looking, clean-shaven, strong jaw. But honestly, there was no appeal for her.

"Yeah, if I remember, you said I was a terrible dancer." He stuck his hand out to her. "Kareena Sharma, right?"

She laughed. "Sorry about that, Sameer. But you were kind of terrible." They shook hands.

He chuckled, but he didn't sound too pleased. Oh no, had she offended him ... again?

"Yeah, well, dancing isn't everything in life now, is it?" Okay, he was undoubtedly offended.

"Right," she said, trying to come up with some way to steer away from any topic that related to moving one's body in synchrony with music.

Right then, the DJ popped onto the stage with a mic. "Hey, everyone! Happy *Diwali*! Let's light up the dance floor and get this party started!"

"Welp!" She heard her sister exclaim, who'd been a silent bystander. She glared at her over her shoulder before pulling her into the enclave of discomfort.

"This is my sister, Reyana. You might not remember her. She was probably still a dumb kid in middle school at the time."

"I was," Reyana said sweetly. She shook Sameer's hand. "Nice to meet you. So how come we haven't seen more of you? Where've you been hiding?"

"Sameer is a big, fancy finance man. He travels to meet with clients most of the year," Pinky filled in for her nephew.

"I work for Deutsche Bank," he elaborated. "And yes, that's true, I travel a lot for work, investigating and overseeing mergers and acquisitions—I'm a glorified auditor," he said self-deprecatingly, making his aunt wince. "And I don't have time for some of the Indian shenanigans—I mean, *parties*." He corrected himself, as Pinky scowled. "I'm barely in New York as it is."

"Interesting," Reyana said.

At least she was trying, Kareena noticed. For all Kareena cared, the guy could fly off to another country and never come back. She was so tired of being set up wherever she went.

As Reyana and Sameer made small talk, Pinky Aunty steered Kareena a little away by the elbow. "Kareena, I want you two to get to know each other."

"I can't imagine why," Kareena said mildly. Maybe she could deflect this situation by playing dumb.

"Can't you?" The little woman gave her a secretive smile and said conspiratorially, "My nephew is ready to settle down and get married."

They both looked at him and Reyana talking.

"Well, to be honest, Aunty, I don't think Reyana is in the market for a husband. She may never be, you know?" She sipped her drink. "I'm sorry if this was a waste of a trip into the city for you." She frowned into her glass, feigning sympathy.

Pinky looked confused but then slapped her lightly on the arm. "*Ki* (what)!? You tease. I don't mean your *sister*." Her small, jeweled hand gripped her arm tightly, crushing the delicate georgette material of Kareena's sleeve. "You! Your parents *told* me you were looking for a husband again. We didn't get far last year, so I'm doing my best to find the perfect boy." She sucked her teeth and said sadly, "It was so sad what happened to your Arjun. And such a good boy, too." She tsked, shaking her head. "Being a single parent is a lot to handle, *nah*?" She bobbled her head. "And you're still so young. You could have more children ... maybe with Sameer?" She glanced over to her nephew, smiling as proudly as any matchmaker who thought the deal was in the bag.

Have more children!? What was wrong with the one she already had? What was wrong with not wanting more!? Kareena wanted to burst her smug-ass bubble so badly. She almost lied and told the woman that she'd been sterilized after Tamannah. What would she think about Kareena for her precious Sameer, then?

But she was the older daughter. She was the one who needed to be polite. So, instead, she steered them back to where Sameer and her sister were talking, her mind working on a way to side-step this, at least for the time being.

Why wasn't she better at lying? Not enough practice, she realized.

"No!" her sister said heatedly as they approached, startling them. "I'm telling you the live-action version was a *dog*! No one had any business trying to make *Avatar: The Last Airbender* into live-action … twice!" She held up two fingers for emphasis in front of Sameer's nose.

"Come on—" Sameer scoffed, and was Kareena seeing things? Because it seemed as if there was chemistry between these two, even though her sister looked like she was about to drop-kick him in the nuts.

"Sameer, *Beta*, what are you doing?" his aunt asked him as she smiled icily up at Reyana, placing herself between the heated conversation about … well, Kareena had no clue what they were talking about.

"Pinky *Khala*, sorry, yeah." He looked uncomfortable with his aunt present now, and he stepped away from Reyana.

Kareena recognized this behavior; she'd seen it too many

times to count—had even experienced it herself. It was that of a responsible South Asian child, in this case, a son, who was trying to do what was 'right'—perhaps go into the profession his parents wanted him to, or, as in this instance, marry the woman chosen for him. But spoiler, he didn't want to. She'd met tons of men like this last spring when she'd been actively working with Pinky Aunty to meet contenders. To save everyone the trouble, Kareena usually quickly sniffed out what their true feelings were about the setup (why be a psychiatrist if you couldn't use it to your benefit?), so they didn't awkwardly waste time. Usually, met with bland arguments, there were a couple of instances when the men were more than happy to walk away from a proposed match.

Sameer smiled placidly and sighed. It looked like he was getting his bearings. Kareena smiled sympathetically. She genuinely felt bad for the guy. She hated this, too.

"Kareena, I'd like to get to know you further, if you're up for it."

"I'm not," she said immediately, wanting to end it there, but went on when Pinky Aunty gave her the stink eye. "I mean, right now. Reyana and I are here to meet with someone for our podcast. You've heard of it, right?"

"I don't know that I have," he started.

"*Spill That Masala*," Reyana offered quickly, beaming. "We talk about all the things living within the South Asian diaspora. It's quite an important topic that has no clear-cut answer. But … it helps a lot of brownies balance what *they* want versus what their family wants."

"Wow. That sounds interesting," Sameer responded thoughtfully.

"But, *Beta*," the matchmaker addressed Kareena, "you aren't going to keep doing that. You'll go back to practicing medicine again, soon, *nah?*"

Kareena's quick answer surprised even herself. "Meh." She shrugged nonchalantly.

It was the Lakshmi-tini she was drinking that was making her act this way; she was certain of it. She glanced down at the orange drink. What was in it again?

Reyana's lips rolled inwards as she held back her smile.

"What is that supposed to mean?" Pinky asked, horrified.

"I'm not sure."

She knew. She was going to go back to work ... eventually. But right now, it was too good to play with this woman. And Kareena had to wonder, where was this boldness coming from and how did she channel it more?

"What kind of job is a ... a..." She sucked her teeth in frustration.

"Podcaster, Aunty," Sameer filled in.

"*Heh* (Yes). Thank you, *Beta.* How will anyone take you seriously, Kareena?"

"Right now, the most important thing for me is to take myself seriously," Kareena answered truthfully, taking on her professional doctor voice. "And to make my daughter my priority."

Pinky Aunty wasn't convinced, a finely threaded eyebrow raised high, almost disappearing into her hairline.

"This *is* my objective, too. Making sure you and your daughter are taken care of." She gestured absently at Sameer, who'd stuffed his hands in his pockets.

"And I appreciate everything you've been doing to help me. But this just isn't the time or place," Kareena said solemnly.

The matchmaker looked like she'd been slapped.

"I'll be sure to let your parents know how this went," she said, a warning in her tone.

"Please do so, Aunty. It was good to see you."

She'd be hearing from her parents very soon. Sheesh, where were more Lakshmi-tinis when you needed them?

"Sameer," she said, placing her hand on his arm apologetically. "It was a pleasure. I hope you can enjoy the party and aren't too put out by the cost of the tickets."

He appeared to have no idea what was happening, but said, "Don't worry about it. I got them comped through my company. They're a sponsor tonight."

"Rad," Reyana said a little too happily. "Hey, if you ever want to talk about Anime and the merits of illustration versus converting them into live-action trash, you should look me up on socials."

For the first time, Sameer's grin was genuine. Pearly white and very straight, the brace face situation had done its job.

"Sure. I will."

He and Pinky Aunty left, but not before the small woman tossed a dirty look at Kareena.

Hot air deflated out of her.

"That could have gone a lot worse," she said, before turning to her sister, and teasing her. "So, *rad*?"

Reyana's face turned beet red. "I know. I was smooth like Ex-Lax, wasn't I?"

Kareena took pity on her. "Hey, I hear the '90s are making a comeback." She bumped her shoulder with her own. "You think you like him?"

"I don't know, maybe." Her sister shrugged and put her hands on her hips. "But, he's meant for you, clearly."

"I'm pretty sure he had eyes for you. But, wait, how the hell did Pinky Aunty know we—I—was going to be here?"

Reyana sighed, tossing her head. "That was all me. I'm so sorry, Kara. I mentioned it to the parents when they asked why I couldn't come down to Connecticut early for their *Diwali* celebrations this weekend. Then Dad mentioned he wanted to give you a call to get you and Tam-Tam to come earlier. Me and my big mouth told him you were coming to this party with me. I think they were trying to bombard you with Sameer in the comfort of our childhood home, but then plans changed. They probably told Pinky Aunty." She flailed her arms in an illustration of how easily words flew around within their community. "And the rest is history. That woman has balls, that's for sure." She grabbed what looked like a scallop sitting in a large clamshell from the waiter's tray, who'd paused near them. "God, I'm starving."

Kareena ruminated over this. Here was the thing: although it was the matchmaker who had bombarded her in a place she least expected it, Kareena would be on the hook. She could already envision the conversation she'd have with her parents. "She's just doing her job," her father would say, bobbling his head. "You didn't even try to give this boy a chance?" her mother would ask, hurt, as if Kareena had rebuffed her, not Sameer. Then, ever the dutiful daughter, she would call Pinky Aunty, set up time for tea, falling all over herself to make sure she could fit into the matchmaker's overly booked calendar. The chance of another matchmaking scheme being thrown at her *while* she was apologizing for this one going south wasn't out of the question. Pinky Aunty not only had balls; they were huge.

Right now, she wanted to feel as free as her sister did, not giving a single thought to how offended Pinky might be. Just living her life the way she wanted to, eating food at a party like she hadn't a care in the world. But that just wasn't her role in the family. And now, old Kareena, the responsible one, the polite one, decided to make an appearance.

"Maybe I should go after them," she said worriedly.

"No way," her sister said with her mouth full. "It's not your fault if Pinky Aunty is butthurt. You had no idea she'd be here. What if, in the off chance, you met a guy here and you two were getting it on, and she bombarded you?" Kareena couldn't help but snort at the ridiculous notion that she'd meet a guy at this party and make out (seriously, had her sister never seen her social ineptness?). Reyana grabbed the server's arm before they walked away, taking another scallop. "Don't you think that would've been way worse? You handled it great. Anyway, forget about it for now. We have to find Devika and lock in this pre-holiday gig she wants our podcast for." Her sister practically gobbled up the second scallop, closing her eyes in bliss. "O. M. God, you have *got* to try these."

Kareena wrinkled her nose. She wasn't into seafood unless it was really good, really fresh salmon sushi. Her mother had beaten her chest and wailed to Goddess Annapurna when Kareena finally told her she didn't like her fish curry.

She crossed her arms over her chest, wanting to address something before it got too out of hand.

"Hey, it's *your* podcast. I'm just … helping until I figure out my sabbatical end date." She grasped her thick hair, pulling it over one shoulder, combing her fingers through the strands—a habit of hers when she needed to think. "I'm going back to work eventually; you know that, right? My patients need me."

Did they? Or did she need them?

"Mhm," her sister murmured. "What about the 'Meh' you

tossed out before? I thought Aunty was going to go into a state of shock and we'd have to perform CPR or something."

Kareena remained silent while Reya grabbed the last seashell from the server's tray, before they scooted off. She handed it to her with a cocktail napkin.

Kareena stood there holding the beautifully presented scallop. It sat in a large white shell—was this its home before it sacrificed its life? She was starting to sound like her daughter, who was on the verge of becoming a vegetarian after learning about animal cruelty at school.

It did look tempting, though. The firm white flesh was browned perfectly, glistening under a drizzle of pink sauce, with pomegranate seeds artfully piled on top. And it smelled divine.

"Seriously, lady, put that shit in your mouth. You don't know what you're missing!"

Kareena examined it again. Then picked it up gingerly between her thumb and forefinger before taking a small bite.

Immediately, rich buttery goodness exploded in her mouth, followed by tart and spicy sweet, then the satisfying little bursts of the seeds as she finished chewing. Was that her humming while she ate?

"Definitely NOT shit," she uttered, astounded and swallowing. "Whoa."

And then she stuffed the rest in her mouth, her eyes almost crossing at how good it tasted.

How had she never tried scallops? Dear God, what had she been missing out on all these years? She was about to ask her sister why she'd never made her try them before, when she noticed Reyana wasn't paying attention. Her gaze was locked on someone behind her.

Oh no, not again.

There was only one other way to nip this in the bud.

She whirled around, mouth still full, not caring how rude she was about to be. But instead of the big-headed, little figure of the matchmaker, she was met with an expanse of crisp, dark grey cotton, and thick, muscular arms crossed in front of a wide chest.

Confused, she tilted her head back, letting her eyes slide up the stiff material, passing over a wide neck with ropey veins and a hint of a thick gold chain, to a strong jaw covered in a short auburn beard. And her eyes didn't stop there because she couldn't stop them if she wanted to. Thick lips curled into a sensual smile, and she paused there, licking her own lips. The husky chuckle that came from those lips reverberated down to her core, and she shuddered, finally looking up to meet the dancing cinnamon brown eyes of none other than Zayn Stavros.

What was he doing here, looking too hot to handle in his simple chef's clothes?

Heat bombarded her cheeks, and her body followed suit, a warmth spreading from the depths of her belly out to her limbs.

"Yummy umami," she murmured, not even sure where she'd heard that, and swallowed the bite that was still in her mouth. "Probably the best thing I've ever put in my mouth." Of course, both statements were wildly inappropriate, and she had no idea where they'd come from.

He grinned, and she couldn't believe she'd said any of that out loud.

"That good, huh?" he asked softly, his voice gravelly. "I'm glad you enjoyed it."

She shivered in reaction.

Her sister lightly shoved her from behind, but it only pushed her closer to Zayn and the heat he emanated. And his smell …

the sophisticated scent of spices and masculine citrus mingling with cooking aromas.

She couldn't help but whisper, "Whoa."

She was awkward; she'd never refute that. She'd always been that way. But why couldn't she pull herself together around this man? He was a hot, hunky enigma she couldn't decipher and it made her a nervous ball of energy.

"Is that so?" he asked, his eyebrows raised.

Shit. He'd heard that?

CHAPTER 8

ᛒ

*H*e heard her murmur a low, 'whoa.' Her smooth husky voice laced with surprise and, if he wasn't mistaken, something that sounded very much like desire.

He couldn't help responding to that, teasing her, as her cheeks flooded a pretty pink, and she bit the bottom of her pouty lips.

He stared into her eyes, enormous and deep brown, soft like velvet, filled with wonder and heat. His chest constricted and fizzy bubbles popped in his veins.

Immediately, he felt a tightening in his pants as she licked pomegranate sauce off with the tip of her tongue, swiping at her upper lip. His eyes freely roamed lower, over the smooth skin of her neck, over the mounds of her full breasts, the heaviness of her silver jewelry a contrast to the delicate flesh almost quivering under his watchful gaze. His eyes raked lower, over her bare abdomen, her abundance of curves, her flesh begging him to roam his palms over, to explore the dips and folds, and to grab in the heat of passion. Her long skirt molded to her rounded hips before it swished out to frothy layers of seafoam green and turquoise, shot with silver and gold. She looked beautiful, like a water goddess manifested from the depths of the sea.

"Zayn Stavros, is that you?" The woman standing behind her asked, forcing him to take his eyes off the vision in front of him. "It's been *forever*! When did you get back into town? Wait, are you catering this event?! How did you know it was us?"

Zayn nodded, smiling at the bombardment of questions, realizing it was Kareena's younger sister, all grown up. She was attractive in that overly stylized chic way, but his eyes begged to return to the other woman, her natural beauty speaking volumes to him.

Kareena stepped back, pulling her thick hair over her shoulder and covering her breasts, to his disappointment. He'd always loved her body, and he'd known when they were younger that she was self-conscious. But now, her fuller curves screamed something more to him, different from the young horniness they'd experienced together. More like the desires of a woman that only a man (him) could fulfill. He had an instant craving to see all of her on display.

"I recognized you from across the room and wanted to come say hello," he said politely, though inside, his directional compass had felt pulled in Kareena's direction. He'd seen Kareena speaking with a man and a familiar-looking small, older woman. Again, he was taken aback and he'd asked himself, again, if he was seeing things, if the vision of Kareena was real. But it didn't matter, because when he observed the man and her, with their friendly body language, and then she placed her hand on his arm, his feet moved automatically in their direction, a sizzling feeling burning in his chest. Though, waylaid multiple times by guests recognizing him, his intent was on Kareena.

"I just got back into town," he said, doing his best to focus on Reyana, but confused that she didn't already know he was back. He glanced down at Kareena, her eyes moving around his face. "You didn't mention it?"

"What?" she asked faintly. He grinned, knowing he was the source of her muddled brain.

"We ran into each other in Midtown about a week ago." He kept his eyes on her as she fiddled with the empty clam shell, stacking her cocktail glass on top.

He reached over, taking them from her, their fingers brushing. Tingles shot up his spine.

He jerked a nod to a server a few feet away, who immediately came over. He dumped the empty things on their tray unceremoniously.

"What!?" Reyana squealed sharply. Zayn did his best not to flinch. He forgot how loud and overly excitable she was. "Kara, you never said anything!"

"I ... forgot," she said weakly.

She forgot?

How was that possible when anytime he wasn't thinking about his inheritance, he was thinking about their random meeting on the street? He was thinking about what she'd felt like in his arms. He was thinking about ... her. However much he didn't want to.

"To answer your question: I *am* working this event." He kept his eyes on Kareena as she looked everywhere but at him. "The restaurant that's catering isn't mine, but I'm helping a former colleague out."

"You know Chef Lauren Bates?" Reyana asked

incredulously, impressed. "Of course you do. You're like, part of that up-to-the-minute cool chef crowd."

"Sure," Zayn answered readily. "Lauren and I went to school together at ICI in Switzerland—the International Culinary Institute." He clarified. "We've been colleagues on and off, and I owe a few favors, so here I am."

"Wow!" Reyana said, clapping her hands together. "Lauren Bates' restaurant, Nosh, is *the* talk of the town!"

"That's right!" Kareena chimed in, looking at him with those wide eyes, her thick, finely shaped brows raised high. "You guys were in that great *New York Magazine* article. What was the title?" She tapped her lips, thinking. "'Nosh: On everyone's lips *and* minds,'" she quoted. "But you created that amazing scallop recipe?" She waved in the direction the server had gone.

"I did."

She nodded, her eyes on his chest again, roaming over his crossed arms, focusing on the tattoo on his inner right wrist—a chef's knife.

"If the scallop was the best thing you've ever put in your mouth," he said, leaning into her, smelling her sweet, herbal, and musky scent. "I wonder what you'll think of the marinated paneer."

Kareena's mouth opened slightly, the tip of her pink tongue darting out and back in.

Fuck, now he was hard.

How was this happening? He needed to get out of there.

"So, everything good here?" he asked, straightening up and pulling the front of his chef's jacket down, hoping his hard-on wasn't apparent.

"Wonderful," she murmured, her dark gaze shyly returning to his.

"Just peachy!" Reyana said, breaking the tension that could only best be described as sexual between him and the woman he couldn't keep his eyes off. "I can't wait to try the cheese dish. If it's as orgasmic as the scallops, put it into my mouth asap. Right, Kara?"

He chuckled at Kareena's reaction, the mortified expression on her face. "Right," she squeaked out, running her fingers rhythmically through the thick strands of her wavy hair.

"Orgasmic was exactly what I was going for." He nodded, still only focused on the woman who seemed to take up space in his brain more than he thought was possible lately. He wasn't sure if he was annoyed or humored by it. Regardless, he was enjoying himself, making his former high school sweetheart squirm.

"Can't wait to put it in my mouth and taste it," she said huskily.

Her darkened gaze boldly met his, and fuck, she was dishing it back to him.

His boner got tighter in his pants, telling him he needed to escape this quietly sexy woman immediately.

He scanned the room behind them and saw a West Indies DJ he knew, having attended his wedding recently. He waved, getting his attention.

"I have to go see to a few other guests."

He turned to leave; relief mixed with something else he couldn't quite put his finger on settled inside him. But he couldn't resist tossing over his shoulder, directed only at Kareena, before fully retreating, "It was great seeing you again … Karma."

He didn't know why he'd said it, but using the nickname he'd given her from high school, an amalgamation of both of her names, 'Kareena' and 'Sharma,' was worth it to see her reaction.

"Same," she murmured, nodding, wonder in her eyes as the corner of her lip lifted in an impish smile.

HE WAS in the middle of directing dessert service much later, when he noticed Kareena in front of the wall of flowers, speaking to the smaller woman from earlier—the one he thought he recognized. It seemed innocent enough, but then the smaller woman waved her arms wildly, her face transforming from placidly patronizing to darkly livid in the blink of an eye.

No one seemed to notice; there was too much going on. A celebrated Indian drum player was on stage, playing in tandem with a hot Bangladeshi-American musician's new track. The music artist experimented with innovative sounds on his new hit single via his laptop as the drummer banged his *tablas* in tandem hypnotically. The captivated audience crowded on the dance floor, shiny with sweat, hair floppy, and clothes awry.

This was turning out to be quite a party, Zayn thought, as he oversaw the desserts laid out artistically on the buffet. No detail was too small, he thought, nodding his head at the servers finishing up as they sprinkled edible flower petals onto the exquisite-looking sweets. Before heading back into the kitchen, he looked over his shoulder at Kareena, wondering if he should say goodbye.

He shook his head, thinking better of it. The more distance he kept from her, the more he could rid himself of this feeling of want. Livid with himself for flirting with her earlier, he ruminated over what the fuck was wrong with him. It was just so easy to flirt with her, though. Their attraction was thick, home-churned butter that required no more than a dull knife to slice. One false move, and he'd end up pursuing her, and for what? There was too much left unsaid between them to make that move. It would be ugly—more than ugly.

But when he glanced in her direction, he caught sight of the smaller woman practically dragging her away from the party, and his curiosity was piqued. First, the woman was deceivingly strong, if she was able to strong-arm a woman almost a foot taller than her, and with more substance. Unless Kareena was letting her, which wasn't far off from what she was like when they were kids—letting the elders tell her what to do.

But the look of rage on Kareena's face, the low furrowed brow, her lips moving quickly, had his feet begin to move in their direction. Kareena had always been known for her patience. So, unless she'd done a complete makeover on her personality since high school, there was no way her buttons hadn't been pushed at the moment.

What the hell was going on?

He caught up with them outside the party, near the coat check, and heard a few words spewed from the older woman's mouth. He held back momentarily, waiting to see if he should jump in.

"—I can't believe you let this happen. Sameer was meant for you, and only you. Do you think I would try to set my nephew up with just anyone? Now, you've ruined it."

"How exactly have I ruined it? You surprised me here. And regardless, I had no idea that everyone was trying to marry me off to Sameer."

The older woman pointed a shaky finger in Kareena's face, her eyes slit. "Don't you speak about him that way."

Kareena put her hands up in defense. "I wasn't speaking about him in any way. It's just—" She huffed out a breath. "I didn't know that you and my parents were in cahoots to have me meet him. He's a perfectly fine person, Aunty. But I wasn't ready. A lot is going on in my life right now. I have my child, and well, you know, I'm figuring my job out. And well ... and ... and..."

Curious, Zayn moved closer. Kareena stuttered nervously before she finally huffed and blurted out, "And, I'm already engaged."

Zayn's feet stopped in his tracks, frozen to the spot at this new information.

"To whom? Answer me at once!" the little woman demanded, her voice shrill.

"You don't know him—he's not part of ... the community."

She was already engaged, for a second time? His heart felt like it plummeted down to the soles of his feet, and irrationally, his anger fired up.

The older woman's nostrils practically fumed with smoke. She grabbed Kareena's arms and attempted to shake her. "I knew none of this. Were you working with another matchmaker?!" Immediately, the older woman went from anger to appalled to what looked like anguish as her face crumpled like a prune and she began to ... was she howling?

The hell?!

Zayn wasn't sure if he should be disgusted or if he should laugh. He was no professional, but either this woman was the best actor who never graced the sets of Bollywood, or she had an undiagnosed personality disorder. He was willing to bet it was a little of both.

"Pinky Aunty," Kareena said, her voice calm now. "I'm a grown woman. I can make my own decisions, you know."

The Pinky woman, whom he now realized was the illustrious matchmaker in the South Asian community, covered her face with her hands. She sobbed loudly, with what looked to Zayn like crocodile tears, and her small shoulders trembling. He had to hand it to her; she was pretty good.

"Your parents are so worried about you, *Beta*. Don't you see? You're falling into a black hole that you won't be able to come back from. First, your husband dies. Then you lose your job." The older woman sniffed loudly over Kareena's protests of taking a sabbatical. "I can only imagine what you did in your last life to deserve this. And now you have your *meye* (daughter) to look out for by yourself. You can't manage! *Tomar meye mushkil* (your daughter is difficult)! Don't you want the chance to have normal children?"

He was stunned, but the look on Kareena's face didn't give him time to ruminate over the woman's horrible words. Her expression had him standing up taller, his muscles tensing and ready for action. She went from trying to hear the woman out, giving her the benefit of the doubt, it seemed, to absolute murder.

He'd never seen Kareena so livid in his entire life. Her chest heaved heavily, the mounds of her breasts puffed over the material of her blouse, stretching the fabric taut. He saw her raise a hand. Slowly, it got higher and higher, until it was above her head, her palm stretched wide. He knew immediately that was the look of someone determined to slap the shit out of the other person. Honestly, from the words spewing from the hateful woman, he couldn't blame her.

He darted to them and, in one swift motion, grabbed Kareena by the wrist and pulled her into him, wrapping her in his arms, keeping his body between her and the other woman as a shield. He held her tight, stroking her back rhythmically. He shushed into her hair, smelling her and feeling her all at once. It calmed his erratic heart down, too.

"It's okay," he said quietly in her ear.

If he knew anything about moms, they were naturally protective to begin with. But if someone so much as glanced at their child the wrong way, fight mode was their automatic code-switch. He would know. His mother had been his biggest champion while he struggled in school because of his attention issues. He'd learned later that he had some form of ADHD, but even as an adult, mother continued to check in with him, though he knew how to manage it most days. She was still very protective.

"Z—Zayn?" Kareena whispered into his chest; her fists balled up tightly between them.

"Yeah, it's me." He exhaled and inhaled, hoping the deep movements of his breath would calm her racing heart which beat rapidly against his own. "Are you okay?"

His concern was only for her, though the small woman kept yapping beside them, more annoying than a chihuahua on steroids. She alternated between asking who he was to admonishing Kareena for physical abuse.

He was about to ask the older woman in what world was it

okay to speak about someone's child so callously, when Kareena took him off guard by saying, "I feel like I'm out of control." Followed up immediately with "I think I tore my blouse."

They both looked down to see a silver safety pin dangling precariously on her shirt, the cause of a large rip in the delicate material.

As the pin swung and finally slipped out, falling between them, Zayn couldn't focus on anything else but her breasts; the ones his eyes kept returning to earlier in the night. More of her smooth brown skin was revealed to his view, along with her lacy brown bra, between the two top hooks, and a huge gaping hole made even bigger by the rip. He had a sudden animalistic urge to lean down and wriggle his tongue into the exposed, tight cleft between her breasts. Would it fit?

Fuck, now he was turned on again.

She wiggled a hand up and covered the hole, to his dismay and his utter relief. She looked up at him with her big brown eyes, soft and sweet, like liquid chocolate, so expressive, and full of something that warmed him down to his bones.

"Zayn—"

Again, the woman asked shrilly, "Who *is* this, Kareena? Tell me at once!"

He was more than annoyed at the absolute monster standing there berating Kareena as if she'd done something wrong. He was confused by his uncontrollable desire for the woman in his arms, who kept popping into his life lately. He was dumbfounded that the most natural feeling he had was to protect her. But why?

In a muddle of emotions that he knew he'd have to unpack much later, he sighed loudly in aggravation. He kept an arm wrapped around Kareena as he turned to the woman, hiding none of his disdain as he said, "I'm Zayn Stavros."

But before he could ask her what her problem was, Kareena jumped in.

"This is my fiancé, Aunty."

MILES HIGH IN THE SKY

PRESENT DAY

the stavros' family jet

CHAPTER 9

꠵

*S*ilence.

That's what Kareena met when she'd uttered those words a few weeks ago, not realizing the significant web of lies that would unfold; seeds of deceit spread haphazardly into the wind. She'd never forget the shocked stare of the matchmaker, how she looked like someone who was about to get pie smashed into her face.

She hadn't dared look up at Zayn. He'd think she'd lost her marbles. For the record, maybe she finally had. Life was throwing her hurdles, as if she were some kind of parkour expert. She'd never been that sort of athlete, though. She'd always been slow and steady, taking the safest, clearest path.

But that didn't feel right anymore. It felt more than wrong, like she was wearing an ill-fitting costume.

And, Zayn—she glanced over at him sitting in one of the private jet's comfy leather captain's seats, as he doodled on a pad of paper, making a list of some sort. He just happened to always be around when she needed rescuing. He was her savior that night, cooling her anger down when she was about to lose complete control. Pinky Aunty needed a good smack, but she was glad he'd stepped in. And she'd felt safe with his arm wrapped around her. She'd felt like she had the spine of someone bolder than her normal self.

She'd had to think fast, before he undid what she'd just put into motion, or in case old Kareena swooped in and fucked things up with her preference for a backbone that resembled jelly. She'd swiveled back to him, pressing herself into his body, and there was no denying that it felt sublime.

Even now, sitting there beside him and staring at his profile, his strong square jawline, with his lip between his teeth as he scribbled, then crossed it out, she could still feel that sublime sensation. How she fit his large, muscular frame perfectly.

One of his legs jiggled, indicating his excitement at whatever he worked on, making him look much younger than he was, more like the teenager she'd tutored. She had the sudden urge to wrap her arms around him and put her face in his neck; tell him whatever he had plans for would come to fruition. She would help him however she could.

That night, she'd boldly stood on her tiptoes, while she slid her hands up his chest, feeling the rock hardness of his muscles, and the heat that bled through his chef's jacket. She swiped across the breadth of his wide shoulders and over his neck, just brushing his prominent Adam's apple that bobbed deliciously at her touch. She'd cupped his face with both hands, his beard scratchy against her palms.

"Don't be mad," she'd pleaded in a whisper, bringing his head down to hers and meeting those sexy, thick lips with her own.

Oh ... to kiss him ...

She'd moved softly across his mouth, feeling the warmth

of him against her, tasting a spicy sweetness, akin to pistachios and cardamom, and the smoky hint of tobacco underneath. Did he still smoke? She'd wondered. He'd smoked in high school, too. He'd stood motionless for a few seconds, shocked, she assumed, at her actions ... until his large hands slid up to her waist, his palms searing her bare lower back, pulling her ever so slightly closer to him. She'd felt every muscle along the front of his body against hers, including the growing stiffness between his legs. Her knees weakened as he'd taken control, keeping the kiss gentle but swiping her lips with his heated tongue. It'd felt anything but pretend.

Oh God. What had Pinky Aunty thought?

Even now, sitting miles up in the sky, she put her face in her hands in mortification. Here she was weeks later, still experiencing the heat percolating in her belly before it dripped down between her legs as she recalled fervently shimmying her hips against his hardness.

She shifted side to side in her seat, trying to alleviate some of the tension in her body.

Zayn lifted his head, his eyes hooded and serious, so similar to what they'd looked like when they parted from that kiss, though then his look had been filled with utter need.

"Everything good, Karma?" he asked, putting the tip of his pencil in his mouth, his mind not completely on her. "Do you want some water, champagne, a cocktail?"

He didn't wait for an answer but flagged the flight attendant down, whom he seemed to be very familiar with. They talked easily, and he ordered himself a martini and a champagne for her.

She thanked him and turned to stare out the window as they

cruised through a sea of clouds in all manner of thickness and density.

"Yummy umami."

That's what he'd murmured after they'd parted, rubbing his thumb over her bottom lip.

She'd been more than embarrassed by that point. He'd repeated back to her that ridiculous statement, taunting her. She'd wanted a hole to open up below her and swallow her. But they'd turned to the matchmaker instead, ready to gauge her reaction.

Kareena had never seen the woman so flustered. Her bony hand was pressed to her chest, the jewels flashing every time she puffed out a breath. Kareena worried she was about to faint. Her face was pale before it mottled to purple. Kareena had momentarily felt a stab of remorse. She hadn't meant for it to look so ... real, so passionate. But it had, and she couldn't have stopped it if she wanted to.

The matchmaker tossed her silver bob, seeming to have composed herself. "Your parents never said anything." She'd addressed Kareena with slit eyes.

"They don't know. It happened so fast." The confidence with which that lie came out of her had been shocking ... exhilarating. There was definitely something wrong with her, and she'd need to find some time to put her psychiatrist hat on and figure it out.

Pinky Aunty, who never missed anything, looked between the two of them, her brow raised. She pursed her lips.

"I'm disappointed, *Beta.*"

And then she'd turned to Zayn.

"How do I know you, young man?" She'd examined him closely in his chef's scrubs. "You look familiar."

"Who says you do?" Zayn had answered with sheer arrogance. Kareena would have found it attractive, except that she didn't need his attitude at that moment.

She'd fumbled and quickly come up with, "Zayn!" while swatting his arm playfully. "You know him, Aunty. But it's been so long."

She'd explained facts that were real: who his parents were, the last time he'd probably been at one of the Indian get-togethers as a teenager. Zayn had jerked his head in acceptance as the other woman nodded in recognition, still giving him a critical once-over. Then she'd glossed over how they'd run into each other recently. They'd caught up, and one thing had led to another. Now, they were newly engaged and completely happy.

Then she'd given Pinky Aunty the highest compliment she ever could.

"You're the first to know. And that's why I'm not wearing a ring." She'd flashed her ringless left hand while Pinky observed her closely. She followed up with, "We plan on telling our families together, soon." Hoping the other woman got the hint. It was a delicate balance getting a woman like Pinky on her side. You couldn't outright tell her what to do, but you could instill empathy in her.

Zayn had been completely silent through all of this, and she wasn't sure if she should cringe or be thankful. There was no way she could come back from this. She might have to certify herself as insane.

"And so, young man, you come from a good Indian family —the Roys. I know them. And your mother's side—I remember, it was quite a scandal when your parents married. But she comes from an old European shipping family—Greek, I think. Successful business people. Lots of money."

Kareena remembered him stiffening beside her. The cringey nature of the entire ordeal surely couldn't get any worse.

"You forgot to mention that I stand to inherit a boatload of money, too, no pun intended," Zayn had said frigidly.

And ... the cringey factor had gotten worse.

"But you cook for a living, instead of being a businessman. May I ask what happened there?"

And *now* they'd just entered into a whole new level of ick.

"No. You may not," he'd said, his deep voice brokering no argument as he'd squeezed Kareena's waist and pulled her closer to his side. But he'd stared down at her, into her eyes, and she thought, things might be looking up, until she realized she couldn't read what he was thinking. He'd said something about toiling all day in the kitchen and needing to be with his fiancé. She couldn't remember exactly because his eyes roved all over her body, making her feel hot and flustered.

She'd known then that he wasn't going to go along with this so easily. Zayn Stavros had always been aware of her tendencies to do as her family wished. The one big reason she'd broken up with him was just that. He couldn't compete with what her parents wanted of her. He'd been so angry, hurt. And there she was, at the age of thirty-six, using him, trying to thwart her parents' plans to get her to remarry. She was pathetic.

She was so grateful that he'd played along, flashing a wide grin, where she knew those two identical dimples existed on each cheek under his beard. But it had made her wonder what was in it for him.

CHAPTER 10

ᔆ o

"*M*r. Stavros, your martini. Ma'am, champagne?" One of their usual flight attendants handed Zayn his chilled cocktail while leaning over to hand Kareena her champagne. The woman lingered a little too long, keeping her body close as she gave him her best come-fuck-me look.

For some reason, this annoyed him more than anything.

"Thank you, Thalia. My fiancé and I appreciate it," he said cordially, a heavy stress on the word *fiancé*.

Thalia nodded, getting the hint, and backed off with a miffed sniff. He couldn't blame her. She regularly gave him blow jobs in one of the two bathrooms on board, and he happily reciprocated on return flights, eating her out, even when they hit turbulence. The bumps making it a challenge he welcomed. But lately, the only woman he was interested in was the one sitting next to him.

Kareena, whose eyes were glued to the window as she appeared lost in thought, sat up straighter and took a sip, making a small sound of approval as she tasted the champagne. It shouldn't sound so sexy to him, but it did.

"Was that really necessary?" she asked, though her face beamed.

He hadn't realized she noticed the cold shoulder he'd given Thalia.

"Really? If you want, I can bring her back over—" He turned, making it seem like he was about to flag the other woman down.

Kareena laughed and grabbed his arm, pulling it around her shoulders. She continued drinking her champagne as she snuggled down in her seat.

"Nah. You're mine."

His chest lit up at her words, and he felt buoyant, like he was floating on his back in the middle of the Mediterranean.

"—for the time being," she finished, sinking that buoyant feeling inside him.

He cleared his throat and continued to drink his martini. He pulled off the three Castelvetrano olives from the toothpick, chomping at the mild buttery bites in one go.

"Tell me about this taverna. I want to know what you're after..." At his frown, she continued, "...and what's rightfully yours, of course."

He nodded and explained to her how special the old taverna was. It'd been on Naxos since anyone could remember; the local watering hole for those who labored and lived on the island for generations. When she asked who the laborers consisted of, he filled with pride as he listed off the fishermen, boaters, olive pickers, oil mill workers, and the estate's staff and groundskeepers. He probably sounded a bit wistful as he spoke, but the part about keeping the taverna on the island, though converting it to a more modern place, made him extremely happy. He'd grown up with many of the people who toiled away on the island. At the end of the day, the people of Naxos helped his family, too. He was extremely grateful for their loyalty, even though some of them had been little shits when they were kids, chasing him around town trying to steal his new bike or skateboard. He realized quickly that they didn't have much, and he shared his things with them, making lifelong friends. So, by doing this, taking on this project, it was his way of giving back, while fulfilling his dream of his own place.

"That's really ... beautiful, Zayn." She shook her head, her eyes bright in admiration.

He felt a little embarrassed. Admiring his good deeds was not why he had skin in the game. These were things he felt responsible for—things he felt needed to be done. He'd explained all of this to her when they'd first laid out all the rules, facts, and outcomes. She knew all about Silas and his greed; about the stipulation of being engaged to get his inheritance. He didn't mention the last part—the marriage portion. Because, quite frankly, he wanted nothing to do with it.

"The taverna is really special. I want to keep the guts of it, the parts that make it so memorable. Like the old bar. It's ancient. I'm going to refurbish it. Hopefully it's not rot-filled."

"Why's it so special?"

"When I turned eighteen, my grandfather took me there, sat me at the bar, and ordered me my first beer."

Kareena nodded.

"It's also where I got my first blow-job ... from the bartender's daughter."

Her mouth dropped, and she closed it immediately, rolling her puffy lips inwards.

"Too much information?" He leaned into her, whispering against her thick hair. "Remember, eye on the prize."

"Not at all," she said, trying not to choke on the last of her champagne. Her cheeks pinkened, and she looked out the window at the clouds parting with the jet's airstream. "If I recall correctly, you'd already told me about the bartender's daughter who'd flirted with you all night on your eighteenth birthday and kept plying you with ouzo shots." She tilted her head and glanced at him beneath her lashes, looking utterly innocent before she added, "And then you barfed all over her when she'd just made you ... you know."

"I told you all that?"

He had. Of course, he had. They'd shared everything (including his first sexual experiences the summer before moving to Connecticut) during the school year and summer of their young romance. So much so that when she'd suddenly ended it, he'd been shocked, having no idea that being apart was her ultimate goal. They'd never once discussed a future without each other.

He shook his head from the memory of being blindsided. The betrayal and anger. They'd been way too young to be discussing such nonsense about their futures, though the hurt never fully receded. Even now, his chest stung just thinking about it.

She nodded. "And, of course, you know my first experience."

He didn't need to ask; it was him. He'd been the first one to kiss her, put his hands on and inside her, the very first to taste her between her lush thighs, making her come in breathy cries. And he'd taught her how to hold him in his hand, grasp him, clutch him, and make him come undone.

The thought sent waves of lust through him, and he felt the crotch of his pants tighten. Not because of the thought of them screwing around as teenagers, but at the thought of fucking around as adults. It wasn't the first time he'd thought about it.

She licked her lips and pulled her hair over one shoulder. She ran her fingers rhythmically through the bluish black strands, deep in thought.

"Kareena," he said low in her ear. Her body shivered in reaction, and from his vantage point, her nipples hardened underneath the material of her dress, perfectly capping the heavy weight of each of her breasts. His hands itched to cup them, squeeze them; find out if they were as soft and firm as he remembered. "We can always cross that line if we feel like it. There's nothing wrong when it's two consenting adults."

GOD, what was he saying? The way he was looking at her, like she was the perfect chaser to his martini, made her insides turn into a fire that desperately needed stoking. She couldn't concentrate on anything but the way his thick lips moved as he offered her something she had urgently—wantonly—wanted since first seeing him again.

Would it be so terrible? They were officially engaged—for the time being. The weight of the platinum engagement ring on her finger, with the enormous solitaire diamond that he'd procured for her at the start of this charade, validated that fact.

Her new self, the taking-life-by-the-balls Kareena, was the one making the case for pure adulterated fun. And why not? Surf, sun, and sex?

"They're basically the three most vital S's for a beach vacation," her sister had said.

Personally, Kareena believed more in Sleep, Sunscreen, and Supplements. But that was rule-follower Kareena.

So, why not? She could trust this man, couldn't she?

He leaned in and nuzzled her hair. "We know it'll be good. What's the harm? Eye on the prize, of course."

He almost had her. He'd almost made his case and won it without practical Kareena barging in to make the argument that it was absolutely crossing THE line—the one that most definitely counted. One that she'd never be able to return from. She wasn't flippant about sex—really had never had the chance to be. Unless she counted the few drunken scenarios in college, and those weren't even fully doing it.

And then she'd been too busy with medical school before getting engaged to Arjun. She'd lost her virginity to him when they got married. Sex with him—well, if 'wasn't so bad' was a category, he'd get a gold star. They'd gotten to know one another through the arranged marriage process, so their wedding night wasn't too weird. It was fine, if not a little awkward in the beginning. But she attributed that to his being reserved with his feelings. In any case, she was seriously lacking in the sex department. But, she had a feeling that if she let her physical needs take over with Zayn—the man who'd always owned a piece of her heart—she'd lose her entire self, and where would she be when they ended things? He held the reins now when it came to what they were doing, whether he knew it or not, and he could easily toy with her and toss her aside once he got his inheritance. The smarter move was for her to keep herself protected. She had her future and her daughter to think about.

She let herself finger the thick gold chain around his neck. It was warm to the touch, heavy as she lifted it and let it drop. She heard and felt his loud exhalation as she continued to trace the weighty metal.

With her heart racing, her back arching in a primal reaction to him, and with the desire in her belly swirling like an inferno, she said, "I think it might be best if we leave it for now, Zayn."

There was a pause, as if he thought she was joking. But then he exhaled again; this time she heard his growl of frustration as he sat back against his seat, running a hand through his hair. But he nodded.

"Yeah, it might be for the best."

The flight attendant from before, the stupid, flirty one who shamelessly smooshed her boobs into Zayn's face when delivering their drinks, swished by them quickly. Kareena couldn't help but notice his eyes follow her down the aisle.

Jealousy blistered in Kareena's breast. She huffed as Zayn unbuckled and got up. He stretched and she stared at his profile, before her eyes roved down his body of their own accord, noticing his arousal through his pants. He was big. She knew that, and seeing the outline of him made her gulp. Nervous? No. She was more turned on than ever.

He made his way in the opposite direction the other woman had gone, towards the restroom. She was relieved for the moment, in mind only. Her body—well, that was an entirely different issue.

CHAPTER 11

꒳꒳

They'd made good time, or so she'd been told. True to Zayn's word, Theo, their captain, landed them with barely a bump at a private terminal in Athens, Greece, within nine hours.

Zayn, his mother, Penelope, and her fiancé clapped and cheered the captain, while Silas frowned and grumbled at their behavior. Kareena's curiosity was piqued. What was with this older man's constant need for entitlement and displeasure? With so much effort put into it, he must constantly be exhausted. She wondered what made him act that way. But, she didn't have time to dwell on that because they were getting ready to deplane.

She felt refreshed, though she shouldn't be surprised. She'd never flown privately, let alone in first class. She might have an idea of what the extremely wealthy were accustomed to, but to experience it first-hand was quite a treat. She couldn't get past the staff's constant attentiveness (buxom Thalia no longer attended them, but a middle-aged man named Nick). Beverages, snacks, or a warm towel were always at hand. Two meal options were given for all of their meals, and a lovely traditional continental breakfast was served early morning. It was by far her favorite. A variety of yummy cheeses, fresh bread, coffee, or hot chocolate, and fruit; she was in heaven. When she'd needed to sleep, Zayn showed her how to recline her already comfy, roomy seat for maximum comfort. Automatically, Nick was by their side with a fuzzy blanket, eye mask, earplugs, and a silky pillow for her.

Could she live on this plane forever?

"You look refreshed and ready for anything," Zayn said, interrupting her thoughts.

She grinned and thought the same thing about him. He'd somehow managed to change his shirt into a fresh white waffle knit polo and navy pants. His hair was wet as if he'd showered, ready to take their fake engagement to the next level (i.e., with his entire family and the people of Naxos).

"Did you take a shower?" She ran her fingers through her hair and grabbed her mirror compact from her purse, making sure she didn't have sleep drool crusted at the corners of her mouth.

"I did. We have two full bathrooms—one in the front and the back. There's a separate corridor that leads to the showers in each of them. Might look more like a sliding door to a linen closet, but they're full, spacious walk-in showers."

Kareena *had* noticed them. The times she'd used either restroom during the flight, she'd poked around. How could she not? When would she ever get to fly on a private jet again?

He continued, "Don't you remember about two hours ago I asked you if you wanted to shower and change?"

"You did? Are you sure?"

He chuckled, his eyes crinkling. "Yes, I'm sure. I definitely remember trying to wake you up. You complained and told me you'd walk me and give me my treat later."

Oh, lord.

Why was she always a moron around this man? Could the Greek gods please lightning bolt her into oblivion, right now?

Now her face was warm. "I…"

But she didn't know how to answer. How did one come back from this? Especially when he was looking at her with a raised, thick brow and licking his lips slowly.

She squirmed in her seat, warmth radiating from her nether regions. She straightened up in her seat before clearly ignoring him and saying, "I'd love to freshen up right now if there's still time?"

He nodded. Thankfully, he took the high road and didn't continue his teasing, though his cinnamon eyes were hooded and unreadable. "There's still time. I'll wait for you here while everyone disembarks."

She nodded meekly and grabbed her carry-on, unbuckling to stand up and slide past him. The plane jerked, and she promptly fell into his lap.

"Karma, we really have to stop meeting like this," he murmured, his big, muscular arms wrapped around her protectively, her body cradled against his solid chest. His deep voice was thick and gravelly as he whispered in her ear. And his scent—the freshness of minty toothpaste on his breath and his masculine citrus smell—intoxicated her. Smooth liquid, hot and insistent, pooled in her panties. Oh God, would she soak through her dress and onto his pants?

She scrambled out of his embrace and tossed her head. She couldn't think straight, and she blamed the long flight and the time zone change. She wordlessly made her way to the bathroom in the back, the sound of his soft chuckles following her.

Inside, she decided she didn't have time for a shower. Instead, she washed her face, brushed her teeth, and applied a quick version of her morning skincare routine. She reapplied her deodorant, changed her underwear, and put on the fresh outfit she'd brought in her carry-on just in case.

She looked at herself in the mirror before exiting, now in a royal blue, fitted tank top, with a slight crop that showed a sliver of skin. She tugged it down a few times, but to no avail. She'd paired it with a tan pleated skirt in lightweight cotton that hit her mid-calves. She had a matching tan cropped jacket to go with it, considering she'd been told the weather wasn't blistering hot now that it was November.

When she exited the bathroom, she saw that she and Zayn were the only ones left on the aircraft. He stood where they'd been sitting, checking his phone, black aviator sunglasses covering his eyes. He looked up when she approached and stared at her for a beat before taking her carry-on from her and motioning her to the exit.

She wasn't expecting the blast of dry heat that hit her once she stepped onto the rolling stairway to deplane. It was definitely arid and hot, and she promptly removed her jacket.

"Shit. It's warmer than I expected. We were just informed that Greece is going through a heatwave for this time of year," Zayn said behind her.

The wind picked up in a gust of hot air, salty ocean, and something musty, which she attributed to the sienna-colored soil covering the landscape and hills in the distance. She gazed at the expanse of stunning, rippling turquoise waves that went on forever. She shuddered at the thought of the never-ending body of water. She hated big bodies of water. They scared the ever-living crap out of her. The idea that she could be stranded in the middle of nowhere with all sorts of ocean creatures swarming about her … she shuddered again. It was one of her worst nightmares that stemmed from a traumatic experience when she was little. And yes, she realized the irony of a psychiatrist who hadn't dealt with a past trauma, but … here she was. Already, panic had a chokehold on her, like hands wringing her neck as something on the edge of her brain began to rapid fire—the beginnings of losing her shit. She took deep breaths, using a box breathing technique she gave many of her patients to calm themselves.

"Mind over matter," she'd repeat to them, and she did the same to herself, as she turned her gaze, noticing dunes and mountains beyond the airport. Thick green foliage and flowers clung to the land, and the lively colors almost vibrated under the bright morning sun. She dug around in her purse for her sunglasses. She continued carefully down the stairs, following the others to a line of sleek, waiting cars.

"Where are we going now?" she asked curiously, getting into the last car with Zayn.

"We're taking the family boat to Naxos. There's a small airport on the island, but we traditionally take the yacht," he said casually, scrolling through his phone again.

"Right," she said as calmly as she could. "How long is the boat ride?"

"It can take up to three hours, but we cruise faster in half the time." He was still going through his phone, mumbling to himself, so he didn't notice that none of what he said quelled her nerves.

She inhaled and exhaled deeply, having a conversation with herself in her head.

You knew this was going to be part of it all. Greece has three oceans bordering it—the Aegean, the Ionian, and the Mediterranean. You can do this. Put your big girl pants on and a lifejacket, and you'll be good to go.

An expletive from Zayn took her mind off, if only momentarily.

"What is it?" she asked.

He grumbled, annoyed. "My social media manager is driving me crazy."

"Um, what? You have a social media manager? Since when?" she asked curiously.

He straightened up and cocked his neck, cracking it. "Well, you know how the life of a celebrity chef is..."

She did know some of it. She had attended a few of his social events through the guise of their fake engagement. She nodded.

"Well, that's only the tip of the iceberg, Kareena. Honestly, I love the cooking portion, but the socializing ... it never stops. I have someone working for me to manage the day-to-day. I hate social media, and my manager loves it, so it's win-win." He shrugged as he finished, not meeting her eyes. She had a strange feeling that he wasn't telling her everything, but the car turned at a small office building and continued to roll to the marina. Now she was back to hyperventilating status as she took in the enormous yachts.

Zayn got out of the car first and helped her out. He left to speak to his family members, and she stood there motionless. The others' excitement carried over to her on the hot breeze, and it only made her more tense. Especially when she looked up to the largest, glossiest white boat, with a big *Stavros Titans* logo on the side, bobbing up and down on the currents that hit the shore. The crew was smiling and filed down the gangplank in an orderly fashion.

"Okay, you can do this." She searched in her bag for her short-term anxiety pills—the ones she'd had a colleague write her a prescription for. She didn't normally take them. However, giant bodies of water called for desperate measures.

"Crap," she muttered, not finding them. She knew she'd packed them; she had actually put them in her cute little compact that she used for this exact purpose.

They must be in her suitcase, which was currently being carried on board by one of the crew members. And then she realized she'd switched out her purse before leaving for the airport. They were still in her other bag in New York—the one she'd decided would be too bulky.

She swallowed once, then twice, and stood frozen as everyone else started to make their way from the curb to the long dock that ran alongside the yacht. She made herself follow, gingerly stepping onto the wooden planks.

Good. They were solid. No chance of any of them splintering and her falling through.

She went slowly, taking her time, breathing in deeply and exhaling with every step. She saw the family and Zayn already up ahead at the yacht, chatting with the crew members who served them shiny crystal flutes of champagne.

Her lovely breakfast from earlier that morning threatened to come up as she gagged. Alcohol on a boat? Oh, hell no.

Zayn was taking two glasses off a tray when her brain emptied of any thought but to get away from the abominable situation she'd gotten herself into. She promptly turned on her heel and made a beeline back down the long dock. She just had to find the car and figure something out. She'd left everything by the boat except for her purse. She had her ID and passport. That's all that mattered, she thought practically, even though she was frantically hustling along the planks over the water. She tried not to look down.

"Kareena!" Zayn shouted, finally noticing she wasn't standing with all of the others nor by the pile of luggage that was being put onto the boat by the staff.

She ran, but damn him, he was fast. Stupid stubby legs, she bemoaned inwardly at her shorter limbs. All of a sudden, something, or things, flew past her in a blur of black. She ducked, her hands over her head.

"What in the hell?" she shrieked. She was continuing on when they came at her again.

This time she fell to her hands and knees, her sunglasses slipping off her head and over the planks, into the deep blue, which probably wasn't so deep, but—really *any* body of water … and all that.

"Hey," Zayn said, his voice louder as he got closer, slowing his gait. He crouched beside her, and *now* was the time for a hole to appear and swallow her up. It was funny how she craved that whenever he was around.

His large, warm hand was suddenly on her back, making slow circles.

"What's happening, Karma?" he asked, concerned. "Do you feel sick? Was it the flight?"

She rolled onto her butt and pulled her legs up to her chest. She dropped her purse and put her head on her knees.

"Kareena?" His concern was rising. "Was it the birds? Did one of them get you? They can be complete assholes, but the swallows are a native bird species around here. They usually migrate during winter."

"The water," she choked out, her face still in her knees.

He sat back on his haunches. "What?"

"Don't look at me. It's so stupid."

"Hey, now." He pulled her arms from around her legs, trying to see her face. She was doing her absolute best not to cry. Why was she such a baby? Why couldn't she love swimming? Why had she let her fears consume her from enjoying one of life's little pleasures?

"Are you still afraid of the water?"

When she didn't answer, he continued. "What happened to the swim lessons I gave you in high school?"

She snorted; she couldn't help it.

He'd managed to teach her a few of the basics, but only after she'd negotiated with him. He'd been smoking back then, too, and she'd been curious (everything about him made her want to try new things), wanting to try a puff. He'd only let her, if he could teach her how to swim. He was aware of her childhood trauma—of being thrown into the pool as a small girl by her swim instructor, with only dinky floaties on. His love of the water made him super annoying, giving her some speech or another about the need to know that specific life skill. So, she'd agreed. She'd learned to float on her back and a crude version of the front crawl, but she never got the hang of it, refusing to put her face in the water. And in the end, he hadn't let her try his cigarettes. He didn't want to lead her down the wrong path.

Frustrating, yes. In retaliation, even though they weren't together anymore, she'd not only smoked a little bit in college (barely socially if that; she couldn't figure out inhaling, and it made her cough painfully), but she never practiced swimming again.

"I take it you never kept up?" he asked, his tone becoming a little schoolmarmish.

"Oh, spare me, Z." But she sounded weak when she said it.

He sat down beside her, resting his elbows on his knees. "Well, as I recall," he looked up at the sky, his sunglasses still on, "you said you were going to move somewhere landlocked eventually. How did that turn out for you?"

She didn't answer. She didn't need to. But come on, New York City was barely an island.

"How about you try while we're here?" he asked casually, as if he didn't care whether they did it or not.

No way, he was not going to use some form of manipulative tactic on her. The same tactic she used with her daughter to get her to do something when she didn't want to.

"I didn't bring a bathing suit," she said vehemently. She would win this one. "You said the weather was turning at this time and the water would be too chilly."

"I did say that, didn't I?" He looked around. "I was wrong."

"Can I get that in writing?"

"Ha," he said flatly. He reached his hand over the side of the dock. "Yep, water feels like miso soup. It's perfection."

"Cold or hot?"

"Cold or hot, what?"

"Miso soup. There can be different temperatures served based on the season."

He dared to shake his head in exasperation. He helped her get up, placing a hand on the small of her back. He picked up her purse and shouldered it. She gripped his arm, not realizing how shaky her legs were.

"I don't think I can do it, Z," she said pathetically.

"We won't jump into swim lessons immediately. How about that?"

"That's not what I meant—though, I'm saying a big fat no to swim lessons."

"*Okay*," he said, drawing out the word. He was speaking to her like a child. To be fair, she was acting like one.

"I don't think I can do the yacht, the boats. Is there a way to stay in Athens? Or, can't we fly to Naxos? Doesn't your family own the island or something? Shouldn't there be a helipad or some shit?" She shuddered in her lunacy.

He chuckled. "Or something, Karma. You can do this."

They were still standing in the same place where she'd collapsed. He was not rushing her, which was a good sign.

"How about I knock you out?"

"What, like Mike Tyson? I hardly think violence is the answer."

He barked out a laugh, and her nerves went from bubbling angrily in fear to a low simmer. She took a deep breath and let it out slowly. She did it again, and after the third time, she realized he was doing it with her.

"That's it, Baby. You got this," he said softly. "I can see if any flights are running from Athens to Naxos. There's a limited number right now. In the meantime, I can get you Dramamine, or something."

She nodded in relief; her brain muddled at him calling her 'Baby.' She shouldn't like it so much, almost as much as when he called her 'Karma.'

"Dramamine is for motion sickness. I need something to make me sleepy. It's the only way. Then I can nap on whatever sea carrier we end up on in case there aren't flights."

"Okay. Sounds like a good plan. You'll tell me what to look for at the pharmacy?"

When she nodded, he said, "Great. Let's go tell the others that we're noodling around Athens for a bit before we make our way over later."

Her shoulders relaxed in relief. She already felt childish, and it sounded like he didn't plan on telling his family about her water fears, which would only make her feel like more of an imbecile.

They both looked over at the family yacht, where everyone stared at them from the top deck. Silas tapped his wrist, indicating the time. His mother's arms were waving, ushering them over, trying to hurry them along. And Pen, well, she was starting down the gangplank, concern written all over her face.

"Noodle," she said, chuckling, trying not to dwell on her fears. "We're talking about Athens, here—one of the oldest cities in the world, with history in every direction." She shaded her eyes and found the Parthenon temple ruins high above, overlooking the city. "And you want to waste time noodling."

"Eh." He shrugged. "When you've lived most of your life here…"

She squished up her face in a mixture of horror and disdain.

"Yeah, I sound like a shit. Let's go see the Parthenon," he sighed.

CHAPTER 12

‫د‬

*D*id they go to the Parthenon to see the ancient temple dedicated to Athena? Did they climb up the dusty path to the Acropolis, Athens' high rocky outcrop, where the temple sat, overlooking the city since ancient times? They sure the hell did. And lucky for them, it was still rather early morning because the off-season could get crowded with visitors touring the relics.

Zayn was pleasantly surprised at how much he ended up enjoying the morning, even though he'd seen the ruins up close too many times to count. The first time was barely a conjured-up memory. He could envisage the printed photos his mother had taken of him as a chubby toddler with his father, walking up the south slope—the same gravelly path he and Kareena wound up to get to the top. Truthfully, he barely noticed them anymore, as they served as just a backdrop every time he returned to Athens.

He saw them anew through Kareena's eyes. She'd never been to Greece, and it was like he was viewing the giant, discolored marble columns, and enormous scattered sun-bleached stones for the first time. The expression of sheer awe when the temple came into view was nothing short of inspiring. How had he taken the expansive history of his homeland for granted? Yes, he loved Greece, but it was the sun and water, the food and culture that got him. Now he felt like he needed to revisit all of the old ruins he'd overlooked in the past. There were small temples and ruins dotted throughout the Naxos countryside. He and Kareena would be there together for twelve days. Other than the wedding events, they had some time to kill. He had a pretty good idea who his enthusiastic travel mate was going to be, too, he thought, staring at her plump backside as she climbed the crumbling steps up to the Parthenon from the Acropolis' flat citadel.

"The air, Zayn," she marveled. "It's thick and musty; old but timeless. It smelled like this when we got off the plane. But here..." She turned around to take in the view of the city below and stumbled on a loose rock. He put his hand out to steady her, landing on the small of her back, on the sliver of skin that refused to remain hidden, even after she unsuccessfully tugged it down multiple times. It was smooth, moist with perspiration, and heated from exertion. "Can you just imagine who else has breathed in this exact air? It could've been Athena herself!"

He wasn't about to correct her by telling her that it couldn't have been Athena or any of the other Gods, as myth was that they breathed a purer form of air that wasn't available to mortals. The absolute beauty and joy on Kareena's face, especially compared to how vulnerable she'd been earlier, on the dock by the water, was something he didn't want to crack. In fact, he could watch her all day. She could erroneously tell him it was actually the Hindu God Krishna whom this temple was dedicated to, not Athena, and he'd be happy to listen to the error of her ways. That was highly unlikely, though. She'd always been a history buff and loved the arts and ancient Grecian and Roman history. When she'd first found out he'd spent his earlier years and then his summers in Greece, she'd peppered him with questions about any and everything.

Despite her good mood now, and his relief that she seemed to have forgotten her anxiety from earlier, he still couldn't believe she'd never practiced what he'd taught her so long ago. She hadn't set foot in the water since then. Oh, she'd told him she went in as far as mid-thigh with her daughter, but she'd never submerged herself fully. The idea boggled his mind.

No one should have to experience the level of anxiety she'd felt back on the dock. Her body had been stiff, cold. All warmth drained with terror. And it was such a contrast to how he'd remembered her as a teenager—placid and calm—the one who could help his mind settle, and lasso in his emotions when they were all over the place.

"Is that—" She covered her mouth with a hand, her gaze in the direction of the museum on a lower hill. The white sun high in the cloudless sky hit the building at an angle so it appeared to be floating on a hazy mirror. "That's the archeological site of a local village, right? I looked it up."

They'd skipped past the museum on her eagerness to see the ruins.

"I believe so. I actually haven't seen it up close. That reflected area is made out of glass, and outside of the front entrance, you can stand on it and see an entire portion of a dig and really take it all in. Unfortunately, the museum is closed for renovations, since it's technically the off-season."

She seemed disappointed but perked up when they got into the Parthenon structure, where she explored every nook and cranny. She exclaimed over the beauty of the remaining friezes, depicting soldiers on horses etched into the stone.

"Come on, slowpoke!" She grabbed his hand and started hurrying to the other side of the vast structure, a hundred-watt smile on her face.

It was contagious, and he grinned back, rushing with her. She'd stopped when they reached the sculpted figures that made up the columns on the opposite side of the temple, some of them missing limbs, portions of their bodies, and facial features. "Whoa," she said under her breath. "It's extraordinary—all of the details and all carved from marble. Do you think way back in the 6th century BC Pericles would've ever imagined that his vision of the Acropolis and all that was built on it would continue to stand thousands of years later?"

Zayn wasn't sure who Pericles was. The name sounded familiar, like all of the old dead men who'd taken part in developing ancient Greece. Luckily, Kareena didn't expect an answer. She continued her commentary, and Zayn enthusiastically listened—not for the history portion—he'd never found dusty old stories that interesting. But her enthusiasm captivated him, and he found himself wearing a small smile as they wandered through the great hall.

She still held his hand, and she squeezed, looking up at him. He couldn't help but notice the uptick in the beating of his heart, which he clearly knew wasn't from the quick jog to the other side of the temple.

A foreign but familiar feeling suddenly hit him. It was so unexpected that he wondered when it had begun to sneak up on him. But, truly, had it? Maybe it'd finally shown itself, had quit hiding in the deepest recesses of his mind, his heart ... hell, his entire being.

With trepidation, he asked himself, was there anything he could do to stop it? He didn't have time to mull it over at the moment, because he was famished and thirsty, and by now, so was she. He suggested they go grab a midday meal, and she happily agreed.

They climbed back down, and twenty minutes later, he led her through bustling side streets, going to a favored place of his in the heart of Athens. Small businesses abounded along an enclosed old stone road, with picturesque shops and cafes crowded up against one another.

He took her to a quaint little restaurant that was one of his preferred eateries, known for simple, fresh flavors. He ordered for them, starting first with what he considered the best Greek tavern salad that combined chunky fresh cucumbers, juicy tomatoes, briny olives, all blanketed in a pungently flavorful concoction of oregano, olive oil, and vinegar. The crumbly, creamy feta cheese on top was locally made, and he encouraged her to try it by itself first.

She took a bite and moaned in bliss, her eyes closing with euphoric illumination on her face.

"Zayn, I could die for this kind of cheese."

He chuckled, a sweet sensation curling in his chest. "You'd pledge your allegiance to dairy?"

Her eyes popped open. "Wouldn't you? There's nothing better than fresh cheese, or melted cheese, or grilled cheese for that matter—okay, yes, all dairy claims me as their submissive."

"I never thought I'd say I was jealous of dairy." He placed his napkin in his lap.

Her shoulders wiggled as she took a forkful of salad, a little bit of each ingredient in her bite. Her cheeks were glowing from the morning in the sun, but he couldn't tell if she was embarrassed that he'd alluded to his physical want for her, or if she was just overheated.

"Dairy has nothing on you, Z." She put the forkful in her mouth and moaned again. "Whoa. The flavors are so vibrant, so explosive, so … so … refreshing. I recognize every ingredient in this salad, but together—"

"Angels sing." He nodded and took a large mouthful, enjoying the tartness, saltiness, and the creaminess of the cheese in one perfect bite.

She nodded in agreement and kept eating.

They shared a bottle of chilled local white wine from Santorini Island, specifically known for the Assyrtiko grape. He explained how the vines were trained to grow low to the ground in baskets, protecting them from the winds and hot sun. The acidic and volcanic soil they grew in gave the wine its complex flavors, which complemented the food perfectly. A smile slowly crept onto her face as he continued to speak, detailing the harvesting and their scientific methods of growth and unique flavors.

"What?" he asked, noticing her toothy grin.

She shrugged and picked up her wine glass, taking a long sip, before saying, "I like that you're a nerd now. I was the nerd in high school. But now we're even."

He was completely taken off guard. But he chuckled deeply.

"What?" she asked, her turn to be confused.

"You just used the past tense." He tipped his wine glass to her. "That's funny." He drank, keeping his eyes on her over the rim of his glass.

"Hilarious," she deadpanned. "Fine. I'm still a nerd. At least I can admit that."

He winked at her, and she threw her napkin at him.

Their server came and dropped off a large platter of small fried fish. The steam looked obnoxious in the heat of the midday afternoon, but he couldn't wait to eat one of his absolute favorites. And he wanted her to try them, too.

But Kareena inspected the platter with dismay.

"Anchovies? Where's the octopus? Isn't that your favorite?"

"You remember that?" he asked, surprised.

"As much as I remember that *Gulab jamon* was your favorite dessert back then." She fiddled with her silverware.

"Still my favorite dessert, no question," he replied softly. Her skin, with its natural soft sheen, had always reminded him of his favorite dessert, and today, after soaking up the morning rays, it had a sensual luster he couldn't stop staring at in admiration, his fingers itching to caress her.

"Octopus, freshly grilled, *was* my favorite," he continued. "But I realize they may deserve to be left alone for the time being." At her quizzical stare, he quickly added, "I promised someone I wouldn't eat them anymore." He left it at that for now, turning to the anchovies, changing the topic. "These were fresh caught this morning. They're marinated quickly in lemon juice and herbs, then drenched in flour and fried in really tasty hot olive oil." He squeezed the lemon wedges over the fish before taking one and popping the entire thing into his mouth. It practically incinerated his tongue and he blew out as he chewed because he couldn't wait. They were the best when hot.

"You eat the entire thing? Guts, bones, eyes, fins…?" she asked, now only mildly dismayed as he popped another one into his mouth, the crunch going perfectly with the hot unctuousness of the fish and tart lemon juice.

"Mmm, mmm, mmm," he uttered. "Try one."

She picked one up hesitantly between her thumb and

forefinger and put the entire thing in her mouth, her eyes on him as she crunched and chewed.

She finally swallowed and took a long sip of her wine, then refilled her glass.

"Well?" he asked, his excitement barely containable. She *had* to have enjoyed that bite.

"I'm sorry to say that you're going to have to order another platter of these," she said primly, pulling the plate closer to her. "These are all mine, now."

"Would you call them orgasmic?" he asked teasingly.

"Close. But not as orgasmic as this talented chef's scallops I recently tasted."

He leaned in across the little iron table, reaching over to wipe a few crumbs on the corner of her mouth. Was it strange that hearing her compliment his food made him hard?

"There's always more where that came from, Karma," he murmured, rubbing her bottom lip with his thumb before sitting back. "I'd love to cook for you, and only you, one day. If you'll let me..." The words just poured out of him. But he didn't regret saying them.

"I might," she said so quietly, he barely heard her, and now the apples of her cheeks were a deep blush, telling him she was indeed embarrassed by his words and attention. He leaned back in his chair and watched her, everything about her keeping his focus.

Yeah, his future self was going to be royally fucked when this was all over. He could already foresee it.

After paying, they strolled around, got delicious gelato, and he left her to do some shopping while he ran to the nearby pharmacy with a list of safe over-the-counter drugs she'd scribbled out for him. Honestly, she might not need anything, he thought as he paid for an antihistamine and Valerian root, an herbal supplement known to help with anxiety. Exhaustion was settling into his muscles from the travel, the heat, and the hike up to see the ruins. She was undoubtedly feeling the same way, too.

As predicted, once they finally boarded the ferry for Naxos later in the afternoon (the next flight from Athens was hours away), she didn't need to take anything. She promptly fell asleep, with her arm tucked into his while they sat in one of the dozens of seats below deck of the ferry. He gently rested her head on his shoulder, making her more comfortable.

CHAPTER 13

১৬

*K*areena sat on the stone bench under the pergola's shade in the quaint garden. Flowers in every color bloomed around her along the perimeter, vying for the sun's attention. Her favorite bloom had always been peonies; the fluffier and delicately pinker the better. But the flowers here on Naxos—bright, almost neon-like, such as the red poppies and the blindingly magenta climbing bougainvillea above her on the wooden structure—were definitely in the running for her favorites.

She breathed in deeply, the air punctuated with herbaceous notes, hints of floral, salt from the sea below, and the mustiness that she realized was the background to any scent here in Greece. It wasn't so different from how she remembered it smelling in India the last time her family went there. It gave her a sense of the old and revered, mixed in with the hustle and bustle of life. It left her with a sense of wonder at the vastness of time and how tiny they were in that extremely long timeline.

She chuckled to herself. She could be so philosophical in these places. But she appreciated them every time.

A raised garden bed of overgrown herbs stood next to where she sat. As soon as Zayn brought her here, he'd run his large hands over the stalks and smelled his fingers, closing his eyes in what looked very much like ecstasy. Then he did it again, but he put his warm fingers up to her nose, and she breathed in the intensity of fresh oregano mired with the warmth of fennel fronds. He pointed out the various herbs often used in Greek cooking: marjoram, dill, and parsley, to name a few. Then he'd tsked before pruning the wildly overgrown foliage and disappearing into the charming villa attached to the garden with a large pile of freshly hand-pulled herb stalks in his arms. He told her he'd be right back, and she heard him rummaging around inside, sounds of clatter interspersed with his deep voice letting out expletives.

She breathed in again. Everything felt calmer here, slower. There was no gridlock traffic, no angry pedestrians and bikers cursing at drivers, nor crowds to bustle through to get where she needed to go, making sure she always left herself enough time for train or bus delays.

Instead, she listened to the distant crashing of the waves below, just on the other side of the ancient garden wall, and the gentle buzz of some of the largest, fuzziest bumble bees she'd ever seen. They were adorable and reminded her of her Aloo, making her smile, her thoughts immediately going to her daughter. She missed her and their pup, but realized she missed the feeling of being carefree, without the responsibility of parenting and dog mom, too. Like clockwork, she'd eventually experience the absent pieces to her heart. In a little over a week, when the novelty of being by herself completely wore off, she'd be getting ready to head back to New York anyway, and back to her life.

Her smile faltered just slightly at the guilt she felt.

She turned her thoughts to the day before, and the turn of events it had taken. Her panic attack was inevitable, and it came on as soon as she caught sight of the ocean, the expanse going as far as the eye could see.

Then Zayn was there, and he'd saved her … again. But she didn't feel a sense of owing him something back, or that she was a burden when he'd sat with her. Embarrassed, yes, but he'd also managed to make her feel normal—that her fear wasn't irrational. It was serious and valid.

She shook her head, pushing her fears away.

The remainder of yesterday had turned out spectacularly.

After going to the Parthenon, they enjoyed delicious local fare (anchovies were now on her list of things she wanted to explore with her daughter—if she hadn't gone completely vegetarian in the time Kareena was away), and then Zayn had left her to do some shopping while he went for her medicine, and thankfully so. She managed to pick out a few outfits that were more appropriate for the unexpectedly warm temperature, including new bathing suits, in case Zayn was really serious about swimming lessons. Part of her wanted him to be, and part of her didn't. The latter, for obvious reasons—she didn't think she'd ever get over her fear of water. But the former because the thought of being in a rather skimpy bathing suit (that was all they had in the shops), all wet, maybe clinging for dear life to him and his hard body, also all wet—well, she was thinking dirty, and she couldn't deny how he made her feel—safe and sexy. Again, she let herself wonder if having sex with her fake fiancé was such a bad idea. He clearly found her attractive, and she reciprocated. What was the harm with two consenting adults, as he'd so eloquently put it?

They'd arrived at the island via ferry, a few hours later, with the sun setting on the horizon, the sky a glorious punch pink that only nature could paint; it was everything she expected and more. He'd had to shake her awake, but when she saw land, she almost wept with relief.

It was mindbogglingly breathtaking; she'd only ever seen images online. Soft white sand met the edge of the sea, now cast in a darker shade of cerulean blue. It looked unreal, except that when she dipped her toes (of one foot only, the other one was solidly on the sand), it was soothing and warm, and very real.

They'd taken a private car to the Stavros Estate, one that had been waiting for them as Zayn had called ahead to communicate their change in plans while on the ferry. As she looked up at the hills and mountains which were black against the now purple sky, she made out tiny buildings at the very tops of some, realizing they were shrines or religious buildings, and she wondered how anyone got up there. How did they live so isolated from the rest of the world?

Having gone up a winding, skinny road—one that hugged the edge of a hill—she felt grateful for the dark, or she'd have been looking down at deep ravines. At one point, the car stopped because a local herder was trying to coax two goats down from a precarious cliff. The driver, clearly a driver for the Stavros family, got out to help him, not even asking Zayn's permission. But then Zayn got out to help, too, and she watched from the car as the three men cajoled down a mother goat and her kid from the giant boulders they'd climbed up, the flashlight shining on them as they bleated.

Zayn apologized for the little delay, to which she could only respond that it was no trouble. She'd been the one to delay their entire arrival by having to stay in Athens.

He smiled in the dark, his white teeth flashing against the shadow of his beard. True, he'd said. But he also went on to explain that the Stavros family always ensured everyone's safety on the island. The relationship was a symbiotic one. For instance, that goat herder's milk made some of the island's finest cheese, including being an ingredient in the cheese she'd eaten earlier that day.

He'd then told her that he'd show her around the property the next day, and she would see for herself how much the Stavroses relied on the locals, and vice versa. She nodded, curious about this side of Zayn. One she'd heard so much about as a teenager, but could never really fathom.

The car proceeded to turn onto a wide gravel road and went through trees that shaded the bright moon above, leaving everything almost in pitch black inside the car. Even the road in front of them was eerily dark, the only light from the headlights.

When the house came into view, it was from a distance, but here the trees parted away to open fields dotted with shrubs. The road became paved and was lit up by lamp posts. The manor itself was sprawling tan stucco and very much in the traditional modern blended architecture of the homes she saw in town— clean geometric structures, but this one was stately and enormous. Like the smaller homes, there were arches and columns on the facades. Numerous outdoor patios and balconies jutted off the edifice, indicating the importance of nature to their culture. It was fascinating in its combination of traditional and modern features, and immediately, Kareena wanted to explore everything.

As they got closer, she noticed the pretty ivory and deep red detailing on each and every one of the numerous windows and doors. The paved driveway circled in front of the home at the main entrance with enormous, rounded, double doors that looked more like they belonged on a fortress or castle.

When they stepped inside, it was to a spacious and airy high-ceilinged entryway that felt warm and inviting, despite the large scale. A wide staircase swept up in a curve to the second floor. Right above them was the most enormous chandelier Kareena had ever seen, dripping with pretty gold leaves and round crystal pieces that bounced tiny rainbow prisms on the ceiling and walls.

Zayn requested they be shown to their room immediately, and up the wide stairs they'd gone, through numerous corridors and turns to a sumptuous suite filled with a four-poster king-sized canopy bed swathed in a pretty white gauze. On the far side stood glass double doors that went out to one of the many outdoor sitting areas she'd noticed earlier. A sofa faced the doors with a low coffee table between. A vanity sat in one corner, and a door which she found out later led to a walk-in closet; another led to a huge marble bathroom with a large separate tub in the middle of the room, and a walk-in shower with all of the jet fixings on the other side.

The floor in the bedroom was a cool stone mosaic in varying colors of beige and covered in off-white rugs and carpets. It was all so clean but luxurious at the same time.

As they unpacked, Zayn casually mentioned that he might take the couch, though the bed was large enough to fit them both—and all of his relatives who had flown over with them.

Because it was late, she didn't argue or try to discuss it further. She brushed her teeth, washed her face, and put her PJs on, letting sleep take her. She'd call her daughter the next day when she felt more settled.

CHAPTER 14

ᔕ8

*Z*ayn was already gone when she woke up. But she knew he'd slept in the room by the bed coverings left on the couch. She'd quickly folded them, along with tossing the comforter over the bed she'd slept in. It was a force of habit for her. The day always felt like it would start better with the beds made.

Before she got dressed, she poked her head out of the double doors. A pretty pergola shrouded in thick ivy shaded a rustic table and two chairs. She spied an ashtray and a cigarette butt, noting that Zayn had already been out there.

The smoking thing—the entire scenario had caught her off guard when he warned her on their way to the first of many charity events he had to attend, that she might hear some things about him that she wouldn't understand or like. He confessed that he'd recently overdosed on uppers, which he normally used to fuel his stamina during long work days. His last stash gave him a bad reaction, and he'd found out the reason was that they'd been laced with something way more toxic. He hadn't known.

She didn't know what to think. First, alarmed that he was still using, he reassured her that he was in the process of kicking the habit. How, she'd asked him, and wouldn't the stress of their fake engagement—all of the details they had to remember, the lengths they were going to—push him to start using again? She'd communicated her worries just as they arrived at the Armory in Manhattan, where the fancy event was.

"I picked up smoking again." He'd said, taking a crumpled pack out of his jacket pocket. "I don't really smoke that often, or at least before all of this happened. But this is the only thing that helps me take the edge off when I feel the need to reach for uppers. It won't be forever, but it's what works for me right now."

The patronizing doctor in her screamed to let out a word of caution, to tell him this was not a healthy habit to lean on. But she knew that smoking was the lesser of the two evils, and even some in the medical community felt it was much preferred if it got him off the harder stuff.

Something deep ached for him. She hated that he was going through this, wishing to help him. But didn't give her opinion. It wasn't her place as she wasn't his real fiancé.

She closed the double glass doors and went to the walk-in closet, reaching for the new yellow sundress she'd purchased in Athens. She got ready, and filled with anticipation laced with trepidation, she went downstairs, taking a few wrong turns to begin with. She finally found Zayn on the first floor, sitting outside where breakfast had been set up under massive sail shades, and situated by an Olympian-sized pool. A few people were already splashing in the water, including his mother and Penelope.

"There you are," he said, his cinnamon eyes crinkling as he smiled warmly at her. "I was about to come find you."

"You need a map to get around this place," she said, sitting next to him at the large round table. Coffee was immediately (and thankfully) placed in front of her before she went up to survey the breakfast laid out buffet style.

After consuming homemade Greek yogurt, melons, soft-boiled eggs, and toast, Zayn took her around the property. It was a lot to take in, and she would never remember all the names to the faces, but she understood his love for the land, which the locals were an integral part of. Many were pleased to see Zayn and were welcoming toward her. She blushed when they asked her about their plans for babies, and told her they'd never seen Zayn happier. But in all, she felt very comfortable with them, even making the one-eyed fisherman crack a smile—the one who she was warned would be a crabby old man and that it wasn't personal.

They poked around the stables full of beautiful horses (Tamannah would love meeting them, Kareena thought wistfully), before they meandered through the dappled olive grove, where she wanted to taste the olives right off the tree. Zayn warned her she would regret it with so much seriousness that she let it go.

The olive oil mill was at the further end of the grove, and they visited it briefly, peering inside the old building. Everyone yelled a greeting to Zayn and wanted to meet the woman far too pretty to be with him (their words, not hers).

Afterward, they made their way to the edge of the property. The cliffside ran the length of the grove, separated by an ancient-looking stone wall. Here, a few varieties of trees grew, and he picked velvety pink fruit off one and told her to try it.

They were clearly figs, and she took a bite without hesitation. The florally sweet flavor knocked her senses right out of her, and she keened in delight with her eyes closed, her hand outstretched for another.

She heard him chuckle, a sexy sound that hit between her thighs, and made her toes curl.

"You really have no idea how sexy you are, Karma," he said deeply, his voice soft.

She'd opened her eyes to him, to his deep gaze, and the fire lit within. The gentleness on his face was mixed with open desire as he watched her.

Her nipples hardened, and she wanted his hands on her that instant. For a brief moment, she wanted to answer the absolute hunger written on his face, which had nothing to do with the land's agricultural bounties. She wondered if this was where they would finally succumb to each other. Where he'd touch her body in ways she'd only imagined. It was there, within their reach. but the moment vanished as quickly as it appeared when they heard voices approaching.

It was Penelope and her mother, Zia, taking a stroll along the property. They were having a quiet moment before all of the relatives descended in a loud cacophony of joyous celebration, music, dancing, and yes, lots of dish-breaking. They stopped to chat, and that's when they all ended up at the pretty villa, a little further down from the olive grove but still along the cliffside— the home that Zayn was to make his when he finally claimed his inheritance.

The two women continued on their stroll, and Zayn proceeded to show Kareena the delightful place. It was like a fairy-tale cottage, but with white-washed stucco walls, stone floors, and honeyed wood. It was bigger than it looked from the

156

outside, airier, with four bedrooms, three full, spacious bathrooms, a large kitchen and dining area, and a bright living area with a wall-length shelf perfect for books and other knick-knacks. Dust and cobwebs layered the surfaces, but the excitement in Zayn's eyes, in his voice, in the prospect of his future made her want to impulsively grab him and kiss him.

And she might have done just that if her phone hadn't buzzed, leading her back out into the garden again. She didn't want to miss it in case it was Tamannah. Or her sister, with a question that could probably wait until later.

It was her father, and it went to voicemail before she could pick it up. Did she want to listen to it? She hesitated before deciding to, as Zayn was busy inside seeing what needed restocking and repairing.

"*Shona*," the familiar voice wobbled. Then her father sighed deeply. "We miss you. We haven't talked to you in a *very* long time. Please call us."

She almost went to dial him back and then thought better of it. Her *abba* had a way of sympathizing with her, but making her feel bad at the same time. She'd realized recently, as she'd thought about her relationship with him, that he absolutely and completely exhausted her. It was a constant struggle of making sure she didn't offend him or disappoint him, and it left her weary. It was emotional drainage, and she needed a step away from him—from both of her parents, though she loved them dearly.

They hadn't loved the idea of her and Zayn's engagement. Though a predictable reaction, it had bothered her more than she thought it would, even though it was all a lie.

Since then, she couldn't speak to them without losing her patience, something she'd never experienced with her parents.

She recalled that moment before the big *Diwali* celebration in Connecticut, when defying them felt insanely good, even maniacally so. In hindsight, it probably wasn't the best timing, as they had to act like nothing was amiss in front of their community the entire long night of celebration. But how could she have known it was she who would unwittingly be the one to open her big mouth and unleash everything? The problem was, once she did, there was no going back.

4 WEEKS AGO

greenwich, connecticut

CHAPTER 15

ॐ

"*T*hey're gonna know."

This was a common phrase Kareena tossed at Reyana as kids whenever the younger girl thought she could hide something from their parents. Admittedly, Reyana had a talent for keeping things from them, but they found some things out, so the phrase wasn't always uttered in vain. And poignantly, after learning about Kareena's secret high school relationship, when their parents began to watch *both* of their daughters' activities more closely, Reyana took glee in dishing that phrase back to her big sister.

So, it really shouldn't have surprised Kareena when she arrived with her daughter at her parents' house on Sunday for the Greenwich, Connecticut, *Diwali* party, and they lobbed a bombardment of questions at her, without any sort of greeting first. Truthfully, she'd expected them to call her the previous day to pull the facts out of her and possibly set her 'straight' if she had ideas about straying from their plans for her.

Both of them spoke at once, making her head spin while she

and Tamannah stood in the front entrance of their home, the vaulted ceiling making their voices echo.

"What happened on Friday with Sameer?" her father asked, while simultaneously, her mother harped, "*Beta*, we know everything."

Her father bobbled his head at her mother and asked in a whiny tone, "*Keno* (why)?"

A flick of his wrist emphasized his annoyance, while his face crumpled in dismay, as though her *amma* had foiled their plans. The bickering between her parents was nothing new. But the fact that her outspoken mother began to speak, but then promptly shut her mouth, was. She shrugged, sucked in her cheeks, and gave Kareena a hard stare.

"Go ahead, answer your *abba*." She crossed her arms over her stained cooking apron, which covered her pretty, deep orange, and gold sari.

All Kareena could think, as she lay a hand on her daughter's shoulder (more to calm herself), was that the matchmaker had spilled everything. She'd assumed the woman would've at least kept some of what happened last Friday to herself. It wasn't her fake news to share. But what had she expected?

She was going to be in so much trouble.

Kareena decided to take the anger route—sometimes that was the easiest tactic. She glared at her parents, gesturing at her daughter, who stood wide-eyed. Tamannaah was at the age where she was a sponge, sopping up every word that came out of their mouths. Her little hands played with the thin plastic, colorful bangles on her wrists, unwittingly rubbing the cheap glitter off and onto the reddish-pink satin skirt of her *lehenga* outfit.

Kareena dropped to her haunches and looked her daughter square in the eyes.

"Tama, why don't you go see if Reya *Khala* is in the kitchen? I'll bet she's already gotten into *Nani*'s special desserts." She winked at her daughter.

Her daughter considered her options, looking from her grandparents to her mother. Then she shrugged and skipped away.

When she heard her sister's excited voice exclaim gleefully from the kitchen, she focused on her parents.

She smoothed down the front of her black and white, large paisley-printed *salwar kameez*. The design of the tunic and matching pant ensemble resembled an abstract painting, and she'd styled it with hanging gold and pearl *jhumka* earrings, along with a thick pearl choker. She felt sophisticated when she'd first put the entire outfit on, pairing it with her Prada ivory leather slingbacks, and pulling her hair up into a loose twist. But now she felt like a truant child as she adjusted the matching *dupatta*, feeling warmer than a moment ago. She was suddenly aware that her feet pinched, her earlobes ached from the bell-shaped, solid gold earrings, and she was getting more irate by the minute.

She blew a wayward tendril from her face and stared head-on at the two people who'd backed and supported her for her entire life. They were making her irrationally angry lately.

"Okay," she said, taking a deep breath and clasping her hands in front of her as she began to pace. "What happened on Friday was that Pinky Aunty bombarded me with her nephew. I wasn't prepared; I wasn't in that 'let me interview you to be my husband, and vice versa' mindset. I was there to, oh, I don't know, enjoy other people my age, socialize with other Indians

… have a good time? *Celebrate the festival of lights?*" Her shoulders were hiked to her ears, and her hands were palm up in supplication as her glance bopped back and forth between her parents.

And the thought crossed her mind before her mother even said it, "You sound like Reyana."

Kareena would normally take offense to that, but at the moment, she said seriously, "Thank you."

Her father's thick black brows creased low over his eyes. He slowly came to her and asked, concerned, "*Shona*, what's the matter?"

He put an arm around her and ushered her out of the front hallway into the family room. They both went to the overstuffed burgundy couch and sat down.

"*Nothing* is wrong," she said more forcefully than she intended, because everything was wrong. She didn't want to discuss any of this. She wanted them to be okay with the fact that they'd caught her at a bad time—that there was a time and place for such things, and not at a function where she least expected a surprise matchmaking attack. She really wished they could figure out on their own that after meeting Sameer, there was just no way in all this world that she could attempt to meet him again, hoping an arranged marriage would result eventually. Because another arranged marriage just didn't feel right anymore. And more importantly, and which she'd keep to herself, was that she still had the shadow of that kiss she'd planted on her former high school sweetheart, still seared on her lips from two nights ago. She'd been the one to initiate it, but he'd been the one to leave her breathless. Since then, it was all she could focus on.

Her brain went back to when Pinky Aunty had thankfully

left, buying her story about the engagement. She and Zayn had stood there, momentarily in silence, watching the shorter woman grab her fur coat from the coat check and walk out, her head held high.

Zayn's arm had felt comfortable around her waist, his warm fingers tickling her bare skin, and she wondered if he knew he was doing it. Suddenly, cool air hit her back as his arm dropped.

He'd run a hand through those luscious, copper locks, mussing the curls further than they already were, and said sardonically, "Well, *that* was weird."

She was edgy. What she'd done there was not only weird, but she'd taken a leap of faith in him, that he would keep going with her lie until the matchmaker left. And he had. But now what?

"Zayn, thank you. This time, I *do* owe you one."

Expecting him to tell her she didn't owe him anything again and walk away as quickly as he could, like last time, her breath had caught in her throat as he crossed his bulging biceps over his chest and said with aplomb, "Yeah, you do."

She'd been unsure where to look—at his arrogant, prickish smirk, which was way sexier than it ought to be, or back at the party, to escape the dangerous heat in his deep, fiery brown eyes.

He'd stared down at her, and his gaze flicked down her body, making her feel like a piece of meat he intended to mar. Was he going to ask her for … sexual favors in return? No. He wouldn't … would he? She needed to keep in mind that she had no idea what he was like anymore. It wouldn't be so far from the mark of what he seemed like these days, dating all sorts of women. But would he stoop so low?

And would she agree to it…?

"Okay," she'd said quietly. "What did you have in mind?"

His eyes squinted as his mouth worked, clearly thinking. "Give me your phone."

"What?"

"I need your phone."

"It's back in my purse at the party."

He jerked his chin for her to go inside, and she went. He followed.

When she got to her table, she grabbed her purse and pulled her phone out. She swiftly turned back around, only to find him standing inches from her.

"Unlock it."

"Why?"

"Do it." When she still hesitated, he said with annoyance, "I'm not sending you a dick pic or anything. I'm only programming my number in."

"Oh." She put in her code and gave it to him. Did he normally send pictures of his dick to women?

While he swiped around, he said rather casually, "For the record, I don't think you're out of control. That woman is a piece of work."

She doubted he had any clue how much that validation meant to her. She'd felt like she'd lost her mind when Pinky had nothing good to say about Tamannah.

A buzz in his pants indicated he was getting a call. He pulled his phone out while handing hers back to her.

"There. Now we have each other's numbers."

She didn't know why, but it thrilled her, and it really shouldn't have.

She swallowed hard. "Okay, but why?"

He smirked at her again. "Because, Karma, I need to figure

out exactly how you're going to repay me. And I want to make it good, so I'll need some time to think about it."

There was that nickname again, the one he'd made up for her in high school. Her heart skipped like that same teenager when it came from his lips.

Then he'd turned on his heel and left without so much as another word. She stared down at her phone to see he'd put himself in as 'Fiancé.'

What in the freaky Friday Diwali *lights was going on?*

"What happened with Sameer Sarkar?" her father asked, pulling her from the strange (but undeniably exhilarating) recollection of that evening.

"Hah! So you did know about that part," she crowed triumphantly. Of course, she knew he knew; she just wanted to hear him admit they'd sent Pinky and her nephew on a fool's errand.

He leaned back, his forehead wrinkled. "Of course, we did. Pinky wanted you to meet him this weekend, before he had to leave the country for work. When we found out you couldn't come earlier than today because of the other party, she had the bright idea to meet you in the city. It was all for your benefit, Kara."

He bobbled his head, absolutely believing he was in the right here.

Oh, to be a man, and an Indian one at that; one who'd never once been questioned for his motives.

"I don't understand what's going on, *Shona*. And…" Her father scratched his head. "I'm worried. You're not acting like yourself."

"Guys. I'm fine. I just don't like surprises. *You* know that!"

True. They knew her to be a planner; someone who needed

to be prepared. What they didn't know was that she'd completely deviated from that at the party, to get out of the ultimate plan her parents had for her—a second arranged marriage.

"And, frankly, I liked Sameer, but not like that. We had no chemistry."

He might have stood a tiny chance if she hadn't run into a certain hot chef multiple times—and the fact that her sister seemed to have more of a connection to him than she did.

Her mother, who'd been standing and listening in the wide doorway, came into the room. She sat down on the other side of Kareena.

"You don't want to give Sameer another chance?" she asked slowly, disappointment in her voice.

The inner turmoil between her old self and her new defiant one had a momentary struggle in reaction to her mother's dismay.

"But Sameer is such a good boy." Her mother went on. "Did you know Pinky and her *boro appa* (big sister) haven't spoken in decades? Now, her sister comes to her for help in finding the perfect girl for him, and who do you think Pinky came up with?"

At Kareena's blank stare, her mother continued. "*You, Beta!* That's how highly everyone thinks of you. Even if this will be your second marriage."

Her new self decided it was time to jump in.

"Well, that can't happen."

She stood up and faced them, her hands on her hips tightly. She squared her shoulders, while her body stiffened into defense mode.

"Why not? He makes a lot of money. He travels, but you

would still see him, I'm sure. Even if you will be busy again with your patients when you return to work."

"Well, you already know why he and I can't get engaged, right?" Kareena said haughtily, tossing her head, her armpits moist now.

Her mother looked at her father with unease.

"Well, *Beta*, we know about that, but it shouldn't matter," her mother continued, pulling at an orange thread on her sleeve.

"It shouldn't *matter*? I'd think that it's a huge factor in why I *can't* get engaged to Sameer."

She stood aghast, completely thrown by her parents' reaction. She knew they didn't like Zayn. But that was a long time ago. He'd made a name for himself. And they couldn't refute his heritage. Even Pinky Aunty knew who his father was … and his mother's family. But the fact that they would have her break her 'engagement' to him, to get engaged to someone they preferred, left a repulsive taste in her mouth.

"Wow. I didn't know you could be so … judgmental, even after all these years."

They could absolutely be judgmental after all these years, but Kareena was hoping they would prove her wrong. Why? Why did it matter this time?

Kareena felt like a part of her was disappearing, and funnily enough, she wasn't bothered by it; more perplexed. The person her family had known her entire life had become a shadow of this new bolder one who seemed to have grown a spine recently.

Her father's head cocked to one side as he stared up at her, his ankles crossed. Her mother looked down at her lap, her hands fidgeting.

"I don't know what to say." She was at a loss. "If I'm already engaged, how could you expect me to break that off—"

Her father stood up abruptly, and her mother shot an alarmed look at her.

"You're engaged?" her father asked, while her mother went to the heart of the matter more quickly.

She thundered, "To who?"

"Whom," Kareena corrected absentmindedly, waving her hand distractedly. "You *know*. Pinky Aunty must have said something when she told you about how everything went with Sameer." She waved her hands further, blood rushing to her face. "You're going to make me say it, aren't you?" At their startled looks, she said defiantly, "Zayn. I'm engaged to Zayn Stavros."

"Kiran's boy?" her father asked, dumbfounded.

"But he … he … has nothing to Sameer," her mother stuttered and stood up, her mouth in a frown. "We thought you were talking about not finding Sameer's looks to your liking— just like you did with Arjun when you first met him. You got over it and made it work. You had Tamannah."

Kareena wasn't sure there was a way around the mortification of speaking to her parents about having sex with her deceased husband. Thankfully, her mother continued to berate her about Zayn.

"But, *why*, Kara? And when did you see him? We knew nothing about this." Leela Sharma sounded demoralized, as if Kareena had dragged the family name through the mud.

But at her parents' stuttering, she asked heatedly, "But you guys already knew all of this, right? Why are you acting so clueless?"

And that's when she realized the error of her ways. They *didn't* know every detail from that night. Pinky Aunty *had* only dished out what happened, or lack thereof, between herself and Sameer.

She stared at her parents, momentarily speechless, realizing she'd put herself in the most twisted predicament she could have ever dreamt up. And shockingly, it was the tenuous peace that dribbled through her that was more satisfying than she could've ever imagined.

PRESENT DAY

naxos island, greece

CHAPTER 16

ও৬

A fat bumblebee droned lazily next to her, and she gently swatted it away as she continued to sit in the garden in contemplation. Her parents had been insufferable after that, wanting to know the details of how she and her old high school boyfriend reconnected. How had it moved so quickly? Why hadn't she said anything to them? Her father had proclaimed that even his old friend Kiran Roy thought his son was a wild card. The younger man had entered a career that was as combustible as they came. He could implode at any moment, given his history of unstable behavior.

She ignored their comments, ignored the breathlessness that whipped through her at his being labelled a 'wild card.'

Something made her decide right then and there that she was doing this. She was going to move forward with this charade. She'd figure out a way to get Zayn to agree later. Would she owe him further? Probably. And it sent a thrill racing through her.

What she'd told them was very topline and vague, a variation of what she'd said to the matchmaker. They weren't pleased one bit. In fact, one could say their lids had blown completely off.

"This is just like when she was in high school," her mother had grumbled, as though Kareena wasn't in the room.

Her father had sucked his teeth. "Please, Leela. You're not helping."

And it did sound like she was still in high school; a repeat of how her parents had acted when they'd first found out about her and Zayn's high school relationship.

"Except that *she's* a full-grown, thirty-six-year-old woman," she'd retorted heatedly. They'd always see her as a child.

More words were said about how bad a match this was.

"What about Tama? Do you really think this is good for *her*?"

Kareena bristled and stood up taller. "I'm her mother. I know what's best for her." She thought quickly. "I haven't mentioned anything yet. I need to be careful with her, especially since she absolutely adored Arjun. I don't want her thinking that he is being replaced. Zayn and I plan to tell her at a more appropriate time … together."

But her father had persisted.

"Just think about it, *Shona*. It's not too late to end this. I'm sure Zayn will understand. Do you think a man like him would want to be a father?"

Kareena exhaled, the storminess of that argument subsiding, leaving her in the garden's quietude as she heard footsteps approaching from the villa behind her. She stood as the man in question approached her.

God, he looked adorable and hunky all at the same time. Cobwebs clung to his shirt along his wide shoulders, and a few were in his hair.

A thought came unbidden as her heart skittered. *Would a man like Zayn want to be a father?*

She approached him and gently pulled away the delicate strands. He smelled incredible, like man, sweat, and hints of aftershave.

"Who was on the phone?" he asked curiously.

She hesitated. "My *abba*."

"Hey, you're talking again!" He sounded pleased for her, even though he knew how her parents felt about him.

"We're not. It went to voicemail, and I only listened to his message. I didn't call him back."

"Do you want to talk about it?" he asked quietly. And her heart beat faster for this man.

"I don't. Not right now anyway." She pasted on a smile. "Hey, at least I'm getting what I want. They're off my back. No meddling relatives and arranged dates. Yay, us!"

"I know it's breaking your heart, Karma. You don't have to pretend with me."

He enfolded her into his strong arms, and she willingly went, her face nuzzling against the soft cotton of his shirt. She inhaled deeply, feeling ... fine. She wasn't speaking to her father, or her mother, for that matter, and she was sad about that, but she was doing okay.

She stepped away from him and tilted her head back.

"Did you get done what you needed to?" she asked, brushing dust off his t-shirt, needing some way to keep touching him because she already regretted telling him 'No,' when it came to sex. She didn't know how to use her feminine wiles to attack him.

Was 'attack' even the right method?

This was unfamiliar territory, and she wanted another

woman's advice. There was Reyana, who'd be more than enthusiastic about giving advice, having previously instructed her to get immediately railed by the hunky chef. Or, her old best friend Sheila, who'd tell her to be cautious because she wasn't completely sold on this scheme, and it wasn't the fake engagement part she didn't like. It was *who* was doing the fake fiancé-ing that she had issues with. She had nothing against Zayn but was concerned with Kareena opening up an older-than-old, possibly expired, can of worms. Sheila had been there over late-night calls filled with sobs and the unfairness of it all. She was the one who'd known first-hand how hard it'd been to get over him.

He nodded, grinning as he pulled a wayward cobweb from his beard.

"I *thought* we would go to the taverna next. It's right below us on the beach. But there's something else I want to show you first, before you head out and do your lady things with Pen and her bridesmaids."

She rolled her eyes, but smiled, happy to be part of the girl group, enfolded in as if she were one of their own.

He took her hand and led her to the garden wall, where, beyond, she knew was the steep drop down to the beach.

"Where are we going?"

"To a special spot that I completely forgot about. My great-great-grandfather had it constructed, if I remember correctly. It's indescribable. You have to see it for yourself."

He kept heading toward the stone wall, and her confusion grew. Where was he taking her? "Are we hang gliding down or something?" she asked nervously.

He chuckled, stepping through an opening in the wall that she hadn't seen from the bench. Before she followed him, she paused, making him stop, too. She noticed a very steep downward stone path immediately behind him, but beyond was nothing but blue sky and ocean.

He turned to look back at her, a secretive smile playing around his lips.

"Is this safe?"

His smile widened, showing his white teeth. "Trust me, Karma. You trust me, right?"

"I do," she said without hesitation.

"Okay. Then let's go."

He took a step down, and she followed, her hand gripping his tightly. She did trust Zayn. She always had.

She realized they were climbing down a steep rocky path, made up of crude steps carved into the mountain. The high wall from the garden continued here as well on one side, following the natural curve of the path as it wound down. The other side was flanked by a thicket of trees and greenery, and the cliffside widened out to steep hills. It was like a secret little tunnel, and her nerves turned into eagerness as she felt like a kid on a treasure hunt.

She let her free hand brush the dusty wall, feeling the safety of its solidness, though portions were crumbling. Her other hand was in Zayn's as they carefully descended.

"Watch out," he said a few times, pointing out holes in the steps where she could lose her footing in her thick-soled slide sandals.

But he must have missed one, because her foot landed lower than she expected, her knee collapsing below her, and she fell into him. Her foot, or rather her sandal, was stuck in the hole, and she couldn't move.

"I got you," he said quickly, maneuvering so that they were chest to breast, and he held her close, steadying her.

HE EXPERIENCED lightheadedness as he held her tight, savoring the feel of her soft form pressed against him. Her warmth penetrated the cotton material of her outfit, through his clothes, and to his skin.

She wore a yellow dress; one she said she'd picked out at one of the shops in Athens. The waist sat high, right below her breasts, with the skirt flowing out below and hitting her above her knees. A little bow was on the bodice, right where her cleavage was, and had been difficult to ignore all morning.

He stayed there for a hair longer than he probably had to, realizing he needed to let her go eventually. He began to pull away.

"Wait," she said. She glided her hands up his chest. The one that had been on the dusty wall left a smudged handprint on his shirt, mingling with the dust from the villa earlier.

"Yes, Karma?" he asked, trying to keep his tone solemn. They were still standing flush against one another, and if he didn't know any better, he might've thought that she'd scooted even closer. He clearly felt his dick resting at the apex of her thighs, as she stood a step or two above him.

She stared into his eyes, now almost at the same level as his. He wasn't sure of her intent, except that she blinked slowly, then rapidly, as if she was contemplating something.

"Eye on the prize," she whispered, and her lips met his.

Surprised, he let her kiss him, not so different from that time at the *Diwali* party that had started all this. Unlike that time, he noticed she was less hesitant. Her lips were insistent as her tongue ran along the seam of his, requesting entrance. He was about to oblige, when she pulled away from him, expelling a soft sigh from her pouty mouth.

"What was that for?" he asked, a little dazed.

Maybe someone was watching them.

He looked around, poking his head above the garden wall to the drop below. Then he peered over her head to the thicket of greenery. Sometimes people tried to climb the cliffs—dangerous, but doable.

"Is there someone out there?"

She shook her head. "I wanted to." she said a little meekly, her fingers pulling at his shirt. "Was it bad? Have I lost my edge as the better kisser out of the two of us?"

He'd been prepared to flirt with her, to rain compliments down on her, but that's not how things had unfolded between them up until now. They'd somehow become friends again. He was coming to care for her, again, and he didn't want to be *that* asshole chasing her with only one thing in mind. He respected her too much for that.

But he couldn't ignore his constant state of arousal when he was with her, or even just thinking about her.

Last night, when he'd finally come into the bedroom that his mother had put them in together (they were engaged, so naturally she would assume they'd sleep in the same room), Kareena had moved around on the king-size bed and was on her back, her arms flailed in different directions. She'd kicked the sheets off, and she was in rose pink satin shorts and a matching pajama top. A few buttons on the top were askew and undone, giving him a generous look at the rounded heaviness of her breasts. Her shorts had ridden up, exposing the beautiful brown skin of her belly and torso. The same brown skin on her legs looked smooth and shiny, as if she'd just put lotion on, and the material was hiked up, exposing more than she might have wished if she were awake. He knew there was no way he could sleep on the other side of that bed.

Yes, she was conked out, but was he confident in his ability to resist her when sleeping in such proximity? He wasn't entirely sure, and he wasn't about to try. He'd taken the sofa on the other side of the spacious guest room, trying to get as comfortable as he could with his large frame cramped into the cushions, and the worst case of blue balls imaginable.

"I'm not sure what you're talking about," he said, squatting down to help wiggle her foot out of her sandal, and then releasing her sandal from the hole it was stuck in. "You're a natural-born kisser, Karma."

When he stood up again, he hid his smile from her disgruntled look. His hand going up to smooth the wrinkles between her brows.

He continued. "Should we test the accuracy of that statement?"

"I think we have to," she said solemnly.

He pulled her up against him, flush again, and this time, he felt sweet heat between her legs as he positioned himself with

his back against the wall. She leaned into him, one of his thighs snug against her core, forcing her to spread hers.

Her breath caught, and he quickly covered her mouth with his, wanting to take that little breath of surprise for himself.

Unlike their closed-mouth kiss from before, he pushed his tongue through the seam of her lips, into her warm mouth, and she complied, opening up for him and twisting her tongue with his.

She moaned and pressed herself into him, putting her weight fully on him, letting go as her arms clutched his neck. He felt her nipples harden, and she rubbed her breasts against his chest, while simultaneously undulating on his thigh, a husky groan coming from the back of her throat.

His cock was pressing against his shorts, and into her belly, and his own hips gyrated against the soft flesh in pleasure.

Fuck. She was hot and ready for it. He could take her right here, right now if he wanted to.

He lifted his head abruptly, catching his breath.

Her eyes were closed, her mouth still open, and he saw the little red marks his beard had left along her cheeks. She breathed heavily as her eyes fluttered open, the dark brown turned almost black, glassy like rare volcanic obsidian found in secret, hidden places on the island.

"I need more information to justify your statement," she said huskily, still out of breath, the top of her breasts puffing over the bodice of her dress. She looked like she'd been ravished, and damn if he didn't feel a sense of pride in that. He was the one to make her come undone like this, to leave her breathless, and clearly wanting more. He was the one who could navigate past her usual calm and proper demeanor and make her wanton.

He pushed a thick strand behind her ear as he asked, "What are you saying?"

Was she changing her mind about them? From the way she was looking at him, he sure the fuck hoped so.

With hooded eyes, her fingers playing with the hair at the back of his neck, tickling him, she murmured, "I'd like to amend my answer about us … crossing the line."

He raised his brows. Exhilaration fizzed through his veins as heat struck the back of his thighs. "Is that so?"

She nodded.

He wondered what made her change her mind. Did he even care? Shouldn't he want to get the sexy woman into bed?

He glanced at his watch, and he frowned, murmuring, "Shit. If we're really going to do this, I don't want to rush us, Baby."

She arched her back and looked up at him, pressing the heat between her legs relentlessly onto his thigh. He groaned low in unadulterated pleasure.

"Do we really need long? Didn't I hear somewhere that you're a total pro at this?" She pouted.

He couldn't help barking out a laugh. She was breathless and a little whiny, and he absolutely adored needy Kareena.

"Who told you?" he asked.

"Doesn't everyone know about you and your … conquests?"

He tilted his head, mulling this over. His hands had been gripping the material at her back, and he released it, smoothing it along her warm skin, squeezing the soft flesh at her waist.

"I've been around." He lifted a shoulder in a shrug. "And I know what a woman wants." He nodded. "Personally, I wouldn't even need thirty minutes. I could get myself off in five flat."

She snorted. "And what about me?"

He leaned down and rubbed the tip of his nose against hers.

"You, my Karma, wouldn't get off once."

"Well, that's shitty." She balled her hands against his chest, displeased.

God, she was adorable, and so fuckable at the moment. But that's not how he wanted things to play out between them.

"Let me finish, Baby." He took a deep breath and stared into the deep depths of her gaze, realizing what he really wanted from her as he squeezed her waist again. "You'd come way too many times to count."

"In just five minutes?" She choked out. "Well, aren't you ... full of yourself."

"I know where my strengths lie."

"You're so cocky," she uttered, but she didn't sound disgusted. She sounded breathless and needy again.

He pushed his still rock-hard dick into her belly. "What gave it away?"

She tossed her head, pursing her lips.

"So, if five minutes is all you need, what's the holdup?"

He pressed his forehead to hers. "In that short amount of time, Baby, I'd take you so hard that your legs wouldn't hold you up properly after I was through with you. And we've got a long day ahead of us." After the bridal party spa excursion, there was a family dinner and dancing at the manor.

She gasped with widened eyes, her cheeks a luscious pink, as she sucked her bottom lip. He gently pulled it out from between her teeth and rubbed his thumb over the wet softness, trying not to think about his cock between those lips.

"Don't even worry about a thing, Karma," he exhaled, getting his bearings. "We'll have plenty of time later. And I'm going to hold you to this new level of 'eye on the prize.' It'll be good for the cause." He wiggled his brows, making her grin spread slowly as she nodded in agreement..

"All right, good," he said as he pushed them off the wall. They wordlessly navigated the crumbling steps, both of them getting their bearings.

He'd be thinking about it all day, he thought, as she was off getting massages, manicures, or whatever Penelope had planned. He'd need to shamelessly jack off later, letting his imagination run wild with what he would do to her supple, sexy, gorgeousness, and then even after that, he already knew that wouldn't be enough. He'd hit the ocean for a vigorous swim until he had plenty of time to pull multiple orgasms from this woman. She had no idea what she was in store for.

The path veered off suddenly, about halfway down to the beach, leading to a flat landing. It looked as though someone had intentionally scooped out the cliffside, creating what looked like a private oasis. The cliff hung overhead, providing shade over lounge chairs on one side. A good-sized lap pool with a holy and frayed tarp covering it was at the center, dug into the solid rocky terrain.

"What exactly is this place, Zayn?"

"It goes to the villa upstairs, which was originally built to house my great-great-grandfather's mistress. He built the pool for her, too."

He walked to the pool. "I'm going to have this place cleaned up while we're here because I'd like to use this for your swim lessons. This way you won't have to be out in the wide-open sea, which scares you, and you won't feel embarrassed by other members of my family who are actively using the pool at the big house."

She clasped her hands in front of her breast and turned to him, batting her eyes. "I'm touched that when you thought of your great-great-grandfather's mistress, you also thought of me."

He groaned. "You know that's not at all what I meant."

"I know." She bumped her shoulder into his chest. "It's really thoughtful. Thank you." She continued to look around. "But I haven't agreed to swimming lessons."

He grunted loudly.

She'd always been stubborn when it came to water and swimming. Why would he think any differently about her now? Didn't she realize it was for her own good?

She turned around, crossing her arms over her chest, making her breasts balloon up. "So you agree, we never agreed on it."

He dragged his gaze from her ample cleavage to her face. One thick brow was raised quizzically, and he knew she was after something. He'd already seen the clothes she'd purchased from Athens, specifically a sexy, skimpy red bathing suit. So what did she want? Truthfully, he'd trade anything to see her in that tiny number.

"Name your price, Karma," he taunted.

She tapped her chin with her index finger. "While I'm here, let me help you with your addiction."

He bristled, taken aback. "What?"

"Well," she said carefully, "If at the moments when you want to reach for pills, you're smoking as a substitute then you have an addiction problem.

"Kareena..." he said with a frown. "I know you're a doctor, but come on."

"I'm not judging you, Zayn. Actually, smoking tobacco is a lesser evil than those pills. I get why you're relying on tobacco for now. But it's not healthy in the long run." She lifted her chin, holding steadfast.

She just called it like it was; she didn't even shimmy around it. It was kind of liberating. Most people were awkward or didn't know how to ask or approach him about it. Her candidness was refreshing.

But *did* he have a substance abuse problem—an addiction? Yeah. He did.

He'd told her about his overdose and subsequent smoking early on and she'd kept quiet regarding how she felt about it all. He knew she wouldn't be completely in line, though. She was a medical professional after all.

"Let me think about it." He decided to leave the option open. There was no harm in considering her help.

"Great!" she said brightly. "Then, I'll go ahead and *think* about swimming lessons." She shrugged and turned away from him. "Personally, I think *you* get the better end of the deal." He saw her shiver as she inspected the pool.

He shook his head, hiding his humor and annoyance at sassy Kareena. She was probably right and just trying to be helpful. She had no skin in the game; they weren't together for real, so she didn't need to care. The fact that she did both exasperated him and gave him a fuzzy feeling inside. He didn't mind, though, because it was how she'd always been with him— supportive and understanding.

But smoking was the crutch that worked for him, and his overdose was still so near in his past. He wasn't sure if he was ready to give it up.

CHAPTER 17

59

*T*hey returned to the manor later and had a speedy lunch. Then Kareena got ready and headed out with Penelope and her bridal party to a Turkish spa in town.

It warmed his heart seeing how Kareena was getting along with his favorite cousin. Penelope was the baby of the bunch, but Zayn had always given her attention, as the others ignored or forgot about her on more than one occasion. He'd been treated similarly at times, as the only half-Greek cousin, who wanted nothing to do with the shipping empire. They'd come to each other's rescue on more than one occasion, and over the years, she became more like a little sister to him. When he'd first introduced Kareena to her at Teterboro Airport, she'd hung onto every word his fake fiancé said, as if she was star-struck. She'd told him on the flight over that she couldn't wait to call Kareena her cousin.

He knew Kareena was in good hands with Pen that afternoon and reminded her as she left to relax because she would need her strength for later. She grinned wickedly at him and said something about testing out his cockiness later before kissing him headily in front of the other women, making them giggle and sigh. Then she left with the group, his heart beating wildly, with thoughts of defiling her clean, herbaceous scent on his mind, and a hardness growing in his pants.

Shit. What was she doing to him? He didn't have any control when around her. It was like they were teens again, when she'd slowly let him peel back her uncertainty about getting physical. The pace they'd gone had only made him crazier for her, naturally. And now, though he hadn't expected it, he felt the urgency more so. Maybe it was because, unlike last time, he knew there was an end to their time together.

The realization was unsettling, and one that kept rearing its ugly head more frequently, just like now, as he watched the cars carrying the bridal party leave the estate. There was a sudden restlessness inside him, sending his thoughts into a jumble. The need to take a swim in the ocean to clear his mind was stronger than ever. And maybe it would also tamp down his constant lust for the woman, too, at least until they could finally do something about it.

He turned on his heel and jogged to the carriage house, where various modes of transportation were parked, including a row of mopeds. He jumped on one, turning the key that was already in the ignition. He drove to the main road from the estate and wound down to a parking area built on a natural plateau above the taverna. He parked and took the stairs on the side of the building down to the private beach.

He observed the waves flowing calmly as he tore off his shirt and shucked his shoes and pants. In his underwear, he headed into the water, needing some of that calmness to rub off on him.

It felt exquisite, as the tepid water moved smoothly over

him. He began swimming laps, back and forth. The tranquil currents allowed him to effortlessly swim miles, pumping his blood, working his muscles, and clearing his thoughts.

He felt much less agitated as he finished up and got out, his feet hitting the dry sand. He collapsed next to his clothes to dry off.

Did he feel something that he hadn't felt for Kareena in years? Undeniably, yes. Being with her felt right, as if he was coming home from being away for far too long. Despite that, he'd already decided that what they were doing by crossing that physical line was living in the moment; nothing more. They would enjoy themselves, and when it was time to part ways, they would do so without nary a lingering emotion.

His chest constricted, protesting the clean-cut strategizing of his mind. He was lying to himself and needed to face that there was more to his future desires than just the taverna sitting behind him.

He shook his head, putting 'them' on the back burner for the moment, as he glanced at the restaurant behind him. Now dry, he put his clothes back on and decided to re-familiarize himself with the place. He climbed up the rickety old stairs onto the deck that took up the entire length of the building's beachside façade.

As soon as he entered the dim and musty open space, the memory of just turning eighteen hit him. His grandfather had laid a heavy hand on his shoulder and guided him to the bar. The bartender recognized them and wished Zayn a happy birthday. His grandfather ordered two Mythos beers for them and toasted Zayn to his first legal beer, though everyone knew Zayn was part of the local teens' party scene on the island.

Zayn looked around the dim interior. It still looked the same.

Dark wood lined the interior, worn and splintered. It badly needed repurposing. The long bar was the same and even emitted a strong, moldy odor that was concerning. He would get someone in to look at it while he was here for the wedding. No point in waiting.

He pulled his phone out of his pocket, brushing sand from the screen. He'd photographed his notes on design and menu ideas from the journal he'd had on the plane. He brought up the images and studied them, comparing some of his visions with what was possible. He made a note that Capiz shells lining the front surface of the bar could work. The wood would look cleaner, sanded back to its natural finish, and the stucco walls only needed to be scrubbed back to their original brilliance. The soggy floor planks needed to go, and the beautiful mosaic stonework he had in mind would look at once cleaner and more sophisticated. He could definitely picture pendant lights creating warmth and ambiance.

He went to the floor-to-ceiling windows and peered out at the deck and its seating arrangement. Everything would have to be refurbished as the old furniture hadn't withstood the elements. Zayn pictured the addition of space heaters so people could continue to enjoy the outdoor area in the cooler months.

His phone suddenly buzzed. It was a text from Aariv.

"How's the happy couple? Any attempted murders yet? Do you need a lawyer?"

Zayn chuckled. If only Aari knew how things were developing in the complete opposite direction between him and his fake fiancé.

Instead, he typed, **"She wants to help me with my substance abuse problem."**

When Kareena said she would only agree to swim lessons if

he let her assist him with this, he couldn't help noticing the irony. The first time they'd had this conversation a long time ago, she'd wanted to *try* his vices, including his cigarettes.

"I'm impressed. She's definitely smart, and it's good that you have some support in that while over there. I hope you consider it. But be careful."

Zayn grunted and shoved his phone back into his pocket, leaving the text unanswered..

He stared out to the horizon. He wanted so badly to push Aariv's stern lecture from his mind. But it incessantly knocked on his psyche, even as he wondered if Kareena was having a good time and couldn't wait to see her again.

She would only be gone for a few hours, so when exactly had he started to miss her company? Was it so ridiculous to think she might feel the same, too?

Things were moving fast between them, and he couldn't control how he felt. Part of him didn't want to slow down. What the outcome ended up being was something he couldn't prophesize. But he'd be a complete dumbass if he didn't heed his best friend's warning. He'd already experienced heart wreckage from this same woman before. Did he want to chance that kind of carnage again?

3 WEEKS AGO
new york city, new york

CHAPTER 18

১৮

Zayn couldn't wait to tell Aariv that he might have found the solution to his problems. Admittedly, the scenario with Kareena had been odd, but also titillating, and he could use it.

They were in the middle of one of their usual Sunday morning pick-up games at the court near Zayn's West Village apartment. They sat on the bench, taking a water break, when he told Aariv about running into Kareena Sharma.

"Zayn," Aariv said seriously, wiping the sweat off his face with a towel. "I need to tell you something, and I need you to not lose your fucking shit."

Zayn had an idea of where his friend was going with this and interrupted him. "Aari, let me stop you right there. I know you've never liked her. Her little circle of friends taunted your cousin as the new *Desi* kid. I know. But everyone is past that, including Mimi. So why are you still so touchy about it?"

Kareena and her friends hadn't been nice to Mariam (Mimi), Aariv's younger cousin, when she'd first moved to the area. At community events, they taunted her for her looks—she was skinny, scrawny, and half white and half Indian. They also made fun of the fact that her parents were divorced, and that she didn't attend the same posh private school as the rest of them. It was bullying if one looked back on it. Aariv had done his best to intervene and protect her when he could. He'd just moved to the US and was preparing for college at the University of Connecticut while also helping to care for his ailing grandmother, so he wasn't around as much as he would've liked.

"It's not that. When I was working with the matchmaker last spring to find a wife—"

"Your wife hunt, you mean?" Zayn said jokingly, grabbing the basketball and spinning it on his index finger.

"Yeah. Well … Kareena and I were matched up. Our numbers aligned, and everything else seemed to fall into place."

"What?" Zayn said, caught off guard. He wasn't sure he'd heard correctly. The basketball spun off his finger and bounced away. One of the other players grabbed it and dribbled it toward the hoop, dunking it.

Aariv's expression was solemn. He wasn't joking. Zayn stood up in a sudden rage. It was like someone held a burning hot poker right smack dab in the middle of his chest. Jealousy burned brightly through him, and he felt a headache coming on.

He dug around his duffel bag, looking for his cigarettes. He'd forgotten them. He swiveled back to his friend.

"Wait a minute, Kareena Sharma? *My* Kareena Sharma?!"

"Is she yours?" Aariv asked quietly.

He ran his hands through his sweaty hair. "Yes—no. Fuck."

The basketball bounced his way, and he kicked it so hard

that it flew over the chain-link fence on the other side of the court.

"Hey, come on, dude!" one of the other players protested. Zayn ignored them.

"I can't apologize for us matching up," Aariv said. "I can't control that. But I was pissed as all hell when the matchmaker and my stepmother sang about her attributes. I was still annoyed about how she and her friends behaved toward Mimi. But I didn't even get a chance to tell her I wasn't interested; she could tell I wasn't." Aariv looked away, rubbing the back of his neck. "It was at a party where Chrissy was the events manager. Kareena saw the way I was acting around her and knew I was already mentally with someone else. She's smart and very observant. I'll give her that."

Zayn considered this new information. "Okay. So why are you telling me this now?"

"I'm being honest with you. The fact of the matter is, she was on a hunt for husband number two at the time. Who's to say she still isn't?"

"I know she's not. We ran into each other before the party— before the will reading."

At Aariv's inquisitive stare, he finally told him about literally running into Kareena in the street.

"She told me straight up that she was against the second marriage."

But he also recalled the fight going out of her, her shoulders slumping, her expression becoming docile, and now he wasn't so sure about this version of Kareena. How many times had he witnessed exactly that when they'd been together as teens? Anything from wanting to go to their favorite frozen yogurt place with a group of friends after one of her tennis matches, to fighting tooth and nail to go out of town with her friends for one of his swim meets at state finals. He'd seen her give up and do what her parents wanted of her. She hadn't given up easily, but she'd given up.

And yet, what about the *Diwali* party and her unwavering willingness to lie to the matchmaker about him being her fiancé?

His friend studied him thoughtfully. "Listen, I'm not saying it's not a good idea. But what if she has another motive? What if she's going to trick you into marrying her for real? Or, what if she's going to take you for everything you've got in return for this arrangement? You were worried about those money-hungry women who might do that ... what if Kareena is one of them?"

Zayn shook his head, bristling. He may not know the woman anymore, but he knew deep down she wasn't like that.

"I'll be pulling all the strings here, Aari. She won't have a chance to 'fuck around and find out.'"

THAT AFTERNOON, still ruminating over Aariv's words, Zayn was in his kitchen, working on his next video. His inheritance, and everything related to it, would have to wait. He couldn't ignore Shelly's barrage of messages (both text *and* voice) and needed to give his fans what they wanted. He'd focus on his fake fiancée and hash out the details after.

He thought about the warning he gave her on the night of the party—that he had her number, and he was going to use it.

It was a little thrilling that he held the reins on this, and he had the perfect plan for her: she'd have to be *his* fake fiancée in return. The plan couldn't be any more flawless. He'd get his inheritance and move forward with his new restaurant. In return, he could continue to act as her fiancé if she wanted, and help keep every meddling aunty and uncle off her back. How hard could that be? He already knew where he stood with the community—they'd never be pleased with his standing in life and who he'd become, but he could handle a few parties and her folks if it came to that.

What he had in store for her was way more involved. As a well-known chef with a packed social and business schedule, she'd need to be on his arm extensively over the next few weeks, just until the will's claims period ended. But in that time, they needed to make it look convincing, and he had every intention of seeing what their continued attraction was all about. Was it crazy? Hell yeah, but there was no way she didn't feel their chemistry, too. He'd witnessed her tells, the flicking of her tongue, her eyes burning dark with desire after they'd kissed. It was strange, the headiness he felt around her. He couldn't remember a time with any woman that made him feel this way —utter, unfettered lust whenever he was in her vicinity. He had to attribute it to the fact that they'd done many sexually risky things together as teens, but they'd never been fully naked, in a bed, with their limbs tangled, and his dick inside her, screwing her until she screamed his name. Would it be out of the question to propose that they do something real about it while they pretend in other aspects? What was the harm if they both wanted it?

He maneuvered his phone in the stand, angling it just right so that his workspace on his countertop was in the shot. He'd already aimed his recording light (the one Shelly gifted him as he would never consider getting one himself) to the perfect position and leaned over to click his phone's record button. In the frame, he stood shirtless, with his studded black leather hood covering his face, and his arms crossed over his chest. His trusty knife was gripped tightly in one hand, and he made sure to grin like the sinfully dangerous chef he portrayed.

He dragged the pile of cooked scallops to him. He'd taken home the meager leftovers from the party Friday night—just enough for the midnight snack recipe he'd come up with spur of the moment for this video's content. He would make his twist on shrimp toast, a famed East Asian Street food, using scallops instead, and incorporating Indian flavors. All of his ingredients were prepped and organized neatly on the counter, the label for the particular brand of spice he was promoting this time front and center.

He chopped the seafood into small chunks, working it into a paste. As he pulverized the meat with his knife, his mind replayed Kareena (he couldn't help it) and what she said about his food. She'd enjoyed the scallop dish very much. He'd watched the pink tip of her tongue lick the equally pink sauce away from her sumptuous pink lips, closely. The way her eyes had widened up at him, like burnt brown sugar, made him think of her licking something else from her lips as she stared up at him, preferably on her knees, where he could see down the front of her blouse and get a good look at her breasts.

Fuck, he thought, she'd always had a great rack. She'd been shy in the beginning, but he'd convinced her to let him see her tits after a few months of dating. They'd been large and round, firm and perky, with small brown nipples that matched her eyes. And they'd tasted even better, he recalled. At first, she'd been hesitant to let him kiss her there. But then she demanded it, enjoying it while he did other things to her she'd told him she'd never imagined.

Damn, and since the party, all of those memories raged back into the forefront of his mind (and his pants), especially when she told him she couldn't wait to taste the other appetizer dish; that she couldn't wait to put it into her mouth. The woman was flirting with him, whether she knew it or not. And she wanted him, whether she knew it or not. He felt himself hardening, and he had to shake off the lust.

Concentrate.

He scraped the scallop paste onto the side of the blade, revealing the consistency to the camera. He had followers who observed his cooking and prep techniques as closely as they observed how his muscles flexed.

He threw the pile with a smack into a clean glass bowl, then added a blend of Indian spices, an egg white, and softened ghee. He donned black rubber gloves with a loud snap before mixing the contents, ensuring the squelch of the moist mixture caught on the little microphone set up next to him.

He pulled off and tossed the dirty gloves with fanfare before sliding slices of fluffy white bread into the shot. He wiped off his knife with a kitchen towel and proceeded to cut the crusts off each slice. He worked with care, but his mind went back to the strange lie they'd—*she'd*—communicated to the matchmaker. It'd stunned him silent. He played along, not sure why, but Kareena kissing him might have had something to do with it. Those sumptuous pink lips of hers slid warmly over his mouth, while her hands cupped his face. She probably hadn't been aware, but her fingers worked through his facial hair, softly caressing, as if enjoying the feel of his rough, short hairs on her palms. And how could he help himself? He'd been imagining kissing her ever since running into her again, wondering if it was as sweetly hot and sexy as he remembered. And it had been, but so much more. He felt the need in her, the way her body pressed into his. He wanted to kiss her all night, and eventually rip off her already torn blouse to worship her breasts—

"Fuck!" he howled, as pain shot through his left hand.

He dropped the knife as blood seeped heavily from an open gash on his index finger. He hadn't been paying attention, and of course, he'd cut himself on something as menial as slicing off crusts.

Thick, red droplets quickly pooled onto the cutting board, soaking the stark, fluffy slices, transforming them into a gooey mess of deep burgundy. He clasped his index finger tightly and grabbed the dish towel from earlier, wrapping it around the wound to slow the bleeding.

Shit, it hurt like hell, with a burning pain searing along his palm and radiating to his other digits. He glanced at his phone and noticed it was still recording. He leaned over, fumbling, knocking it over, and finally turning it off. Shelly would need to edit the shit out of this video, he thought, with humor. And then he laughed outright. He hadn't cut himself like this in ages, and he'd done so now because his focus was all over the place. The problem was Kareena. She was back in his orbit, and his mind had no room to focus on the literal tasks at hand.

Jesus.

Her on her knees, her pretty mouth full of his dick, was a fantasy he couldn't refuse that he wanted to make real. He'd need to tread lightly, however. He needed her more than she needed him if she agreed to a real fake engagement. He had more at stake with the possibility of losing his inheritance. Was her situation dire enough to warrant committing to something so crazy like this with him? Who knew with Kareena? Though of strong character, he recognized even now, from their brief run-ins, that she could still fold easily under her family's pressure.

There was only one way to find out. He'd need to come up with an agreement so tempting that she couldn't refuse.

CHAPTER 19

ﺱﺩ

*Z*ayn stood outside Kareena's Tribeca home the
following Wednesday. The elegant brownstone sat
in the middle of a picturesque street, straight off a NYC
postcard. Pretty homes were decorated for Fall with fat potted
mums out on their stoops in an array of autumn colors, along
with perfectly placed gourds, pumpkins, and Halloween decor.
Young families were already on the sidewalks with excited kids
in costumes running ahead to the end of the block, where he'd
just come from. That portion of the street was closed off to
traffic for a Ghoulish-themed fair, already alive with hubbub
and activity.

He'd barely pressed the doorbell to her brownstone when
the door flew open. Instead of Kareena, he looked down to see a
solemn little girl in a furry tan costume—a costume that was
recognizable only for the fact that the scratchy fur was the same
he remembered holding for Kareena as she got her bearings
from the truck incident.

Zayn was startled, having already been told the little girl
wouldn't be home.

After he'd cut the fuck out of his finger and managed to finish up his video, he'd received a text from Karma. He'd programmed her into his phone with that old nickname because what else would he call her? Strangely, it seemed meant to be that they'd run into each other at that particular moment in his life. That nickname was appropriate in more ways than one.

Her text read, **"We've got a problem. How soon can we meet?"**

He realized this might be less straightforward than he thought, and he'd called her, catching her at a time that seemed crazy, but she managed to hold a conversation. In the background, he heard growling and shrieks.

"Hold on a minute, Zayn. Sorry." She yelled away from the speaker, not even bothering to cover it, "Stop antagonizing each other! Please go to the other room. Both of you."

What, or who, was growling, he wondered. Surely it couldn't be her daughter?

"Oh my freaking stars, it's been a day," she said breathlessly. "Sorry." He heard her inhale deeply before letting air out in a sharp whistle. "Okay, so…"

She explained to him that she'd inadvertently bungled up by telling her parents what she thought they already knew—that they were "engaged." That Pinky Aunty had, for once, not spilled the beans that weren't hers to spill and had kept that portion of Friday night to herself. Her parents were livid, she'd said.

Of course, he'd thought. He'd never be good enough for their precious firstborn.

"So…?" he'd asked, needing her to spit out whatever she was thinking so he could propose his own plan. She owed him.

"I want us to really fake an engagement, Zayn. I need them to get off my back once and for all."

She was making this way too easy for him, he'd marveled. But he needed to ensure she was on board with what *he* had in mind.

"Why?" he'd asked cautiously, though genuinely interested in her answer. Was this new level of boldness real, or would it expire when the going got too rough?

"I'm a freaking thirty-six-year-old woman, a mother, a widow. I'm on sabbatical from my job ... a sa-bbat-ical!" she almost shouted.

"I know what a sabbatical is, Kareena."

"Great. Then, as my fake fiancé, you can explain that to everyone who's treating me like a child. Like I've totally lost control of my life. When really, can't a person take a moment to breathe and figure herself out—"

She'd stopped abruptly.

"I get it," he said softly. He'd felt a similar pressure from his father when he didn't know what to do with his life. But thankfully, he had his mother to support him and a passion for cooking.

"Right," she'd said, mollified. "Of course, you do. Zayn. Would you—how do you feel about—" She puffed in irritation. "Look, I know it ended badly before college. But, we're past that, right? What's your schedule like? How do you feel about a real fake engagement?"

He'd almost laughed at how casual she sounded, and really how similar their lines of thinking were.

"So, you're asking me to continue to be your fake fiancé?"

"I know, it sounds ... pathetic."

"Not at all, although this isn't what I had in mind when I said I'd be calling *you* for payback."

She'd groaned. "I'm sorry. Is this another favor you can add to the never-ending list of favors you've already done for me?

He chuckled. "I'm more concerned that you're asking for my help for the third time in only a few days. What's in it for me?" He wasn't going to make this easy for her. He knew what he wanted, and it very much stood in line with what she wanted, but he wasn't going to tell her that yet.

She'd guffawed. "Technically, it's been once per week since that truck incident—a *Stavros* truck, might I add."

"Pfft. I already paid for services due by saving your life, remember?"

She laughed, but sounded defeated. "Okay. Well, I don't know, I thought since you and I have a history, and already know some things about each other, it was worth a shot—"

"Hold up, Karma. Let's not be so hasty."

Why did it feel so good to call her that? Probably because he knew she was blushing and trying not to smile on the other end, recalling her playful grin from the *Diwali* party.

"I *do* think I can help," he continued. "In fact, I know I can. But you have to be willing to do something for me in return."

"Whatever you want, for however long we decide; dick pics and all."

"What?" he'd asked in confusion, not sure if she was joking, or even if he'd heard correctly.

"Nothing," she'd said quickly. "Tell me what I have to do. I'll do it, you know."

"Ah, Karma, I wouldn't be so dismissive about all of this. What I have in mind will require a lot."

"It will?" she'd asked quietly. "What is it? Will I have to sleep with you?"

This caught him off guard. "Are you kidding right now? I can't tell."

Would she have to sleep with him? By God, what an exchange; one he couldn't refute that he'd already fantasized more than a dozen times. Was she fantasizing about him, too?

"Let's just say I wouldn't throw you out of my bed."

She snorted loudly, and he grinned, remembering that sound; how her mother told her she sounded like a farm animal and to be more ladylike. He was glad to hear it, indicating she'd not complied.

"Gee, thanks," she said testily.

Was Kareena Sharma bothered that he'd not said he wanted to jump straight into bed with her? Interesting. He'd need to file that away for later use.

"Listen," he said, "what I need from you is for you to act as *my* fake fiancé, too, but in my very social, B-level celebrity circles, and when around *my* large and intense family."

Then he explained quickly about his inheritance and the engagement stipulation, but promised to tell her more if she accepted.

"So anything from a few weeks to two months? That means the possibility of spending Thanksgiving, Christmas, and New Year's as a fake couple..." she seemed to be talking through it to herself.

"Scared to kiss me on New Year's Eve?" he asked mockingly.

"As if. You know I was always the better kisser, even if you were my first."

He remembered, and judging by the kiss a few nights ago, she was still pretty damn good.

He shook his head. He needed them both to focus on the details.

"Timing-wise, I'd need that level of commitment. Do you think you can handle that?"

She was silent, and he wondered if she was already going to bail before they'd even begun.

"What about my daughter?"

That threw him for a loop. He'd forgotten about the daughter.

"Well," he said carefully. "That's up to you. I'm not great with kids. I don't know that many…"

"I know. I'm just thinking out loud."

In the end, she made the decision not to tell her kid, which he thought was smart. This was already a sticky business; why make it more complicated? If he ever came up in conversation, her excuse would be she was helping an old friend with something important. Technically, not a lie, and for some reason, he felt better knowing that, even though he'd never met her daughter, and didn't really ever plan to.

They'd decided to meet mid-week for him to tell her more and hash out the details. She'd assured him that her daughter wouldn't be there, so the fact that a child was answering her door had him worried.

Her face was painted dog-like, with a pink snout around her mouth, a black-tipped nose, and fine lines for whiskers. A headband with two tan felt ears held back a thick mess of dark brown hair.

This was indeed Kareena's daughter, he thought. Even in the costume, he saw the resemblance to her mother was uncanny.

Judging by the spooky festivities he'd seen upon arrival in her neighborhood, he guessed she was headed there, too. He studied her as she looked wide-eyed up at him.

It took him a moment to compose himself before he said as calmly as possible, "Hello. I'm Zayn."

Was he supposed to shake hands with a child? He wasn't sure. But she beat him to it, sticking her small hand out.

"I'm—"

Abruptly, she was knocked over by a flash of golden fur that barreled through the pocket doors behind her and into the foyer, a leash attached to it. A second later, Kareena appeared, gripping the other end. She did not look happy.

The dog-girl caught herself on the doorframe as the little beast headed straight for him, proceeding to attack his legs. But Zayn held his ground as grunts, sniffs, and whines ensued from the funny-looking French bulldog.

Kareena, still holding the other end of the leash, tried to stay in one spot as the dog circled him. But, naturally, she ended up circling him out on the stoop landing, too, as she firmly let out commands for him to stay, to sit, to heel, which only made the dog nuzzle its head into Zayn's shoes, and bark in utter joy.

Zayn watched in amusement and caught the little girl's gaze. She burst into giggles, and he couldn't help but smile at the ridiculous situation.

When Kareena was standing close enough for him to feel the warmth emanating from her disheveled appearance, the leash was wrapped around his legs at least three times, making it impossible for him to move. There was no more lead to pull on, so she and the dog stood there in a sort of staring contest, eyeing one another. And Zayn took a moment to study her in her natural habitat.

Her thick hair was up in a ponytail, wavy tendrils messily framing her face. She wore a black mohair sweater with a wide neck that exposed the expanse of her smooth brown flesh, dipping slightly in the front, where he caught a hint of cleavage. Though not a tight fit, the fuzzy material clung to her curvy form. She wore jeans and was barefoot. Her toes were painted a pretty red.

He breathed in deeply at their nearness, at her relaxed state. Witnessing her within mundane daily elements felt intimate, especially since they no longer knew each other. And even that deep breath felt intimate because the smell of her—herby and floral, musky, and sweet—came crashing into his senses. He shouldn't like it so much, especially as he was there for a fake engagement that had nothing to do with chemistry, unless he encouraged it, and would result in them parting ways eventually.

"Aloo," she said firmly, squatting down quickly to lecture the animal. The dog flopped at Zayn's feet, using his black, Chelsea-style boots as a pillow. A big pink tongue lolled out, periodically licking the shiny leather surface, and he thought the animal indeed look liked its namesake, the word for 'potato' in Bangla.

Kareena unwound the leash from around Zayn and stood up. It was then that she must've realized how close they were standing because her pretty eyes widened, and her dusty pink lips opened in surprise. A blush crept into her cheeks.

"I'm so sorry about this." She shook her head and took a step back. "I wonder sometimes who is leading whom."

She laughed huskily, and he chuckled. "Usually, it's the cutest one out of the bunch who's the boss." And he couldn't help winking at her.

२०

"*Mommy* thinks Aloo has a screw loose somewhere," Tamannah spoke up, lunging to sit next to Zayn's feet, scratching behind their dog's ears.

"Is that so?" Zayn asked, his deep voice easing warmly through Kareena, making her shiver.

That wink, had she imagined it? Wasn't he upset that her daughter was here? It was a last-minute change in plans, and she'd texted him as soon as she found out, but he must've already been on his way.

He looked amazing, of course, in just a grey crew neck sweater and black jeans, with a black, worn leather bomber thrown over. Really, he could be a Calvin Klein model, and she couldn't stop ogling, making it difficult to keep track of what he and her daughter were talking about. But she caught on to his last comment. "You know, animals have their own personality traits. Seems like Aloo is more mischievous than anything. She just needs a little guidance."

"He," Tamannah quickly corrected. And Aloo rolled onto

his back, exhibiting an edited version of his crown jewels for the newcomer.

"Ah. Sorry, little man." Zayn knelt and rubbed his belly. "I had a horse in Greece where I grew up who was just like this. She could be trained, but she had a wild spirit."

"You had a horse?" Tamannah asked wide-eyed and in awe … Kareena was pretty sure she looked the same, too. She needed to reel in whatever conflicted emotions roiled inside her. Though he was as hot as sin, and the attraction she felt for him pleaded for attention, she couldn't risk falling into that (her unused nether regions begged to differ). He was here for a business agreement.

Zayn nodded. "Her name was Pegasus."

"Pegasus. Isn't that a flying horse? *My* name is Tamannah, by the way."

"Oh, sorry," Kareena said apologetically. Where were her manners, and the basic rules of social etiquette, for that matter? There was too much going on, and her daughter's last-minute presence was throwing her. She hadn't wanted to get her involved, but maybe there was a way to save this. "This is my daughter, Tamannah." To Tamannah, she said, "This is Zayn, an old friend of mine."

"Are you going to be my new dad?" her daughter asked curiously, still on the stoop, petting Aloo.

Kareena stared at her daughter, horrified. She literally felt the blood drain from her face.

She couldn't view Zayn's expression, but he continued to pet their dog's velvety belly, rhythmically.

"Mommy! You should see your face!" Tamannah shrieked, giggling, covering her mouth with her small hands. "I'm only *kidding*."

"Tama, that was not funny in the least," Kareena said with relief, her heart pounding on high alert.

Zayn abruptly spoke up, and she noticed the half-smile on his face. "I don't know, it was a little funny."

"See, Mommy. Ms. Lindsey was right." She turned her attention to Zayn. "Ms. Lindsey is my therapist. She thinks my mom has a lot going on in her life. She told me to try to be helpful when I can and to make her laugh more."

"TMI, Tama," Kareena mumbled, flustered. Why were kids always so honest? Because they hadn't been roughed up by life, yet, she thought.

"But isn't he an old friend of yours? And aren't friends supposed to be there if you need them?" Tama asked slowly, as if spelling it out for her mother.

The innocence of her child would have made her smile in wonder if the truth of her statement wasn't so stark and in her face.

Zayn spoke up again. "That's exactly right, Tamannah. Your mom is actually helping *me* with something. We're friends who go way back." He looked up at her thoughtfully; his gaze bright and warm as he nodded. He chuckled, murmuring, "Your mom and I ran into each other after a long time. She invited me over to … meet you and Aloo."

Nice catch, she thought, as she blew a wayward strand from her face.

"Thank you," she mouthed with an embarrassed smile. Their gazes locked and held for a brief moment, a warm connection stirring and keeping them there.

"But how did you know I was going to be here? I was supposed to go to the Halloween fair with my friend," her daughter said matter-of-factly.

"Beta," Kareena interceded breaking their stare. She should've known better. Her daughter always noticed the small details. "Let's finish getting our shoes on and go to the festivities before it gets too dark outside and they deflate the bouncy house."

That got her moving. She scrambled up, saying, "Zayn Uncle, you have to see this fair. It's so creepy cool!"

Kareena once again zoomed in on her daughter, startled. Did she just call him by the respectful term of a close male family member or friend? For some reason, this made her both proud of her daughter's politeness and angry at herself that she'd put the little girl in this position in the first place.

She knew she couldn't foresee plans falling through, but she'd blame herself a million times over if, when all of this was through, her daughter so much as showed a scratch from it. Maybe it wasn't such a good idea to go through with this. What kind of mother was she?

You're a good mother.

She had to remember that she was doing this so that her parents didn't force a new husband on her *and* a new father on Tama. Her daughter didn't need a new father. She was doing just fine and thriving.

She'd stand by her initial rule—her daughter would never know about this. It would stay between her and Zayn ... and his entire enormous family ... and her parents ... and quite possibly the South Asian community.

Oh, for fuck's sake. This might be harder than she thought.

"Do you think I could meet Pegasus one day?" her daughter continued, her fascination with this new person in her life her only concern.

"Well, she's not alive anymore." Zayn stood up.

Tamannah's face fell, and he quickly followed up with, "But we have an entire stable full of horses on my family estate in Greece. Maybe you can meet them someday."

Her expression lit up, and she skipped into the apartment.

What exactly made him utter those words had Kareena scratching her head for days. She had no intention of bringing her daughter, let alone herself, to her potential fake fiancé's homeland. It would never get that far. She didn't want to directly (or indirectly) encourage a relationship between the two, which could result in heartache for her tender daughter when this all ended.

Before following Tamannah into their apartment, she murmured, "I'm so sorry about this, Zayn. Tamannah's plans changed last minute." She cringed because it sounded like an imaginary excuse, but it was the truth. "But, now you see what I contend with daily. Between this crazy little guy and the antics of your average seven-year-old, I'm pretty much outnumbered."

He nodded and chuckled, but he remained aloof, muttering drolly, "Didn't expect the dog, that's for sure."

Yikes. This was not turning out the way she'd imagined. Damn, Marigold's mom. Abby said she would take the girls to the fair. Kareena had triple checked with her, making sure she was good on her offer, because the woman tended to be flakier than the butteriest of croissants. But not even an hour ago, the other woman texted that her plans had changed with no other explanation. Kareena had no choice but to take Tamannah, who'd been looking forward to this for weeks.

She asked if he would like to reschedule their conversation, but he opted to go to the Halloween fair with them. It was creepy and crazy after all, and he couldn't miss it. He loved Halloween.

She smiled placidly, though her inner self groaned. She would need to juggle a conversation with Zayn that had the importance of a covert operation, while simultaneously ensuring her daughter didn't hear a drop of what they were up to.

A little later, they finally stepped outside. She'd rushed Tamannah in getting her shoes on, even though the girl went as slow as molasses and wanted to show Zayn her room.

Somehow she'd convinced her that all the candy would be gone, to which her daughter, actually more observant than your average seven-year-old, eyed her with slit eyes but complied anyway.

Outside, Tamannah explained her costume to Zayn in the waning golden light, with the sky streaked in deep orange. Aloo was on a tight leash and alternated between sniffing new smells at their feet and sitting as she passed down dog treats to him. Tamannah held up one of Kareena's old, non-working cell phones and an empty to-go coffee cup with 'Dog Mom' printed on one side, explaining that she was dressed as Aloo's mom.

Zayn's deep chuckle warmed Kareena to her bones, even as a chilly gust cut at her cheeks.

"Oh, Mommy, we forgot my other puppy baby!" Tamannah's cute painted face turned into a deep pout.

Kareena said firmly but gently, "We've already been over this, Tama. You've got so much to carry. How are you going to also carry the little stuffy? I don't want you to lose him. He's special to me, remember?"

When the little girl's face went from pouting to glowering in the blink of an eye, Kareena knew she was going to be in for it. She almost turned around to go get it when Zayn stepped in.

"I have an idea," he interrupted. "How about you tell me

about this special puppy, Tamannah. Why's it so special? Does it have superpowers?"

He looked at her daughter like she held the answer to life's secrets, though his tone was casual. Then he abruptly turned on his heel and walked in the direction they'd been heading in the first place. He stuffed his hands in his jacket and continued to take relaxed, easy steps, only shooting her daughter a glance over his shoulder once before going on his way.

Tamannah's bottom lip, the one that had been trembling, was now caught between her teeth. She barely glanced at her mom before following Zayn, skipping to keep up.

Holy smokes! Amazed, she followed, too, staying a few feet behind while she kept Aloo from nosing around smaller kids whom he wanted to make friends with.

It made sense, she thought. Zayn was similar to Tamannah —somewhere on the spectrum. Alarmed at first seeing the little girl (Kareena had noticed when she and Aloo crashed out the front door), he now carefully maneuvered her daughter away from tantrum territory. Maybe he had no idea that he'd even done it (he'd already admitted he didn't know kids), but he did it seamlessly, and now Tamannah gleefully spouted about the special toy her mom had owned forever, and why it meant so much to her—

Oh, for the love of oversharing kids. *Shit.*

She'd caught up enough to hear her daughter say, "And she says it's super special because someone super special gave it to her."

Zayn was attentive, his head bent slightly down to listen. He nodded and asked, "Someone special gave your mom that stuffed animal?"

"Yeah. She said it was a long time ago. The water scared her, and her friend gave her the little yellow dog."

A grinning witch stood in the doorway of a little bookstore, and she beckoned Tamannah over. Zayn stood there, his face quirked in confusion, an auburn brow raised.

The memory rushed back to Kareena, and she was momentarily trapped in a current of teenage angst. She'd been afraid of setting foot on the whale-watching boat during their senior class trip in Los Angeles. Her fear of the water had kept her from going with the rest of the kids. A few of them decided to hang out on the Santa Monica pier and the boardwalk, where he'd won the stuffed dog, a cheap little thing, in an arcade to cheer her up.

"Only one piece, Tama!" she called after her daughter, as she saw her rifling through the black plastic cauldron the witch held.

She dared not look at Zayn, even as the mortification of what that little stuffy meant, and the fact that she still had it, made her want to turn and run. He must think she was an idiot.

She tightened the sash of her favorite mauve peacoat, then pulled up the wide collar around her chin, attempting to keep some of the wind at bay. "Why didn't I bring my scarf?" she muttered to herself.

Maybe, just maybe, he wouldn't remember that incident—a pipe dream, of course.

Warmth crept up her neck and onto her cheeks, noticing that he now wore a funny half smile.

Hoping to redirect whatever thoughts were circling inside his head, she said, "I apologize about my daughter being here. She and her friend were supposed to go to this fair together, but," she shook her head, annoyed, "her mom decided to change plans last minute."

"You've already apologized. It's fine," he responded.

She nodded.

"The yellow stuffed dog?" he finally asked, and then looked down at the tan dog wagging his little tail at his feet. "That's not the one I gave you in high school, while in LA, is it?"

He glanced at her profile as she stared at her daughter, still choosing her candy. The apples of her cheeks were so hot she could probably go over and help the chestnut man on the corner roast chestnuts at his stall. Her throat worked, and she had trouble swallowing.

Finally, she squeaked out, "Of course, it is. Why would I ever get rid of something so precious to me?"

He nodded but said nothing more as they continued to walk down the storefronts decorated for Halloween in thick cobwebs, lit-up carved pumpkins, and skeletons and ghosts of all shapes and sizes. Parents carted their costumed kids from one store to another, ensuring they received the urban version of Halloween and trick-or-treating.

"So, this fake engagement between us … I have some stipulations," he said, his deep voice low and close to her ear, as they watched her daughter skip from shop to shop, following behind.

Her pulse picked up at his nearness, and she inhaled his masculine citrusy scent. It almost smelled like the same fragrance he'd worn in high school. A sophisticated amalgam of lemon and bergamot with musky undertones and nothing like the cheap Axe body spray that permeated the halls from the other boys.

She nodded and tried not to close her eyes in bliss, telling her overly excited heart to take a hike, as she responded, "Lay it on me."

"I have a list of social events and family obligations I need you to attend with me ... and we need to make it look convincing. Can you do that?"

She fluttered her eyes open, realizing that Zayn watched her with a sexy half-grin. Could she make it look convincing—their connection, their attraction? Yes, she didn't even need to try.

But she couldn't resist asking anyway, "Like what?"

He stepped nearer and put his arm around her waist, his heat warming her through her wool coat. He leaned into her ear, and just that intimate movement made her shudder. When his deep voice spoke, her breath quickened.

"Just like that, Karma. You're doing exactly what I need you to do. Act as though I said something naughty in your ear, and pretend that you love it, and you love me. Let's keep our eye on the prize."

She needn't pretend about ninety percent of his requests. There would be no problem convincing other people, considering the way her heart hopscotched inside her breast. It was convincing herself not to believe his actions, like how he purposefully blew her hair gently away from her cheek, and how his warm breath against her neck made her weak in the knees, that would be the bigger issue she'd have to contend with.

CHAPTER 21

ॐ

"Through *New Year's*? Are you sure you can keep that up?" Reyana asked. "Wait, don't answer that. When you're determined, nothing stands in your way."

Kareena was with her sister and her oldest friend Sheila, having met up a few days later at one of their favorite coffee shops. Sheila and her had been the closest out of the four girls who'd made up their high school clique called the Ivy (as they planned to attend only Ivy League universities, naturally; spoiler, they all did, but not all of them lived up to their South Asian parents' expectations).

She and Sheila continued to stay in touch, and Kareena knew all about her friend's messy divorce and her career shift from hard-assed real estate attorney to aspiring yoga instructor in training. It seemed that Kareena wasn't the only one having an identity crisis.

Unsurprisingly, her sister wasn't fazed at the idea of a fake engagement. It sounded more like it could be one of her hair-brained schemes, rather than Kareena's. It was the length of time they had to pretend that floored Reyana, because her sister had the attention span of a fruit fly.

"The bigger question is," Reyana continued, blowing on her hot chocolate. "Have you gone bonkers? What about Tama?"

She *did* make a good point about her daughter, though.

"She won't know. She already met him—totally a fluke." Kareena shook her head, stirring her coffee. "And we told her that he's an old friend I'm helping."

"Wow. Okay. You guys have this all figured out. What if she finds out?"

Kareena stared hard at her sister, who wore blue contact lenses to match powder blue streaks in her long hair. "She's not going to find out, Reya, *okay?*"

"What about the parents?" Reyana said, unfazed by Kareena's tone.

"*Amma* and *Abba* think she'll know eventually but have agreed not to say anything to her. I told them Zayn and I would tell her together when we're ready."

God, she hoped her parents would respect that wish.

Her sister had the same line of thinking. "Here's hoping to that lofty goal." She raised her hot chocolate in a salute before slurping loudly. "Their lips are looser than mine."

"Someone has looser lips than yours, Reya?" Sheila asked, returning from the restroom. Her long, thin form was wrapped in black knit overalls covering her yoga clothes underneath. She had a class later.

"Our parents," Kareena filled in.

"Not inaccurate," Sheila replied blandly, sliding into her chair and dunking a green tea bag into her cup of hot water.

Her friend would know. Kareena had mentioned Sheila's career change in passing, and Sanjay and Leela Sharma had inadvertently told Sheila's parents. Since that unfortunate event, Kareena had been trying her best to curb that kind of behavior—the one where she felt obligated to tell her parents everything.

Thankfully, Sheila hadn't been too upset with her about it, though it resulted in her not speaking with her parents anymore, as they were already upset about her divorce.

"Fill me in," she requested, and Kareena explained everything she'd already explained to her sister, including what she would have to do to help her fake fiancé.

"Wow. That's … a lot. I guess it's kind of genius so that you won't have mediocre men continuously paraded in front of you, and being forced to choose one. Heaven forbid we die single." Her friend rolled her eyes.

Kareena nodded. "Exactly."

"So, what about your mini-me? How is this all going to work—"

"Hey, wait a minute," Reyana interrupted. "Sure, no one was as perfect as Arjun. But guys like Sameer aren't all that bad." Her face reddened furiously.

Kareena grinned. Her sister definitely liked Sameer.

"Uh-oh. Are you into one of these mediocre men?" Sheila asked, sharing a teasing glance with Kareena. "Please, do spill."

"Nope." Her sister shook her head vehemently. "I plead the fifth. This is about Kareena and her fake engagement. Hey, you know what?" her sister said excitedly, changing the subject. "This could be like that movie, *The Holidate*. Super cringey, and kind of terrible, but your fake fiancé could be your date to all sorts of holiday events. It's totally the same, minus the fake engagement part."

"So, not the same at all," Sheila deadpanned, blowing on her tea before sipping it.

Kareena barely heard the two women. She stared outside at the leaves falling, curling, and whispering at people's feet in nature's form of jeweled autumn-toned confetti. How was the weather already changing? It felt like only yesterday that Tamannah just started her new school year. Life was passing too quickly, and she wasn't enjoying it to its fullest, she thought morosely. She used to not care, but maybe it was because she had so much time on her hands now, or perhaps because she understood life's fleeting time in this world due to Arjun's unexpected passing.

"Kara," her sister pulled her from ruminating. "Tell Sheila *who* you're faking it with." She wore a sly grin.

Her friend directed her piercing gaze at Kareena. "Spill."

"It's not a big deal." She squared her shoulders, clearing her throat. "Zayn Stavros," she said indifferently, but inside her nerves wracked when she said his name out loud, and it also sent waves dipping up and down her spine. Her chest felt light, and she tried to hide her smile.

"It's not a big *deal?*" her oldest friend said aghast. "Are you being for real right now?"

Kareena shrugged and looked away. Sheila had always been as levelheaded as her, so the entire fake engagement thing probably sounded cuckoo enough already. But now aware that Zayn was involved ... her best friend likely thought she needed to be committed.

"And you knew about this?" Sheila asked Reyana accusingly.

"Hey, I just found out while you were in the bathroom," Reyana complained. "If you ask me, we've stepped into the multiverse. If it's a sign that Kareena is less than perfect in the eyes of our parents, then I'm all for it."

Everyone knew how much her parents didn't approve of Zayn. Not then, not now ... probably never. And yet, Kareena didn't care.

"Girlfriend, is this wise?" Sheila asked cautiously.

Kareena's shoulders slumped. "*Et, tu*, Sheils?"

"She's already speaking in Greek tongues, Sheila. Me thinks my big sis is more than obsessed with the return of her old flame, and this plan is just a decoy."

"Shut up, Reya. And it's Latin, you, Buttmunch." God, her sister really had the capacity to turn her back into a teenager again. Thank goodness her daughter was at school and nowhere in sight, or she'd never hear the end of the stupid term 'buttmunch,' where it originated from, and why it was appropriate or inappropriate in its current usage. "Where were you freshman year of Latin? Or, did you skip that class, too?"

Reyana stuck her tongue out before getting up to peruse the pastries at the front of the shop.

Sheila adjusted her black knit beanie over her jagged chin-length bob. "Buttmunch, or not," she said seriously, "Reya might be right. You were crushed when you had to break up with him. I know you said you got over him, but ... *did* you really?"

Kareena could understand her friend's reaction. It was no lie that for years after she broke it off with Zayn, she couldn't even stand to hear his name mentioned. It'd hurt too much.

"I did. How else would I have married Arjun?" she said with more confidence than she felt. Here was the thing: she thought she was over him—no, wait, that wasn't right because she *was* over him. Her friend and sister were confusing her.

"You should've seen the way she acted at the *Desi Ignites' Diwali* party a week ago. Oh my God, Sheila, it was like she lost all function of her brain," Reyana said as she returned with a giant black and white cookie and slid into her seat.

"No, I didn't!" Kareena shot back, absolutely aware it was true. Her body had taken over that night, wanting to get closer to him than any other male in forever. "He's really great at cooking now—a huge, famous chef. His food is incredible. His flavor pairings—"

"There she goes again, about to orgasm just talking about his food."

"Stop it, Reyana. You're being childish."

"I'm not the one denying that she thinks her ex-high school boyfriend is one mega hottie, now."

Kareena rolled her eyes. "Joke's on you. I always thought he was a hottie."

"I've seen pictures of him in *Entertainment Daily*. I'll bet his abs are more eight pack than six," Sheila commented.

"I'd bet good money that they're more like a twelve," her sister said, chuckling. "O. M. God! That totally reminds me— have you guys seen this new social media sensation? He's a hot chef, too—wait, let me find him." She grabbed her phone and swiped quickly. "Here. *Sinful in the Kitchen*. He's got a huge—"

"Wouldn't cooking in the nude be a kitchen hazard?" Sheila cut in. Kareena laughed.

"Knife, Genius. God, you two are terrible," Reyana said with disgust. She held her phone up for them to see. In the video, a tan, muscular man wore a black mask hiding his identity. Shirtless, he flicked his chef's knife (and it was indeed large) around dangerously while putting together some kind of sandwich.

Everyone at the table murmured about his sex appeal. They all jumped when he tossed his knife in the air, and collectively exhaled when he caught it by the handle with his other hand. His movements were fast and sleek, and the tendons along his forearms and the muscles on his biceps tensed deliciously as he worked. He had what looked like veins tattooed from one shoulder that spread down his entire arm to his wrist. With each movement he made, it looked alive, like lightning striking along his sculpted muscles. Something was written in detailed script, right under one of his pectoral muscles, but it was too small for Kareena to read.

Her phone buzzed, and she glanced at it, but not before she glimpsed the knife tattoo on the inside of one of his wrists.

Her breath caught. Desire licked at her, right there, in the coffee shop, while her sister and friend tittered, still studying the video and the unidentifiable hot man. Was it the tattoo that did it for her? She'd noticed a similar one on Zayn's wrist. Did most chefs get something similar to commemorate their culinary talents? She wondered again what other tattoos her former high school boyfriend's beautiful body might display.

She looked at the missed call on her phone and saw that it was her father. She flipped her phone over. She'd get back to him later, not in the mood to argue with him when her decision was already made.

"What if he wears that mask because he's a dog underneath?" Sheila commented, looking closely at the small screen.

"I refuse to believe that," Reyana said matter-of-factly. She pulled her phone back, a little miffed. "Anyway, Kareena, tell us more about your pretend engagement. Is there going to be a party?"

"Don't be weird, Reya. It's fake, remember? I'm not even sure there's any point in getting both of our parents together."

She tapped her lips absentmindedly, thinking. Time had not healed all wounds on her parents' part from almost twenty years ago ... mainly her mother. Why make everyone overly emotional with something that wasn't even real? And then she'd have to work around her daughter ... nope, not necessary.

"So, why is New Year's so important?" Sheila asked, finishing her tea.

Kareena recalled the details shared with her. "Zayn's grandfather wants him engaged by then, or by the end of the claim's period to his will (whichever comes first), so that he can get his inheritance. According to every single Stavros who knew the old man, no one is going to contest the will. So, I imagine we won't have to fake it past Thanksgiving."

"Interesting," Sheila said, thoughtfully, no doubt racking the former lawyer side of her brain. "And in return, you get breathing room from meddling matchmakers. Okay. I think I can get behind this," she said, nodding. "And Tama?"

Kareena nodded. "She won't be involved at all. To her, he's just a good friend, which is not entirely a lie." She sighed. "Everyone thinks I need to get remarried and that she needs a father. But what in the actual hell? She's come a long way since Arjun died—we both have. There was a moment when I thought it might be a good idea, but I was numb from the loss of him, and then the crap that happened at work sent me into a tailspin. Now that I'm a little more clearheaded, it just doesn't feel right for us anymore."

Sheila grabbed one of her hands and squeezed. "Heard."

"If Princess Tam-Tam wants a new dad, she'll tell you, *and* she'll pick him out herself," her sister said. Kareena laughed, nodding in agreement. "Now, can we get back to the inheritance?" Reyana continued. "Is the hot Greek going to inherit millions?"

"I don't think so." Kareena wasn't certain on that part. "He did tell me there's some land and an old restaurant that's at stake on his family's property back in Greece."

Reyana wrinkled her nose. "*That's* why you're helping him?"

Kareena nodded and couldn't quite explain this need to help Zayn. Sure, he'd recently helped her out (more than he could possibly ever know) and would continue to do so by acting as her fake fiancé. But it was the way he spoke about the out-of-date restaurant that had swayed her. The eagerness in his tone as he relayed his plans of transforming the eatery into a contemporary dining experience so he could make the old man proud had convinced her. She admired his dreams. Was it possible that she was trying to atone for how she'd treated him so long ago? Yes, but more than anything, she wanted this for him.

"Fate," Reyana said with a knowing nod. "You two were destined to meet again because there are no coincidences in life. Two people needing fake engagements at the same time who happen to already have a past? You can't make this shit up!"

"Nothing is going to happen, so you can stop thinking that."

"But what if you finally get laid?" Sheila asked nonchalantly, checking her phone. "Oh, I need to run—"

"*Sheila!*" Kareena cried in mortification. That was just between her and her best friend.

"Crap," Sheila said, slapping her hand over her mouth. "I'm really sorry, Kare-bear."

"Wait a minute. What?" her sister asked, her attention fully snagged on this new bit of information.

When Kareena didn't answer, Reyana urged on. "Wait a sec. How long has it been, Kara? Don't tell me since Arjun—*since* Arjun?"

"Okay, you don't have to tell the entire coffee shop," Kareena muttered, glancing around at the other patrons who scarcely looked up.

"Okay, Sis, this is serious business. You need that hunk of an ex-boyfriend turned fake fiancé to rail you good and hard at some point." Reyana folded her hands primly on the table. "Preferably sooner, rather than later, before you forget what your c-u-next Tuesday is for."

Kareena waved her hands in front of her face, cringing. "Please stop. This is merely a type of business transaction—one that benefits us both. He's going to be my plus one to every community party from now on (if I get invited to any), so no more matchmaking," she said with surety. "While I play the part of his fiancé so he can gain his inheritance. And, who knows if he has anyone on the side." The idea made her nauseous, but it wasn't totally off the table. They hadn't brought it up. Maybe they needed to…

"I hope not. That'd be rude," her sister said.

"It's fake, Reya. What part of that don't you understand?"

"So, what kind of events are we talking about?" Sheila asked curiously.

"Restaurant openings, charity events, and some family get-togethers. How hard could it be? I already know his parents."

"Yeah, but you don't know *him* anymore," her sister interjected. "He's changed, Kara. He used to be more friendly. Now, I don't know, he seems cut off."

Kareena had already thought that the first time they'd run into each other again. But she'd noticed inklings of his old self somewhere in the new man. "It's not a big deal. We'll get more comfortable with each other. It's like riding a bike, you know?"

Reyana's brows danced. "Interesting choice of words."

Kareena ignored the comment because the fluttering in her chest wasn't just nerves. It was something else she didn't want to dredge up—their history and sexual connection; a tension that seemed to hold on tenuously, even though so much time had passed.

"Put your heart-shaped eyes away, *Choto Bon* (Little Sister). I need you to keep your big mouth shut and not let the parents or family members find out and especially keep mum around your favorite niece."

Reyana nodded solemnly. "Cross my heart and hope to die."

Kareena glanced sharply at Sheila. "You, too, Sheila."

Sheila pretended to zip her lips closed. "Not a problem. You know I'm blacklisted from community events—self-imposed, of course, but who needs the stares and gossip? *And* you've probably talked to my parents more than I have in the last year." She began to pack up her things. "For what it's worth, I'm really proud of you, Kara. You're taking a stand against your family, for once. You've never had the chance to be on your own, you know?"

"I'm never alone." She mused. "And having a mini-me has definitely made it tough, though I wouldn't trade anything in the world. And it seems like I'll be busier than ever now."

"Yeah, well, this is a time for you to figure out what *you* want, *without* parental involvement," Reyana chimed in. "I'm proud of you, too."

Kareena rolled her eyes. She'd always known what she wanted growing up. They just happened to be the same things her parents wanted for her—minus the part about Zayn. But she understood what her sister and friend meant. She'd never deviated from the plan to become a doctor and marry the man chosen for her. And who'd planted the idea of going to medical school in her head in the first place, if not her parents? Now was the time to press pause on whatever trajectory she'd been on, before they decided more things for her.

PRESENT DAY
naxos island, greece

२२

"*Y*ou look amazing, Mommy!" Her daughter's voice sounded high and tinny over the video call.

She bounced on her bed in neon multi-colored pajamas with the words 'Bruh, I'm in Second Grade' printed across the front.

"You do, too, Baby," Kareena said. "I like your new pajamas."

"Thanks! Reya *Khala* got them for me today."

Tamannah bounced on her bed again, clutching her stuffed panda bear. Aloo was somewhere in the room; Kareena heard him whining at the sound of her voice.

"Can I see the little man?" she asked.

Tamannah nodded enthusiastically and told her to hold on.

She heard her daughter huff and puff as she finally lifted Aloo to the screen. His giant snout and pink tongue were the only things she could see, but he licked the screen, nonetheless.

"Are you being a good boy, my little potato?" He barked loudly. "I miss you, too, little man. Make sure Reya *Khala* doesn't burn the house down."

"Hey, I resent that," her sister said, having come into the room. She took Aloo from her daughter and sat back on the bed with him on her lap. "The three of us are having *the* best time, if I do say so myself. Henny's got nothing on me."

Reyana was watching Tamannah for a short while, as Henny, Kareena's house manager/part-time nanny, couldn't for a portion of the time Kareena was in Greece. Though Tamannah definitely loved Henny, having known her since she was a baby, Reyana was the fun, cool aunt, and her daughter was getting to that age where those things mattered.

"I don't doubt it," Kareena said seriously. "You're the best aunt she could have."

"You know that having a good relationship with your aunt is almost as important as the relationship with your mom, right?"

Kareena wondered what social media post her sister had seen that on, but she could only agree.

"I do know that," she said solemnly. "Thank you again for watching her tonight."

"You know I love it. Luckily, Sameer is out of the country for work, so I could do it."

"How are things with you two?"

A few weeks ago, Reyana had revealed that she was seeing Sameer. She really liked him and thought it might go somewhere, except that he didn't want to share with his family that he was dating her. This had appalled Kareena. Sameer was a full-grown man and needed to grow a pair. Reyana acted like it was no big deal, as she never cared what the South Asian community thought of her, but Kareena sensed that Reyana was more phased this time around.

"It's the same. But it's … whatever." Her sister clammed up, which meant there was more to the story that Kareena would need to delve into when she got back.

Reyana changed the subject. "Your tan is smokin' by the way."

"Thanks." And Kareena did something she'd never done in her entire life. She didn't follow it up with some variation of, 'I think I got too dark. Amma is totally going to say something, I just know it.'

She didn't want her daughter growing up thinking that people's worth was based on their skin color. She'd lived too long feeling less than, trying to please her mother for something she couldn't ever change. She had a darker complexion than many in her family. It'd always been a subject of contention whenever she spent too much time out in the sun or didn't put on enough sunscreen, which was *not* how sunscreen worked in the first place. One year, when she was still in middle school (middle school!), a relative had returned from India with a skin-lightening cream. It was a top-selling product and had been for years. Even her mother had been insulted by that and thrown the tube in the trash, to Kareena's relief.

"And I love that zig-zag dress. So chic, Kara. I hardly recognize you. You're practically glowing!"

Kareena beamed. She felt great, relaxed after the girls' spa day yesterday. They'd gone to a traditional Hammam Turkish bath house and been subjected to all kinds of treatments.

She was in the middle of telling Reyana about the vigorous scrubbing portion of her spa day when her daughter's face butted into the screen.

"Mommy, I need to ask you something."

"*Beta*, don't be rude. I'm still talking with Reya *Khala*."

"It's okay. Ask away, Princess Tam-Tam," her sister said, sitting back and nuzzling Aloo.

"Mommy, are you being as helpful as you can for Zayn Uncle's restaurant?"

This was the reason she gave Tamannah for travelling to Greece with Zayn—that she was going to help her old friend with his new restaurant. Technically, not a lie, so she didn't feel guilty about it.

"I'm doing the best I can, Tama," she said with seriousness.

"Good. He deserves the best help he can get from his friend. I have another question."

"I'm listening," Kareena said, hiding her smile. Her daughter had come to appreciate Zayn in a very short amount of time, even though they'd barely spent much time together.

"Mommy, is Zayn Uncle eating octopus while you're there helping him?" Her daughter was so solemn that Kareena dared not chuckle at the randomness of the question.

She actually took the time to think about it, though. "I don't think I've seen him eat any while I've been here. But why, Tama?"

"Well," her daughter sat back down on the bed, pushing her poofy hair behind her shoulders, getting comfortable, "he told me on that one day he watched me—remember, when you had to go to work for something, and he was the only person who could do it?"

Kareena definitely remembered. She'd had to go into her office last-minute on a Saturday to meet with all the heads of administration and Human Resources, along with the practice's legal representation, to discuss a possible lawsuit involving her patient who'd attempted to take their own life.

Zayn had called that morning with details about a trip to Greece, but she wasn't listening because she was too preoccupied with figuring out child care. Quickly, he sensed she was distracted and asked her what was wrong.

She'd told him her dilemma, and he said he could move some things around to come watch her daughter for a few hours, if she wanted.

"Really?" she'd asked, flustered, astounded he'd even offer. "What if Tamannah finds out about what we're pretending?"

"Give me some credit here, Kareena. I kept our secret in high school," he reminded her.

True.

"I know, I just mean that my daughter is pretty inquisitive. What if she asks you a question and you inadvertently tell her—"

"She won't have time. We'll play some games, make some snacks, and do whatever seven-year-olds do. I'm sure she'll have a list a mile long."

For someone who didn't know kids, he seemed to know her daughter.

"I knew a very precocious seven-year-old once a long time ago. My favorite cousin, Penelope," he'd filled in.

"Oh." She hadn't known how to respond to that. She'd known he had a gaggle of cousins, but that was all. "What about the dog?"

"That little potato?" he'd scoffed. "Don't even worry about him. I've had pets before."

"Well, don't be too lovable," she'd blurted out, before she could think better of it.

He'd remained silent for quite some time.

"Well, I doubt they'd fall in love with me so quickly," he finally said, "but stranger things have happened." He'd chuckled self-deprecatingly, and she wanted to tell him that she'd fallen in love with him the moment she saw him at that summer barbecue in New Jersey almost twenty years ago. She dashed that ridiculous thought away as he said, "We're going to have to bend the rules a little. Are you fine with that?"

"I have to be. I need to get to that meeting. My career—" She was going to hyperventilate. The stress was overwhelming her. She was absolutely going to get fired.

"Don't worry, Karma. Everything will be fine." He already knew about her work dilemma, and she appreciated his words, though she wasn't entirely sure he understood the intricacies of what an impending malpractice lawsuit meant for her future.

But true to his words, everything *had* been fine. The situation diffused itself during the meeting. The patient's attorney admitted they'd re-reviewed the case files and Kareena's patient notes, and knew they were looking at an uphill battle. It sounded like the attorney had experienced the blowing of hot air from this particular client before. True, they might seek a settlement outside of court, but for now, Kareena's conduct wasn't being taken into consideration.

When she'd arrived home, she found her house a little wrecked, which was nothing new. She hadn't been able to keep things as tidy lately, and Henny did what she could, leaving the house spotless before she left for the day, but her daughter, combined with their dog, insisted on getting into everything. Plus, Henny didn't work on the weekends, so having a messy home on Saturday and Sunday had become Kareena's norm.

What was comically bizarre was that she'd found her

daughter dressed in her pajamas already, even though it was only four o'clock in the afternoon. Tamannah met her at the double pocket sliding doors that led from the front foyer to the living area on their first floor.

"Shh, Mommy. Everyone is asleep." Tama held a finger up to her mouth, and her eyes were enormous.

Confused, she peered over to the couch and saw Zayn fast asleep, a portion of his long legs off the cushions, too tall for the normal-sized couch. The dog was cuddled up against him, snoring almost as loudly as the man.

"What happened, Tama?" she asked, trying to keep a serious face, as she tiptoed in at her daughter's urging.

As she got closer to the couch, she saw that he had brightly colored stickers all over his beard and forehead. The dog did, too.

"We were playing 'Have you Ever' and *I* kept winning," her daughter whisper-shouted.

Kareena wasn't so sure her daughter had been playing fairly. With only two people, it was doomed from the start.

"I'm really good at it. Zayn Uncle is terrible, and every time he answered no, I put a sticker on his face. Oh, and Mommy, he was so tired because when we took Aloo out for a walk, he did that silly hide-and-seek game," Tama continued rambling. "Zayn Uncle didn't know how to retract the leash, and Aloo kept bouncing from one bush to the next in the park, pretending to hide. You know how he does that, but we still see him, but he thinks he's so clever and hidden?" Her daughter had giggled, and Kareena had smiled knowingly. Frustrating when they needed to be somewhere, but it always made her laugh because Aloo was so confident that no one could see him, but so eager for them to 'find' him, that his entire roly-poly body wriggled cutely. "Zayn Uncle got tired trying to catch him, and he was already tired when he got here. He said he and a chef friend were trying new recipes to make octopus. And then I told him you can't eat octopus. They're the smartest creatures in the world!"

"So, he's definitely not eating them?" Her daughter asked, abruptly bringing her back to the present. Her face was very close to the screen, intent on getting an answer.

"As far as I know."

Tamannah bounded off the bed. "Good. Because he promised me he would never eat them again." She ran off on some mission, and Reyana and Kareena shared a look as the dog also jumped off the bed, following her.

"What in the world—" Kareena started. It was her daughter whom Zayn had been talking about a few days ago in Athens when he said he'd promised someone he wouldn't eat it anymore, though it had always been his favorite.

Something inside her breast stumbled. Like her heart stopped beating for a nanosecond, then started up again. He'd really promised that to her daughter?

"So, this glow you're sporting," her sister said, tossing her thoughts into disarray. "Is it *just* the massages, or is there more to it?" She wiggled her brows.

After finishing up the call with Reyana, Kareena left the manor to find Zayn. She'd admitted to her sister before hanging up that yes, being around him set her panties on fire. She didn't tell her that her intention was for him to put that blaze out between her legs immediately, especially after that kiss yesterday on the stony path.

She hadn't seen him all morning, but the note he left next to her pillow, with his familiar handwriting that still looked the same from so long ago, had clear instructions for her.

> Dear Karma,
> I hope you slept well. You have no idea how hard it was for me not to wake you up and continue what we started yesterday. I know you were exhausted after the spa day, so I left you alone. I needed to be at the villa this morning anyway to clear some things out. But later today, be ready for a workout. Meet me at the private pool after your ladies' only wine tasting lunch. You'll need to be suited up because we're starting your swim lessons ... among other things. I thought about your offer from yesterday, and I do want your help with my problem, as long as there's no group therapy involved (I can't stand that shit). Anyway, today WILL be a full-body workout, which I'm confident you can take, given the amount of sleep you've had (jetlag is a bitch). See you soon.
> Your swim instructor extraordinaire, Zayn

Her pulse quickened in trepidation at being in the water. But longing left her limbs weak as she imagined herself submerged with him. The idea that her swim lessons were a thin veil for what they were absolutely going to do made her stomach flip and set a pulse thumping between her thighs. She almost felt like a teen again with a giddy horniness that nearly caused her to skip across the olive grove. And deep down, she was more than pleased that he accepted her help for his problem, though it was outside the scope of their charade. She could support him with this; this was what she was good at.

Last night, to her mortification (and devastation), she'd fallen asleep after the spa day. The steam baths, facial, vigorous scrubs, and massages had taken much out of her. But so had the chatter and questions from Penelope and her bridesmaids. There were eleven of them (including the bride), and all were sorority sisters at Stanford. When they found out Kareena had pledged Delta Gamma at Columbia, they swarmed in on her, like flocking to their long-lost big sister. DGs were a sister sorority to theirs, Delta Sigma Theta. They peppered her with questions about her college life before honing in on her and Zayn. When had they met? When was the wedding? Was Zayn as good in bed as rumored (where Penelope screeched, covering her ears)?

They were all face down on massage tables by the beach, and because she couldn't escape, Kareena answered as best as she could, including telling a bold lie about Zayn's sexual prowess (which she was pretty sure wasn't a lie at all). She relayed the truth about their high school romance, followed by their break-up because her parents disapproved, and how she regretted it to this day (also true, she realized). Then she glossed over their recent unexpected run-in and falling in love all over again.

"*Wow*," one of the girls sighed dreamily. "That's *so* romantic. It's like you two have always been connected— nothing could ever cut your bond."

The other girls sighed in unison and agreed.

The comment startled Kareena. She couldn't have said it better herself. She'd always felt linked to Zayn. Even though they hadn't spoken to each other in decades, she'd always felt like they were tethered. She'd always thought that even if they never met again, their bond would always remain. And she realized it was because he'd given her new experiences, companionship, self-confidence, and a sense that she was more than just the obedient daughter. He'd made her feel wanted and beautiful, even though she'd never seen herself like that. He understood her, too, though their upbringings had been vastly different. It was most definitely a one-in-a-million kind of connection. She realized then, with her face down on the massage table, that they *were* given a second chance. Not only for her to make amends for how she'd treated him back then, but for so much more. Maybe this was their chance to be together again, even if for a short time, and any lingering nervousness about getting physical with him slid away.

Later, she'd returned to their suite, her brain humming with thoughts of Zayn on top of her, inside her, coaxing her in his deeply sensual voice. She told herself she'd lie down for a few minutes before getting ready to meet him later for dinner.

But she hadn't woken up minutes later. Rather, it was the next morning, with the bright Mediterranean sun already up for hours, alone. His handwritten note next to her pillow pacified her, with promises for later that afternoon. She was also relieved that Zayn was considering her help.

Knowing she would have a big lunch, Kareena had decided to skip breakfast and spent the morning slowly getting herself ready for the day. At noon, she headed to the winery on the other side of the island for the ladies' lunch and wine tasting, where she learned what she'd missed the previous evening from Zayn's mother and some of Pen's friends.

Dinner was followed by a live six-piece band with lots of dancing. It was raucous, and dishes were smashed, much to the housekeeper's chagrin. According to Zayn's mother, there was an entire storeroom full of plain dinnerware to destroy, provided by the wedding organizer, but people threw down the fine China in their exhilaration.

Kareena was disappointed to learn of this. She'd wanted to take part in some of that.

"My dearest," Sofia soothed her. "You'll have plenty of chances at the rehearsal dinner and the wedding itself, only a few days away now." She smiled warmly. "Some people think Greeks don't actually throw down dishes when celebrating, but we Stavroses are all about it."

"It's the *real* drama you missed," one of Pen's bridesmaids said sneakily.

Sofia told the girl to hush, and that piqued Kareena's curiosity.

At the admonishing look Sofia gave the younger woman, Kareena teased, "Okay, you have to tell me what else I missed, Sofia Aunty. And if you don't, I can always ask Zayn..." She smiled slyly. She was so happy in that moment, taking a sip of the delicious crisp white set before them.

Sofia took a deep breath and began.

"Well, you know how these kinds of big family events can get. In our society, it's tradition to ply the engaged couple with ouzo shots. Poor Penelope was drunk in no time. She picked an argument with Silas." Sofia winced. "She said she hated Silas. He'd never cared about her after their father died. She wanted Zayn to walk her down the aisle. He'd always been more of a big brother to her than any of her own brothers. Mind you, she has four."

One of Penelope's bridesmaids, unable to stay quiet any longer, happily finished the story. She said Silas was totally out of his mind after that. He not only shouted awful things about

Zayn, but he claimed that Zayn's engagement to Kareena wasn't real.

That had confused Kareena. "Why would he say that?"

"Because of the ring," the girl said smartly.

Now she was even more confused. She stared down at the enormous Tiffany diamond on her finger.

What does this ring have to do with anything?

"It's beautiful, Kareena. But it's also a problem," Sofia murmured, seeing Kareena's confusion.

"You're going to have to spell it out for me, Sofia Aunty," she finally said.

Sofia explained that Zayn's place in the family was special. Almost everyone loved him, and he had a particular way with the locals, too. Her parents, his grandparents, adored him. Not only did his grandfather want him to have the taverna and someone to share it with, but his grandmother wanted his future wife to wear her engagement ring—an old family heirloom passed down for generations.

This unsettled Kareena. Zayn never mentioned this detail, even though it seemed critical to their situation, and any detail when it came to them was like a chicken bone to a dog with Silas. He'd go after it and chew it until it shredded to pieces (or got lodged in his throat, which had happened once with Aloo, and what Kareena wouldn't wish on anyone, though Silas was beginning to look like a contender).

Sheesh, what was wrong with her? Her protective instincts were showing, and they were for Zayn. But why? Clearly, he'd not told her about the ring, so then … what? If anything, she was completely in the dark here and would need to ask him about this to ensure they were on the same page. But really, he was the one with an inheritance to lose.

At her quietness, Sofia said hastily, "Oh, but Zayn has always mocked these old traditions, though we've told him how important they are to our family. I'm sure you two have discussed it. I wonder if he'll come to his senses any time soon. It would only make things easier for everyone—especially with my father's claims period ending very soon."

"What?" Kareena asked, startled. This wine tasting luncheon was throwing her for more than one loop.

"No one has come forward to claim anything. My father was very good at making sure everyone was taken care of." She'd flagged the sommelier down and asked for another full pour. "Now, about the ring—truthfully, we'd all love to see it on your finger, since as Zayn's intended bride, it was meant for you."

Well, there it was. She wasn't ever going to wear that ring because she wasn't ever going to be a Stavros bride, was she?

Kareena tried to pretend that this new information didn't bother her, but she wasn't sure it had worked as Sofia seemed to keep her eye on her the rest of the lunch. Once the confusing and unfortunate wine tasting ended, Kareena had gone back to her room. Shaken by everything she had learned, she decided to call Tama and Reyana—they always helped her recenter herself.

Feeling better after that conversation, she breathed in the fresh air as she opened the garden gate, passing slowly through the blooms and herbs, their scents tickling her nose in the heat.

Though she felt calmer, she had to admit she was curious about the entire thing. She loved this kind of stuff—inheritances only bequeathed upon engagement; the involvement of heirloom jewels (she'd learned from Sofia that the diamond was gifted from a Greek royal in return for services given in the early nineteenth century, and she wanted to find out why). However, this felt more and more like it was turning into one of those outlandish Regency romances; the kind she secretly read under her covers at night as a teen—minus the romance. All of this might seem exciting—only adding to the escapism of what she was doing in Greece in the first place—except that it irked her that Zayn never mentioned this crucial family tradition that *everyone* knew about. Was she not significant enough to know this information, too?

She chuckled at her foolishness, because, here was the thing: 'they' had become a little less clear-cut than when they initially started this pretense. She realized it had all been a product of her imagination. It meant nothing when he called her by his special nickname for her, or that he kissed her like he meant it, called her 'Baby' like he felt it in his bones, or even promised something significant to her daughter. Withholding that precious family heirloom confirmed that it was all business on his part.

"That's okay," she muttered to herself, pushing down a discomfort that felt a little too close to betrayal. She reached the rocky path to the pool. "This is what we came here to do, and you're totally fine with that."

It couldn't be helped if his family (namely, Silas) withheld his inheritance based solely on the ring and all of the truths it signified. It seemed like Zayn couldn't care less about that— another stipulation by his family.

God, this was now starting to sound like a Tolkien novel. She wouldn't be surprised if his family had been involved in some kind of epic battle.

All right, she needed to adjust her frame of mind and the idea that had crept into her psyche without her being totally aware of it until now. This whole thing was making her feel things she wasn't supposed to be feeling. Annoyed at herself? Absolutely. But she perked up because all of this didn't mean she couldn't still enjoy this, right? They could still have fun together in the meantime. She could treat this like a luxurious vacation.

She nodded an emphatic 'yes' as she went down the path carefully. She deserved pure, unadulterated sex with no strings attached—although the strings might already be attached...

২৩

*W*hen she got to the private pool, Zayn was already there. To her shock, she saw that the old tarp was gone and the pool was pristine with fresh water. Pretty shiny blue tiles lined its inner walls.

But that's not what got her. Zayn stood with his back to her, shirtless. He had on cargo shorts he was in the process of removing, and when he did, he was in the most delectable hunter green swim trunks, more like boxer briefs than the looser, baggier style that guys wore in the States. The thoughts that had been arguing inside her head just minutes ago completely vanished.

It was hard not to stare at his glorious, almost naked body. He was so muscular that it made her marvel at the gentleness he had for her, and the times she'd witnessed him with her daughter and pup.

Every move he made, every shift in position, even while folding his shorts on top of his shirt, made the muscles under his tan skin shift smoothly. It was riveting. *He* was riveting.

When he turned around, his wide chest looked even wider, made so by the tiny swim trunks. A light pelt of auburn curls dusted his chest and thinned to a line that went between his defined ab muscles (definitely an eight pack, Sheila had been right), and disappeared into his shorts, where she clearly saw the outline of his bulge. His legs had a dusting of hair over his enormous thighs and down his solid calves. Everything about him screamed his masculinity, and her lady parts answered wholeheartedly in a throw-me-over-your-shoulder-and-take-me kind of way.

It felt more liberating than she ever thought it would.

He was a Greek God come to life. She was certain of it, and her heart skittered around in her chest. It felt like her stomach had bottomed out at the thought that she was the object of his desire.

She debated briefly whether to try to reel her lust in when he said, "Stop looking at me like that, Karma. Or zero swimming lessons will happen, but your muscles *will* be sore."

Her breath hitched. She responded with a "You promise?" Unable to hide her admiration for him. She was pretty sure drool was pooling at the corners of her mouth now.

Her eyes caught on his ink on display, and here, at this moment, her pussy clenched. Okay, so she was definitely a tattoo-on-a-man kind of woman, but only if it was this man, she realized.

She knew about the chef's knife on his inner wrist. She'd seen the lightning vein on his arm that wrapped around his bicep and went down to his wrist. But she now saw that it spread up to his shoulder and wrapped all the way around.

He walked closer, and she saw writing on his chest on his

left side, making something tug in her brain. There was something familiar about the placement ... had she seen it before? Yes, she was lust drunk, and maybe her brain was misfiring and she was imagining it. He was so sexy and big, and even the thick gold chain around his neck flashing white in the sunlight made her shudder.

When he stood directly in front of her, she clearly read what was etched in cursive, directly under his heart. The word 'Karma' curved below his pectoral muscle, as if cradling that vital organ of his that exuded life's blood, literally, but also held the key to all of one's emotions.

She shivered.

When she finally looked up at his face, the expression he wore confirmed something she also felt and had known for a long time: they would always have a piece of each other's hearts.

"Zayn," she whispered, closing up the space between them. She traced the beautiful script of each letter with her finger. When she got to the end of the 'a,' he grasped her hand and clutched it to his chest.

"When—" she broke off. "Is this—?" Her throat clogged, and he blurred in front of her as her eyes filled with tears.

"It is. And I had it done after you broke up with me. It got me through some tough times, even though I hated you through it."

She inhaled sharply at his harsh words.

"But hate is the other side of the same coin, Kareena. I loved you then, and what you did broke me. But I never wanted to forget you—us."

A tear slipped down her cheek, and he caught it with his

thick thumb, swiping it away. "I don't think you know how hard it was for me to give you up," she finally choked out.

Good God, she was screwed. The ramblings of thinking that they were firmly in just fuck-buddy territory for the short time they were together completely disappeared.

"Kareena," he said softly, one hand cupping the back of her head as the other wrapped around her, bringing her close. He kissed her deeply, pulling her into a haze of wonder and lust, but something else altogether that she wasn't ready to admit yet. "My Karma," he whispered against her lips before sliding his tongue into her mouth sweetly.

The fragmented thought about his tattoo under his heart was forgotten as she focused on the man in her arms and what he was doing to her physical senses. The burning desire burned hotter than ever, and she wanted only him.

HE COULDN'T SEEM to get enough of her. His mouth ravished hers, and she moaned deeply, her hands sliding up and around his neck, her fingers combing frantically through the hair at the nape of his neck.

It was the way she'd looked at him, the desire wrapped with need and an emotion he didn't know he wanted from her after seeing his tattoo—the one that signified her and was etched close to his heart, that consumed him. Vulnerability crossed her pretty features, and her eyes, black with want for him, had filled with tears, and he didn't like it one bit. Hurting her was so far from what he had planned.

Yes, he'd hated her back then, and through the years until he could finally put her aside and move forward with his life. But he knew it had never left him. He wasn't insincere when he told her that hate was the other side of the coin to love. They were similar in the extremities one felt with either one—how much they consumed a person. Hate had left him hardened and heavy, with no thoughts of ever finding "the one." Relationships were for romantics, not him. Now, with her in his arms, he experienced a weightlessness, a lightness of the coin flipping. It was the long-forgotten sensation of wanting someone with his entire being.

His hands slid from her waist to the small of her back, pulling her flush to him, as he fisted the light knit material of her cover-up. He needed it off. He needed to feel her skin.

He grasped at the sides of her dress, pulling it up as their lips remained locked, only parting to drag it over her head, tossing it aside.

He brought her back to him, feeling the smooth, cool nylon material of her bathing suit, only slightly aware that it was the new bright, sexy red one he'd seen before. His hands roughly spanned her body, only catching slips of material, with a low back and cut high at the legs. His hands swept up her front to her utter gasp of surprised pleasure, to find a deep plunging neckline. He took a moment to lift his head and push her away, wanting to see her in so few clothes.

She stood there, arms at her sides and her back arched, making her large breasts jut toward him, barely covered by the 'V' in the front. The curves on both sides of each one peeped from the material, her brown soft skin a delectable contrast to the red nylon sheen.

Lust raced to his cock, and his mouth salivated. Her nipples were hard, and he wondered if they were as beautiful and tight as he remembered. Little dark brown orbs that matched the color of her eyes.

Her waist curved in before her hips flared out, rounded and soft, and perfect for him to dig his fingers into and leave his mark. He stared at the apex of her thighs, a slight mound that he knew had to be wet and slick with her lust, though there was no telling with the slight material covering her there.

"Zayn," she whispered, her dusty pink lips plumper now, having been ravaged by him. "I want you."

He licked his lips, trying to slow down the pounding of his blood. His cock throbbed tightly against his swim trunks, and her gaze was focused there as her chest heaved quickly.

She licked her lips, too, and began to peel off the straps of her bathing suit, letting it pool around her waist. She folded her arms across her breasts, hiding herself from him.

"I want you, too, Sweetheart."

She nodded and looked down at herself. "My body—I've had a child, and I breastfed, and my body—"

He stepped back to her and lifted her chin so she could look at him. He saw the worry there and reached up to smooth the tension from her forehead.

"You're more beautiful than I've ever seen you, Kareena."

He slowly pulled her arms away to see her nakedness, groaning gruffly as his hands slid up her body and reached for her breasts. The warm flesh overflowed in his large hands, and he squeezed them gently, making her arch her back further. She was so fucking sensual and so responsive to him.

He dragged his lips down her neck, down her chest, and kissed the top curves of each breast, noticing the faint, silvery stretch marks there that marred her beautiful brown skin. He licked each one tenderly before lifting a heavy breast to his mouth to kiss a peaked brown nipple. Goosebumps raised around the small areola as he licked her before pulling her nipple into his mouth, sucking her sweet flesh, biting tenderly down on her.

She moaned raggedly, her hands in his hair, her warm breasts in his face, and God, he wanted to fuck her into oblivion right there.

"Kareena," he groaned, standing up to his full height. He swept an arm under her knees and carried her dazed to one of the cushioned loungers.

He placed her gently down and paused to look at this beautiful woman so open and wanton for him. Her breasts spilled. Rising and falling quickly, and he couldn't help grasping each one again and squeezing.

"These tits are as gorgeous as ever." He tugged lightly at her nipples. She keened and bit her full bottom lip, closing her eyes as she widened her thighs around him.

His hands went to the material bunched at her waist, and he tugged it down, over her pelvis and curvy thighs, down her legs, and finally off her feet.

"Damn," he said under his breath, staring at her fully naked.

Her bounty of dips and curves was laid out before him, and he was like a hungry man coming home from a long time at sea. The curve of her belly was evident, and he loved that, his hand going to feel the soft flesh under his palm, noticing silverly stretch marks on her dark skin here, too. But it didn't detract from her beauty and sexiness. It only made him want her more. He wanted to claim her as his. He wanted her to forget ever knowing another man inside her. He wanted to be the next and only person to have her, and maybe even put a baby inside her.

Fuck. Why was that thought at once so alarming and hot?

Her large eyes were hooded, as she lay there unabashed, though her hands gripped the sides of the lounger.

"Relax for me, Baby. I want to see you. All that I've missed these past years."

Her chest rose and fell a little less frantically as her hands loosened their grip.

"Spread those thighs for me, Sweetheart," he said, not able to hide the need in his voice.

Her pussy was covered with a dark strip of black hair. When her legs widened, he saw wetness coating the insides of her thighs and the folds of her pussy, brown like her skin, but turning a dark pink as she spread wider, glistening with it.

He let out a growl, an animalistic sound of primal ownership.

She smiled demurely, but her eyes were filled with heat. "Now let me see what I've been missing all these years," she murmured huskily.

He nodded and obliged, ripping his swim trunks down and kicking them away.

SHE LICKED HER LIPS, staring at his hardness, long and thick, sitting in a nest of auburn curls. He grasped himself and pumped a few times, and a stark white pearl of precum beaded out against the tip of his crown. Everything about him was so big, and on instinct, she rose quickly, sitting up, leaning in to lick his tip, savoring his saltiness on her tongue.

He let out another growl, deep and primal.

His hand shot out and weaved through her hair, holding her head away from him.

"Don't." His voice was tight, like he was being strangled.

She automatically felt like she'd done something wrong. She hadn't been with someone she wanted this much since the last time they'd been together as teens.

"I'm sorry, I—"

"Don't you dare apologize." He sounded like he'd run a marathon. "I want you to suck me. I want my cock so deep in your mouth, down your throat, with those pretty lips tight around me, that you'll gag. But not right now. You're not ready … neither am I. I'll come so fast in your mouth that you'll choke."

She nodded, reaching for him again, heat spreading, making her hotter, thankful for the cool shade the cliff overhang offered.

"Kareena, I want to be inside you first. I want to come inside you."

His words made it hard for her to breathe, as her eyes stuck, glued to his massiveness. The veins along his length were engorged, and new pearls of precum appeared.

A new burst of moisture coated the insides of her thighs. She was so turned on that she was spontaneously leaking with her own arousal. She needed to let him fuck her mouth at some point, wanting to see him come undone like that.

But right now, he wanted to come inside her. Did that mean he wouldn't use a condom?

The idea was so unsafe, so wrong, and yet she wanted it more than ever. Wanted to feel his length inside her without a barrier. She wanted his hot cum sliding into her, overwhelming her, leaking out of her.

It was the most intimate of acts, and she couldn't imagine not doing this with him.

"Zayn, I'm on birth control, so pregnancy isn't an issue. And I haven't had sex since Arjun—"

"Don't say his name." He was suddenly angry. "I don't like knowing another man was inside you."

"Zayn," she said calmly, as if speaking to a child, caressing his muscular thighs. "You're who I want. I don't think I've ever stopped wanting you. But, he was my husband, it was only natural."

She was talking about her deceased husband while she lay naked and horny with another man. Was she breaking some kind of unnamed rule for widows? She wasn't sure, and she couldn't help it. If Zayn didn't put that enormous cock inside of her soon, she might lose all her nerve and run away. She needed this. She needed him.

He nodded jerkily, his thick lips set. "I'm clean. I'm responsible and get tested regularly."

Jeez, how many women had he slept with? She felt like a completely inexperienced fool in comparison.

"Don't even think it, Karma." His voice was gentle now, deep, gravelly as he began to lie on top of her, forcing her to lie back, too, the cool canvas hitting her back.

"Think what?" she asked, tracing his jaw, the roughness of his beard scratching her palms. She drew her fingers along the lightning tattoo on his shoulder, then skimmed over his firm pecs, gliding down over his nipples, to trace the karma tattoo, marveling again that it was her he had in mind when he got it.

"I find it an extreme turn on to know you haven't been with many others. Do you know why?"

She shook her head, her hand grazing down his hardened

body, making her buck her hips into his hardness as she let out a raspy moan. God, she needed him.

"Because I get to defile you. I get to be the one to teach you how your body can take my cock, my mouth, my tongue. I'll show you filthy things if you let me. But they'll feel so damn good, Baby, you won't even think they're dirty by the time we're through. You'll beg for it all the time."

"It's only been one other person, Zayn," she whispered.

His eyes closed as he groaned. His hand skimmed across her breasts, over her hip, and to the apex of her legs, cupping her with a possessiveness that made her spread her thighs even wider. He squeezed her flesh, and his long fingers swiped ever so slightly through her back crack, so quickly that she thought she might've imagined it. She moaned at the strange sensation and she believed him when he said she'd be begging for it. She wanted him to do that again. When he asked, "Would you like that, my sweet Karma?"

She nodded, having trouble swallowing. She was panting now like *she'd* run a marathon. Would he want to fuck her ass? God, the thought was terrifying and intriguing all at once.

"Mm, my Karma, so sweet, so dirty." He leaned down to kiss her heatedly as his hand began to massage her.

When he lifted his head, she murmured a reminder, "But I already know some of how I can take your mouth and tongue." Her hand slid along his hard body to grip his cock and squeeze. She forgot how thick he was. Her hand barely grasped all the way around him. She swiped his precum with her thumb. "Remember that time in my bedroom, when you made me come for the first time with your fingers, and then convinced me that your tongue would be better? So I let you eat me out?" she said this all innocently, matter-of-factly, as if she was reminding him of that time they went and got TCBY yogurt after her tennis match, trying the newest flavor on the menu.

He groaned. "Jesus, that memory shouldn't turn me on so much," he rasped, his mouth claiming hers again, making all reminiscences leave her brain as she focused on his tongue forcing itself inside her mouth again and his big, hard body on her.

She couldn't get close enough to him. She needed him inside her, now. And she urged him by grinding her hips against his hand to do something.

He obliged by slipping a thick finger between her folds before entering her, while his thumb found her clitoris and circled it. It was like he had muscle memory and could conjure up her physiology without trying, as he was doing everything more than right. Or maybe he just had way more practice with the female body.

"So wet, Baby. So tight." She remembered these exact words from a teenage Zayn. He slid another finger into her, coaxing her to stretch. But the next words, she didn't recognize. "You're going to take my big cock so well, Sweetheart. And you're going to love every second of it."

She was about to agree with him when his fingers reached higher and found that spot that had made her come undone so long ago.

"Zayn!" she cried, her eyes closing as her inner muscles constricted quickly, little pulses that were picking up speed and building up a deep and heady sensation. She gripped his arm, and her hand on his dick went slack, as he pumped her, this time with three fingers.

"Yes. That's my girl. Come for me," he murmured, his voice deliciously low against her ear. She arched her back as her hips undulated against his hand, the sound of her slickness loud in the little area by the private pool. Now she understood why the Stavros relative had built this place for his mistress. It was the perfect place for wild outdoor sex.

God, it was liberating. Experiencing these things out in the open with him. Anyone could find them, but she didn't care.

"Mmm, you have no idea how many times I've fantasized about you, Kareena." He leaned down and sipped one of her nipples into his mouth, sucking and licking, teasing, making her skin raw, before he switched to the other, while his hand continued to work her, slipping in and out. Now he had four fingers inside her—four thick, long fingers that deliciously stretched her wide, reaching in deeply again. "Yes, Baby. You're going to take me so good."

It was the dirtiest of promises, and it made her cry out and pant. She hadn't felt this alive in forever. Her entire body undulated now. Her breasts shook, her belly quavered, and lightning licked at her as she exploded into a thousand pieces, crying out so loud that her voice echoed along the cliffside.

"That's it, Karma. Let go for me. I'll take care of you."

She was back to hiccup whimpers when she finally came back into focus, and she realized he'd shifted his big body and was now lying fully on top of her, keeping his weight on his arms.

"I'm going to eat out that sweet pussy of yours," he promised in her ear. "But first, let me put my cock in you. Let me fuck you the way you should've been fucked for all these missed years."

Was he like Homer writing his version of a sexual poem? How he'd missed her for so long and couldn't wait to bury himself inside her and stay there forever? It would be an instant classic; she was sure of it.

"*Yes,*" she whined, and she couldn't believe that was her. She sounded so needy.

Zayn chuckled, agreeing with her. "My needy girl." He shifted his weight to his elbows on either side of her, pinning her. He used one hand to guide himself to her opening, rubbing himself against her, his precum mingling with her slickness.

She groaned, completely losing it, gripping his shoulders tightly.

"Fuck, you feel good," he panted. "I can't be gentle, Baby."

She pushed some of his hair back away from his forehead as she stared into his heated cinnamon eyes and the concern worrying his handsome face. "Then don't."

He took one reassuring glance at her before covering her mouth with his and slamming himself into her fully.

She felt like she was being ripped apart at first, but the pain quickly dulled as she got accustomed to his size. The muscles inside her flickered along his hardness, and the sensation was so satisfying she moaned, arching her back so that her breasts flattened against him.

It was like they understood one another; no words were necessary. He continued kissing her as he began to move, pulling out, as if he was going to completely disengage from her, and then sliding all the way back in. It was indescribable. No man had ever been this deep inside her.

"You good, Karma?" he grunted in her ear as he continued moving in and out of her.

"Better than good," she gasped as he slid his hand under her ass and forced her pelvis up into him.

"Move with me, Baby."

She pushed her pelvis up into him and began to undulate, and she didn't think he could get any deeper than he already was. She groaned at the sensation, needing to feel him there unceasingly, and undulated her hips faster, her insides screaming for more, her body getting damp with sweat.

He chuckled. "So impatient." But he got the hint when she reached up and nipped his bottom lip.

He moved faster, his weight still on an elbow, a hand gripping her ass cheek. Then he reared up, sliding his hand to her thigh, angling it around him as he pounded into her. She keened in pleasure at the new sensation, and the lounger groaning under them.

"Fuck, I love doing this with you, Kareena. You're my wildest dreams come true."

She would have agreed if she could, staring at him and trying to memorize his muscular body, his handsome face contorted in pleasure as he worked her to ecstasy. No words came as pleasure lit through her. She heard herself squealing over and over again in tandem with his grunts, his movements, and the squeak of the lounger that she hoped wouldn't collapse. It all only turned her on further—the wildness of what they were doing, the roughness that he took her with that she only appreciated.

"Zayn," she gasped. "Zayn!" she whimper-screamed.

"Yes. Say my name, Kareena." He bit out harshly, sweat beading his forehead. "I want to fuck you from behind, I want to fuck you in the shower, in the pool, on the beach. I want to fuck you in my bed and make you come so hard you never forget whose name you yelled."

He owned her. There was no other way to describe it. She belonged to him, whether she wanted to or not. The thought came unbidden as her body exploded and she saw lightning streaks raining down behind her closed lids.

"Zayn!" she shrieked again, feeling her inner muscles clenching him like a vice as she came once more. And this time, she heard him groan deeply, saw the pleasure contort his face as his eyes closed, his mouth go slack as he moaned so loudly it took her breath away. His cum slipped inside her, filled her up, and seeped out as her thighs squeezed him to her while he whispered, "My sweet, sweet, Karma." Over and over again.

CHAPTER 24

২8

*K*areena sat in front of the vanity in their estate suite, wearing just her robe.

Tonight was the rehearsal dinner. She couldn't believe how quickly time had passed. It'd already been five days, and by this time next week, she'd be back in New York.

Pushing that disheartening thought aside, she thought about how great things had been, though a few odd hiccups popped up. She believed they were in the clear about the validity of their engagement. And she'd got to get to know his family. Plus, she'd been treated like a queen bee by the estate staff and the locals, and gotten to see parts of Greece she never thought she would.

Had she learned how to swim yet? Not a lick. But other licking had happened that both she and Zayn were more excited about than anything.

Her cheeks heated and turned pink as she glanced at herself in the mirror. Was that really her? She looked relaxed and rejuvenated. Her skin was darker, tanned with a sheen, and even her hair looked thicker. Had it been the sun, surf, and sand, or the pumping of Reyana's version of Vitamin D into her system? Or, maybe it was something more ... resurfaced feelings that refused to stay buried from so long ago, for a man she hadn't been able to fully let go of.

Yes, she knew she was in big trouble. She'd developed feelings for him despite her many talks with herself. She stared at the Tiffany engagement ring sitting on the table, picking it up and sliding it back onto her finger.

Was there any way to alleviate the warm sensation budding inside her breast at the thought of Zayn and their new intimacy, despite knowing it would be over soon? He'd also confirmed yesterday what his mother had told her earlier about the claims period ending more quickly than expected. They wouldn't have to pretend for much longer after she got back to New York. By Thanksgiving, it might all be over.

And yet, she couldn't stop thinking about him and how he'd made her feel so sexy and satisfied ... and wanted. She couldn't have asked for a better first 'swimming lesson' from him, she thought with humor.

With limbs still sweaty and tangled, he'd pulled out and flipped onto his back, demanding she sit on his face. To which she absolutely declined. No way was she going to put her weight on him and possibly break his jaw in the process. If what she'd just experienced was any indication, and true to what he'd told her on the dusty path, her legs would be complete goo. There wasn't a chance she could hold herself up while he licked her into oblivion.

He'd replied, "Fair enough." And had said he'd make his request when they were in bed with a headboard for her to hold on to. Which only lit up her lady parts again. But then her stomach rumbled, and they both realized they were famished. Before they got up and dressed, she asked him about the family ring, unable to keep from knowing where his head was with it … and possibly her.

"Traditions like that aren't important to me, Karma," he'd said a little stubbornly, his fingers pausing their walk up and down her spine. When she urged him to reconsider because it could only build their case against Silas' doubts, he'd groaned in frustration. "It's just an old piece of jewelry that a king gave to our family. Apparently, the Stavroses offered a fleet of ships during the Greek War of Independence. It doesn't—*shouldn't* matter anymore."

The breath of his casualness had left her speechless.

So, the family *had* been involved in a very important battle, and were way more illustrious than she could've ever imagined. Well, it was no wonder he hadn't considered that noteworthy ring for her. She and he were phony, and she needed to keep reminding herself about that overarching truth. He might not be one to consider marriage presently, but one day, someone would be important enough to him to wear it.

She gazed at herself in the mirror with a frown. Now, why did that feel even more disheartening than the fact that her time in Greece would be over in a matter of days?

They'd climbed up to the villa, hand in hand. And when they stepped inside, she gasped with delight. He'd done more cleaning and clearing out that morning. The place was free of dust and cobwebs, and he'd had furniture moved into the living area and the largest bedroom.

The kitchen was sparkling clean and stocked. He pulled out

ingredients and a cutting board, prepped the counter, and announced he was going to cook for her. Was she okay with a simple fare of traditional Naxos stewed beans topped with crumbly fresh feta and freshly made pita bread from the bakery?

He was certainly making it harder for her to focus on the fact that whatever they were doing had an expiration date. And she didn't want to think about how he'd revealed his hatred for her after she'd dumped him, but that love was the other side of that same coin. That had left her breathless and more confused, because this man was continuously making her heart beat faster for him. And then he'd gone and proposed cooking for her; he, a well-known chef. She got all giggly like a teenager.

"Everything okay, Karma?" he'd asked, a twinkle in his eyes as he noticed her huge smile and giggles. He'd pulled out beers for them, cracking them open.

She'd gulped hers, relishing in the light, refreshing flavor, and said something about getting to live every woman's fantasy.

He'd inquired what that was as he tied an apron around his waist, which only made her giggle more, and he frowned. "What? Do you think this is funny?" He'd asked, looking down at his cooking apron.

Then he'd slowly stalked her around the kitchen island, and it was like they were kids again, lighthearted, and carefree.

When he'd caught her, he backed her up against the island, their bodies flush with one another.

She couldn't help admitting that it felt like high school all over again—her enormous crush on him while she was his tutor, not knowing that he had one on her, too. And when he first cooked for her over one study session, her eyes had been filled with stars.

He'd asked what she thought now.

She'd blushed but held his gaze while uttering truthfully, "Stars galore. The entire galaxy, in fact. I can't believe you, this professional, celebrity chef, this ... complete hunky hottie, wants to cook for *me*. I'm nothing special."

And he'd told her she was wrong. She was more special than she realized. She'd helped him get through the last hard year of high school. Even after that, thoughts of her had gotten him through culinary school. She'd been his first believer, and he'd kept that close to him.

She'd gulped down emotions, recalling what he'd said about the tattoo under his heart.

They'd held each other's gaze for a beat as questions about them floated around the kitchen, along with the delicious smell of his stew. But he kissed her hard on the forehead and went back to the stove.

He'd changed the subject, proclaiming she'd shake in ecstasy when she tried his beans, making her laugh in fits all over again. He'd rolled his eyes and couldn't believe what a juvenile mind she had. She'd wiped tears from her eyes as he brought the spoon he'd dipped in the stew to her mouth for a taste.

True to this statement, she'd closed her eyes in bliss, savoring the warm sauce as it settled onto her tongue with simple ingredients that melded together in a symphony of flavors.

"Zayn, you're a magician," she'd complimented, her eyes still closed. She heard the distinct click of the stove and the clattering of a lid.

When she'd opened her eyes, he was taking his apron off, throwing it on the counter. He grabbed her hand and pulled her to him, kissing her deeply, the taste of the stew on both of their tongues.

"Do you understand how hot it is when a woman loves your cooking? And not just any woman—you, Karma."

He'd dragged her out of the kitchen and up the stairs, throwing her onto the king-size bed in the largest bedroom as he shucked his clothes off. He helped her with hers, and when they were fully naked, he rolled to his back with her on top, encouraging her to take the lead.

She'd leaned down and kissed him, completely turned on by his need for her to take control. And it hadn't taken long, both of them too excited for foreplay. She'd lined herself up to him and sunk onto his hardness, her body shuddering as she took him inside all the way, already ready for him, her head thrown back and her eyes closed.

"Oh my God," she'd moaned. "Zayn, you feel *so* good inside me." She moaned again, low in the back of her throat, and began to undulate on him.

"God has nothing to do with it, Baby." His hands gripped her hips tightly. "It's just you and me, mere mortals."

They'd come as one, his hands grasping hers, lacing their fingers together.

She stood up from the vanity abruptly, not able to look at herself, knowing that her face was even more fiery as her body became wound up and hot, thinking about being with him. What was she going to do when this was all over?

Don't think about that.

She went to the closet and pulled out the pale grey satin floor-length dress she'd brought for the rehearsal dinner. The dress code was fancy cocktail.

Her sister's comment while she'd packed for her trip was

that it was very *a la Fifty Shades,* making her wonder at the appropriateness. But now she was glad it was sexy. She wanted to look good for Zayn. And it was also one of the most comfortable dresses she'd ever worn. But maybe that was because it resembled more of a satin nightie than an actual dress?

She slipped it on, marveling at the way it hugged her body perfectly. Her rounded hips were supple and smooth under the lustrous material; no sign of thigh dimples in sight. She looked glamor chic, even with her too-high waist, larger hips, and thicker thighs (construed as muscular, but they were still thicker than the average person's).

Her sister had also asked at that point if she was sure about going to Greece. Kareena had told her absolutely. Sadly, the last conversation she had with her parents made the decision for her. They were still disappointed in her engagement with Zayn and couldn't see how she would make it work. They also used Tamannah as a reason why he was the wrong choice—how could he ever be the right father for such a special child? That had done it for her. And she told them not to call her until they could come down from their condescendingly superior ivory tower to join her in the real world. So, when Zayn mentioned the Greece trip again in passing—when she had less on her mind than an impending lawsuit against her—she asked why he hadn't asked her to come.

His response about wanting her to be there—for the sake of their fake engagement, of course (eye on the prize and all that) —didn't matter. He knew she had a lot going on in New York that she couldn't get away from.

She'd been touched that he'd already thought this through, but by God, she could really use some time away, and she told him to ask her anyway. And he did, a little bitingly with irritation because he probably thought she was going to say 'no.' She responded that she'd be more than happy to attend his cousin's wedding with him in Greece and to advise her on what to pack.

She'd felt buoyant with her decision, though it was so far from anything she would have done in her past. As a psychiatrist, she always advised her patients to make sure they took care of their needs first because only then could they be a better spouse, daughter, son, sister, brother, etc. She'd *never* once taken her own advice, and she desperately needed it now. Her life was a chaotic top, spinning out of control, and she worried about when it would finally fall over, motionless with no more spin to give. The only good things were her daughter and the podcast with her sister. And Zayn. Yes, the fake engagement and the staggeringly busy social schedule had taken her mind off the stresses in her life. She needed a break from being a mother—she was mentally taxed as a single parent. She told herself, like she'd told numerous patients in her career, she wasn't a bad mother for needing a break from her daughter. The fact that she was taking a break from her meant she would be an even better mom by the time she got back.

Zayn had been stunned and asked numerous times if she was sure. She'd laughed and said she was. And he'd given her the itinerary of events, which admittedly would be a lot. He advised that, as it was November now, it was getting cooler in Greece, and to pack layers.

Reyana had told her while she packed, "You deserve some fun in your life right now. The engagement might be fake, Kara, but that doesn't mean you can't *actually* have a good time.

Maybe see if you can get some "Vitamin D" while you're out there. You're always talking about taking your supplements."

Why was it always the least person you'd expect to give you good advice, the one who was always right?

She went over to the three-way mirror in the guest suit to get a better view of herself in the grey dress. She turned to view her back. The crisscross knot situation at her upper back was not only an eye-catching design element, but it also functioned to hold her breasts snugly in place.

Her butt looked good, too. No indentations, just smoothness under the sleek satin, with a hint of half-moons hinting at her ass-cheeks where the fabric became a little more fitted, before it flared out ever so slightly.

She accessorized with pretty white gold crystal drop earrings she purchased on a shopping excursion with Penelope and the bridesmaids earlier that day, after another all-girls expedition in town, this time to get manicures and pedicures. She clasped the matching crystal and white gold Y-shaped necklace, smoothing it over her chest, making sure the crystal sat snugly within her cleavage.

She pinned back one side of her hair behind her ear, leaving her hair thick and wavy. The look was nothing short of a 1940s bombshell. She looked and felt good.

She squared her shoulders as she exited the suite. Zayn had left earlier in the afternoon for a boating excursion with the men and the groom. It was going to be a long day for him, and he wouldn't be back in time for cocktail hour.

Or, at least, that's what he'd told her, but now here he was at the bottom of the steps, dressed absolutely divinely in a dark grey suit, white button-down, and a silver tie. He was about to come up the stairs when his eyes met hers, and he paused.

Could one feel a whoosh of anxiety *and* a sense of calm simultaneously? Because the way Zayn stared up at her, the way his mouth gaped open, had her reeling with a heat that rushed over her, almost knocking her backward. She gripped the banister tighter, willing her knees not to buckle. That wasn't the look of a man pretending to be engaged to her. That was the look of an absolutely carnal man, and she was his possession.

It felt more than right to her.

CHAPTER 25

२८

*H*is breath caught in his throat at the sight of her. For the millionth time since he'd asked her to be his fake fiancée, he couldn't take his eyes off of her. A heat spread through his chest, and it felt like lightning struck him right above his 'karma' tattoo.

He'd thought the dress was simply elegant when they were unpacking. Turns out, it was deceivingly sexy, though sophisticated in style. The fabric clung to her flesh, hugging her every curve in a way that felt a little too sensual for a family event.

Her skin, already glowing healthily from enjoying the sun these past few days, now gleamed a deep bronze against the material's luminescence. With each movement, as she carefully continued down the stairs, the dress went from dove grey to light rose to a silver blue. And her hair, so thick and full and shiny, was so black that under the din of the lights above, it held that blueish tint to it, the one he'd noticed the moment he'd met her decades ago. She'd kept the style fairly simple, except for pushing one side back behind her ear, showing off the smooth skin on the expanse of her neck and chest, only decorated minimally by a pretty white gold necklace and matching earrings. Tan lines were apparent along her shoulders and back, and it sent a wave of lust through him. He couldn't wait to glide his tongue along her warm skin later, tracing those contrasting-hued lines.

All in good time, he thought, rushing up to her. They ended up meeting in the middle of the wide, curved staircase.

"You're stunning, Karma," he said, knowing that no words could justify the admiration he held for her. "That dress," he shook his head, at a loss for words. Instead, he let out a low whistle, his eyes snagging on every one of her curves.

She rolled her lips in at his reaction, trying to hide her grin as she replied a thank you.

He put his arm out for her to take as he led her down.

"I think we make a pretty good couple, don't you?" she asked under her breath, a little nervous.

"I do. In more ways than one," he teased her, but he spoke with truth. These last few days had clinched something deep for him. He wanted her in more ways than one. It started with a physical want back in New York; a curiosity to be with her physically after the smallest taste had revived his hunger. But their time in New York, and then in Greece together, the shared moments of joy, laughter, even angst—discussing their hurts from the past, made him know deep down that he didn't want to end this with her when this was all over.

The details would be tricky. They weren't teenagers anymore, and there were other factors to consider. But they could figure things out, couldn't they?

As they reached the bottom of the stairs, he glanced

sideways at her, wondering if he wanted too much from her. He hadn't hinted at any of this, and his mind was already trying to hash out the details—his presence necessary in Naxos for the restaurant, her need to be in New York for her daughter, her family, and even her pup.

Focus.

He had to get through the rest of this trip and gain his inheritance before he could address 'them.' But he knew it was definitely a goal he intended to work on. When he knew, he knew, just like so many other decisions he'd made in life.

The resounding applause from the guests surrounding them as soon as they arrived at the bottom of the staircase shook his thoughts. Immediately, cheers and shouts of congratulations abounded.

"*What* is going on?" she asked with a bemused smile.

"You didn't think a family like mine would *not* celebrate our engagement, did you? My mother and Penelope planned all of this. Penelope and Brutus were happy to share their rehearsal dinner evening with us."

"What!?" She tensed up. He'd always known she hated being the center of attention.

"Relax, Karma," he said in her ear, the delicate shell tempting him to bite the soft flesh. He put a hand to her back, just to steady her, and the heat of her skin was barely contained by the thin dress material. "Just think about how great this dress will look on our bedroom floor later." He purposefully didn't use the term "eye on the prize." He was pretty sure that wasn't the only prize he sought anymore.

She hummed lightly in the back of her throat, and he witnessed her shoulders easing up as she relaxed. Damn. His hands itched to palm every inch of her, and fuck if this wasn't going to be one hell of a night. But he forced himself to concentrate on one more surprise for her, and he hoped she would take it well.

He'd ruminated over this detail since he'd announced their engagement to his family weeks ago. Everyone was happy for him, for the most part, and everyone asked him if she was wearing the family ring.

Admittedly, he'd always scoffed at the idea of it. To him, it was an antiquated tradition, one that was persistent in a time (the present) when the family was doing more than well, unlike after the Greek War of Independence in the early part of the 1800s. Much of their wealth had gone to help the war effort, including the donation of a huge fleet of ships. After the war ended, many treasure coffers, along with ships and land, were bestowed upon their family in thanks for their loyalty and services, helping them reestablish their commerce and wealth. The diamond, a two-carat old mined stone, was pulled from one of these coffers and set into a beautiful gold ring designed to look like olive branches, circling and coming together where the prongs held the stone. It was a symbol of the strength and goodwill of the Stavros name and had been passed down through three generations to brides coming into the family.

Zayn had already received an earful from his mother, but Silas was the one who really ate at him about it, maintaining that there was no way his engagement was real because Kareena wasn't wearing that family ring—the one their *yia yia* (grandmother in Greek) had bestowed on him for his bride. He'd gone so far as to even say that, as a half-Greek, he didn't deserve all of the special treatment and gifts their grandparents had given him. That's where Silas was wrong, though. It was *because* of his half-Greek status that his grandparents had taken more interest in him, observing that many of the cousins, as kids and led by Silas, had begun to give Zayn a hard time. They ignored him or made fun of him, and it wasn't until he was about six or seven that he realized it. He made friends with the local kids instead and spent more time with his grandparents, who held no animosity toward him. That was how he'd come to be very close with both of them, and why everyone thought he was their favorite. Maybe he was, but he'd certainly spent more time with them than any of his other cousins.

So, he realized as soon as they set foot in Greece, he'd have to face the small but critical fact regarding the family heirloom. He'd not mentioned it to Kareena because, honestly, he'd forgotten about it until his mother brought it up to him. But he knew that once back in the motherland, not only would the rest of the family wonder, but so would the locals, and he needed this to look as real as possible ... until he could make it as real as possible.

Fuck, had that thought just crossed his mind? He grinned. He wanted to make it real—whatever it was that he and Kareena were doing.

He thought about when she asked him about the ring, and he knew his mother had been behind her knowledge and questioning of it. As the eldest daughter of his grandparents, she couldn't understand his reasoning, and he could tell she was hurt by his refusal to carry on the tradition. And it was so like something his mother would do—telling Kareena about it and getting her to talk to him.

He felt like a complete shit when she'd come to him, right after they'd had incredible sex out in the private patio of the villa, their bodies still sweaty and entwined.

He knew she was vulnerable as she hesitated in asking him.

He might have sounded irritated about his rationale for why he'd never told her about it. In reality, he was pissed at himself for not preparing her to be asked about it by quite possibly any of the hundreds of family members that had descended on the island by that point. He could only imagine her shock and having to cover it up in front of his mother whenever that conversation had occurred. He suspected it must have been earlier that day, at the ladies' wine tasting and lunch. He chastised himself for being so foolish and putting Kareena in that position.

He'd already decided that he would have her wear it. He wanted her to, wanted to see it on her finger, if just to answer the question of "what if" which had lived with him since he was a teenager and first fell in love with her.

He just needed to get to the Athens First National Bank and retrieve it from the family safe. He'd done that earlier in the morning, using the men's fishing trip as an excuse, and knowing she'd be busy again with another bridal excursion.

He took a deep breath and turned to her, his arm still around her. "I have one more surprise for you."

She looked up at him with questioning eyes. "Another one? You know I don't love surprises."

"Trust me. I think you'll like this one—or, at least I hope you do."

Maybe he was making too big a deal about what he intended to do next, but there was no knowing unless he followed through.

He took her hand with the Tiffany engagement ring on it and pulled the pretty but flashy ring off, pocketing it.

"What—" But she stopped when he pulled an old jewelry box out of his pocket that had seen better days.

Without a word, he opened it, and it creaked with age. Inside was his grandmother's ring. It sparkled as if it was breathing fresh air, now back out in the open. He pulled it out and stuffed the box into his pocket, wordlessly slipping it onto her finger.

"Zayn," she whispered, "Is this your family ring?" She was alarmed.

That wasn't a good sign, he thought before she murmured, "I can't," and motioned to remove it. The room broke into applause, and "*Opas*" resounded from every corner, making her stop and stare wide-eyed at his large family.

Despite her expression, seeing her wear his family's ring filled him with satisfaction and pride that swelled his chest so large that he murmured an '*Opa*' under his breath, too, only for her to hear. His first thought was that she should've been wearing this ring a long time ago. He knew that was foolish. Their timing hadn't been right back then.

"I don't know if I can wear this, Zayn," she whispered with worry. "Isn't this meant for true Stavros brides? I understand why you didn't have me wear it in the first place since we're pretending—" He put a finger to her lips, stopping her. He didn't like that word describing them anymore.

"Kareena, please wear it. It would mean the world to me."

She looked at him for a beat before nodding. "Okay," she said so softly he barely heard her.

She examined the beautiful gold detailing. "It's beautiful," she murmured.

"Well, well, well," a familiar voice boomed behind them. They both turned to see his father approaching them with his arms out wide.

Kiran Roy was a man shorter than him in stature, smaller in

build, and slightly portly around the middle. His personality, though, one that was larger than life, made him seem bigger.

His eyes, the same light brown as Zayn's, danced with joy. His black and white peppered hair was thick, though thinning on the top, and he'd swept the remaining locks over the shiny bald spot he'd been self-conscious about since Zayn could remember.

"It's about time, Papa. When did you get in?" Zayn asked, happily surprised.

He hugged his father heartily.

"Ah, just a few hours ago. You know me, always working. I plan to retire soon, though. Mark my words. I've had enough."

He turned to Kareena.

"My child. I'm so happy you and Zayn have found one another again."

Kareena bowed her head with her hands clasped together at her breast. "Namaste, Uncle."

Kiran's expression softened, and he pulled her hands from their position of respectful greeting to give her a proper hug. "You're to be my daughter soon, *Beta.*" He stepped back and pushed her gently toward Zayn. "I must speak with your *abba.*" This last part he said a little concerned. But his face brightened when his wife joined them, a waiter behind her carrying four flutes of champagne on a tray.

"Kareena. You look wonderful, my dear." Sofia kissed Kareena on both cheeks. "I'm sorry I couldn't give you a proper engagement party. But I'm so happy and proud that you're wearing your rightful engagement ring." Her eyes were filled with tears as she inspected Kareena's hand with her mother's ring on it.

She turned to the waiter and handed a glass to everyone, keeping one for herself.

"Please, Sofia Aunty, this joint party is more than enough for our engagement. Thank you. It's so thoughtful. Where's Penelope? I have to thank her, too."

"Present!" Penelope sang, approaching them with Brutus following closely behind. "Kareena, we're more than thrilled that we could do this for you and Zayn. Just look at how much Zayn adores you. There's no way I wouldn't give you and your love a moment to shine tonight, especially when you told me how you two met up again and fell hopelessly for each other for a second time!"

Zayn couldn't stop grinning. It all felt so real; that it really was his and Kareena's engagement party. And damn if it didn't feel right.

His father stepped onto the bottom step and shouted above the din of guests, "A toast, please. Everyone, a toast?"

As everyone quieted down, he raised his glass and said to Zayn, "To my Zayn, and his Kareena. Their destinies finally aligned, thank goodness. Congratulations on your engagement."

Guests murmured congratulations in both Greek and English, while some cheered, and many others yelled "*Opa!*" again, while some shouted, "Kiss, kiss, kiss!"

Kareena's cheeks turned scarlet as Zayn handed his glass and her glass to his parents. He pulled her close and kissed her gently but firmly, dipping her for a brief moment to everyone's joy, before pulling her up again and releasing her pouty lips. She looked dazed and utterly filled with joy. Her eyes shone brightly as she laughed. She was the most beautiful woman, and he was going to make sure she was his for good.

Later, after dinner, more toasts, and speeches, only a few people lingered over dessert.

They'd eaten out in the field next to the olive grove, under a massive white tent. It was adorned with twinkle lights and pretty little chandeliers that tinkled in response to the breeze that lifted from the ocean and mingled with the sounds of waves crashing in the distance. It was a beautiful night, a little calmer than the last family gathering when Penelope, drunk on too much ouzo, had decided to rip Silas a new one.

Zayn hadn't been too surprised by Pen's behavior. Silas had never been nice to her. It bothered him that he couldn't walk her down the aisle, but it was Silas's right, as their father had passed away years ago. Part of him believed that Silas took pleasure in being the one to give her away, though she preferred Zayn.

When she'd screamed at Silas that night, Zayn had pulled her aside to calmly thank her for her words of praise (he wasn't being facetious in any way; he appreciated Penelope's support and love). He'd then advised her that it didn't matter who walked her down the aisle. He'd always be there for her, and that what she really had to look forward to was her future with Brutus. She had tearfully nodded, then promptly heaved, and barfed her entire supper right next to his feet. He'd led her to the bushes and rubbed her back as her slight frame shook, throwing up the contents of her stomach. Then he'd handed her over to Brutus, who carefully took her back to their room.

Shit, what a night that had been. Her outburst, though probably warranted, was unexpected in the setting it had occurred. It only enraged Silas further, and he'd been even fouler in the past few days, sneering at Zayn, trying to provoke him with taunts of entertaining multiple talks to sell away his inheritance. At one point, Zayn had to ask him if he was a man or a boy, because his behavior was shitty and childish, especially when they should be focusing on someone else's wedding celebration. What cut at Silas even further was that he ribbed him about the family ring, still maintaining it was just a piece of jewelry that meant nothing anymore, though he knew he was going to have Kareena wear it.

He sighed and stared at Kareena's profile now, as the evening wound down.

People were scattered about the estate, a sort of peaceful excitement filling the air, aware that the big day was tomorrow. Music from the old ballroom drifted out to them from open windows. Unfortunately, it wasn't a beautiful string quartet, or even that of the local six-piece band that had performed a few nights ago. Someone had set up a karaoke machine and was belting out pop songs, one after the other. Currently on rotation was a catchy song about a pink club in LA, and the singer who liked to dance on the stage of said club.

It was a good song, but the singer was butchering it.

Kareena leaned in to him, her head on his shoulder. "I hate to say it, but it sounds like a cat is being actively skinned alive at the moment."

Zayn chuckled. "I'll make sure to tell Pen how much you like her singing."

Kareena lifted her head off his shoulder; her mouth was open wide in shock. "You're kidding. That cannot be Penelope."

He nodded. "She always thought she'd be a singer one day. But her talent was never in perfoming. She's the genius in our family. She's graduating from Stanford early."

Kareena was shocked all over again. "What!?"

Zayn nodded. "She's truly very smart. Perfect SAT scores … I know how much that means to you."

She punched him in the arm. "Hey! Cheap shot." She'd been obsessed with test scores in high school. It was a time when that's all she and her friends had cared about, though Zayn couldn't have cared less.

He gathered her close, nuzzling her hair. "The cheapest. I apologize." He kissed her forehead. "Do you want to turn in?" He asked. "I know a few things we could do if we're not too tired."

"Zayn, how are you not exhausted after today? Wasn't sailing all day tiring?"

He kissed the curve of her ear and inhaled her fruity and herbal muskiness. He wouldn't tell her about his trip to Athens. "I haven't had a taste of you today. I need you, Sweetheart. It doesn't matter how tired I am."

"Is that so?" she asked, the tremor in her voice indicating she felt the same. "I think we can make a quick getaway, don't you?" She glanced around covertly, which was hysterical because they were the only ones left at the long table, except for his aunt Alva and her cranky little poodle, Demetri, and one or two other guests.

The candles in their glass votive holders were dwindling, with some already completely extinguished. In the dim light, he stared at her as she took one last sip of her coffee. His family's ring flashed on her finger, and it was on the tip of his tongue to ask her to make this all real—not necessarily the engagement part, but the 'them' part—when her phone buzzed in her purse.

"Oh! I forgot," she exclaimed. "Tamannah was going to call to tell me how her day went. They had a spelling quiz today." She pulled her purse to her chest. "Do you mind if I take this first?"

He shook his head. "Not at all."

Maybe he should be relieved that they'd been saved by Tamannah. Was he moving this too fast? Was being home, surrounded by his family, and partaking in a huge romantic wedding, clouding his judgment?

He watched her get up and leave the tent, looking for a private spot to talk to her daughter, and he realized that no, he was not moving too fast. It all felt right, even the daughter and the crazy dog.

CHAPTER 26

२७

*K*areena found a quiet spot outside the tent, though really, did she need one? People were retiring, and dinner was over.

Before calling her daughter back, she took a minute to breathe. The salty air felt refreshing on her face, and she could dust off her thoughts, the perplexing ones that had arisen when Zayn surprised her with his family's ring. What was he doing by putting it on her finger, in front of everyone, and then expressing that it meant a lot to him?

What was happening between them? Every day closer to their endpoint felt like they were becoming closer in their intimacy.

She couldn't help staring at the heirloom ring for maybe the hundredth time since he'd slipped it on. It was gorgeous and cleverly designed to make the gold olive branches the ring portion as they circled to the front, with the diamond in the center, as if they were holding it, hiding the dainty prongs underneath. With too many facets to count, the diamond sparkled even more than the giant Tiffany ring from before, and had an old-world charm that she knew was hard to come by these days. She had to admit that it looked really good on her, and it felt even better. For the time being, she'd go along with wearing it, and she'd ask why later. She needed to keep things straight in her head, even though she felt herself falling further for him. Was it possible he felt the same way? Was this his way of showing her his sudden turn of emotions?

She exhaled deeply. They'd have plenty of time to figure it all out once the wedding was over and their charade wound down.

She pulled her phone out of her purse only to realize it wasn't her daughter who'd called, but her sister.

"What do you want, *Choto Bon?*" she said pleasantly, after her sister picked up on the first ring.

"Well, *you* sound happy."

"Mm, something like that."

"Wait, has the railing commenced?" Reyana urged.

"I already told you, I don't kiss and tell." She wasn't about to fill her in on the line she and Zayn had crossed. Reyana already knew way too much about her life.

"You know by not telling me, you're basically admitting that you're doing it, and it's amazing." Her sister said knowingly.

"Sure," Kareena replied, keeping mum. "So, what's going on? Why are you calling? It's not ... *Abba* or *Amma,* is it?"

Shit, why hadn't she called them? This was the longest she'd ever gone without speaking to them.

"No. They say 'hi' by the way. I have got to show you something. I'm sending a video over via text."

"*Reya,*" she whined. "Is this about the podcast? Can't it wait?"

"It's not about the podcast, or ... maybe it is," she said thoughtfully. "And no, this absolutely cannot wait."

She rolled her eyes at her sister's dramatics.

"I have to go, Kara. Sameer's plane just landed. Just check it out. You won't be sorry. Love you, Bye!" Her sister hung up.

Kareena looked at her phone screen and waited for the video to pop up. When it did, the text her sister sent with it read, **"I'm telling you, this guy would be a perfect guest on the podcast."**

Kareena rolled her eyes. Reyana was talking about the faceless hot chef. She'd been stalking his social media profile, examining every video because his new following looked like a shooting star she wanted a piece of.

Another text came in. **"Look familiar, Karma?"** followed by the video.

"Huh?" she said out loud. "What are you talking about, you weirdo?"

She clicked the video, and immediately, the hot chef her sister had been obsessing over filled her screen. The familiar black mask covered his face and neck as he prepared a snack. Except this time, he was in a different location than what appeared to be his apartment in his other videos. He looked like he was in an older kitchen, with a large iron stove range and warming ovens behind him. The lighting wasn't great, but one could still make out his flexing muscles and his majorly muscular body, which was probably all that anyone looked for anyway, she thought, studying him.

Instantly, understanding hit her, almost knocking her over. It wasn't just from the tattoos on his body that were exactly like another hot chef's that she knew so intimately and had traced her fingers over numerous times recently. It was the man's physique that she knew immediately. The way he moved as he sliced and diced with speed and precision. She'd seen him live and in action only a day ago. As he picked up a large melon, she recognized the way he gently handled the round fruit because it was similar to the way his large hands eloquently palmed her breasts.

Maybe she was seeing things, she thought for a split second. Or maybe she was being a dimwit because it was obviously Zayn, in a hooded mask, cooking up what looked like a scrumptious dish. He flash-fried calamari before shoving it into familiar fluffy pita (the kind they'd had at lunch yesterday), and drizzling lemon juice and marinara sauce, then sprinkling it with freshly chopped oregano. He cut up the melon and served it wrapped in tissue-paper-thin slices of prosciutto.

Though the video was dim, she clearly read the writing under his heart. The 'karma' script was so apparent now that she wondered how blind or dumb she'd been before to have not put the pieces together. Maybe she was both.

She'd told her sister about that tattoo after finding out about it, and the others on his body, though she'd never told her how she'd found out. Reyana, already obsessing over the masked online chef, had figured it out.

She shook her head in bewilderment, even as her body flooded with desire when *Sinful* took a large bite, groaned, and smiled devilishly, licking his luscious lips.

The question wasn't how blind or dumb she'd been to notice it was him before, though. She wanted to know why the hell did he, in his scary mask, shirtless and cooking, turn her on so much? Where exactly had this kink come from? And seriously, what was wrong with her?

To say she was turned on after finding out that Zayn had a secret alter ego, and that secret alter ego was none other than *Sinful in the Kitchen,* was an understatement—massively so.

She couldn't find him fast enough. She dragged him, surprised and chuckling, from his chair, into the house, past the bride-to-be's terrible singing, and up the stairs, her heart beating frantically. She was wild for him and needed him naked.

Never mind that he hadn't told her about this. Fuck the facts that she now knew why he had a social media manager. God, if her daughter had been presented with these clues, she would've put the pieces together quicker than you could say easy peasy lemon squeezy. Thank God her daughter would never know about this, though. She was seven.

Kareena dragged him into their room, the bed already turned down and the lights set to an intimate low. She slammed the door and pushed him up against it. For such a large man, he didn't put up a single finger or fight despite the way she was woman-handling him.

"Karma, this is a new side I really like—"

She attacked his lips with her own, shutting him up, while she pulled at his tie, untying it like a maniac, and slipping it from around his neck. His smile against her lips told her he was more than happy to partake in whatever had code-switched her from family woman to feral woman.

She unbuttoned his shirt as his hands slid under the straps of her dress, tugging it down around her waist. He deftly unhooked her bra, tossing it to the side before cupping her breasts, groaning in pleasure as he squeezed them.

Her mind still only on one thing, she pushed his hands out of her way as she jerked his shirt from his pants and unbuckled his belt. She stumbled on the button and zipper, and he moved her hands aside to undo them himself. Then he let her continue.

Without warning, she slipped her hands beneath the waistband of his underwear and pushed them down, taking his pants, too. She dropped to her knees in front of him and stared at his hardened cock for a beat, his precum oozing deliciously from the tip. Then she put her mouth on his tip and sucked, making him emit a low groan.

"Kareena," he said in wonder, his hands threading through her hair, pushing pins out from their holding place.

She tasted his thick pre-cum, the salty muskiness, and opened her mouth wider, taking in more of him. She paused, making sure she could breathe, before she pulled back and then continued forward again, more of him going down her throat.

"Baby," he gasped, his hands tightening in her hair, taking control as he held her in one place while his pelvis bucked, fucking her mouth.

The corners of her mouth stretched, burning from his girth, and she knew she couldn't handle any more of him. So she clutched his base with her hands, rubbing up and down, as she let him fuck her mouth.

"Kareena," he groaned. "Fuck, Baby," he hissed.

She moaned around him, encouraging him. She wanted him to lose control. She didn't know what was driving her need to suck his cock, but ever since being with him that first time, it was like he'd flipped a switch inside her—a kinkier side was now in charge. And the fact that he was secretly the social media hot chef? Fuck she was more than frantic for him.

She bared her teeth and scraped along his veiny length, and he moaned, long and deep, before jerking his pelvis faster against her face, her mouth taking him fast and hot, until he forcefully pulled her away from him. But he held her close so that his hot cum spurted out of him and hotly onto her neck, coating her, dripping down and over her breasts.

JESUS FUCKING CHRIST. What the hell?

His breathing was jagged, and he tried to even it out. He slowly became aware that he still gripped the back of Kareena's head tightly, and some of her strands were wound around his hand.

When he looked down at her, he saw the sexiest, most beautiful woman in the world, on her knees in front of him, having let him fuck her face, and now covered in his sticky cum.

The vision would be burned in his brain forever.

"God, you're so beautiful," he said, gently unwinding her hair from his hand.

She shook her head, suddenly bashful, her hair now in the sticky mess of his cum.

"You don't think you're beautiful?" he asked as he helped her stand up. Her dress pooled to the floor, and all she wore now was her silver heels, a tiny tan thong, and his cum, coating her neck and the flesh of her big, round breasts, like white thick frosting drizzled heavily over succulent coffee cake.

He quickly stepped out of his pants and simultaneously toed off his shoes while pulling the rest of his clothes off.

She made a motion to move, and he stayed her with a hand on her arm. "Stay there. Give me a second."

He pulled off his socks, now completely naked. He took her hand and led her to the large three-way mirror in one corner of the room.

"What are we doing?"

"Come," he urged. "See what I see when I look at you, Sweetheart."

He positioned her so she stood in front of him. He looked at her looking at herself, her gaze perplexed.

His hands glided up her over her fleshy hips, squeezing, before moving up to her waist.

"Look how sexy you are, Karma. I've never been with a sexier, more vibrant woman."

She turned her head and cupped his face, bringing him closer to her for a kiss. He obliged, kissing her back, sipping her lips, licking her before pushing his tongue into her mouth.

She sighed into him as one of his hands glided down her soft belly, into the front of her underwear. His fingers slid through her folds, slick with her need, and began to gently massage her clit. He used a feather-light touch, moving back and forth quickly along her tight little bud, making her arch her back, her ass pressed into his dick, her ass cheeks hugging him.

She moaned as she felt him harden between her plump cheeks, closing her eyes. He released her lips and told her to open them back up.

"Watch, my sweet girl. Watch how you come, and how fucking gorgeous you are."

She turned her gaze back to the mirror and took in the

glorious sight of herself, her legs spread with his hand down her underwear, working her pussy. Her breasts, coated with his now drying cum shook and bounced with her every movement, as she ground against his cock while he kept working her clit.

In fascination, he watched her hands slide up her body and fondle her breasts, plucking at her nipples as she moaned, her eyes on what they were both doing to her beautiful body.

The look on her face almost made him come undone. It almost made him fling her onto the floor to bury himself deeply inside her. Because as he watched her, her eyes got more hooded, glassier, as if she was high on a drug. Her mouth became slack, and she fixated on herself, her breasts, her belly, his hands on her, and down her underwear. She moaned, undulating, her pussy weeping against his fingers, until she screamed his name and came, her body shaking from the force, as her knees buckled.

"So beautiful, Karma. So sweet and so beautiful." He whispered in her ear as he held her, and she shook from the force of her orgasm.

He maneuvered her so her hands were on the mirror, and he bent her forward before pulling her underwear down, to expose her slickness to him. He palmed her ass and slid three fingers inside her, stretching her, making her shudder. She moaned as he added another finger inside her, stretching her further for good measure. His cock was painfully hard now, seeing her like this, with her luscious ass in the air. He replaced his fingers with his throbbing hardness, entering her still quivering flesh. Her heat and her pulsing muscles sucked him in, as her moistness coated around him.

"Damn," he hissed, feeling utter and complete bliss as he slid all the way in, her inner walls rippling along his length.

"Zayn," she gasped, arching her back, her neck, so that she could now see his face reflected in the mirror.

"Yes, Sweetheart," he said, meeting her gaze. "We're so good together. You know that, right? You see that."

She nodded, and he grabbed her hair in one hand, pulling to arch her back further, while his other hand settled on the small of her back.

He didn't take her slowly or tenderly. He was fast, intense, and erratic, and it was so hot he wanted it to last forever. She screamed his name as her ass shook, coming all over again. He came, too, a surge of lust that constricted the back of his thighs so hard his knees almost buckled. He gripped her tightly, no doubt leaving bruises, as he released and emptied himself inside her. He didn't think he'd be able to come again so quickly. Fuck it was good with her. Better than good.

Afterward, he ran a bath for them, and he helped her clean up. He used a fluffy, soapy sponge to gently wipe off his cum. Then he shampooed her hair, gently massaging her scalp, as she leaned back against his chest.

In between sighs of pleasure, she said, "I've never done anything like that before, Zayn. I've never been a voyeur to mine or someone else's pleasure."

He rinsed her hair out with warm water, and as the suds ran out of her hair into their bathwater, he asked curiously, "You've never watched porn before?"

"I have. But it's not the same thing. This was way more sensual. Erotic, but beautiful. And intimate. I never thought watching myself come, my body moving like that would push me over the edge."

He chuckled. "Now you know how I feel when I see you

come. It pushes me over an edge I never want to come back from."

He put the showerhead down and wrapped his arms around her, burying his face in her neck.

"Kareena—" he stopped. He took a deep breath and went on. "Kareena, what if we keep this going when we get back to New York? And not just the sex part. I want to keep seeing you, for real."

There. He'd spit it out. Now the ball was in her court.

Her shoulders tensed, and he waited for her to say 'no,' that maybe her life was too difficult. He had arguments ready if that happened. Shit, he was willing to fight for a chance to just try this with her.

She sat up and turned to him, a sweet smile on her face as her dark eyes lit up. "I thought you'd never ask."

She placed frothy soap suds on his nose before she leaned in to kiss him deeply.

CHAPTER 27

२९

"Oh my goodness. Just look at those two. They're so in love, and Penelope looks absolutely divine."

Kareena loved weddings, especially when the couple was completely and totally in love. It was as if the world got to glimpse inside what their love for each other was like. Her wedding, though a joyful occasion, hadn't been like that. It wasn't that she didn't admire her husband, and he her, but they'd never reached that level of getting lost in one another, not like Penelope and Brutus. Not like how she was falling for a certain someone.

She turned to look at that certain someone sitting beside her at the wedding reception. He leaned back in his chair, his arm slung over the back of hers, with one ankle crossed over his opposite thigh. He wore a lightweight tan suit with a white linen button-down underneath, a few buttons undone, looking completely sexy and relaxed. He wore the same boutonniere in his jacket as the groom—a pretty sprig of baby's breath— having walked his Aunt Zia down the aisle. But his eyes weren't on the newly married couple. They were on her, warm and bright, and burning with an intensity that was very difficult to pull her gaze away from once he'd captured it.

"Zayn," she said. "Are you looking? They're just so into each other. It's so romantic!"

"I'm looking, and I see and feel what's happening between them." His eyes remained on her. "And she's the most gorgeous person I've ever seen in my life."

She blushed furiously, about to pull her thick hair over her shoulder and run her fingers through the strands, needing a minute under his stare. But she forgot she'd put her hair up for the occasion.

They were sitting in the same tent from last night, in the same field that bordered the olive grove, but this time it was transformed into a beachy theme. Seashell chandeliers hung in place of the crystal ones, clicking and clacking happily in the ocean breeze. Tall tapered white candles were lit, replacing the small glass votives from yesterday. Bleached starfish, seashells of every size, and what looked like large iridescent pearls (she wouldn't be surprised if they were real), were strewn amongst them, all at the center of the round tables, dressed in pretty lace crocheted table cloths, versus the long communal table from the day before. It was romantic and ethereal, and perfectly designed to look both effortless and luxurious.

Penelope and Brutus were dancing their first dance. The floor was covered in sand from the beach purposefully, and most everyone had removed their fancy footwear.

The bride wore a simple white silk chemise dress with spaghetti straps that had the most beautiful, intricate lace embroidery along the low back line. Her long veil with the same lace embroidery along the edge floated whimsically behind her as she walked down the sandy aisle earlier on the beach. She still wore it, but it draped over her arm, away from the ground, so she and her husband could twirl around. Her strawberry blonde hair was in a simple low chignon, and she'd kept her makeup natural and dewy. She looked like a heavenly, barefoot nymph. The groom wore a finally tailored light grey suit, no tie, but a pretty pink handkerchief square, and a wispy bunch of baby's breath, the same flowers his bride had carried as a romantically overflowing bushel with pretty grass stalks. His pants were rolled up at the ankles as he was shoeless now, as well.

Attire was beach formal, so Kareena packed a two-piece Indian *lehenga* to wear for the occasion. It was pretty cornflower blue with a long skirt in layers of breezy chiffon, with a slit on one side that hit her mid-thigh. The wide waistband made her waist look smaller, and it had pretty white flowers embroidered around it. The top was of the same material and a halter style, with the same delicate white embroidered flowers along the neckline and shoulders. It reminded her so much of the Roman Greco designs she'd seen on antique pottery that she'd thought it was perfect to wear for the occasion. She'd left the scarf piece in her room. She put her hair up in a loose twist, with tendrils framing her face, and kept her jewelry simple with diamond teardrop earrings, a matching diamond solitaire necklace, and gold bangles. She'd paired the outfit with strappy, shimmery cream sandals, but as the ceremony was on the beach, and with the sandy ground underneath the cool canopy, she, like everyone else, was shoeless.

The cheers and whistles as Brutus dipped Penelope gracefully had Kareena blinking rapidly, as she realized she'd been staring into Zayn's eyes, entranced.

"Now who's not watching the joyful couple?" Zayn asked. He winked, and she leaned over and kissed him. How could she not? This man—he was making her happier than she'd ever dreamed of being, every second she spent time with him.

He wanted to pursue their relationship in New York, and she'd been floored when he announced that last night, while enjoying their bath. She'd wholeheartedly agreed because that's what her heart was telling her, too. There was no way she could end whatever this was when she left Greece. They'd become more than just friends, and they were even more connected than before.

"I want to show you something later," he said mysteriously.

"Oh my God, are you going to try swimming lessons with me again?" she asked teasingly, cupping his bearded face tenderly.

He chuckled. "I'm never going to give up on that with you." He leaned forward so he could wrap his arms around her.

The fact that he cared about her safety, even though she still vowed never to immerse her entire body in water (unless it was that giant tub in their suite), made her heart flutter even more madly for him. He looked so adorably hunky with his thick lips curved into a grin; it was all she could do to keep herself from hopping into his lap and ordering him to take her somewhere and have his way with her.

"It's the taverna," he said.

She smacked a hand to her forehead. She'd completely forgotten about the one main reason they'd started this ruse in the first place. With so much going on, she hadn't even seen it, and was more than curious about the place Zayn hungered to have as rightfully his own.

"That's right. Yes, please. I want to see it, and I can't wait."

He leaned in and kissed her, his thick lips soft on hers.

The applause from around them made them break away. The newlyweds finished their first dance and encouraged everyone onto the dance floor with them. He stood up and pulled her to her feet, to the dance floor, where others had already congregated. An upbeat song came on, and he held one of her hands and began to shake his body, urging her to move, too.

She laughed as he twirled her around and brought her close to him, then pushed her back, still holding onto her, her skirt swishing around both of them. She felt alive in that moment, and he shared the same look of fervor.

When the song ended, the DJ announced that the next song was for the old timers. But it wasn't an old song that blasted through the well-hidden speakers. The familiar beats of Justin Timberlake's "SexyBack" filled the tent, and Kareena and Zayn looked at each other with mouths open, horrified. Then they doubled over in fits of laughter.

"*This* is *old*!?" she asked. But Zayn started dancing again, gyrating his hips in his light tan suit pants and white button-down shirt, having already tossed his jacket aside earlier before they got up to dance.

"I know. We're practically geriatric," he commented sexily in that deep voice of his as he gyrated low, close to her, holding her hips. His face was level to hers, and he looked into her eyes as he held her tight, now lifting his shoulders in tandem. "Do you remember senior year, the class trip? This song was everywhere. You danced to this song at the Beanery in LA, when we snuck out. I couldn't take my eyes off you."

"I remember," she said, remembering that he'd been watching her dancing with her friends, his eyes hooded and heated, as they were now. "What a night," she said wistfully.

"You had fun though," he arrogantly said, wiggling his brows comically.

She nodded, giggling. "My first, and only fake ID. And I can't believe we never got caught."

He wiggled his brows again. He'd been the one to get them all their fake IDs on their senior class trip. He knew a guy because ... of course he did. Zayn was the new cool kid who'd lived a globe-trotting life full of excitement and experiences that the other teenagers could only dream of.

She couldn't resist saying, "You were so hot, back then, Zayn. But now, you're even hotter, you're practically *sinful*."

He rose to his full height and pulled her body flush against his. His hands roamed down to the small of her back, and he had them both gyrating now, her flesh pressed against his solid form.

"You're pretty sinful yourself, Karma." He leaned down and kissed her dizzyingly, before moving to her ear and sucking her lobe into his warm mouth.

She tried not to lose what she had in mind while he did sinful things to her on the dance floor. She couldn't *not* tease him now that she knew about his alter ego.

When he continued nuzzling her ear, she tried another tactic.

"Do you think you'll ever make those scallops for me again? I'd love to watch you make them. I love watching you cook. It's so—so, sexy in the kitchen."

"You liked that, did you?" he asked, his tongue gliding along the curve of her ear, making her shudder.

"Yes," she said, a little breathless, trying not to lose it in front of his family. "But what I'd really want to do is watch you cook shirtless, while you toss around that big knife of yours. You wouldn't have to say a damn thing, but I think I would lose it, just watching you act so ... sinful in the kitchen."

There. There was no way he wouldn't know what she was talking about.

He stopped dancing and held her close. She couldn't see his face, but she felt him release a hot breath and heard him curse low.

"First of all, Karma, there will be no tossing around of any chef's knives."

She pulled back from him and stared up at his face. It was quite serious when he followed up with, "I try to follow all safety protocols no matter where I'm food prepping and cooking. It's so easy to injure yourself badly if you don't pay attention." He rolled his eyes and shook his head, a look of annoyance on his face. He lifted a hand to show her the large scar on his index finger. "*This* happened when my mind was ... elsewhere and not focusing on the task at hand."

She inspected it and placed a kiss on it as he continued, "And it's important to follow safety protocols, no matter what I'm wearing or not wearing."

She couldn't help it; she burst into giggles as she clutched his hand.

"Safety is funny to you?" he asked a little dangerously.

"No. Of course not." The thrill that shot up her spine should not be so enjoyable.

"How did you find out?" He finally asked, continuing to dance again. A slower song came on, the languid bass floating above them. They glided across the sand-covered floor.

"I know this person who won't let things drop. She's like a modern-day Enola Holmes."

"I don't know who that is, but I can only assume she's a

relation to Sherlock Holmes. I'm guessing you're talking about your sister."

Kareena nodded, grinning. He knew she and Reyana were close.

He shook his head. "Someone was bound to uncover my secret."

"I love that you have this alter ego, Zayn," she continued enthusiastically. "It's good for you to let all parts of yourself shine. And it's also a positive outlet for any source of stress or anxiety in your life."

"Thank you, Dr. Sharma. What do I owe you in return for this short, possibly unnecessary therapy session?"

She held his stare, her heart thumping wildly in her breast. She wanted to see his reaction when she said breathlessly, "You have to cook as *Sinful in the Kitchen*, but your only audience is me."

CHAPTER 28

२ ৮

*T*he entire rest of the wedding was a blur for Zayn. Kareena seemed as serene as ever, enjoying the rest of the evening, even after she'd told him she knew he was *Sinful in the Kitchen*, and that she wanted him to cook for just her as his alter ego. She'd leaned up and whispered in his ear that maybe she could be naked too, and he could use his big knife on her.

Now, he wasn't opposed to sex play in the kitchen, but big chef knife play? His dick should not have hardened so quickly in his pants at the thought of her naked under his knife. But it did. And it stayed that way, only deflating to a semi-hard the rest of the night.

He barely tasted the beautiful, delicate lemon curd of the five-tiered wedding cake, taking bite after bite from Kareena's huge slice as she kept feeding him and extolling the virtues of lemon in desserts. He didn't pay attention to the final toasts. He gave one, but who the hell knew if he'd said what he'd planned to about young love and growing old together. He only watched as Kareena enthusiastically threw down and smashed plates towards the end of the night, her hair starting to come out of loosened pins, her face dewy, and her eyes bright. He wanted her like he'd never wanted anyone before, and he wanted to do to her *everything* she wanted him to, masked as his dangerous and salacious persona.

When she linked hands with other guests to excitedly perform the traditional Greek *Syrtos* dance of celebration, he pulled her away and dragged her all the way back to the villa. The entire time, he said nothing, while she protested, asking him what was happening; that she'd left her shoes, and that she wouldn't get to wave off the happy couple.

He swooped his arms under her and threw her over his shoulder to protect her feet from the gravelly path to the villa. While she squealed and now protested his carrying her, he told her she'd have plenty of time to say goodbye to the happy couple, as they weren't leaving for their honeymoon for a few more days.

When he got them to the villa, he switched the lights on in the kitchen, just the ones that were over the prep counter in the middle of the room. He sat her down on the wooden counter and told her not to move a muscle.

"But—"

He put a finger to her lips and said harshly, "Shush. I'll be right back."

He didn't mean to sound so severe, even dangerous, but what she'd requested was the only thing on his mind now, and he chased the high of wanting to perform for her all night.

Her eyes became enormous, and she shut her mouth, nodding. He gave her a stern look before hurrying to the stairs on the other side of the room and up to the large bedroom. He'd hidden his executioner's mask in the back of the closet. He pulled it out, running his hands over the leather and stiff black material.

He threw it on the bed, and shucked off his clothes, leaving just his boxer briefs on. Then he donned the mask.

He came down the stairs slowly, taking his time, not wanting to startle her, but he knew that was the game they were now playing. He entered the kitchen, and fortunately for him, she hadn't moved a muscle, with her back facing him.

He walked stealthily to the counter and was now a few feet behind her when he pulled his knife drawer open, alerting her to his presence.

She jumped and turned around, her face filled with apprehension, her eyes enormous, seeing him wearing the mask and completely naked except for his boxer briefs. But then she relaxed with a sexy smile, and her hooded eyes beckoned him.

Her skin gleamed under the lights, her shoulders rounded and smooth. That would be his first move, he decided, as he came around to face her with his trusty chef's knife. It glinted dangerously under the pendant lights.

He tossed its weight back and forth between his hands as he took her in. She licked her lips and ran her hand up his arm, the one with his lightening tattoo.

"If this gets too scary, Karma, what safe word do you want to use to get me to stop?"

Her hand stopped, and she frowned. "I won't get scared," she said confidently.

"You never know. I thought I wouldn't need a safe word when I went through a short-lived BDSM phase, but I did."

Her frown turned upward in surprise. "You had a BDSM phase?"

What had he unleashed in this woman? Her eyes shone with excitement. "One kink at a time, Sweetheart."

She nodded quickly, gulping audibly. "How about…" she looked around the room, and her eyes landed on the bowl of figs on the dining table. "Fig."

He nodded, then said, "Take your top off."

She quickly reached for the hidden side zipper of her top, pulling it down. She grasped the hem of the filmy material and tugged it over her head and off. The movement pulled the loose pins from her hair, and they fell onto the counter in soft "pings," as her hair fell in waves around her shoulders.

She wore a strapless bra, and before she could make a move to remove that, he stepped between her legs, forcing her to widen them, bunching her skirt up around her thighs and waist. He smelled her muskiness, the sweet herbal notes dampened by sweat from being outside in the heat all day. It only made his dick harder. He gripped his knife firmly in his hand, and ran the dulled side of the blade, barely skimming her sheened skin along her collar bones.

Her breath hitched. He did it again, but this time going in the opposite direction, and she arched her back, pressing her skin into the metal. A small prick of blood emerged.

"Careful," he whispered, as he leaned down to lick off the deep red liquid beading at her neck. The metallic taste coated his tongue, and he swiped over that spot again for good measure, even as the bleeding stopped.

"Zayn," she said softly, pushing him away slightly so she could unclasp her bra and toss it aside.

Her breasts hung heavily. Her perfect small brown nipples were peaked in her heightened state, the small goosebumps standing up around each one.

"So beautiful," he murmured, the knife flashing as he poised it over the curves of her breasts, pausing a moment to gauge her reaction. Her eyes were hooded, glassy, and her breathing quickened. He rested his knife, blade side up, onto the soft top mounds and barely skimmed her skin with the dull side of the blade.

She gasped because, though it hadn't cut flesh, it was still cool, sharp metal against her velvety, warm skin. He felt the blood rushing inside him, his cock straining against his underwear.

Fuck, he was so turned on by this—by her reactions. She leaned back on her hands, the pink of her tongue licking her pouty lips, jutting her breasts toward him, her eyes on his knife.

He used the pointed edge to lightly glide down a breast and circle the nipple, flicking the hardened bud gently and removing it quickly.

She moaned, her eyes closed, now, her breathy exhales loud in the silence.

He lifted the knife and did the exact movement to her other breast, and her hips bucked off the counter in reaction.

Wordlessly, he skimmed the point to her sternum and down slowly, very carefully, to the waistband of her skirt.

He stepped back and ordered her to take her skirt off.

She opened her lids and looked at him, her dark eyes dragging down his bare chest to his abdomen, to his cock, where his precum soaked through his underwear. She licked her lips again, staring at him straining against his underwear.

He smacked the flattened side of his knifed on the counter beside her, startling her.

"Pay attention, Sweetheart. Remove. Your. Skirt."

She nodded and went to the hidden hook and zipper at the

side and undid them. She shimmied her hips, pushing the frothy material down her thighs and over her knees, where, bunched up already, it fell to the floor.

Now she was in flirty little sheer baby blue-boy-short style underwear. He saw the dampness soaking the inside of her legs and the slip of barely-there material at the apex of her thighs. He growled in appreciation.

"Do you love this underwear?" he asked suddenly, his eyes darting all over her nakedness, his voice gravelly and deep. With the ominous black hood over his face and neck, it should scare her, but she only shivered in pleasure, arching her back.

She didn't know what he had in mind, but she said, "Not particularly." She sounded breathless as she anticipated what he'd do next.

He used his free hand to grasp behind one of her calves and pull her forward. Then he did the same thing with her other leg. Now she was sitting with part of her butt hanging off the counter.

The knife was enormous and glinted sharply as he stepped closer and kicked her skirt aside.

He ordered her to lie back, and she did, the wood smooth on her back. He stepped in closer between her thighs so she didn't fall off the counter.

She both felt and heard him breathing harshly as he concentrated on slipping the knife underneath one leg opening carefully. From her position, she saw his wrist flex, and she heard the fine material rip all the way up to the waistband.

He did it to the other side, and then his free hand spread her cut underwear below her.

"Just like flaying the finest of meat," he whispered proudly, and Kareena wondered how sure he was using that knife on her. He seemed like he was very sure of himself, but she wanted to encourage him anyway.

"I knew you could, Chef," she said as sensually as possible. Glancing down at him.

"Hm, I like that," he said darkly, looking over her exposed skin.

She wasn't sure what he was referring to. Did he like that she called him 'chef,' or that she was completely naked and open for him?

"Yes, Chef," she said again, her chest heaving heavily. She felt liquid burst from her between her legs, and she clenched his thighs between hers.

"Relax, Sweetheart," he said, pushing his free hand between himself and her pussy, caressing her wetness. "Mm-hm. Perfectly wet and warm." He brought his fingers to his mouth and sucked on them. "Yummy umami," he said dangerously, his eyes burning brightly behind his mask.

She wanted to feel mortified that he still remembered that silly term she'd blurted out so long ago, but it didn't sound silly coming from him. It sounded dirty and sexy.

He hooked one of her legs behind him and stepped back again, giving him space to work with his chef's knife. He kept a hand on her thigh, anchoring her there. Kareena's blood churned loudly in her ears as he used the same point, dull side down, that he'd used to flick her nipples. He placed it on her belly under her belly button.

He looked up at her. "Shall I continue?"

She nodded, her pulse beating thickly in her veins, her chest rising and falling fast with anticipation.

"Yes, Chef," she said breathlessly.

He lightly dragged the point down her belly flesh, through her pubic hair, where the tip caught gently on the thick lip of flesh that hid her clit. She sighed shakily, knowing she was completely at his whim. More liquid oozed out of her.

"God, Baby. You're so fucking wet." The sharp point disappeared from her flesh, but he carefully maneuvered the knife so that the dull side of the blade scraped at her inner thighs, the metal sweeping lightly against delicate skin. He lifted it, staring at it with intensity, then showed her. The knife gleamed shiny with her wetness.

She groaned, letting her head fall back, and her hips bucked up of their own volition. He was being so careful with the knife, and it was turning her on more.

"Be still," he barked. And she forced her hips to settle, keeping still.

He pushed her other leg wider so he had access to her completely. And she felt it—the point of his knife circling the opening of her pussy, lightly, barely touching her. She dared not move, but the riskiness, the danger of it, made her shudder.

"Be still, Sweetheart," he whispered lovingly. "I don't want to nick this most precious flesh."

She nodded and waited. The knife kept feathering her delicate flesh, the experience more erotic than anything she'd ever done. She moaned deeply, her core clenching, needing something there to satiate her, fill her up.

"*Please*, Chef."

His movements stopped. "Please, Chef, what?" he demanded.

"I need you inside me. I need..." Her words died on her lips as she heard the clatter of his knife beside her on the counter.

He grunted, going down on his knees as he pulled her even further off the counter until her wetness was flushed against his hot mouth, having pulled the bottom of his mask up.

And oh lord, if she thought the knife play was titillating, she was in an absolute other realm of erotic pleasure experiencing his mouth on her for the first time since they'd been teenagers.

He licked and sucked; sucked and licked, his fingers spreading her, pushing her flesh up so he could access her clit. The tip of his hot tongue circled it over and over again, until he sucked on the small bud, alternating between licking and sucking there, too.

"Chef!" She whined, her hips undulating crazily.

He didn't stop. Instead, he anchored her hips down onto the counter with his forearm to still some of her writhing. The sound of his licking, of his wet mouth on her wet pussy sounded obscenely erotic to her ears.

When his hot tongue entered her, she screamed his name. His thumb had now found her clit, and he circled it while his tongue focused on fucking her, his face buried against her heat, his beard chafing her delicate flesh.

The pressure began to build. It increased so fast that when she came, she wasn't ready, and her legs would have tightened around his neck if he hadn't expertly shifted his hands quickly, holding her thighs wide open.

Wave after wave of pleasure hit her and coursed through her, and he pulled his face away from her, standing up, as her body arched off the counter. Her moans of ecstasy sounded like those of a crazy person.

"Fuck, you're the most gorgeous woman in the world," he

grunted, just as she felt his thick length slide into her, widening her, stretching her. She groaned in pleasure as his length went in deeper, further, reaching where his tongue couldn't (no offense to his tongue; it was exquisite). When he'd slid all the way in, he didn't wait to move; he pulled out and thrust back in with force, a grunt from the back of his throat punctuating every move.

"Yes," she whined. "Harder. Faster."

"My needy woman. After everything, she only needs this cock."

"Yes," she moaned, every nerve ending sparking inside her, and her muscles clenching him in tempo to his thrusts, as her hips met his.

"Damn," he grunted, sliding an arm under her back and lifting her so that they were chest to breast. He groaned into her as she squealed, experiencing shock waves inside her from the new position. He was so much deeper and higher up than he'd ever been.

"Yes, Baby," she panted, rocking her hips against his, as he ground up and into her. Her arms wrapped around his neck, feeling the slickness of sweat there. He'd removed the mask, and he looked for her lips, capturing them in a long, heady kiss that took what little breath she had. He released her mouth, and when she sucked in air, everything shattered inside her, lightning licking at her, heat surrounding her—them, as she shuddered over and over again, holding him tight. She heard a high-pitched scream, and she realized it was coming from her, as his hands gripped her ass now, squeezing her cheeks as he bore into her even harder and faster.

"Just ... a ... little ... longer," he said through clenched teeth, his face contorted, his eyes squeezed shut. "Fuck. I'm there!" He shouted, his body stiffening, his cum shooting inside her and seeping warmly, stickily out of her, coating her inner thighs that were pressed against him.

"Ye Gods, Kareena. If we died now, I'd be the happiest fucking man on the planet."

CHAPTER 29

২৯

*K*areena rolled onto her side and met a solid, warm wall. She smiled, her eyes still closed as she walked her fingers along the firm, muscular arm attached to it.

When her eyelids fluttered open, she found Zayn on his back, one arm folded behind his head, the other she realized was wrapped around her. He was watching her with a concentration that took her breath away.

They were naked, with the white sheets tangled around them. They'd spent the night in the cozy villa after he'd had his way with her in the kitchen, using his chef's knife and wearing his ominous black hooded mask, giving her the dangerous side of him she so craved.

Her body felt completely used, maybe a little abused, but it was of her own urging. She loved it. She stretched her arms overhead and let out a pleasant moan, looking forward to the day.

"Kareena, last night—" He sounded tense.

She rolled over on top of him and covered his mouth with

her hand. "Shush. It was…" She shook her head, looking for the right words. "Perfection. I wanted it."

He smiled under her hand, his beard softly scratching her palm. "I don't usually bust out knife play with my sexual partners."

"You don't?" she asked, taken aback. The way he'd used that knife, slowly and carefully running the blade down her flesh, without nary a nick, except for that one on her neck, had been more than titillating. It felt like he'd done it before.

"Never. I've thought about it. But I worry I'll be too rough and injure my partner."

"You didn't hurt me," she reminded him.

"I know. It was … I don't know. It was such a turn on to see you like that, under my knife, but I knew I wouldn't hurt you. And Jesus, Kareena, seeing you come like that …" He let out a low whistle. "The way you put all your trust in me —" He broke off. "You don't know how much that means to me."

She felt him harden beneath her, and she smiled impishly at him, taking in his handsome face, his mussed auburn curls. The way the sunlight bounced off the white stucco walls and illuminated him made him look like the Greek God he was to her.

He slowly rolled her onto her back, laying his big body between her thighs. "Kareena, I'm falling in love with you all over again."

Her breath hitched at the use of the big L-word. Her mind dove in five hundred different directions, and before she could even curb her thoughts to find a response, he leaned down and kissed her with some much tenderness that tears sprang to her eyes.

She knew without a doubt that she was falling in love with him again, too.

This time, in the bright early morning light, amidst the tangle of sheets, he made love to her, slowly and sweetly. He moved inside her at an unhurried pace, his gaze on hers, their eyes locked as he took his time to build her pleasure. As soon as she felt like she'd climbed the highest peak to the very top and was about to fall into bliss, he picked up his pace, dropping with her, moaning into her neck, kissing her, and nipping at her.

She held him tightly to her; her arms wrapped around his wide shoulders as they came back down to earth.

"I'm falling in love with you, too, Zayn," she whispered truthfully against his damp hair, into his ear.

He sighed in content and rolled off her, taking her with him.

Later, he called the main house and asked that their things be packed up and dropped off at the villa. They'd both decided to stay there for the last few days in Greece.

Their things were delivered to them while they ate a light breakfast of yogurt, fruit, and coffee. Afterwards, they showered and dressed for the day, and he excitedly led her down the craggy staircase path, stopping at different points along the way to share kisses and whisper what their possible future could be like until they reached the beach at the bottom.

"Oh my God, Zayn!" she exclaimed, taking in the scene before her with the turquoise waters meeting the powder blue sky. Mountains dotted the horizon, and for once, she wasn't freaked out to be so close to a big body of water. "This is breathtaking! I can't believe I haven't seen this yet."

"I know. But once you said yes to being a part of Penelope's bridal party plans, you were cooked. I knew there was no way to wheedle in time to show you it all properly." He shrugged, nonchalantly, so handsome in his lightweight linen button-down, his hands stuffed into his khaki shorts, knowing that Penelope came first; this was her week.

She nodded, and he took her hand, leaving the waves gently rolling onto the white sandy shore behind them.

They went to the wooden stairs that led to the wide outdoor deck. The iron tables and chairs needed some love, he explained, and the umbrellas needed replacing, and he envisioned installing tall space heaters in the chillier months to continue keeping people coming.

"And they will," she said, looking out to the sea and turning around to look up at the cliffs the taverna was built into. "This place is a treasure. A complete paradise. I can't imagine anyone not wanting to come here."

Zayn pulled her to him. "Thank you."

Against his chest, she asked, "For what?"

"For always having my back. For supporting me in my dreams."

She leaned away from him to stare up into his eyes, the ones that danced and lit up with so much emotion.

"I'm only stating the obvious," she said solemnly. "You're so talented, Z. It doesn't matter what you do or where you do it. It's going to be a success no matter what."

He snorted. "Tell that to the chef I trained under in Amsterdam. That tyrant told me I was worthless every day, and that my food belonged in the garbage. Luckily, I had Lauren there, too. We kept each other going."

She stilled, remembering that Chef Lauren Bates and Zayn had an integrated past while they made it through their culinary education.

Now, why did her breast sizzle with jealousy? Zayn had just admitted he was falling in love with *her*, not Lauren Bates.

She couldn't look at him, only finger his collar and gold chain when she asked as neutrally as possible, "Are you and Lauren close?"

He exhaled, his chest moving with it. "Yeah. We were there for each other, and have been working together on and off since."

"Do you think I could meet her sometime?"

He didn't say anything, as he stilled, until she felt it. The rumble in his abs, the shaking of his solid chest before he laughed—a large belly laugh that echoed along the cliffs.

"You're joking, Karma, right?"

She looked up at his face. He wiped tears from the corners of his eyes.

"I don't understand—"

"Baby, Lauren is a man."

Confused, she uttered, "But I thought—wait, isn't Lauren a female name?"

He shook his head and chuckled. "I guess in some societies. But Lauren is a dude, I promise. If he's not, well, I have no idea what the hell his long-ass string of girlfriends thought when they were in bed with him."

Well, now the silence that followed only added to her feeling of idiocy.

"Were you jealous, Sweetheart?" he asked gently, pulling her close, stroking her back.

"Well, I—" Honesty was the best course here, she decided. "Maybe a little."

"I can't lie and say I don't like it if you're jealous. It feels pretty damn great." He squeezed her to him. "But you have nothing to worry about, especially when it comes to Lauren."

She nodded, her cheeks hot in embarrassment.

"Now, can I tell him? Because he'd find this shit funny as hell."

"Hey!" She smacked his solid chest. "I was being vulnerable here. The least you could do is be a little humbled by it."

He grabbed her hand and clutched it to his chest. "I'm sorry, Karma. I'll do better next time. But please, just let me have this one." He snorted deeply again and chuckled.

She rolled her eyes and sighed. "Fine."

When they went inside, he pointed out changes he wanted to make, what would stay, and his vision for a more modern interior, with nature brought inside.

"There's the old bar." He pointed toward the back of the restaurant, where she saw the long dark wood that did indeed look old and very heavy. "I'm having an inspection soon, to see what is hazardous and what's not. Spoiler, I think I'm going to have to gut out a lot of this." He looked around.

"It'll be okay, Zayn. It'll all work out and be better than before."

He nodded and led her into the kitchen through the large swinging door next to the bar area.

"*OH.* NOW I UNDERSTAND." She contemplated the old, cavernous kitchen that literally was from another time.

Dust moats floated down around her, lit up by the sliver of sunlight that crept in through the small windows near the ceiling. She looked too immaculate in this dingy old place, in her white sundress with big, pretty purple irises all over in a watercolor effect. Her hair was in a high ponytail and gleamed blueish black, even in the dim light. The ring on her finger, his family's ring, caught his eye, and he couldn't stop staring at this woman. It was like that time he'd first met her, when his volleyball had hit her in the leg. She'd been sitting on the sand reading, in a similar white dress. He'd been so distracted by her that it was he who'd missed the shot aimed for him.

"What's that, Karma?" he asked, realizing she was giving him a thoughtful stare.

"This is the location of your last Sinful video! Here," She moved to the old wooden prep table in the middle of the room. "This is where you had one of those mobile burners, and you fried up the calamari. And you had your cutting board here and cut up the melon and wrapped them in that thin prosciutto."

He chuckled. "You got me. I couldn't keep my fans waiting. My social media manager would have had my head on a platter. No rest for the weary, and all that shit. I'm not a fan of social media. You have to always be on." He ran his fingers through his hair. "Don't get me wrong, it's been a great money-maker and great branding partnerships, despite the eroticism of it, but it can get to be a lot."

"What are you going to do when you open this place? Will you still be *Sinful in the Kitchen*? Or will he retire?"

He mulled this over. "I'm actually not sure."

She nodded. "You've got time to figure it out. Now tell me about the menu you've planned." She looked as excited as he felt. He enthusiastically launched into the Indo-Greek fusion cuisine he was putting together. He'd need to have everything taste-tested, but he was confident with his flavor pairings.

"It sounds like you have it all figured out. This is going to happen, Z." She nodded eagerly and clapped her hands together.

"The name is the only thing I'm unsure of."

"What do you have in mind?"

"Nada. I can't come up with something that feels meaningful."

"Hmm. Let me think on it."

She asked him what exactly he was trying to evoke with the name.

"The mutual relationship of Indians and Greeks since ancient times. I want people to know that people like me have been around forever. That the blending of two cultures can create something beautiful."

"That's poetic," she said admiringly.

It was later, when they'd left the taverna, after they'd taken the moped he'd left parked in the parking lot a few days ago—with Kareena clutching him as they zipped down the winding road to town, her whoops of excitement in his ear—after they'd parked at the market to get supplies for dinner, that she snapped her fingers and said she had it. She pulled out her phone from her little backpack and looked something up.

"Indoi-Yavanas," she said. "Or, Yavanas-Indoi, whichever combination you prefer. But I think the first one has a nice ring to it."

"What are we talking about?" he asked, in the middle of choosing seafood for the pasta he wanted to make. They were standing in front of Liannis' seafood booth, the older man bagging up fresh clams, listening to them curiously.

"So I remember in my college Western Civ class that we learned about a relationship between ancient Indians and ancient

Greeks. They influenced each other's cultures, even back then. It's exactly what you're looking for, Zayn."

She looked down at her phone and continued. "The Greeks back then called the Indians 'Indoi,' and the Vedic Aryans—I could go down a rabbit hole with research on that, but I won't for your sake—" she said blandly, quite aware she nerded out on ancient history. "Anyway, they called the ancient Greeks 'Yavanas.'"

She looked up at him with a shine to her eyes, and a hundred-watt smile that was contagious.

"Bah." The cranky one-eyed fishmonger said, pointing at the fresh enormous shrimp. "You want?" he asked him.

"Wait, why 'Bah?'" Kareena asked, tilting her head.

Liannis, who was normally never questioned for his opinion, widened his one good eye, the one that wasn't hidden behind his old brown leather eye-patch that had seen better days. His cheeks reddened as he said, "Only Greek food here, Missy."

"But why, Mr. Liannis?" she asked.

Zayn had to hide his smile. She called him that because Liannis was his surname. No one actually knew what his first name was. And Kareena preferred to address him like this as a sign of respect. She'd done it the first day she'd met him, almost a week ago.

Liannis didn't seem to mind, either. At first, he was taken aback, thinking that perhaps the young woman was making fun of him. But her sincerity won him over. Zayn had a feeling Liannis thought Kareena was too good for him. She probably was, but Zayn would never tell her that.

"Missy, only real Greeks live here. No new flavors necessary. Keep things the way they've been for centuries."

"But Mr. Liannis, what purpose does that serve? Obviously,

some people don't identify as fully Greek *do* live here." She gestured toward Zayn. "And what about me?"

"You?" Liannis raised one brow.

"Yes." She took the bag of fresh-caught shrimp and handed it to him. "What if I moved here to live?" She didn't look at Zayn when she said this, and he noticed her cheeks flushing prettily. "I'd miss my culture's food. And sure, I could go back to Athens and find a fabulous Indian restaurant, but why not try something new with similar flavors to what I'm used to? The same could go for the native Naxians. And don't forget about tourists. They would only come to Naxos more during tourist season and spend more money at the local shops." She looked over at the seafood sitting on ice. And then at the little hotplate he used to cook up some of the food for people needing a quick snack. "You might need much larger catches of the day to feed more people coming to the island." She shrugged. "I don't know. Call me crazy, but I think it could all be a great thing for everyone involved."

Liannis harrumphed but said nothing more. His one eye blinked rapidly at Kareena as she smiled and paid.

They walked silently back to the moped, hand in hand. When she swung onto the back with him, she whispered in his ear, "I think I broke the one-eyed fishmonger."

He shouted out a laugh. "I think you did, too. I've never seen him at a loss for words when he's passionate about something. And let me tell you, he *hates* my restaurant idea." He shook his head, still thinking about the way Kareena had gone on. "That was a pretty little speech. Where did it come from?"

She leaned her body into his back and sighed. "I don't know. It just appeared out of thin air. But I suppose it's how I feel every day in the US, too. I've found my people, those who are Indian, and we have the same or similar cultures. But sometimes you still feel different. No one can truly have the same experience that you have. And ... it's nice to have something that relates to your specific experiences, what you grew up with. And maybe others can learn to experience and appreciate them, too. I don't know. My sister's podcast delves into this. It's been on my mind a lot."

He nodded, making a mental note to ask her more about that later. He was curious about it, and it sounded like she really found it fascinating, too.

CHAPTER 30

৩০

*I*t had been a perfect day. Before leaving town completely, they stopped for some local favorites— crispy, light *spanakopita*, with a melt-in-your-mouth spinach and feta filling, while also splitting a *gyro* sandwich stuffed with juicy lamb and crispy French fries.

"So, tell me about the end of the claims period," Kareena requested before taking a bite of the sandwich and making small noises of delight as she chewed, closing her eyes.

Zayn couldn't concentrate on anything else. Yes, food was his life, so it made sense that watching someone enjoy what they ate would give him immense joy. But watching Kareena was a whole different level of pleasure. Nothing was better than seeing a sexy woman (his woman) eat her food with gusto. After she swallowed, she opened her half of the sandwich and dumped more *tzatziki* sauce inside, completely covering the fries and meat.

"This sauce is insane. I've had it before, obviously, but when it's fresh like this, holy yummy umami." Her brows danced, and she took another bite, and the sauce oozed out, leaving a white smear at the corner of her mouth. She flicked her tongue to get it, but some remained.

He leaned in and wiped it off with his thumb before putting it in his mouth and sucking off the garlicky cucumber yogurt sauce.

"So?" she asked, after swallowing and sipping water.

"So?" He'd already forgotten what they were talking about.

She chuckled. "The claims period. What's going on with it? Your mom mentioned it was ending sooner than expected." She sipped her water again. "Does that mean we won't get to kiss as a fake engaged couple on New Year's Eve?" She pouted.

"Maybe not as a fake engaged couple, but there will definitely be kissing," he said, wriggling his brows. "My mother is correct. The claim's period is much shorter than we expected. I spoke briefly to one of the attorneys at the wedding. Old *Pappous* left things neatly squared away, all bequests accounted for and not a thing out of place, just as everyone predicted. It looks like the earliest we can end our charade is shortly after you get back to New York … right before Thanksgiving."

Her expression was thoughtful. "And Silas hasn't bothered you about our engagement?" She twisted his family's ring on her finger. "Your inheritance is yours?"

"He hasn't bothered me. He's barely spoken to me since our 'engagement party.'" He air-quoted. With the fanfare he'd displayed putting the family ring on Kareena's finger, Silas absolutely didn't have a thing to say to them now. Though Zayn wouldn't be surprised if the ill-tempered cousin still spouted foul words about how undeserving he was of *any* Stavros property.

SHE REACHED OVER and grabbed his hand. "That's great news, Zayn." She shook her head in amazement, her heart bursting with joy for this man. "You did it. You're going to get your restaurant!"

He squeezed her hand. "*We* did it, Karma. Thank you for helping me with this. After you leave for New York, I'll meet with the attorneys in person to confirm the timeline. Silas will have to be there too, and I can't wait to see the look on his face."

She nodded. "So, when I get back to New York, I'll need to explain 'us' to Tamannah. But, I'd love it if you were there with me to do that."

Zayn agreed. He said he probably wouldn't be able to get back until a week after her, which was fine, since she had her own loose ends to tie up with her parents. Her guilt about not talking to them was mounting more as her time in Greece was waning. She wasn't quite sure how to handle all of this with them.

Zayn ran his thumb back and forth over her hand, his expression thoughtful. "Can I tell you something?"

Her pulse quickened at his tone—the hesitancy, the hushed quality. Was he going to change his mind about them?

Why did her mind always jump to the worst?

She dashed that thought away. But nodded and waited for him to tell her what was bothering him.

"I think Tamannah already knows we're more than just friends."

That was not at all what she was expecting.

Relieved, she began to laugh, but at his serious expression, she asked, "Why?"

"She's smart, I get that. I saw that the moment I met her during Halloween. She reminds me a little bit of well … me." He scratched his bearded chin. "I'm not saying I'm smart—"

"Stop it."

"I mean: smart like that. She's brilliant. I don't know why I should be surprised; she's your daughter. But she definitely notices things that others might not notice. I remember being like that, before life got in the way."

Kareena considered this. "Tell me exactly what she did or said to make you think that."

He grunted. "As soon as you left for your work meeting, she accused me of staring at you too much."

She didn't know whether to laugh or to be annoyed with herself, thinking that they could pull the wool over Tamannah's eyes. It was like the girl had X-ray vision.

Zayn went on. "She said, and I quote, 'Stop looking at my Mommy like that.' I had to ask her to explain, and she said, "Like she's the prettiest lady in the world and you want to kiss her."

Kareena sat back in her chair, dumbfounded. "That kid…" she mumbled, before she burst into laughter. Zayn began to chuckle, too.

"Well—okay! Then telling her about us might be easier than I thought," Kareena said, still giggling. But she stopped as a thought occurred to her, something her father had said way back when she'd first told them she was engaged to Zayn. "Are you fine with having my daughter in your life?"

"Do you think I'd *want* to be in your life if I wasn't?" He asked back immediately, his brows furrowed. She'd offended him.

"I'm sorry. I just have to be sure. Tamannah has been my world since she was born. She'll always be my first priority."

"Understood. I wouldn't expect anything less." But he remained silent after that.

She leaned forward and grabbed his hand again. "Tell me what you're thinking. Are you really okay with all of this?"

"Kareena, I promise you, I am. I can handle it. I want to, if it means being with you. I was just wondering something."

"Yes?"

"Does this mean I can try to be lovable to her, now? I'm pretty sure I've got the dog covered."

She grinned, getting up and sitting on his lap to kiss him. "I couldn't stop you even if I tried."

Soon after, they went back to the villa and put their groceries away. Zayn coaxed her to get her bathing suit on and come down to the beach with him. She'd shaken her head and said a firm no. But then he mentioned Tamannah again.

"I don't think you're playing fair, Zayn Stavros."

"But, wouldn't it be amazing if she knew you'd overcome your fears while here, Kareena?"

She huffed, "I hate you."

He pulled her into a hug. "But, do you really?" he teased.

"Yes," she said, muffled against his chest, even when her head shook 'no.'

It took a few attempts, but she got in up to her waist. Even he knew that was a major feat. He got her onto her back, and she remembered how to float, but was still nervous about it. He kept his hands under her, skimming her back so she knew he was there, while also telling her he had her. Nothing was going to happen to her.

They lay in the sand on towels, after that, drying off, watching the black swallows up in the sky. Initially, Kareena grumbled about the hateful birds, but then she quieted down and followed their movements keenly, like him.

Something had been unsettling him since they'd admitted their feelings to each other. He'd tried to kick it out of his head, but it persisted. Now, in their lazy quietude, he had to ask her because he had to know if it would be different this time around with them. It shouldn't matter; they weren't teens anymore, but with Kareena, it would always matter.

"Kareena, what about your parents? Your father?"

She pulled her gaze from the small black dots high in the sky and turned to gaze at him.

"What about them?"

"Will they ever approve of us?"

She sighed, turning her gaze back up to the sky. He stared at her profile, her rounded pink cheeks, her thick brows. Every detail was something to adore. He reached over and glided his finger over an arched brow.

"Honestly, Z, I don't know." She closed her eyes. "I have so much to catch them up on. It feels weird not having spoken to them this entire time. I do feel guilty, don't get me wrong, but I'm glad I forced it. I don't like their judgmental attitude. It's held me back in many ways—ways I wasn't even aware of. I know I need to fix this with them, but I'm not sure how." She sighed heavily. "I might give them a call tomorrow, just to check in, especially with my dad's cardiovascular issues. I haven't heard anything from my sister, but I need to hear that he's okay. I miss them. I miss their voices."

He knew he could never come between her and her parents, though he'd been treated unfairly by them in the past. He wasn't about to argue with her, but he wished she would consider waiting to speak to them until she got back to New York. He selfishly wanted her all to himself without the anxiety they caused infiltrating their happiness bubble.

"What I know right now is that I want this," she continued, sliding her hand to his and grasping it. "I want you."

"I want you, too, more than anything in the world."

He always had. But he thought he'd lost her a long time ago.

"Do you believe in destiny, Kareena?" He suddenly asked, tucking an arm behind his head as he looked up at the birds again. "I've never believed, but everything that's happened in the last few weeks has me thinking otherwise."

Her laughter ended in a snort, and she sighed. "I guess there can be some truth to it."

"Come on, Karma. Tell me that we aren't each other's karmic eventuality."

"Did you just make that up?" she teased.

"Think about it, there's no way that an outside force like destiny, or the fates as they call them here, isn't involved, especially after twenty years apart."

She didn't say anything for a while, as her fingers threaded through his.

"I think … I do believe in it, or in something that pushed us back together. All I know is that whatever it is, I'm grateful to be able to have a chance at loving you again."

He agreed. They might not know the ins and outs about how they'd make it work, but they knew this was their second chance to try.

CHAPTER 31

৩১

*I*t was the middle of the night when her phone rang. If it were Zayn, he'd put it on silent and roll over. But she was a mother, and her first concern was always her daughter. He understood that and waited for her to answer.

But it wasn't about Tamannah. It was her mother calling about her father. He'd had a massive heart attack and was rushed to the ER. Kareena, now fully up, was pacing the bedroom in just one of his old t-shirts and underwear. He watched her as she did her best to quell her mother's hysteria while tears started to run down her face.

Zayn didn't know what to do, and he sat back, letting her pace the floor as she spoke rapidly to her mother.

At some point, she'd left the room and had gone downstairs. He followed her and sat on the couch as she finished up.

When she hung up, she looked lost and defeated. Her eyes were ravaged red.

"He might die." She wasn't even looking at him when she said this. It was as if her body was here, but her mind was somewhere else. "It's all my fault. I should've never—"

Then she startled, realizing he was there.

"What can I do, Kareena?" he asked, getting up and going to her. He took her shaking hands in his, trying to warm them up. Then he pulled her into his arms, rubbing her back. Her body felt cold now, too.

"I need to go to him," she said, her face muffled against his bare shoulder. "I need to get out of here!" She pulled her hands away from him and hurried upstairs.

He followed and found her pulling drawers open, throwing things in a pile on the bed. He watched her from the doorframe as she pulled her suitcase from the walk-in closet and opened it, dumping whatever was piled on the bed into it.

"Hold on, Kareena. Let me see if I can get you a flight. The family jet—"

"No. I'll fly commercial. It's fine."

He found the soonest flight out of Athens. A red eye that would get her back into New York and then Connecticut by the next day, late in the evening.

"Okay. You're all set. I'm sending you the itinerary."

"Thank you," she said quietly, looking around the room at everything but him. "I'll pay you back, I promise."

He came to her again and pulled her in for a hug. "You never have to pay me back. I want to do this." He rubbed her back. "Everything's going to be okay, Karma."

She was silent and still before she pushed him away. Her expression was dark. "You keep saying that, Zayn. But it's not. Everything is not going to be okay!" Her voice had gradually increased, and now she was shouting hysterically, her eyes wild. "This is all my fault. Don't you see? I made him worry. I was the one who left the country without even checking in on them. That last call—" she broke off, tearing her hands through her tangled hair. "What if I never get to speak to him again? What have I done?" She keened, her fist at her mouth. "I left them, I left my daughter, and I'm here gallivanting around ancient ruins, eating amazing food, and pretending at an engagement with a man they never wanted for me."

Tears spilled down her cheeks and onto the front of her shirt again.

Zayn was trying to process what she was saying. "I don't understand, Kareena." A burning sensation swirled in his chest. But the fear that was taking hold of him was stronger.

The darkness he remembered from so long ago began to unfold inside him, as though waiting patiently in the corner for this very same event to happen again.

The thought came unbidden, and he wanted so badly not to have conjured it, to erase it from his mind. But it was like a stain that wouldn't go away. She was going to leave him … again.

"They'll never accept you, Zayn." She went on looking at him, but it was like she wasn't seeing him. Her hands were balled at her sides. "And you know what, maybe I won't be able to either. I'm not strong enough to stand up to them and do my own thing. I *need* them in my life." He could barely understand her as she spoke through big gulps. "I can't lose him, not after I just lost Arjun."

That was the flame that ignited the small wick of jealousy he carried for her first husband, exploding like a high-octane Molotov cocktail. The burning sensation was like a butcher knife to his heart. He almost reeled back from the pain of it, from what she was trying to tell him. He would never amount to her father or her deceased husband.

He wanted to growl and throw furniture. Kick and scream

that it wasn't fair—like he used to do as a child and adolescent when he didn't get what he wanted—when he couldn't understand the opposite outcome of a situation where he'd done everything right.

But he needed to hold it together. He wasn't a child anymore. He wasn't an adolescent still developing his brain mechanisms for impulse control. He would not lose his shit. And he could never raise his voice at Kareena. He loved her, no matter what, and it hurt even more to see how broken she was that she thought she'd done this to her father—her family, than her cruel words.

"Fucking get out of here, then," he said quietly, harshly, through his teeth. "If you can never accept me, us, then just leave."

It was the complete opposite of what he wanted her to do. He didn't want her to leave. He wanted her to open her arms and tell him she was mistaken; that they would figure this out together.

But instead, she nodded silently, her soft hiccups the only noise punctuating the room. "Zayn, I—" At his darkly quiet expression, she cut herself off, and turned her back, continuing to throw things into her suitcase, her breath shakily loud in the room.

While she finished packing, he called her a car and texted her the information.

Then he pulled a shirt on and shorts and left the villa, slamming the door in the process.

He wasn't sure if she was going or staying, and for the moment, all he needed was to get away from the one place he'd found so much happiness with her in—the place that he thought held his future, and deep down, maybe hers, too.

A few hours later, after walking all the way to town to find any little convenience store that was open and sold cigarettes, he found one and came back, rushing quickly. But the villa was empty.

ONE WEEK LATER
new york city, new york

CHAPTER 32

৩২

"*W*elcome back, listeners! If you're just tuning in, this is *Choto Bon* (little sister) and *Appa* (big sister) live—yes, you heard that correctly—we are L. I. V. E live here with *Spill That Masala* podcast. Usually, we prerecord, but you're in for a special treat today. We've partnered with *Desi Ignites,* New York's premier South Asian Social Networking Group, for their Make the Magic Happen pre-holiday season kick-off. You know how it is—once Thanksgiving rolls around, you lose what feels like a year off your dating life … that is, unless you meet someone here! And let me tell you, this is one heck of a love fest. There are games, speed-dating (if you need to find that perfect stand-in holidate—we've all been there), and even a fortune teller who'll read your astrology, but won't try to match you up with their most eligible single niece or nephew … I promise … unless that's your thing. The highlight tonight, *I* think, is the raffle. Enter to win a romantic New Year's Eve dinner for two at New York's iconic Tavern on the Green and get tickets to their swanky party that includes a cozy carriage ride with a bottle of champagne and a wool blanket. You and your special someone can enjoy Central Park in the crisp air. Even I'm amped for that. I plan to throw my name into the pot after this show."

Reyana winked at Kareena, who was sitting across from her.

"Now, let's get back into it. Before our short break, we had a caller phone in upset about something she just found out about her new live-in boyfriend, and she doesn't know what to think. Tell us what's what, *Appa*."

Kareena nodded at her sister, feeling a moment of lightness, a peak of sunshine through the dark, stormy clouds of her state lately. She was grateful the other woman had convinced her to do the live special that evening, even though it was all about 'love,' a subject she kept forcing out of her mind. At least this was about helping *others* with the L-word, allowing her to take the focus away from her problems.

She glanced down at her notes and leaned into the mic.

"Alright, so, this guy," Kareena read. "Has all the green flags flying high. He's financially stable, loves his parents, but isn't about to let them decide his future. He even refused the arranged marriage they tried to push on him! He's kind, likes to travel, is well-read, and there's phenomenal chemistry between the two of them. He sounds too good to be true, right? Well, he might be because the man is ... (she paused for effect), a certified party clown on the weekends."

The cough she choked out was a weak cover-up for the laugh-snort that eventually escaped.

"Say what?" Reyana deadpanned into the mic.

"He dresses up as a clown and entertains at kids' parties. He even makes balloon animals. And I think—" she read her notes. "Yep, he can juggle, too. He sounds ... sweet, and great at multi-tasking, *Choto*."

She had to cover the fuzzy mic so her laughter wouldn't be broadcast over the airwaves, as her sister guffawed with a horrified look on her face.

It felt good to be laughing again. The heaviness weighing her soul down seemed to evaporate, if only for a moment. It'd been days since she'd been able to so much as smile. Maybe all would be right in her world. This was her forte—helping people. She was made for this, not for sitting on the receiving end. Enough time would pass, and she could move forward, slowly, but surely.

Reyana rolled her lips inward but giggled anyway. "Sorry, this isn't funny. We're here to help our fellow South Asian Americans, right? So, our caller's problem is that the whole Bozo the Clown thing makes him less attractive to her." She paused, then said thoughtfully, "I don't know. Listeners, what do y'all think? It's tough. On the one hand, the guy is a diamond in the rough—perfect relationship material. But the clown thing … *eesh*—isn't that going into big yikes territory? Like, I'm not gonna lie, clowns are legit scary."

Reyana shivered while her eyes rolled dramatically to the back of her head. "What your take, *Appa*?"

Kareena could get one's fear of them—she'd read an entire study in medical school about the negative psychological outcomes of clowns. But she'd been to plenty of kids' parties with her daughter to experience ones that were less creepy, nicer, and friendlier.

"I don't think it's so bad. He likes to entertain kids, and someone okay with hanging with kids is A-okay in my book."

It was. The countless men she'd dated (or been matched to by her family) had turned out to be less than shy about their opinions on kids and the fact that she had a seven-year-old. But then again, some jumped in, taking the time to understand kids and the quirks they came with; those were the ones who deserved understanding, love, and more. They certainly didn't deserve someone walking out on them without a backward glance—

Her sister brought her back to their caller by saying, "Should she be mad at him for lying to her? Or is that a moot point? The bigger question is, should it matter about the clown thing? He sounds like a solid guy, one she wouldn't have to worry about fuckery behavior—" She sucked air as her eyes bulged, another thought coming to her. "But wait, what if he's more about the clownery than the fuckery? Like, what if he can never be serious about anything, and cracks jokes, or creates balloon animals to get out of a sticky situation?"

"Get real, *Choto*," Kareena said, trying to reel her sister in from stepping off the deep end with this. It was amusing, sure, but they needn't make a mockery of someone else's love life. These were real people with real problems.

"*I am*! There are major dogs out there, clowns, too, no pun intended … but seriously, do we know why he's into this? Does he have a weird affinity for clowns? Would he bring his rubber nose and red wig to bed and make his girlfriend partake in … X-rated clownery?"

Kareena had to keep a straight face. Any crack in expression would only break her, and she'd be rolling in either fits of laughter or crying in a big puddle of tears on the floor (her emotions were all over the place since she'd arrived back in New York). This was why she preferred to pre-record their shows. Their producer could edit out the unplanned bits.

"He does it as a side gig to make extra money," she answered, solemnly, again trying to get back on track. But this was how they did things on their show and why so many had started tuning in—Reyana went a little berserk with the stories, and Kareena, the professional psychiatrist, brought her calm and serious take on the situation. Right now, she had to admit she was quite taken with this 'clown's' achievements. "That's how he's been treating her to fancy dates, and recently a surprise weekend in Paris, and honestly, what's so wrong about a person's side gig? As long as they aren't doing anything cringeworthy."

She'd been with someone who'd had a very successful side gig. Some might think it was cringeworthy or silly, but Kareena had been more than enthusiastic about it. She'd found it utterly sizzling hot.

Reyana clapped her hands together, leaning back in her chair with a huge smile.

"Ding, ding, ding. I think we have a winner, even with the clown thing. But listeners, we want to hear from you. Text us and tell us what our caller should do; should she let him continue with the side gig? Should she be mad that he kept it a secret, but she's reaping the benefits? Or should she pack him up and send him to the circus with the other clowns? Text us at..."

While Reyana wrapped up the segment, Kareena swiped open her iPad and looked up the next caller waiting on their feed. It was Aryan S., a thirty-three-year-old computer engineer, who still lived with his parents in northern New Jersey. He wanted to know why every woman he met on dating apps immediately ghosted him after he requested a preliminary compatibility test over Google Meet. What was so wrong with wanting to see if their energies meshed before forking over good money on a date that might end up being a bust?

Had she read that right?

Good God … the absurdity. But did she really have the right to judge? She'd just been one half of an over-the-top scenario that had combusted in her face.

Yeah, but you did it to yourself, didn't you?

She leaned into her mic, about to introduce the caller, when Reyana swooped in.

"Wait, *Appa.*" Her sister sat up in her chair. "If you don't mind, we got a last-minute email and it's *real* good." She grinned mysteriously, and her green colored contacts sparkled, making her look a little demonic, with the matching green dyed streaks in her hair. "I think our listeners are going to want to hear this."

Chills instantly raced along Kareena's skin, even as she nodded. Maybe it was because they usually decided on the show's line-up together, and more importantly, Reyana was now avoiding eye contact with her.

She reminded herself that this particular episode was different. They were live on air, where anything could happen. It's what made it so fun to listen to, Reyana had so eloquently argued, convincing her they should do it. And Kareena was determined to give this a shot; anything to keep her mind off of how she'd left things back in Greece.

She shook her head, trying to focus once more, ignoring the goosebumps that rippled along her skin while catching their producer, Vikram's, eyes outside the glass booth. He shrugged disinterestedly and turned away. No surprise there, she thought. Vikram was a distant cousin who only chipped in with budgeting, equipment, and advertising, and barely spoke three words to them. He needed the experience for his resume as he finished his journalism master's at NYU.

"Alright, is everyone ready?" her sister asked before clearing her throat theatrically. She began to read, while Kareena sat back to listen.

To the Spill That Masala Wonder Duo,

This is bizarre, but no more bizarre than what got me here, so here goes: I need your advice. First, let me say that I've never done anything like this. I've never let feelings come into the mix. 'Love' and I don't work. There was a time years ago when I thought it might. But it didn't, so I've never put myself in that dark place again. Because, why? Why go through a self-made hell? People turn into whiny suckers when emotions get in the way. How do I know? I just joined that cult.

But the problem is, she came into my life again, which made me hope. It was karma, and she knows it. We're so fucking good together. So why the hell am I alone?

I don't know if I can take another round of this—yeah, we've done a different version of this dance before. Help me understand; am I the crazy one? I thought it was for real this time.

I might sound like a damn psycho when I admit this, but I can't let her get away with this. I don't want to. And, I'll be fucking honest; my drive for anything in life is shit—food has no taste, air has no meaning, and water has no sustenance. Hell, even my future plans I've had since I was a kid give me no excitement. I'll move forward, because what else have I got? But, do I let her go for good? I think I know the answer, but I'd like another hot take.

Anguished and more than PISSED-OFF,

Sinful in the Kitchen

Reyana sucked her teeth and tut-tutted, while Kareena stared at her in horror, barely able to breathe.

At first, she felt sympathetic to the writer, listening closely to how she could help. But as it unfolded, the chills manifested into alarm. The scenario sounded too freaking familiar. By the time the email ended, panic had curled its way around any feeling she might have felt only minutes ago.

Was this happening? Had her sister actually read that letter out loud, on their podcast—the one time they'd agreed to go live? And more importantly, had he really sent that email to their show?

She reached over and grabbed the other woman's iPad, scrutinizing the screen. The letters danced before her eyes, a blur of stark black on white. She only registered the word "karma," and she knew.

"What the hell!?" She mouthed as Reyana squealed into the mic, still avoiding her glance.

Kareena's panic manifested into hot white anger.

"Listeners, can you believe *Sinful in the Kitchen* reached out to us with this moving email? Am I delulu, or is this the same hot, unidentifiable chef who's taken over social media with his cooking videos showing off his amazing knife skills, *and* his rock-hard abs and pecs, because—yeah, dude cooks shirtless. Whew, I think his tats do it more for me than his mouth-watering food." She fanned herself with her hand. "He puts the 'cock' in concoction." Reyana chortled heartily. "Anyway, for those of you who don't know—and if you don't, you must be living under a rock—he's half Indian, so it's legit he reached out to *Spill That Masala*. But I had no idea he was in love—and so tortured. He said, and I quote, 'food has no taste.' That's huge coming from him." She finally met Kareena's livid gaze. "What do you think, *Appa*? What kind of woman crushes a man's soul like that?"

Though Reyana spoke excitedly, she also had the courtesy of looking a little meek, especially when Kareena pinned her with a murderous glare. Satisfied, sure, but short-lived because the nausea roiling inside her was threatening to spew up the matcha latte she'd had earlier. So, she remained mum, but not by choice. She literally had no words to respond because her brain had short-circuited the moment her sister finished reading the email.

This was a wholly new occurrence. Expecting the unexpected was what Kareena did in her career as a psychiatrist.

But *this* ... what she was experiencing now, in the booth with her sister, was a whole other level of crazy because it was personal. She had no idea how to respond, except for wanting to tantrum loudly like her seven-year-old when she didn't get her way. She tried taking soothing breaths, trying to get a handle on the situation.

"Guys," Reyana went on, filling in the dead air, and now she was nervous. Good. "I think *Appa* needs a minute. This is way racier than she thought. You know, I think we *all* need a minute."

For the record, Kareena had no words for many reasons, juicy gossip not being one of them. But as soon as she found them, she'd let her sister have it. Her blood rushed noisily in her ears, and she balled her fists, trying to suppress her continuing rage. She wouldn't make a scene, though. They were in the tiny fishbowl of their podcast booth, right in the middle of *Desi Ignites'* big pre-holiday event with hundreds of people milling around.

"But think about this before we jump into a short break: who is '*she*'?"

Reyana's brows wriggled as she rocked in her seat, her head bobbling. Kareena wanted nothing more than to wipe that eager expression off her sister's dumb face (preferably with a good smack).

"All right, y'all, if you aren't in tune with us, this is *Spill That Masala*, live at the *Desi Ignites NYC's* Make the Magic Happen pre-holiday mixer right here at City Winery," Reya continued in her sleek podcast voice. "Come join us, say 'hi,' get some pics, maybe meet your future partner in crime—*welp*! I mean, the love of your life! We'll be right back after a short break."

Vikram gave them the thumbs up, and they clicked off their mics, removing their headphones. Kareena was so ready to pounce on her sister.

She couldn't, though, because immediately, party guests and smiling fans tapped the outside of the booth, wanting to take selfies through the soundproof glass. The podcast duo smiled and posed, though inside Kareena was dying to ask her sister just what the hell she was doing by reading that email on air for everyone and their cousin's cousin to hear. Yes, they were all about 'spilling the tea,' but not when it was private.

"Can you believe how lit this party is?" Reya asked through her toothy smile as she waved and flicked a peace sign and then a hand heart. "Aren't you glad Devika reached out to us? Look at all these brownies trying to find love! And we're helping them. I'm so proud of us."

Kareena rolled her eyes, but couldn't disagree. Devika Ali had signed them after *that* Diwali party for a live episode for the group's pre-holiday mixer. It made sense. Both the podcast and the networking group had the same audience, one who waded through the complex issues of the South Asian American diaspora while navigating personal and professional relationships. It was the perfect partnership, and both sisters had agreed on the spot to do it. But now … Kareena was beginning to have more than just doubts.

After posing for what seemed like endless pictures, Kareena finally found her voice.

"What the *hell*, Reyana Madhumita?" she spat out. When she used both of her sister's first names, it meant she was at the level of there-is-nothing-you-can-do-or-say-to-make-this-better kind of rage.

She sat back in the hard plastic chair, crossing one leg over the other. Her top leg jiggled uncontrollably, mimicking her patience, which was trying its best to exit the booth.

Reyana continued waving at people, but finally sat back in her chair. She imitated Kareena's posture.

This made Kareena's head spin even further with fury. As kids, Reyana used the mimicry tactic when she did something naughty and couldn't come up with a good enough explanation.

"I know you're pissed, Kara. It was last-minute, and you had no say in the decision to read it on air."

"I'm more than pissed."

Routinely, taking a lot of the younger woman's shenanigans was second nature. It had to be. As the family's older daughter, Kareena was expected to be a beacon of guidance for her younger sibling. But not right now. Reyana had deliberately crossed a line. And for what? More listeners? More subscribers?

"You couldn't possibly expect me *not* to take his email seriously, could you?" Reyana continued. "The man has over

500,000 followers on Instagram alone. He's a celebrity where it counts. This is a total win for us."

"So, that's all you care about. The podcast. Never mind throwing loved ones under the bus—"

"I'm sorry, Kara. I really am. But yes, this podcast is my baby. Think of the lives we've helped, and how this story could inspire others."

Reyana's mission was to help South Asian Americans figure out the obstacle course that was the diaspora in which they lived. She wanted them to be okay with the fact that there were no rules and no one solution when meshing cultures together to find happiness in love, family relationships, friendships, and careers.

Her sister went on, "I want it to keep growing. We can only do that if we have really unique stories."

"Gee, thanks."

"I swear I'll make it up to you." She leaned forward in her chair in earnestness, fiddling with her mic. Kareena waited, knowing there was more. Finally, she murmured, "And I want to help you with this."

There it was.

Kareena huffed at her sister's talent for going from wheedling to syrupy sweet in a matter of seconds—a behavior only a younger sister could ever master with success. Before she could respond that she didn't need Reyana's help, and she could shove her podcast where the sun didn't shine, Vikram popped his head back in, giving them a fifteen-second heads-up.

Her sister put her headphones on, looking a bit apologetic, while Kareena jammed hers on her head. Vikram gave the signal, and they switched their mics back on.

"Hey, hey! We're back!" Reyana chirped. She gestured to

Kareena to say something, as her green contact-colored eyes widened comically, bug-like, silently pleading.

Kareena took a deep breath, willing herself to quash the juvenile desire to remain sullenly silent. They were on air. She was a medical professional, dammit. She needed to act like one.

"You guys." Her tone warbled, but she cleared her throat, "*Choto Bon* hit it on the head. Getting an email from someone like *Sinful in the Kitchen* completely threw me. And you know I'm the level-headed, calm one out of the two of us." Admittedly, this last part came out oozing with sarcasm. "But … wow … this guy listens to our podcast? I'm … shook … I'm moved … and I'm kind of in awe."

She knew her sister saw through the fake enthusiasm. She knew everything that happened between her and Zayn the moment they met in the waiting room at Greenwich General Hospital. Reyana had expected Kareena to come home for this, but was stunned by her actions. She sat silently as she listened to her explain that she'd had to leave him. That what she'd done was the impossible. Her parents couldn't handle her going off script, and now their father would possibly die.

Reyana had patted her back, letting Kareena cry into her shoulder about losing her husband, now possibly her father. She'd shushed her and let her sob, and when Kareena was finally able to lift her head, Reyana only had one thing to ask.

"Who told you Dad was dying?"

naxos island, greece

CHAPTER 33

ගග

"*B*ut … wow … this guy listens to our podcast? I'm … shook … I'm moved … and I'm kind of in awe."

She was in awe, Zayn thought, closing his eyes to the sweet, husky voice as it washed over him. Her words came out lower-pitched and echoey through his phone's speaker, but they still held the same warmth and tranquility.

"Well, Karma, I'll always be in fucking awe of you," he said to himself, his voice gruff with emotion.

That was the thing, no matter what she did to him, no matter how she behaved, she flowed over him in a sense of the familiar, like water when he headed out to the ocean for a much-needed swim to clear his head. She'd always been able to do that to him. He'd lived half his life aware of that fact.

As she continued speaking, it was as though she were there with him, in the kitchen of his villa, her curvy body almost irresistible not to touch, while she sat close to him on the countertop where he'd be prepping the fresh ingredients they'd purchased from the market. Her smile would be bright, her eyes dancing, and her laughter more melodious than any music.

But now, he sensed the gloom in her tone, and immediately his tranquility shook, like a sand castle that finally toppled into the lapping surf after holding on for so long. The thought of them not together wrenched his gut and set his anger ablaze.

He reached over and switched off the podcast, even though it was the closest thing he could do to be in her presence, as the show aired live at the moment from New York. Now, all he was left with were his thoughts screaming deafeningly in his head within the silence of the kitchen. What was he thinking, listening to that email being read on their podcast in the first place? Why had he even sent it? What exactly was he hoping for? For her to open up in agony and admit that she was wrong?

Yes.

A small seed of hope had dug deep into his heart, and it fought to break free, grow, and thrive. Instead, it was smashed to smithereens with disappointment. She'd never change.

He thumbed through his music library and found one of his favorites, Ziggy Marley, and hit 'play.' The unhurried reggae beats instantly fill the room, the bass bouncing off the roughened white stucco walls. He nodded his head in tandem as the melody lifted him, not tolerating the darkness he felt inside —the one that begged to be unleashed. He'd get through this. He'd done it before.

From the corner of his eye, the aquamarine water shimmered like a treasure trove of jewels under the Mediterranean sun and sky. His surroundings reminded him that even though his heart was in agony, he was at least in paradise, and the place he called home.

Black shapes darted by his open window. If he blinked, he might've missed the flock of swallows that visited daily. He was confident that they were the same birds that returned every morning, routinely flying overhead, rotating, and wheeling a complex choreography in the sky. Part of their dance had them speed dangerously close to his window, then swerve away quickly, changing course out to the ocean. He wondered if they'd done this when the villa stood dusty and empty, and this was just their normal routine. Or if he and Kareena, staying there, though briefly, had coaxed their curiosity. He could watch them for hours as they dipped close to the water's surface, something in the vast deep cobalt, mystical, or not, beckoning them. The regularity of their behavior was calmingly hypnotic when so much in his life was in upheaval.

After a few moments, the swallows disappeared into the cottony clouds above, and reality hit him in the face. Fuck. He'd sent that email to get her attention, though a small part of him did want some advice. He was worried about getting through this yet again. He'd been a kid the first time, broken-hearted at nineteen. How was it that now, at thirty-seven, he felt even more shattered? Hadn't he learned his lesson the first time?

He reached for the ripe, crimson tomatoes lying on his wooden countertop. The clear red juice spread across the cutting board as metal sluiced through the fruit's skin, giving him that sense of peaceful satisfaction when beginning his food prep. While he chopped, he considered his dilemma. He needn't look deep. He wasn't one to hide his emotions in any aspect of his life. Anyone who knew him closely recognized he never shied away from what he was feeling—whether good, bad, or ugly.

Only a week ago, they'd talked about destiny. He'd poured

his heart out to her, thinking she felt the same. As it turned out, he was wrong. He'd been blindingly delusional. He honestly believed that what they'd done, the steps they'd taken to help one another get what they wanted, could lead them back together. Now, more than once, since it all went down, he'd thought that maybe the fates above were telling them something else: they *weren't* supposed to be together with every meeting. Their destiny was that old saying: "... two ships passing in the night ..." and would remain that way.

He let out a litany of expletives and forced his thoughts away. He'd done this before, and he *could* do it again. He'd go back to something else, something that wasn't *her*.

He continued with his work, chopping and slicing in tandem to the music. His trusty chef's knife, the one he'd had since culinary school, the one he's used on her recently—

Focus.

The monotonous cut and slide over the board, the hollow ringing of sharp metal on wood, only added a sense of inner quiet stillness. His blood ran cooler, a lazy gliding stream, versus the raging river from moments before. Food preparation was his emotional mediator, keeping him from hurtling himself into destruction.

"I don't care if it hurts. I'm tired of lies and all these games," he sang along to one of Ziggy Marley's songs.

No words sung were more accurate than at that moment. He wondered if she could—would, ever feel it, too.

He continued to hum, working through menial tasks, his mood lifting by a fraction. Before he knew it, an entire pile of sliced and diced cucumbers, tomatoes, radishes, and red onions stood tall, staring back at him on his countertop. He had no space left to begin prepping the leafy greens that awaited untouched at the other end of the counter.

"Fuck's sake," he muttered, diving for the drawer that held his *mise en place* containers.

It wasn't the first time he'd gotten lost in food prep and probably wouldn't be the last. He'd learned to focus on the task at hand, but sometimes he lost track of the process while *within* the process. Was it a problem he could control? Absolutely. Was it something that sprang up when he didn't have a handle on other parts of his life, 1000 percent.

Zayn pulled the "glorified deli containers" out, smiling despite his shitty mood. It was Kareena who'd called the plastic clear tubs that, way back in high school. Since then, he'd always thought of them as that. He slid the vegetables into them, sealing and labeling them, before stashing them in the back of his fridge. He left enough out to make his version of the famous Horiatiki Greek Village Salad for later that day.

"Ya, Zayn! I hear." A deep scratchy voice boomed from the garden outside.

Zayn wiped his hands on a towel and stepped out into the shaded greenery. The older man with a familiar weathered face and a worn leather eyepatch stood amid the thick, fuchsia bougainvillea that climbed along the wooden pergola. Dainty yellow laurels and fiery red poppies were beginning to fade as the weather finally cooled in the past few days, indicating they would get a rainy autumn in Greece after all. The older man swatted a gnarled hand at the fat, languid bumblebees that floated too close to his face.

"Liannis," Zayn said in surprise. "You're early."

"If you want, I go," the man grumbled, pulling a

handkerchief from his pocket and wiping his sweaty neck and mottled face.

"No, no. I appreciate you coming up here and letting me take a look at today's morning catch first."

Zayn was going to move forward with his restaurant opening. It was the only thing positive he had going on for him, even though the idea felt daunting. It was the only thing that he knew could help him overcome the feeling of desolation and anger.

He was in the midst of menu planning; the same menu he'd described to Kareena when she'd seen the taverna. His next step was gathering ingredients and putting them to the test with his flavor profiles. If they were a success, he could proceed to sourcing.

He moved to the table where the crate sat. The ice dripped through the slats onto the gravel below as he inspected the tight silvery scales of branzino, skate, and other fish varieties. He leaned over the bounty, taking a deep whiff. The fresh ozonic smell reached his nostrils, making the wheels in his head begin to spin. He suddenly envisioned a crudo dressed in fresh herbs, fennel, citrus, olive oil, capers, and radishes for the meal he was planning later for himself and his parents. He could almost taste it on his tongue.

"I'll take the sea bream and the red snapper," he said firmly. "And two pounds of the anchovies."

Liannis grunted. "And the *chtapódi*?"

Zayn pined for octopus grilled over an open flame, smothered in lemon juice, as much as the next Greek. However, a small girl's reprimand stuck firmly in his head: what right did humans have to eat the most intelligent creatures on the planet?

"I'll take the calamari."

He'd leave the brainiac cephalopods for another time until he could ease his guilt about the massive quantity of octopi he'd eaten in his life.

"Where is she—your *gynaíka* (woman in Greek)?"

Zayn busied himself with bagging up the fish he'd chosen, while Liannis stood there, peering around, scratching his head.

"Not here."

"She couldn't stand your cooking, either." The fishmonger grunted, nodding in approval as Zayn paid. Zayn grunted in return. The entire island must know that she'd left a week ago. So how was Liannis just asking about this now, as if he didn't know already?

The older man's expression softened.

So, he did know, but he was trying to offer some sympathy. Zayn didn't say anything. He didn't want to get into why she wasn't there, and he sure the fuck didn't want anyone's sympathy.

"Ah. Well, my boy, perhaps she breaks your nerves. It happens," the older man said soberly. He hefted the crate from the table.

"She could never irritate me, Liannis."

Yes, she could. But he didn't want to admit how much to the crotchety old man and thus feel the pain his own chest cleaved open every time he thought of her.

The older man nodded solemnly.

"Then what?" His one good eye squinted as he packed up his things.

Zayn shook his head. "Only the gods can tell us," he said, cynicism dripping off his tongue.

"Bah!" the older man said as he left.

He knew the gods were a silly notion, even though the idea

of their all-consuming power still fascinated many who only believed in one God, even to this day. Zayn wasn't religious by any means, but if the gods really did exist, he'd ask—no, demand an explanation for their torturous games, because love was positively not made for mere mortals. It was a Herculean task that only a few could achieve and though he was known to defy all odds in his past, he didn't know if he had it in him this time around.

new york city, new york

CHAPTER 34

᥆8

*K*areena rolled over onto her side and reached out, looking for a solid, muscular wall. Instead, she found something soft. She hugged it to her, snuggling in. It distinctly had some give, and she hugged it tighter, starting to get comfortable again. But it morphed into something warm and wet. Weird, she thought, but she couldn't complain because it was soothing. Suddenly, she felt weightless, her body bobbing, or floating, or maybe a combination of the two?

Liquid sprayed onto her face, and she sputtered, swatting at her cheeks and opening her eyes. The baby blue sky was above and dense with powdery pink clouds, reminding her of big scoops of strawberry ice cream. They went as far as the eye could see, her gaze traveling to one side to follow their course, her head turning to find them meeting the straight line of the horizon that continued forever. Nothing but the expanse of deep cerulean blue was below it, and when her ear clogged up with liquid, she realized she was floating in the vast open sea.

Panic immediately set in, and her breathing became shallow. If she didn't find a way to calm down, she'd have a *panic attack because nothing was more frightening than being cast alone by herself in the middle of the ocean ... especially since her version of swimming was barely dog-paddling.*

Her panic travelled to her limbs, thrashing about in the water until large hands floated up to her back, rough and warm on her skin. They caressed her under the surface, dissipating the terror that took hold of her.

She turned her head in the other direction, knowing it was him, before he fully came into view.

Zayn stood in the ocean with her, his broad chest glistening with water, little droplets clinging to his chest hair, as the currents lapped around them. The white of his smile was blinding, as was the gold chain around his neck. Thick, damp auburn locks were combed back from his handsome face as he looked down at her tenderly. His deep voice was gravelly and steady when he said, "I've got you, Karma. I'd never let anything happen to you."

She nodded and relaxed fully, reassured in the knowledge that Zayn was here, with her, in the water, and she realized they weren't even that far from the beach. Behind him, she saw the surf hit the shore, rolling gently toward the sandy dunes.

He said something about feeling the water and becoming one with it, and she gurgled with laughter, trying to take what she now realized was her swimming lesson seriously. But she kept giggling, and he chuckled, too, his hands moving warmly, seductively down her sides only to find her ticklish spots to make her giggle further. She was breathless, and enamored, and so full of joy that she overlooked that he'd switch places and his back was now facing the horizon. Something dark loomed over them—a shadow cast, hiding the sun, and she said something about how the rain must finally be rolling in. He responded that there was no rain in the forecast for that day, reminding her that it was unseasonably warm for that time of year—fall in Greece.

The shadow loomed larger, darker, blocking out the clouds and ribbons of blue sky. The last thing she saw above was a flock of the islands' crazy birds—swallows—as they sped one way, then the other in a pattern that her eyes couldn't quite catch, making her dizzy. The shadow continued to get bigger, approaching quickly now, until she realized what it was. The most enormous black wave she'd ever seen barreled down on them. She was fully submerged under water, bubbles surrounding her as she thrashed before coming up for air. She sputtered and caught her breath, looking around her, looking for him, but he was gone. Now panic filled her again, but this time she couldn't breathe because Zayn was nowhere to be found.

She awoke to the sound of a bulldozer. The vibrations jarred her, and all she saw was blinding neon white before she took a sharp inhalation.

Her pulse galloped unsteadily, as questions swirled inside her head. Where was she? What time was it? Where was Zayn? Slowly, realization set in—she was in her bed, in her bedroom, in New York, and covered from head to toe in sweat.

It was a dream, she told herself. It was just a dream. She caught her breath as she smooshed her face into her pillow, the pillowcase hot and damp. Actually...

It was a nightmare of epic proportions that involved her biggest fear, which was drowning, but it was a warped version of a happy scenario that involved Zayn. The thought of him being swept away in the ocean pained every single nerve ending in her body, and she instantly knew this feeling; it was not so unlike her freshman year of college.

It wasn't difficult for her to decipher what the dream meant

—she'd had to review dream case studies during her training and how they correlated to a person's mental function. Also, during her practice, patients had come to her with vivid dreams they wanted decoded.

Short psychiatric answer: She was under stress while repressing (in her case, denying) emotions for someone she cared about. It was a classic case of REM Rebound and manifested in vivid dreams of epic proportions.

Long answer—and she groaned. It would take months—years—to figure out why she was such a coward; why she couldn't make a single straight choice without always fearing how her family would react. Or ... would it take that long? Regardless, she didn't want to think about it right now, especially when the bulldozer vibrations were getting louder, making her head spin.

As soon as she opened her eyes, though, she immediately regretted it. She threw a hand over them to shield herself from what looked to be a sunny, bright late autumn morning filtering through the blinds.

"Rude," she croaked at the joyful sun, enraged that the weather was choosing to be mild this year, everywhere it seemed. She wanted blustery cold right now, so she could feel the sharp wind on her face; anything to dim the sharp pain in her breast.

She realized she'd forgotten to close the blinds last night. Which meant she'd changed with them open, letting any Peeping Tom in her Tribeca neighborhood get a show.

At once, the pounding in her temples began. It was as if a teeny tiny version of her daughter had taken up residence in her head and was beating away at her play pots and pans, like she used to do as a toddler.

"*Make it stop*," she moaned as the throbbing continued, and the bulldozer vibrations suddenly stopped with a loud snort. A warm body adjusted itself next to her foot, and then took up the loud noise again, but this time punctuated with whines and growls.

It was Aloo. He was curled up against her foot, down near the corner of the bed. He was dreaming, most likely chasing that one black squirrel that continuously taunted him in the park.

She gently reached for him, pulling him to her and stroking his silky, soft fur as she tried to shake the discombobulation of her nightmare and what had happened the previous day. But seriously, first, what time was it? Her daughter could come home at any minute. She lifted her head to look at her alarm clock, but it thudded heavily back onto the pillow. It felt like it weighed a ton. For the moment, all movement was futile.

She was hungover.

She remembered pouring herself a full glass of old white wine from the recesses of her fridge as soon as she stepped through the front door of her brownstone, not even bothering to take off her coat or shoes. Aloo had greeted her with enthusiasm, and she knew she needed to take him out for a short walk to relieve himself. But not after she had a few gulps of the cool wine to calm her seething anger.

She remembered taking him out; he did his business, and she didn't let him dilly-dally, like she usually did, her patience worn thin. When she'd come back home, she gave him a treat and promptly continued chugging her wine. She must have finished the entire bottle if her head currently felt like a watermelon being split open.

Then she'd ordered from her favorite Thai restaurant. Had

she even eaten? She thought as she slowly attempted to rise from bed.

"Fuccccck!" she hissed. Aloo shifted beside her and began to awaken. He burrowed into her before rolling onto his back, waiting for his morning belly rubs as his snout widened into a huge yawn.

"Me too, buddy," she said tiredly, rubbing his pink velvety tummy. His tail thumped happily against the mattress.

"Okay," she said to both herself and her pup, who eyed her while he panted loudly. "I need to get up." She turned to her dog and asked, "Aloo, what the hell happened last night?" He cocked his head to one side as if considering her question.

She groaned and pushed herself up to sitting, pausing for a moment before fully standing. She needed to get moving. It wouldn't do for Tamannah to return home from her sleepover to find her mom nursing an epic hangover.

At least she'd gotten her pajamas on, she thought, looking down at herself in her white cotton pajamas printed with Aloo's face all over them (a co-present from Tamannah and her sister last Christmas). Though the buttons weren't even buttoned up the front, and she was braless. Great, she *had* given the neighbors a peep show.

"Whatever," she sighed, leaving her bedroom and going down the stairs to the first floor where the kitchen was. She smelled the rancidness before she saw the cold Thai food leftovers still sitting on the counter.

"Okay, so a major case of the drunchies *did* happen," she said in disgust, wrinkling her nose. Drunk munchies were a thing of her past, or so she thought.

Open containers were spread haphazardly, as if a drunk person had opened them, which was accurate. Her favorite, Pad

See Ew, with the fat rice noodles drenched in a tangy, sweet, brown sauce, was a congealed mess, dripping down from the countertop to the floor.

She pinched the bridge of her nose and closed her eyes to the chaos, needing a minute or ten. But then heard the distinct sound of claws clicking hurriedly across the hardwood floor before the loud inhalation and chomping of food.

"Aloo, leave it!" she cried before opening her eyes to find him licking off the remnants of brown sauce from around his snout and sniffing the floor for more. Then he looked up at her as if he'd done something right, his tail wagging so vigorously his little butt wriggled back and forth, too. His mouth was open in what looked like a grin, and she couldn't stay mad at such a sweet face. "Okay, but you're not going to feel great later," she warned, reaching for her coat, the leash, and shoving her sockless feet into her Uggs. Aloo barked excitedly and followed her as she walked to the front door.

As she got him outside and they made their usual three rounds of the block, the events of what happened yesterday began to materialize—before she'd downed the entire bottle of who-knows-how-old wine. She remembered the email her sister read. The damning one that blamed her for someone else's misery. And you know what, she decided she'd deserved it. She was a heartless droid who would never be able to follow her destiny. She was a coward.

CHAPTER 35

৩৫

YESTERDAY THE DESI IGNITES PRE-HOLIDAY MIXER

*F*ive minutes after that awful email was read on air, they wrapped the show. Reyana hinted that they'd have some advice for the hot chef in their next episode and to stay tuned.

As soon as she stepped out of the booth, Kareena breathed more easily. The tiny space was too confining. There was nowhere for her to hide from all of the feelings she thought she'd walked away from as they unbottled themselves chaotically within her.

Seeing the cheerfulness of partygoers only made things worse, though.

Where were the miserable people who thought love wasn't real, the ones who side-kicked with their more positive friends, only there for the food and cash bar?

The heaviness sank into her chest again. Maybe she'd been

too quick to agree about jumping back into the podcast and coming to an event with endless shiny, happy people.

Sheesh, she was a psychiatrist known for going beyond the usual prescription of meds. She liked to use therapeutic practices if her patients allowed her, and yet, she'd put herself into a social situation she might not have been ready for. To say it was triggering was the understatement of the century.

Her sister caught up with her and babbled nonsense, trying to figure out ways to address the email. But because Kareena already knew how they were going to handle it (tell him to move on; he deserved better than someone like her, someone who was braver than she could ever be), she walked faster. Admittedly, her heart skipped a few beats at the thought, before an ache so sharp jabbed sporadically behind her breastbone that she couldn't breathe. She put a hand over her wounded heart. Could one have a heart attack from a self-inflicted broken heart? The pain was similar; she'd read up on it from some medical journal. She'd need to do some research on that once she got back to work.

Work. She was supposed to go back after the New Year. Everything was set in motion. She'd read the email from HR when she got back from Greece. She should be relieved that she'd have a schedule again. She'd have her patients and their problems to focus on instead of the manic emotions whipping around inside her.

The idea depressed her.

Silent in her turmoil, and needing space turned out to be impossible. Guests from every direction stopped to talk and take pictures. And then *Desi Ignites'* director, Devika, practically attacked them in excitement, a photographer trailing behind her, snapping photos. The bubbly woman gushed about their show and how thrilled she was about their partnership.

"*Sinful in the Kitchen's* email—tell me you didn't plan that?" Devika asked excitedly, her face beaming, looking from one sister to the other. Her hands clutched both of their arms as she bounced on the balls of her feet in excitement.

Automatically, Kareena's core clenched hard, thinking about the online hot chef persona. And now her stupid rebellious brain couldn't stop replaying the time he'd been on top of her, wearing that same mask because she'd practically begged him to, when she found out it was him, while doing salacious things to her, handling her body like a piece of expensive meat. And she got off on it, writhing uncontrollably beneath him—*dammit*! Her brain would need to go through a process of sterilization to forget about him—and them. She dashed the visions away, trying to concentrate on Devika and Reyana.

"Completely last minute, Devi," Reyana said proudly, reaching for the drinks a waiter handed to her and passing one to Kareena. She fussed over the cuteness of the presentation with cranberry colored liquid infused with swirls of edible glitter in martini glasses. Deep blood red maraschino cherries were threaded onto toothpicks, floating in the murky liquid.

"Oh my God, it's surreal. You ladies are so 'it' right now, and I'm happy to share this space with you! By the way, Kareena. I heard you were engaged! I saw it in *Entertainment Daily, New York Edition.* Why didn't you say anything? God, Zayn Stavros is one fine catch. Let me see the ring!"

Kareena hid her hand behind her back and smiled awkwardly. Her engagement news was abuzz at the party. Devika wasn't the only one to congratulate her that evening. People had seen photos of her on Zayn's arm, in numerous news sources and media outlets, from when they attended the dozens of social events he'd warned her about before they left for Greece.

"Come on, Kara. Show her the ring," her sister taunted. She'd already gotten flak from Reyana when she'd returned in tears, spilling her woe-is-me story, but still wearing his family's ring on her finger. Kareena was mortified. She hadn't even realized she'd still had it on; she couldn't believe she'd left the country still wearing his family's priceless heirloom.

And yet, she couldn't bring herself to take it off quite yet. She was pathetic, and she knew it. She chalked it up to keeping up the engagement charade. No one knew that they had been faking it in the first place. Zayn's inheritance end goal very much still mattered to her, and after everything, she didn't want to let him down on this one thing she could control. She knew he would find it in himself to continue with his dream restaurant. He was action-oriented. He'd always been known as a grab-life-by-the-balls kind of person.

Kareena brought her hand out, and Devika gasped at the gorgeous piece of jewelry.

"Oh my God, let me get a closer look!" She pulled her hand closer to her, forcing Kareena to step forward. "It's gorgeous! It looks so … old and vintage, and the facets … there are so many."

"It's an old mined diamond and a family heirloom," Kareena said softly, admiring the ring for about the millionth time.

Devika's eyes were large in admiration. "Me thinks this rivals a certain pop star's engagement ring from her football-playing man. It's certainly not as big, but it has the same old-world charm. Well done, you! And congratulations."

Kareena murmured a thank you, and the three of them posed for a photo-op before the photographer dragged Devika away.

As soon as they were alone, Reyana rolled her eyes and flatly said, "Okay, you can yell at me now. I probably deserve it." She pretended to duck as she lifted her arm to shield her face.

Kareena exhaled sharply. She imagined herself sitting quietly with only herself for company in the garden by the cute villa. The ancientness of her surroundings, the smell of salty sea, fresh air, and fragrant blooms, all combined with the mustiness of time, begged her to. And it led to a quietude and peacefulness inside her.

She tried to channel that feeling, but instead she sharply said, "Don't be so dramatic," memories of tranquility miles away now. She looked up at her sister, annoyed that the younger woman was always determined to wear towering heels, forcing Kareena to crank her neck to look at her. "I know you did it without spite."

She sipped the pretty concoction in her hand, choking on the tartness. She coughed and continued, "Sometimes you know what's better for me than I do. But right now, I need boundaries. I've already made up my mind."

Reyana studied her closely, and Kareena turned away, not letting the other woman scrutinize her.

"For what it's worth, I *am* sorry I put you on the spot like that. But don't you see what it means? His feelings are valid, and ever since high school, he's been your destiny—"

Kareena put a hand up, silencing her. "Stop."

She couldn't do this right now. Not when her father was still fragile and recovering in the hospital. Nor while taking care of her daughter as a single mother. And then there was her career to get back to … She didn't have time for destiny, or fate, or karma, or some other future-telling entity. What she needed right now was to focus on what she'd always known—that she was a rule follower, not a rule breaker.

Her sister sighed—a little too theatrically, in Kareena's opinion.

"Fine. But even Tam-Tam likes him—Aloo, too. Don't you want to fix this? You're so great at helping other people. What about helping yourself?"

"Reya, my kid is seven, and Aloo is a dog. Treats and good belly rubs are his love language, and really, he tends to love everyone."

"Nuh-uh. Aloo can totally be a little turd when he needs to be."

He could. He'd barked away many a random stranger on the sidewalk who only wanted to say a quick hello, or give him a little pat on the head, including a terribly mismatched date set up by her parents. She'd known it was off from the get-go when the guy had been okay with her continuing to work, *if* it was part-time after they were married. She wasn't sure what kind of vibes she'd been giving off because the man dared attempt a goodbye kiss while dropping her off at her door. Aloo had snuck around her legs and growled and snapped the man away, thankfully.

Okay, fine, so her argument didn't hold. While her roly-poly, blonde Frenchy could indeed be choosy (and many times for good measure), her daughter was worse. Stubborn, with a temperamental streak and quirky standards, getting her to even meet anyone new was a challenge, let alone getting her to like them. But Tamannah had done both with Zayn.

Kareena continued before Reyana had time to point this out.

"And not everything is as simple as that. He…" She couldn't say his name out loud just yet. "And I, we're too different."

It sounded pitiful, even to her.

"Um, bullshit," her sister responded. "I've never witnessed you more carefree than in these past few weeks when you were 'pretending' with Zayn!"

She flinched at hearing his name aloud.

"Hey, just because you took one semester of drama in college doesn't mean you're the only one who can act in this family. It was fake. You know it, I know it, *and* it left me alone from every meddling family member."

"Liar."

"It *wasn't* real!" She emphasized, her tone swelling as her cool composure slipped.

Because she knew that even though it started as fake, it became way more real than either of them expected, just like old times, but about a million times better. It was as if they'd never parted.

And how did Kareena handle it? Well, she didn't. She'd left him again. This time, denying him and everything they'd experienced all over again. And it was worse than the first time she'd done this to him. She'd said that the man he'd become, the life he'd created for himself, all of the struggles and challenges he'd faced to get where he was, would never be acceptable to her parents, and … to her.

She was a cold-hearted bitch.

"Tell me you weren't happy again. Come on, lie straight to my face if you have to." Reyana taunted. "Tell me he's not the greatest love of your life."

"My daughter is the love of my life," Kareena said quietly, shifting the topic. "The fact of the matter is that I was fine *way* before I needed this scheme, and shit." Tears sprang to her eyes, and she wasn't sure if it was because of Zayn or her father. "Look what happened."

"That wasn't your fault, Kara," Reyana said in a hushed tone. "It had to do with his stent thingy from a month ago. Dad is doing okay. He's recovering well. Even you saw that."

She had. She'd gone straight to the hospital after her flight landed and seen for herself that her father was out of surgery and calmly sedated. She'd also found out that her mother had been completely hysterical about the matter.

"*Abba* had a heart attack while I was away, playing this ... charade with Zayn. Mild or not, you don't think *I* pushed him over the edge?" Kareena asked in disbelief. "I'm the daughter who never steps out of line, and I went so far as to leave the country—and the words I spoke to him before this all happened—"

She broke into a sob. She'd been selfish. She'd caused him undue stress, and in his already weakened state, the heart attack was inevitable. It frightened her so much—the thought of losing her father *and* disappointing him—that she dropped everything that had developed back in Greece, including the reconnection to Zayn.

"Oh my God, Kara," her sister said, trying to keep her patience. "It wasn't your fault. Stop thinking the family revolves around everything you do."

"I don't think that!" Kareena swiped at her tears. "What a shitty thing to say."

But a small part of her did think that. All Reya had ever done was cause her parents grief. Kareena was the only daughter who made them proud—the one they could count on.

"Sorry," Reya said meekly. "But I think you need to get your head out of your ass."

"Oh, that was much better," Kareena scoffed. "Don't forget I lost my husband not even two years ago, and now *Abba* ..." It was too much to bear, and her face crumpled all over again.

"Listen. To. Me." Her sister gripped her shoulders and faced her. She shook her slightly. "You can't blame yourself every time something happens to the parents. They're adults. *You're* an adult. You have *got* to cut that umbilical cord at some point. And, you know, I have mad respect that you and Arjun made it work, but were you knock-your-socks-off electrified? Like, what about the love, and the sex, and the passion—"

"I did love Arjun." She lifted her face and sniffed. "But not like what you're talking about. Not everyone finds that pie-in-the-sky kind of love, Reya. It's just facts."

"Okay, *Doctor*. I get it. But, as I recall, you hadn't had sex in what ... years before Zayn came back into your life again? How thick were those cobwebs down there?"

Now, Reyana was just being cruel. She rued the day she'd ever admitted her actionless status of the sexual variety to her.

"You're crossing a line, *Choto Bon*," she said, through gritted teeth, dashing the tears away that kept slipping down her cheeks.

Unbothered, her sister continued. "Well, someone has to, Kara. You're so passive. You let people make decisions for you. Now you have a chance to do something—act on something— and you chicken out, going back to your basic life from before."

"Hey! That's not fair. First of all, marrying Arjun wasn't a choice."

To which Reyana tipped her head back and hooted, because, in her opinion, everyone had a choice.

But Kareena went on. "We did what was expected of us, the first born in our families. And how can you call my life basic?"

Her voice had increased by more than a few notches, and the curious looks from others made her lower her volume as she hissed, "I have an incredible kid, a stable home, and a great career. It was *my* plan in the first place to get the parents off my back, so how can you call me basic?" Why was she getting so angry? Basic was good. Basic didn't cause her family any heartache. Basic was safe. "What more can I ask for? I'm thirty-six. It's more than most women have achieved nowadays." She finished, pulling out her patronizing big-sister tone while side-eyeing the other woman.

"Are you seriously turning this on me?" Reyana sneered. "I *love* my life," she proclaimed her voice escalating, too, as she described single life, job-hopping, and a variety of experiences people only dreamt about.

Guests were now gawking, the hot new podcast duo arguing. One with striking green streaks in her hair, matching green eyes, and a loud glittery outfit for a cosplay party she was going to later, and the other—Kareena. Chic, yes, but standard thick, wavy black hair, ordinary wide-leg jeans, and a simple white tee under a black blazer. She *had* thought to throw on thick gold hoop earrings and black boots for the occasion at least. Fine. She was a basic bitch, and she was just fine with that.

Who could compete with Reyana anyway? She'd always been attention-seeking and was loud, always in for a good shock factor. But her life was unstable and crazy.

Kareena, on the other hand, had always flown under the radar. It was just easier that way. She'd sought her family's approval and made her life choices based on what didn't cause ripples. Ripples only caused waves, which could turn into a disaster. She'd just lived it.

She exhaled a cool hiss of air, forcing the negative energy out of her. She would not make a scene. That's not what she did; it wasn't who she was. They would talk about this later in private when they'd both taken a beat.

"You're hiding behind a safety net, Kareena. You're lying to yourself if you think going back to your job and the way things were before him will give you the same kind of satisfaction. You talk about authenticity, living your best life, all that bullshit you spout on our podcast, things you've told your patients ... you can't even believe them for yourself. You're ... a sham."

And just like that, a switch flipped and myriad layers of frustration exploded from Kareena's pores—mottled and scorching hot. If she weren't out in public, she'd have thrown back her head and let out a scream.

"SHUT. UP." She snarled instead.

Reyana nodded enthusiastically, and by God, it felt freeing to say that to a willing person.

"That's it. Let it out, Kara."

It hadn't come from nowhere. The combination of defeat, sorrow, and what her role in life was—her responsibilities versus the other option that didn't make sense but felt right had been circling and duking it out for her attention for far too long. Things were chaotic, a jumble of jigsaw pieces that someone had swept off the table onto the floor, like her daughter did when she couldn't make the pieces fit. All Kareena wanted was the simplicity back where the pieces clicked perfectly together. She wanted her parents to be happy and healthy, and she wanted to carry on in a way where she knew what was expected of her. What she didn't need was a reminder that there *was* more to her small, little life. That she'd tasted a delicious fraction of it recently, and not everyone was on board with it. And that a certain someone she'd been denying for more of her life than she wished to admit, played a leading role in all of it.

"You have every right to tell me off," Reya encouraged.

"*Arrrgh!*" she growled, hurtling her glass to the floor.

It smashed into glittery, sharp shards, flying everywhere. Kareena didn't care. Her need to clean up (her usual tendency) was nowhere to be found.

Her chest heaved heavily, and she wasn't sure who she was, but damn, it felt good.

"Okay, okay," her sister said soothingly, ignoring the gawkers. She wrapped an arm around Kareena's shaking shoulders and ushered her outside into the cool November air. "It's okay. You're okay." She raised her arm to the string of yellow cabs whizzing by. "Let me get you a cab home. Do you want me to come with you?"

Kara shook her head. "I need to be alone."

She gratefully got into the cab that had slid in front of them, promising to call Reyana in the morning.

She leaned her head back on the sticky leather headrest. Thankfully, her daughter was at a sleepover. She needed to be by herself, especially when Tamannaah was still mad at her, wondering where Zayn was. Her seven-year-old was as determined as they came.

Kareena needed to think and re-compartmentalize everything. She was overflowing, the seams of the walls she'd put up coming apart with the one person who'd always been someone she thought she couldn't have. But she did have him, not once, but twice, and instead of following her heart, she'd followed ideals put upon her.

She didn't deserve him.

She twisted the ring on her finger, finally pulling it off and putting it in her purse for safekeeping until she could return it to its rightful owner.

She thought about the email he sent the show, while the city zipped by, already dressed up for the holiday season with multi-colored lights, and celebratory holly and red bows. Thanksgiving was right around the corner, and she suddenly missed him so much, she felt hollowed out.

She wondered how Zayn could still want her. She couldn't for the life of her understand how he didn't hate her after everything.

naxos island, greece

CHAPTER 36

৩৬

*Z*ayn took the shortcut down from the villa to the taverna. He needed to get there quickly. Gossip was like a spark from an open flame that landed in the bushes. It went from containable to a wildfire gone berserk if not caught quickly enough.

So far, he'd already heard from people all over town that they knew Kareena had left in a hurry; that her father was ill, and now, Liannis included. He could continue to brush it off, but the contractor he'd hired to investigate wood rot in the taverna had notified him that he was being denied access to the property.

An ominous feeling hit Zayn. So far, he hadn't met with any objections in accessing the place. So, why now? What was going on? Silas had been his usual cranky self at his sister's wedding, though eyeing him and Kareena with displeasure, even when she wore the family ring.

The ring. *Fuck.*

In all of this, he'd forgotten about it. He hadn't even thought to look for it after she left, his mind a black hole for the past week. He hadn't even cleared out the things she'd left behind at the villa, yet. He shook his head. One thing at a time.

His brain worked rapidly on coming up with ways to deflect anyone who happened to find out that his fiancé had not only left in a hurry, but it seemed she wasn't coming back. But no one knew they'd been faking it, so there shouldn't be this need for panic. He hadn't heard from Kareena, but he could only assume she was continuing their charade. How would it benefit her if she were back with her family and *not* engaged? He could just imagine her parents picking right up where they left off, parading one prospective husband after another in front of her until she was bored to tears. He wasn't sure if he liked that idea, though she might deserve it. No. He hated that thought. It made him want to break something.

Halfway down the stairs, he passed the little footpath that broke off from the route down to the beach. He had to ignore the small pool where he and Kareena had finally succumbed to their attraction, and then everything that happened afterward.

Sand kicked up as he reached the bottom, and he rushed over the small dunes, eating up the space quickly with his long legs until he reached the taverna. He bounded up the rickety old stairs onto the deck. The umbrellas attached to the tables were closed tightly, but they warbled precariously as the cool wind picked up. With the clouds rolling in, dreary and grey, fall had finally announced itself and descended upon Greece.

He entered the restaurant through the heavy door, finding no one in the dim place. He rushed past the old bar to the kitchen, hoping the text he received was mistaken; that perhaps the contractor and his crew were in the back, either setting up their equipment there or checking out the wooden fixtures in the storage room. But no one was there either.

He pulled his phone out and called the contractor.

Alex picked up on the first ring. "Zayn," he said gruffly. "You see now what I'm talking about?"

"I see that no one is here. What am I paying you by the hour for?" he asked, frustrated.

"I told you, my guys and I came in and set up, and then we were told to leave or the *astynomía* (Greek for police) would come and kick us out."

Zayn pinched the bridge of his nose with his fingers, feeling a headache coming on.

"Tell me who told you to leave." Though he had a pretty good idea who the culprit was.

The sound of voices outside the kitchen, echoing in the high-ceilinged space, caught his attention. Whoever they were, they must have come from the second entrance by the parking lot.

"Let me call you back, Alex."

"You're the boss, but—" he hung up on the foreman, striding through the kitchen door, not giving a shit that it banged loudly against the wall, threatening to tear off the hinges, startling everyone.

All of the lights had been turned on, and immediately, his gaze zeroed in on the familiar, stiff stature of his cousin, Silas.

"And just what in the hell is going on here?" he asked, trying to keep his tone mild, even pleasant, though blood whooshed to his head. He had a feeling he wasn't going to like what his cousin was about to say.

"Zayn," Silas said, dressed in an impeccable navy three-piece suit. His smile was more of a grimace.

The others, two women and three men, all suited up, stopped speaking. Zayn crossed his arms over his chest, waiting.

"Give us a moment," Silas said, addressing the group.

He walked into the kitchen without a word, and Zayn followed. Inside, Silas was already at the central prep table, gliding his hand over the old wooden surface, his lip hiked in disgust.

Zayn wished the man would get an ungodly number of splinters just by that small gesture.

Silas looked around the kitchen, at the cooking stains behind the old iron stove, the grim lighting, and the rusty old walk-in refrigerator toward the back.

"I'm not even ashamed that this place is going to be demolished."

"Silas, tell me what's going on, and then we can discuss what's a shame or not." He crossed his arms over his chest. He would not lose his cool with him.

"The hotel development company sent over a few of their executives. They're here to tour the property."

"For what purpose?"

"You know why, Zayn."

"It's not for sale, Silas. I made myself clear back in New York. I'm honoring *Pappous's* wishes. Or are you deaf as well as pig-headed?"

The other man smiled humorlessly, clasping his hands behind his back.

"You know pigs are considered very intelligent creatures."

Zayn grunted.

"Since your engagement is ... *off.*" Why did he say that with such disdain? "The property goes back into the estate, with that *skatá* (Greek for shitty) little olive grove, even that dusty old villa." He waved his hand carelessly. "I'd like your things out of there by the end of the week."

Zayn felt a rage like he'd not felt in a long time. It was so similar to that feeling of helplessness where he couldn't do a thing about the decisions being made for him; that someone else was holding the reins, determining his future. He felt like a humbled, confused kid, trying to figure his erratic emotions out. By God, it felt an awful lot like when Kareena had broken up with him the first time as kids. And now, she'd done it again, exiting in the middle of the night, leaving most of her belongings.

Now this. He was cursed.

He wanted to lunge at his arrogant cousin, dressed so smartly in a fancy Italian suit, his shoes so shiny one could see their reflection in them. But he balled his fist and pounded hard into the wooden surface of the old prep table. The crack was loud and satisfying as the wood splintered under his knuckles. His cousin barely flinched.

Pain shot through his hand, up his elbow. But it was dim in comparison to the ache in his chest.

How could she have left him like that? They only had a few more days before the end of the waiting period. It wasn't just the heavy feeling of defeat that his cousin would win. It was that, after everything Kareena and he had gone through, though based on a lie, had turned real. He'd come to care for her again. He'd fallen in love with her, though he doubted he'd ever really stopped from the first time. Things had happened quickly, true. They'd gone from pretend kisses to tight, sensual embraces, as though they could never part. And when they'd finally let their physical attraction take over, because how could they ignore the heavy, intoxicating weight of it, hovering around them ready to strike without warning if they didn't do something about it, he felt whole.

And she'd said as much, too.

Her exact words had been, "I've never felt this way about anyone before." And then she'd blushed furiously and ducked her head into his shoulder as they lay warm and naked, their limbs tangled in his bed. "Actually, that's a lie. I've felt this way before. It was just so long ago that I forgot how good it could be."

She'd reached up and kissed him tenderly, her lips roving over his as she'd climbed on top of him and they'd gotten lost again, her taking the lead, the sweat on her body a heady musk that was a drug to Zayn. The moon outside the window was bright, casting shimmering rays into the room and bouncing off the roughened white walls, lighting her up like the goddess of his world that she'd always been.

He tore his hands through his hair. Rage and despair, those two feelings were a constant, cruel duo that always reared their ugly heads when it came to this woman.

She was a liar.

He'd never be someone to her. Her words—the ones about her parents never accepting him, and the realization that neither could she, had gutted him. After everything, he still wasn't good enough. Did she agree with her parents? More importantly, had she always seen him as such? Their fake engagement was a means to an end for both of them, but deep down, Zayn couldn't deny that being brought together again was their second chance. He wanted her to be his for good. Had he become obsessed? Maybe a little. But, she'd always been his.

"I know you're disappointed, Cousin," Silas said, cutting through the misery that mocked him.

Zayn stood up taller. He couldn't let this other man defeat him. His mind raced. Think Zayn, he urged himself.

Focus.

He exhaled, finding the answer. "What makes you think our engagement is off? Kareena's father is in the hospital. She needed to go to him."

His cousin answered smugly, "Did you think you could pull the wool over my eyes like every other Stavros? I *know* your engagement wasn't real. And to think you gave that woman *Yia's Yia's* ring," his cousin said with disgust. "You committed the biggest falsehood ever, all in the name of honoring *Pappous.* But how would the old man feel if he knew you lied about everything?"

"What are you talking about?"

"Honor, Zayn. Here in Greece, we have honor. You think you're so high and mighty, trying to protect the land and the people," he sneered. "But lying and making up an engagement to get something that's not yours is the biggest dishonor to our family. What would the old man think of you now? I doubt you'd still be his favorite."

"Tell me, who the fuck told you our engagement was fake. I'll rip their fucking head off!" He was losing it.

"You'd never hurt anyone like that, and especially not my source. They're reputable, so you can go ahead and pack your things and get out of here. You have until the end of the week."

Zayn's fist hit the old table again, a loud thwack that reverberated throughout the kitchen. Now the surface was cracked down the entire length, exactly how Zayn's heart felt. He lifted his hand, shaking it as droplets of blood stained the wood. He stared at the two dent marks; two reminders that the same woman had left him twice, and that she'd not only taken his dreams with her, but his heart as well. He regretted the day he'd ever proposed a fake engagement to her. Because now, he'd lost his integrity, too.

new york city, new york

CHAPTER 37

৩৭

*K*areena stepped out of the shower, wrapping a fluffy towel around her. Taking a longer-than-normal moment to stand under the blast of hot water, rinsing the remnants of her hangover down the drain had done wonders.

She went to the mirror and wiped the fog with her hand. She dried off and slathered on body cream, then got dressed, throwing on relaxed jeans and a dark pink sweater.

Her sister called her a few times, but Kareena let them go to voicemail. She wasn't ready to face what Reyana was trying to tell her. A sham? Really? Maybe she was right, but she didn't have to admit it just yet. She already felt bad enough for leaving the way she did.

She was in the middle of combing her tangled locks when the front door downstairs slammed harder than was necessary for any door to be slammed. Kareena knew she was in for a battle with her little girl. She heard stomping, the distinct sound of heavy boots on the wooden floor and stairs, as her daughter went to her room. There was a quiet pause before her bedroom door slammed, making her jump.

'Drama-Tama.' That's what her parents called their granddaughter when she threw temper tantrums. Kareena always hated it. Seven-year-olds had tantrums. In Tamannah's case, she had trouble regulating her emotions more than others; hence, she had more than the average number of tantrums for a child her age, but with understanding, one could head them off. And conveniently, her parents had forgotten that Kareena and her sister had had their fair share of tantrums when they were little. Kids' brains aren't fully developed until their early twenties.

She heard a whimper and scratching at her bathroom door, and she opened it, looking down. Aloo sat, quirking his head to one side, his big puppy dog eyes a little gloomy.

"I know, buddy." She squatted down and cuddled him, scratching behind his ears.

"Seven-year-olds, Aloo. You can't live with them; you can't live without them." She laughed drily as she said this, aware that it only got worse as kids grew into tweens, then full-blown teenagers.

"Well, let's get this over with."

She put her pup down and finished with her hair. Then she made her way cautiously to her daughter's room. She took a deep breath and rapped lightly on the door.

Immediately, her daughter cried, "Go away."

"Tama. I want to speak to you, please."

"No!"

Kareena sighed and tried the knob, but it was locked.

"Tamannah," she said firmly. "Unlock this door, now. We don't lock doors in this house."

She waited and counted to sixty. She was about to go and

grab a screwdriver to jimmy open the lock when she heard the distinct unclick, and the door opened.

The little girl trudged back to her bed and threw herself onto her Hello Kitty duvet.

Her muddy rainboots were still on, and Kareena did her best to ignore the fact that her daughter had broken her 'no outdoor shoes in the house' rule.

Their dog sped into the room and jumped on the bed beside Tamannah, licking her face. The girl let him, petting him gently.

Kareena leaned on the door jamb and asked, "How was your sleepover at Marigold's?"

"Fine. We watched the new K-pop animated movie."

"Again?! How many times have you watched that together now?"

"Ten times," her daughter said absently. "And we did the gummy bear hack. But we didn't wait long enough for the bears to freeze, so they were more jelly than frozen. I told MG that was going to happen, but she didn't listen." Her daughter sighed. "They were still really yummy. Can we try it here, Mommy? The next time Zayn Uncle comes over? I think he'd really like them."

Kareena exhaled heavily and came into the room. Every time she heard Zayn's name, it was a shot to her fortitude and her heart.

She took a seat in the furry white beanbag chair in the corner, getting comfortable.

"I'm glad you brought him up. I'd like to talk to you about him—us."

"Why isn't he with you? Why didn't he come back to see *Nana*? Doesn't he like *Nana*?

The rightful question in this scenario should be, 'Why

doesn't *Nana* like Zayn?' But Kareena wasn't about to tell her daughter that.

So she thought for a moment about what she could say to Tamannah. "Well, he had a lot to do for his new restaurant." She gulped, understanding that the way she'd left, sooner than they'd agreed, could affect his ownership of the restaurant and everything entailed with it. If anyone had happened to hear their argument, then everything would be null and void for him. They should've never done what they did. Too much had been at stake, more for him than her, though she now realized her heart was on the line. They'd become so close, so quickly, a natural pairing of homemade creamy, salty Greek feta cheese and a deliciously crisp Assyrtiko white wine.

She shook her head, getting back on track. "So, he couldn't come."

"Were you able to help him with what he needed?"

"I—I think so." She said hesitantly.

"Will he come when he can?" Tamannah asked hopefully.

"I don't know," she said truthfully.

"Why?"

"Why what, *Beta?*"

"I thought he was going to be my new dad."

"Tama, you were joking about that, remember?"

"I know. I *was* joking. But the way he looked at you, Mommy. I just knew he was the right one to be my new daddy."

Kareena was shocked. This is what Zayn had been talking about.

"How exactly did he look at me, Tama?"

"When he came over to babysit me and Aloo, he looked at you like you were the prettiest person he'd ever seen, and he wanted to kiss you. When you left for your meeting, I told him to stop looking at you like that because it was weird. And he said he would try, but he couldn't promise it. Mommy, why could he promise me not to eat octopus, but not promise to stop looking at you like that?"

Kareena's throat had closed up. She didn't know how to answer her daughter.

"I liked him. He was funny. He played games with me. He listened to me when I talked about all my thoughts jumping around in my head and how I can't catch one and say it when I want to." Her daughter's skinny arms flapped around as she tried to explain herself. "And I was going to see his horses in Greece."

Kareena's heart clenched tightly. She never wanted to hurt her daughter.

"I know."

"And Marigold's mom said she saw a picture of you and Zayn Uncle in a magazine. She told me you two are engaged."

"What?!"

Damn that nosy mother.

"I told her 'nuh, uh' and she said she saw it with her own eyes." Her daughter stared at her mother curiously. "So, why isn't he here?" She began to count on her fingers. "If he looked at you like you're the prettiest girl in the world, and he couldn't promise to stop, and MG's mom saw a picture of you two engaged in a magazine, I thought maybe you did really love each other, even though you told me you were only friends."

She looked at her little girl as thoughts crashed inside her head. First, it never ceased to amaze her—her daughter's keen sense of observation. She'd basically seen the truth about how Zayn and she felt about each other, when even they, the adults, hadn't known it yet.

Second, her annoyance at Abby, MG's mother, was unfounded. She couldn't really blame the other woman. Neither she nor Zayn had figured in the press photos, and whoever saw them. If anything, it had only helped their cause where it counted.

She cleared her throat, answering Tamannah. "It got too complicated." Her chest felt like it crumbled to ash. *She'd* made it too complicated. "And you can't believe everything in magazines these days."

"Why?" Tamannah got up from her bed and came to her, plopping herself in her lap and curling her limbs around her so she hugged her, chest to chest.

She wasn't the one to speak about love or complications. She'd run from them. So, she changed the subject. "I had to come back for *Nana*. He's very sick. And ... I think he worried when I was gone, and he..." How did she explain to her daughter that she didn't want to disappoint her father, didn't want to hurt him, but had probably done so anyway by her actions? Because how did she still feel this invisible tether to her parents, this need to please them, even in her thirties, when she knew with her entire being that she never, ever wanted to treat her daughter that way? It was a weight that she'd proudly carried for most of her life, but now, it felt more like a heavy ball and chain.

"But *Nana* has *Nani*. She's with him, and he'll get better." Her daughter smooshed her face into her chest and breathed in before she said, "And you don't have anyone in case your heart gets broken and needs fixing."

Tears sprang to Kareena's eyes. Seven-year-olds, she thought again. You can't live with them, and you can't live without them, especially this one. She hugged her daughter tightly. For someone so young, she was already worried about her mother dying alone, and it crushed Kareena further.

"I have you, though. And you're my heart. You're my everything."

She didn't mean it to sound like her daughter would be caring for her in her old age. But more than anything right now, she wanted to focus on them because the little person in her arms was her world, a part of her.

"You haven't seen *Nana* since he got sick. Should we go see him this afternoon? Take a drive to Greenwich?" She asked into her daughter's soft poufy hair.

"Yeah!" Tamannah shrieked, clapping. Then she sprang up and danced around, wanting to make pancakes for lunch. She skipped out of her room, and eager Aloo was hot on her trail.

Kareena's smile faded as she realized she'd done exactly what some of her patients did, and she never failed to call them out on: deflected the issue. She didn't explain what had happened between herself and Zayn. And she wouldn't. She would never tell her the details, but she hadn't been completely honest with her. All her daughter knew was that her mom had come home in a rush and gone straight to the hospital to see her *Nana*. Then she'd returned the next day, encouraging a normal routine with work and after-school activities.

When Kareena had finally seen her father in the hospital, she'd sat with him for hours. He was sedated and sleeping comfortably. She held his cool hand while studying his skin tone, so like her own, but now faded with pallor. There was a moment when he woke up, his eyes opening slightly, and his lips curled up, recognizing her, before he was out again. That had been a few days ago, before the entire podcast debacle, and she was due to see her father again this weekend. He was doing much better as she'd called multiple times daily to check in with her mother and her father's doctor.

What Tamannah didn't know was that Kareena's mind had spun with guilt as she sat looking at him. His once tall and strong stature looked positively shrunken in the hospital bed.

Her mother had come in with coffee, and Kareena had taken it with shaking hands, gripping the paper cup.

"He's happy you're back, *Beta,*" her *amma* had said, putting her hand on her shoulder and squeezing. "I am, too."

She'd sipped the coffee, the powdered creamer tasting stale as it coated her mouth. And she'd automatically nodded, and said, "Same."

But it felt like she'd left more than a piece of herself back in Greece.

naxos island, greece

CHAPTER 38

৩৮

"*I*'ve reviewed all of the documents, Zayn. It doesn't look good." Aariv said over the phone. Zayn heard people talking in the background. "Or rather, everything looks solid and binding from the estate holder's point of view. Finding a loophole to get a partial component of what was to be your inheritance is like trying to find a needle in a haystack." He spoke again to someone in the background before saying to him, "There's no way to contest this, unless you're willing to spend an ungodly amount of money and time."

"Where are you?" Zayn asked, irritated. He shouldn't be so annoyed that his friend also had a life outside of his own messed-up one.

"Court case. The jury is about to return."

Aariv said something to someone again, but it was muffled, before telling him that he had two minutes before he needed to go.

"Well, thanks for looking over everything. I'm going out of my fucking mind right now." He ran his fingers through his hair as he sat on the last few steps of the craggy stone path, his feet sinking into the wet sand. It had rained quickly moments ago, and the weather fit Zayn's uneven temper perfectly.

"Zayn, I'm sorry about Kareena." His friend sighed. "You know I warned you about her."

"Not the best time to say I told you so," he growled.

"I'm not saying that."

"You've never liked her, so how can I be sure you've been upfront with me?"

And maybe Zayn had been too trusting. Or had he? Nothing had felt off between them. But this sudden switch in her was confounding, and if this was what things were going to be like if they'd had a future together, he probably would've given up then, too. There was no way he could compete with her family and their opinions.

So why did he still love her when she couldn't accept him? The plan had been too good, he thought, kicking up wet clumps of sand. Even he'd been convinced by their act.

"Zayn?" Aariv asked.

Lightning threaded the sky, lighting up the churning cobalt waves to an electric flash of white.

"What?" he grumbled.

"I have to go. I'll touch base later. Don't … fall back off the wagon, okay? You'll figure it out. I'll help where I can. Let me comb through the claims' expiration date. Maybe there's wiggle room. Perhaps we can find more time—"

"For what, Aari? It's a lost cause. What am I supposed to do, find another fiancé?"

"We'll figure it out." And his best friend hung up.

He shakily reached for his pack of cigarettes. With the emptiness in him, he needed them more than ever now.

He lit up and quickly inhaled and exhaled while he sat

looking at the dark blob of clouds in the distance. The hazy shadow underneath indicated a heavy rain shower heading his way.

"Zayn? What are you doing out here?"

It was his mother. She and his father were standing under a huge golf umbrella protecting themselves from the on-again, off-again rain.

He didn't answer. His father left the safety of the canopy and came to sit next to him.

"Sanjay *will* be fine, Zayn. Is that what you're worried about?" At his silence, Kiran asked, "Are you missing Kareena? She'll be back when she can."

"I don't think she will," he murmured, putting out the cigarette in the sand.

He stood up. "Let's go eat upstairs in the villa. The taverna is off limits at the moment."

His father and mother looked confused. The building was all lit up as Silas was meeting with another round of executive goons.

Shit. This property really was worth more than Zayn could've imagined if multiple companies were vying for it.

He sighed heavily. "I'll explain over lunch."

They sat around the oval table, the food he'd made barely touched as he told them everything.

"So, I'm doing as well as can be for someone about to lose their future," Zayn said, having explained the fake engagement, falling in love with each other, and her leaving him, because she blamed herself for her father's heart attack. Now, because Silas found out their engagement wasn't real, Zayn was going to lose it all.

His mother was speechless, but his father tipped his head

back and laughed heartily. "It was a good plan. Perfect for a Bollywood film ... or a Greek tragedy!" He slapped his thigh and continued to chuckle, making his rotund stomach wobble underneath his burgundy sweater vest.

"Kiran," his mother admonished. "This is serious." She turned to Zayn. "Why would you lie like that?"

"I didn't have a choice, Mama. The will ... what was *Pappous* thinking writing that stipulation in?" He'd asked her that question more times than he could count since the reading weeks ago.

Her answer was the same every time, just like now, "No one knows what he was thinking, Zayn. And I'm sorry that it happened. He loved you so much. He always knew you would shine brighter than any of the others. He saw a genuineness in you and knew you would take care of the heart and soul of our land. He really did want you to find your soulmate to share it with."

Zayn grunted. He couldn't understand it, and he probably never would.

His father cleared his throat. "Incidentally, I did speak to Sanjay before he had his heart attack."

"Oh yeah? And what did Kareena's father have to say?" He stretched his long legs out in front of him under the table and leaned back in his chair. "Except that he still hates my guts."

"He never approved of the engagement in the first place."

"Were you surprised, Papa?" Zayn asked sardonically.

"I was, *Beta*." His father sipped his tea. "Fake engagement or not, we all believed your love for each other at your engagement party because it *is* real. I told Sanjay that a love like what you two share is unstoppable. So what's the point of trying to stop it? It'll only break families apart. My advice to him:

don't let what happened to me and my relationship with my family happen to him and Kareena, because it *will* happen. She's not a girl anymore whom he can tell what to do. She needs to be able to live her own life and make her own decisions, and she'll do it, with his approval or not."

Kiran spoke from experience. Having married for love, he'd defied his family. To this day, a rift still stood between them and his father.

"But here's the thing: after everything, she *did* leave me," he said angrily. "And it sounds like her father isn't going to die, and she still hasn't said one word to me. No call, no text, no letter. Nothing."

He'd been a moron for sending that email to their podcast.

"*Beta,* love isn't easy." His father shrugged and frowned. "Even if you don't get your dream, the future you've wanted, you can still get the person you love back. And then you can start making your own dreams and future together."

"Are you seriously telling me to go after her?" He asked incredulously. He ran a hand through his hair.

"Help her see she made a mistake," his mother said softly.

"You agree with this, too, Mama?"

She'd always loved Kareena, always rooted for them. Had been sickened when their young love had broken. She always thought Kareena's father was a villain, and this entire situation only seemed to prove her point. Though there was definitely more to it than just that.

Sofia nodded.

"Aren't you disappointed that I didn't secure my Stavros inheritance?"

"I *am* sad for you on that matter. But, it is what it is. You've always found a way to make your dreams come true.

I'm more upset that you and the person you love can't make it work."

"*She* doesn't want to make it work," he spat out.

"Zayn, give her some time. Her father was in the hospital. She was afraid she would lose him. She has her daughter to think about, too. I have a feeling she has more to her than succumbing to her family's wishes. She might just need a little more time figuring everything out."

Zayn pushed his chair back, the legs scraping loudly on the floor, as he stood up.

"I don't want to have to convince her," Zayn said harshly. "She should want to be with me no matter what."

greenwich, connecticut

CHAPTER 39

ও২

*K*areena and Tamannah arrived at her parents' house later that evening. Thankfully, Henny was available to watch Aloo while they were gone. It was too much to bring him this time, though her parents adored him. Her father needed no distractions at the moment.

She parked in the wide driveway and shut off the engine, resting her head back on the seat as she stared blindly at the familiar house. It was a large pink brick home with black shutters and black wrought iron detailing that looked like almost identical to the other homes in their cul-de-sac.

The street lamp posts cast a dreary glow along the empty street. She noticed no lights on inside, except for the porch and the ornamental garden lights that lit up the lawn and her mother's pride and joy: her snowball hydrangea bushes that lined the front of the house, still hanging on through fall.

She glanced back at her daughter in the rear-view mirror. Tamannah clutched her favorite panda bear to her, as she slept, her head lolling to the side in a position that would give any adult a painful neck the next day. She'd urged her daughter to put her pajamas on and brush her teeth before she climbed into her booster seat in the back, knowing Tama would nod off after about thirty minutes of non-stop chatter, and listening to her favorite tunes from animated movie soundtracks.

She sighed heavily, wanting only one responsibility at the moment—to be the parent for just now. As soon as she walked into the house, it was a tug of war between parenting, helping her elderly parents, and being treated like she was still a young girl. Thankfully, her *amma* still had her health, and her father would get better; he had no other choice if Kareena had anything to do with it.

A tap on her window made her jump. It was Reyana. Her long, green-streaked hair was tucked into the hood of her oversized beige hoodie. She wore matching sweatpants with fat, reflective orange stripes down each side of the baggy legs.

Kareena put a finger up to her mouth, pointing to Tamannah in the back. She got out of the car without stirring her daughter.

"You haven't answered any of my calls or texts," Reyana said, her arms crossed over her chest. "Are you alright? Did you go straight to bed after the show yesterday?"

"I'm fine," Kareena said, avoiding her gaze. "And I eventually fell asleep."

"It's just that you kind of lost your shit last night."

"You would, too, if you were confused about … so many things."

"Kara," her sister said mournfully, and hugged her. "It's okay. Any chance you want to talk about it now?"

"No," Kareena said immediately. Her emotions and her wants were not her focus at the moment. She had her father to worry about. "When did you get here?"

"This morning." Reyana stepped back, dropping her arms. "I helped Mom set up the downstairs guest suite."

"How does he look?"

"Pretty good, all things considered. Still very weak. But I'll let you see for yourself tomorrow when he's awake." She stepped to the back of Kareena's car. "Here, let me help you get your stuff and get inside."

Kareena nodded and pressed the button for the automatic trunk door, and it opened. Reyana grabbed her overnight bag and Tamannah's backpack while Kareena unbuckled her daughter's sleeping form, hefting her into her arms. She didn't even stir, probably exhausted from her sleepover the night before, where actual sleep was the last thing on the kids' minds.

They went in through the front, and Reyana led the way to Kareena's old room up the wide carpeted stairs. Being there brought back reminiscences galore, especially when she was hit with traces of some of her favorite perfumes she used to douse herself in, like Ralph Lauren's Romance, and a very short stint with Curious by Brittney Spears. The cloying sweetness still stuck in the dark recesses of her room, melding with the stale smell of passing time.

She put Tamannah in her old full-size bed, tucking her in and pulling the daisy-printed duvet over her. She left a lamp on in case her daughter awoke disorientated, then she left the room quietly with her sister.

They headed back downstairs to the kitchen, where Kareena saw an open beer bottle on the island.

"Want one?" Reyana asked her, going to the fridge.

She shook her head. "I drank way too much crap wine when I got home last night. Is there any seltzer in there?"

Reyana pulled out a can of lime seltzer, the generic brand

their parents bought in bulk from the big box store they loved. Kareena took it and cracked it open, sipping thirstily as the bubbles raced and scraped down her throat.

"Where's Aloo?"

"Henny is watching him for us."

"That woman is a Godsend. You need to give her a damn raise."

"I know," Kareena agreed. "If her son and daughter-in-law ever decide to have kids, she'll go back to the UK to be the perfect English grandmother, and my life will be a chaotic mess."

"It doesn't have to be," Reyana said, flipping open her iPad case, the screen illuminating her face.

"What do you mean?"

"You can pick up everything and move to Greece. You have the settlement from Arjun's accident. Tama would be more than fine there. It's not a third-world country; you can find care for her special needs if it comes to that." She swiped around on the screen. "You *can* choose your own adventure, you know."

Kareena felt a bloom of hope before she popped it, and it deflated.

"I'm here for *Abba*. What did his doctor say?" she asked, aware that she was usually the one on the other end of this questioning, providing the answers.

Reyana sighed and read down a list of medications, dosages, proper rest, and pertinent physical activity when he was ready. So far, he'd taken the bypass surgery well. He was healing properly, though he was stubborn and wanted to do more than he could. He was already annoyed about the fact that he couldn't be in his room upstairs. He loved his bed, the one where he could control his side's temperature and firmness, and if he had to, his wife's too (she was the snorer in the relationship).

Kareena chuckled. "*Abba* doesn't know how to be a patient." She sipped her seltzer. "I guess the fact that he's being as stubborn as a goat tells us he's doing all right."

Reyana nodded and smiled. "Stubborn as a goat, but as weak as a baby lamb. Kara, I'm still confused about why the stent didn't work in the first place. Isn't that usually the simplest and most effective way to help with blockages?"

"Googling, lately?" Kareena teased.

Reyana nodded seriously, and Kareena sobered up and explained as best as she could. Her specialty was psychiatry, but that didn't mean she didn't know about the cardiovascular system, having to have studied it extensively like every other med student.

"When it comes down to it, you don't know how the body will react. Even *Abba* is aware of the risks as a cardiologist. But the positives outweigh the risks in most cases."

She then told Reyana what she'd learned from their father's doctor when she'd visited him in the hospital a few days ago after his surgery.

He'd survived a stent thrombosis. It was an occurrence that could happen anytime, from shortly after the stent placement to months later. Their father was the latter case.

"Layman's terms, please," her sister interrupted drily, and not for the first time, when Kareena and their father, even their mother, got to talking shop in medical terms only they understood.

Kareena nodded. "Right. It's a blood clot that forms around the stent location. The stent is a little mesh tube that widens the artery for blood flow. Basically, it failed because of the blood clot, which prevented blood flow and oxygen to the heart. That's why he had a heart attack and needed bypass surgery. Thank goodness he recognized the symptoms early on to have *Amma* take him to the ER."

She'd been told by everyone when she got there that her father had been experiencing severe chest pains before arriving at the hospital.

She was surprised at how tranquil she was, but realized it was the medical professional in her that kept her from spinning out of control. Sometimes explaining things to people about medical issues, even if they pertained to family members, calmed her down because it was factual, not emotional. She'd alternate to spiraling again, no doubt, in a few moments.

"Anyway, it sounds like he's doing better. *Amma* went a little overboard on the phone. I really thought he was on death's door. But you never know when a loved one goes under the knife."

Such a funny statement, she thought, her mind flashing back to being under Zayn's big chef's knife while they had sex in the kitchen.

"So," Reyana said, making her throw a wet blanket on all the sensually hot things she'd done with him, because really, what was wrong with her brain at the moment? "It was the stent that caused his heart attack."

"The blood clot, which no one could predict would happen," Kareena corrected, sipping her seltzer, glad she could regurgitate medical information so she could *not* think about other inappropriate things.

"And … not your fake engagement and jetting off to Greece with a guy they didn't love for you, but you seem to really care about—that didn't cause his heart attack, just so I'm clear."

438

And just like that, her pulse jump-started in exhilaration at the mere mention of the time she'd spent with Zayn on his family estate on Naxos. It was nothing short of spectacular. She had a feeling she'd be mourning the loss of him and the experience for the rest of her days on earth.

What was her life? Why couldn't she have what she wanted? She didn't resent coming back to take care of her father. But she regretted having to leave Zayn, and the utterly weightless sensation of being with him and being loved and adored.

She set her can of seltzer down a little too hard. Fizzy liquid jostled out onto the counter.

"Why are you doing this, Reya? I feel guilty as is." She swiped the liquid with her hand, pushing it across the marble. Guilt for her father and for Zayn.

"Because you're not thinking clearly right now. Your grief, or guilt, or the combination of the two, is driving your emotions right now. But it's all so irrational. You're the mental health doctor, why can't you see that?"

"So you're calling me a bad psychiatrist, as well as a sham?" Her eyes filled with tears. "Don't you see? I can't lose *Abba* after losing Arjun." She shook her head, dashing away her tears. The thought would leave her life tilted permanently. She'd always had a strong, supportive man backing her decisions, helping her when she faltered.

"Not what I said at all. You're just clouded in your judgment, and you want to hear what only fits within your narrative," her sister said, finishing her beer and rinsing the bottle out before putting it in the recycling bin.

Kareena was shook. When had her sister gotten so … pragmatic?

"I'm going to bed now, Kara. I'm wiped out. I'll see you

tomorrow." She turned to leave but tossed over her shoulder, "I hope you get some rest, but I really, *really* hope you have dreams filled with a certain hot chef and his huge … knife." She waved and smirked as she left.

And there was the Reyana she knew so well, she thought, as she watched her sister leave.

Honestly, all she was having lately were hot chef-shaped dreams, but they were riddled with ominous plots.

Absentmindedly, she ran her thumb over her left ring finger, feeling the ghost of the engagement ring there.

She'd been floored when he'd given it to her the night of the rehearsal dinner, publicly exchanging the new Tiffany ring for this more special one, remembering the sincerity and warmth in his eyes as he pushed the cherished piece of jewelry onto her finger. It had seemed that it was only the two of them there in that moment, that everyone around them had floated away, as she couldn't look away from him, making her believe the tangibility of their arrangement.

She missed that feeling. She missed the way he made her take herself less seriously. How he relished the small things in life, like a plate of well paired, simple flavors, or the feel of the ocean on his skin. If she were being truly honest with herself, she craved him, more than anything she'd ever craved in her adult life.

She wanted to wear his family's ring for good. He was the one person who saw her, made her laugh, and allowed her to feel safe without being demeaning. And what had she done? She'd left him with the ugliest words imaginable, words that she had no idea how to take back.

She wanted to run and hide with shame when she thought about how she'd alluded that he'd never be good enough for her because he wasn't good enough for her parents. She'd lashed out cruelly in fear of losing her father, so closely after losing her husband, that she pushed him away—the one person who made her feel whole, and who'd always seen her and loved her.

What had she done?

CHAPTER 40

80

Kareena tapped lightly on the guest room door on the first floor of her parents' home. The weak voice on the other side told her to come in.

She went into her father's recovery room. It looked a little different, with a portable table next to the bed, lined with her father's medication, a stack of crossword puzzle books, a cup of weak tea, and a small plate of Parle G biscuits.

Her father sat up in bed in his forest green velvet robe. He looked pale and fragile as he hugged a red, heart-shaped pillow to his chest.

"Hi, *Abba*," she said. "Look who I brought with me."

She held Tamannah's hand, who came into the room uncertainly behind her. As soon as she saw her grandfather, she rushed to him.

"*Nana!*" she cried.

Kareena reminded her to be careful, and the little girl stopped short at the bedside.

"It's okay," Sanjay said, putting the pillow aside. "*Ekhane asso* (come here)." He urged his granddaughter to come hug him. "I won't crumble, *Beta,*" he said, both to Tamannah and to his daughter.

"*Nana,* what is that?" Tamannah asked, pointing at the pillow. "Can I have one?"

Her father chuckled and for sure it sounded less robust than before. "Tama, you wouldn't want this pillow."

"But why? It's a heart. I *love* hearts."

Her father leaned into the girl. "This is a special pillow for heart-attack patients. It was given to me by my doctor and the nurses to help stabilize this part of my body after surgery." He pointed to his chest. "Do you know why?"

Tamannah didn't even think about it before she answered, "Because that's where your heart is. And the doctor had to open that part up to get inside and fix it."

Sanjay rubbed the top of her head. "Such a brilliant girl. Yes, you're right. And I'm still a little weak there, so the pillow helps support me, so I don't do something foolish like go and undo everything the doctor did."

"Was there a lot of blood? Did you see it?"

Sanjay tried to hide his smile from Tamannah's thought process. He thought about it before saying, "I'm sure there was. You know I'm a heart doctor, too, correct? I have to open my patients up to fix their hearts. But thankfully, I was asleep for my surgery. I don't think I'd want to see myself being … performed on."

"Yuck. You're right, *Nana.*" Tamannah made a grossed-out face. "I'm glad you're better. I have so many puzzles I want to work on with you."

"You do? Well, where are they? Do you know how bored I am? I need your difficult puzzles and you to keep me company."

"Mommy?" she turned around to Kareena. "Can I go get them?"

"Of course," Kareena said, sitting on the edge of her father's bed.

"I'll be right back, *Nana.*" She ran out of the room.

Her father adjusted the belt of his robe, before picking up the plate of biscuits and offering them to Kareena.

"Biscoot tiscoot?" he asked, the way he used to ask her when she was a little girl.

She shook her head. But he persisted, bobbling his head until she took one.

"Your *amma* keeps giving me snacks. I can't eat all of this. I have no appetite at the moment."

"*Abba,* you need to eat something."

"Oh, I did. I had an egg white omelet and whole wheat toast earlier. And a mixed fruit cup. I'm still full, *Beta.*"

She nodded, nibbling the crunchy, mildly sweet glucose biscuit.

"How are you feeling?" she asked.

"Like I got run over by a truck."

And *wham*! Kareena was hit with the memory of first seeing Zayn again after so many years, when he'd saved her from almost getting run over by the Stavros moving truck. It felt like *her* heart was having an attack of its own, beating furiously and thumping in her ears, which were heating up with embarrassment, as were her cheeks.

"Are *you* okay, *Beta?*" her father asked, sensing her heightened emotions.

"I am," She choked out. "I'm … just so glad you're okay."

He lifted his teacup and slurped the liquid before saying, "I missed you very much, *Shona*. Please do not do that to me—us again."

She felt meek for a moment before she straightened up. "I can't promise you that."

"I know you were upset, but that's no reason not to call your parents back, especially when you are almost on the other side of the world." He sounded like a petulant child.

"I'm sorry about that, *Abba*. But you have to see it from my point of view. I need to be able to make my own choices and find what makes *me* happy, especially now when I'm raising a child who looks to me for guidance. I want her to grow up strong and independent, and to know herself inside and out one day, preferably sooner than I did."

He nodded, ever so slightly. "You're not a child anymore, Kara. I know that. I saw very clearly that by you being with Zayn again, and running off to Greece—"

"I didn't run off."

"Let me finish." He spoke quietly, and she nodded. "By you going out of the country with him, advising us that we needed to stop being so judgmental and then you would speak to us again…" He looked like he was searching for the right words, and there was nothing as vulnerable as seeing her father, a man she'd worshipped her entire life, a man she'd taken advice from without any question in her formative years (and then some), looking so frail, and a little unsure. "I knew that we had gone too far. We had asked too much of you—a woman who is a mother, and a doctor, born and raised an American, who should be living her own life. You have to understand, we didn't grow up like that, *Shona*. But we came here to give our children opportunities that we may have never had. One of those opportunities is 'choice.'"

She was stunned. She let out the breath she'd been holding, thinking she would need to argue further.

"I'm glad, *Abba*. Because I'm here while you get better. But I am going back to Zayn."

The words felt better than good as they came out of her mouth, even though she knew deep down that Zayn may never forgive her, never take her back after her behavior. She wouldn't blame him one bit.

Her father solemnly nodded. "I was thinking, Thanksgiving is next week. I think we will keep it small. But would you like to invite Zayn? We could see if he passes your mother's cooking test for rice?"

Was her father trying to make a joke? And had she heard correctly? Was he inviting Zayn?

"I'm not sure he can get away," she lied. "But I can ask him."

"*Thick ache* (okay). Please do. You know, I talked to his father—before all of this." He gestured to himself and around the room. "It sounds like he is doing very well for himself and opening a new restaurant on the family land?"

She nodded, her throat clogging up. She had to look away as she murmured, "That's right."

No one knew that she'd broken things off with them, right? So by this point, Zayn had to have confirmed his portion of the inheritance.

"Well, when you speak to him next, give him our best wishes, and we hope he can come for dinner. Oh, and, *Shona*, would you like to ask Sheila to come, too? You know, she must be so lonely after her divorce. And I hear her parents aren't speaking to her. I might hear from them about my actions, but if you would like her to come for Thanksgiving, we would gladly have her."

"Really? You don't care about what people are saying about her?"

"I do care. I don't like that they are talking about her. A divorce is between two people, and it sounds like her former husband treated her horribly and with little respect."

That was the gist of it, but he really had no idea. Sheila's ex-husband had a PhD in mind-fuckery and put her through a miserable time in their few years of marriage. She'd already vowed off marriage for good.

"I'll definitely ask her, *Abba*. I know she'll appreciate it."

He sighed, a smile brightening his tired face. "I have a new outlook on life, *Beta*. I want to be more considerate of others and welcome them with open arms."

Kareena stood up and went to her father, gently hugging him.

Tamannah came bursting back into the room, a pile of puzzle boxes under her arm.

"Here they are. I think we should start with the dog one first." She promptly opened that box and dumped the contents all over Sanjay's bed.

Her father spun his head in mock dizziness. "So many pieces, Tama. I'm so glad you're here!"

Kareena left them to it. She said she would come check in on them in half an hour.

She went to her room and took her phone off the charger. She found Zayn's number and stared at it. What if he didn't want to speak to her? What if he didn't pick up ... ever? What if he was already with another woman?

Okay, she needed to scratch that last thought and give the man more credit. He was in love with her. He wouldn't do that.

She wasn't sure how to reach out to him, so she said the only thing she could think of that was the least emotional. **"I have your family's ring. I'm so sorry. I'll figure out a way to get it back to you."** Then she deleted that and typed, **"Would you want to come over for Thanksgiving?"**

That was a curveball out of nowhere, wasn't it?

She deleted that, too, and typed simply, **"I'm sorry."**

That was the truth anyhow, and how she was feeling. She hit 'send' and put her phone away, vowing not to look at it for the rest of the day. She doubted he'd get back to her, and again, she wouldn't blame him.

naxos island, greece

CHAPTER 41

8ک

*Z*ayn pulled his swim trunks on and grabbed a wetsuit. The weather had dipped to cool, turning out to be a typical autumn in the Cyclades. But he still intended to go into the ocean. He needed a swim to clear his head from his parents' advice, Silas's shit, Kareena … everything.

Zayn had still been perplexed as to how his cousin found out about him and Kareena faking their engagement. And Silas, ever the pompous ass, still wouldn't tell him. Zayn questioned if the man really had a reliable source.

It didn't matter anyway now. The clock had run out on the claim's period. By midnight that night, he'd forfeit everything over to the estate.

He looked around the room, keeping his emotions at bay as he was faced with Kareena's abandonment. It'd been days since she left, and he couldn't bring himself to remove any of her things just yet.

She'd left several of her belongings behind. Her flashy red bathing suit was still flung over a chair, having been left there to dry. In the bathroom, her toiletries were in the same place she'd organized them in when she first arrived. When he flung open the closet, he saw she'd left all of the beautiful clothes she'd purchased from the local shops that first day in Athens. He didn't think he could feel any lonelier than in a room full of someone's belongings who didn't want to be there anymore.

He felt like he was confined, seeing her everywhere, but her presence was like a ghost—a thing of the past haunting him. What he needed to do was go out and get into the water. He needed to think, and a hard swim that worked his muscles to the bone, leaving his body in a state of total exhaustion, was the therapy he craved. The private pool wouldn't do. Too many memories with her, and he needed to be in the actual ocean, fighting with the wild currents, tasting salt, finally becoming one with the choppy waves. The water would be down to the low 60s Fahrenheit. Not the coldest, but the beaches would be empty, and he'd have the place to himself.

He turned his phone on to check for any messages before he pulled his wetsuit on over his trunks. It buzzed with an incoming message from hours ago.

It was from Kareena.

"I'm sorry." It read.

He stared at it, not sure if he was reading the simple words correctly. Was that all she'd written? Fuck, those words could mean anything. Was she sorry for leaving? Was she sorry for breaking off their fake engagement? Or was she sorry for breaking his heart again?

He inhaled deeply and closed his eyes, counting to ten before exhaling. Damn this woman—an enigma he wanted to burrow into and figure out. And then he cursed himself for continuing to want to after everything.

He decided to text a response that had nothing to do with her apology.

"How's your father doing? Is he okay?"

He wanted to add, "Are you okay?" but he thought better of it. He wasn't ready to ask if she was ok, because if she answered that she was, that would mean she was fine with the decision she'd made, and he'd have to basically go fuck himself.

Leave it, he told himself. He threw his phone on the bed in frustration.

He was just pushing his arms into the tight nylon of his wetsuit when the frantically loud knocking at the garden door got his attention. He zipped up the front and bounded down the stairs.

"Just a second!" he shouted, striding to the door. He jerked it open, wondering who was bothering him this early in the morning. The sun had barely left the horizon.

It was Penelope. She looked pale and meek.

"Pen? What is it? What happened?"

He ushered her in.

"Could I have some tea?" she asked weakly, sitting down at the dining table.

He stared at her for a beat before moving. "Sure."

He filled the electric kettle and flipped it on. "Chamomile? Ginger?"

"Chamomile," she said, staring at her hands in her lap.

He nodded and fixed her tea, and brought it to her. She dunked the bag a few times, then left it to steep.

"Zayn. I love you like the big brother I should have had." She was close to tears.

"I know. You're the bratty little sister I never asked for," he teased. When she didn't laugh, he asked, concerned, "What's wrong? Is it Brutus? Did that bastard already do something to upset you?"

"No. Oh my God, Zayn, no. He's waiting for me at the big house. We're leaving for our honeymoon in a few."

"So what's going on?"

"Don't get mad, okay?"

"I'll get madder every second you don't tell me what's happening," he said, starting to lose his patience.

She nodded and pulled her teabag out, but didn't take a sip. "After the wedding, Brutus and I were at the manor, right? Killing time in the few days until we had to leave for Thailand —today."

"Right."

"Well, Brutus wanted to see the taverna—we've been so busy that we hadn't had the time. So we snuck in one night. We brought champagne—we got a little wild and did some stuff—"

He held up his hand, getting the picture. "I know you two are married, but I do not need to hear that shit."

She nodded. "We came out to go skinny dipping in the ocean. The moon was so bright that night and it was so romantic. And that's when we heard yelling coming from the villa—here—where you two were staying by that point."

He understood immediately. "You heard Kareena and I fighting."

She played with the rings on her finger, worrying her new wedding band around and around. "We didn't mean to. But I guess your windows were open, and there was no way not to hear the shouting. Brutus thought it might be an emergency, so we ran up the steps and, well, we heard everything."

"I'm sorry you had to hear that."

"Was it really all fake then? You guys seemed so genuinely in love."

"Yeah, we're pretty great actors aren't we," he said bitterly. "But you couldn't help it. There was no way you couldn't hear us."

"Well, here's the part that might make you regret ever loving me like a sister." She took a deep breath. "Silas and I got into a fight the next day, and I told him you were always the best one out of all of us. You're like a brother to me, and that, even though your engagement wasn't real, he should've let you have your inheritance fair and square."

Zayn leaned back in his chair, taken aback as the words sank in. So that's how Silas found out. And he knew exactly why Zayn would never rip the head off his informant.

"It's all right, Pen," he finally said, in reaction to the big, fat tears rolling down her cheeks. "I mean, it's not," he sighed, "but you were emotional, and you're still young. If I've learned anything from Kareena, it's that a person's brain is still developing in their early twenties."

It was something she'd said numerous times in passing.

"Plus, it's Silas. That man could make a nun commit murder."

That only got a half-hearted smile out of his young cousin. "I'll make it up to you. I promise. Just watch. You'll see."

"Don't do anything drastic, Penelope."

"But, don't you want your inheritance?"

He didn't waver when he said, "It's a little late for that at this point. By midnight tonight, the claims period is over and Silas folds the taverna and everything else, including this place," he looked around, "back into the estate." He sighed. "In all honesty, what I really want is my fake fiancé back, but for real this time."

He didn't know what made him say it, but he knew those words to be the truth. Penelope looked at him, with sadness in her grey eyes. "You guys *do* love each other. When love is involved, why can't people make it work?"

"Sometimes it's not that simple, Penelope."

"Shouldn't it be though? That's the one thing we as humans know. We feel it in our bones when a person is meant for us. And if there are problems, we work to fix them, right?"

After she left, and apologized more times than he could count, he stalked out of the house and down the stairs to the private beach. As soon as he hit the sand, he broke into a run and dove head first into the chilly dark waves.

He barely let the foam kiss his back before he headed further down under the surf. He kicked harder, touching the bottom with his hands before turning his body and kicking up to the surface. He broke through and sucked in air before going under again, shooting himself through the currents like a bullet, making his body sleeker by keeping his toes together, and his arms in front of them in an inverted 'V,' with his chin tucked.

He wasn't sure how much time had passed before his muscles started to lose their strength. He returned to the sand, crawling to a spot to dry off on his back.

He looked up into the sky and saw the flock of swallows, wheeling like cartwheels in the air. His eyes followed them as his mind raced and he caught his breath.

How could he blame Penelope for this? She and her brother had a tenuous relationship. Silas had always treated her like an afterthought. The fact of the matter was that maybe, in the grand scheme of things, Zayn wasn't supposed to have the taverna and everything that went along with it. His grandfather had made such an insane stipulation that perhaps it had always been his intention to keep that property within the estate. Perhaps his motive was for Zayn to go out and pursue love. The old man had always been a romantic. He'd loved his wife, and a small part of him died when she went.

He sat up, resting his elbows on his knees. "*Pappous*, what the hell was going through your mind in those last few weeks when you rewrote your will?"

No one would ever know. All anybody could go off was what they knew in the present. For him, it was that he loved Kareena Sharma. He'd never stopped. It was time to go and reclaim his karma once and for all.

THANKSGIVING
THE FOLLOWING WEEK
greenwich, connecticut

CHAPTER 42

8২

"*A*nd so dear listeners, the holidays aren't just about getting together and spending time with family and friends. It can also be a good time to reflect on things we want to make right. Maybe there's a lost love out there, or someone you may have wronged—or both. With the New Year almost upon us, don't we all deserve another chance at a fresh start?" Kareena finished reading from the scrap of paper in her hand and then looked up at her sister. "What do you think? We could throw this in somewhere for the holiday episode. I thought about putting in a Scrooge reference, you know, about regrets, but I'm not sure." She took a deep breath and asked tentatively, "But do you think a certain someone might listen to that and know that I'm sorry?"

Both of them sat in their pajamas in the back den. The fire burned cozily in the grate of the gas fireplace while the Thanksgiving Macy's Day parade was on TV. Though none of them actively watched, the tradition was to have it playing in the background as people woke up, had coffee, and lolled about before cooking.

Right now, Tamannah was the only one sitting on the couch watching in awe as the parade of floats went by on the flatscreen hung above the mantel. Sanjay was on the couch, too, but had fallen asleep. Leela had already started cooking, the smell of fried onions beginning to permeate the house.

"I don't know, Kara." Reyana yawned. "Wouldn't it be better if we just addressed his email on our next podcast, instead? You should see the comments from listeners. Everyone is dying to know what happened with Sinful's romance saga. We could tailor it to how you feel, now." Her sister stretched. "Or, you could just call him and tell him you're sorry."

"I kind of already did. But it was via text."

"What did he say?"

"He asked how *Abba* was."

"And what did you say back?"

"That *Abba* was doing better and recovering."

"And then what?"

"And that's it."

Reyana yawned again. "Sorry, that entire text conversation just put me to sleep."

"*Reya*! I don't know how to do this."

"Are you really asking me for advice on relationships? Wait, don't answer that. I might not be in a serious relationship, or found 'the one,' but I think I've definitely experienced more than you."

"Wow. Thanks."

"Mommy! The Rockettes are going to be on soon," her daughter yelled from the couch.

"Tama, you don't have to yell. I'm right here. And *Nana* is napping." The older man didn't even stir, but was sleeping peacefully with deep, even breaths. Kareena had already checked.

"Ooo, the Rockettes! I can't miss those lovely ladies." Reya said, plopping down between Tamannah and Aloo, and cuddling both of them. Aloo, who was snoozing, wriggled out of her grip and promptly turned around with his butt facing her, before going back to loafing.

"Thanks, little man. I love you, too," her sister said, scratching his back.

"When that's done, Tama, can you go in the kitchen and get some breakfast?" Kareena asked, crumpling up the paper with her notes scribbled on it.

"But what if I miss Santa Claus?"

"I won't let you miss Santa Claus," she said, firmly. "He comes on at the very end anyway."

Tamannah was slowly but surely transforming their family into a it's-never-too-early-for-Christmas kind of family. She was adamant about putting her grandparents' tree up the day after Thanksgiving. All of the trimmings and ornaments were already brought down from the attic, including the fake tree in its box. Kareena's hard 'no' was getting a real tree, which Tama pouted about. But it was too much work, and she wasn't in the mood this year. However, she was more than happy to go along with her daughter's wish of continuing family cheer, moving right on from turkey day to celebrating holly, jolly, old Saint Nick. Who didn't love looking at a decorated Christmas tree for as long as was decently possible?

The day was one of those that felt like it went on forever, but still flew by. Kareena could actually experience every moment, savor the memories while baking pumpkin pie, or helping her mother make *Gulab jamon,* which the older woman insisted on having last minute, or while outside playing in the piles of dry fallen leaves with her sister, daughter, and Aloo.

When Sheila arrived, a beautifully wrapped box of pears and chocolates in hand as a gift to her parents, the sun was starting to set. Golden hues touched every surface outside, and it was glorious.

They sat out on the back deck, enjoying the last hazy hours as the sky turned from orange to fuchsia, violet, and cobalt blue. It reminded Kareena so much of the brilliant flowered blooms in Zayn's garden on Naxos that she sighed loudly and shakily.

"So, I take it you miss him?" Sheila asked, sipping her spiked hot cider. The smell wafted in the chilly air toward Kareena, and she inhaled the cozy scent of autumn and Thanksgiving, closing her eyes. Someone was burning an outdoor fire, and the smoky warm essence mingled around them.

"I do," she said, her eyes still closed. "But I don't know how to make it right."

"Do you love him?" her friend asked quietly.

She nodded.

"Is that the engagement ring?"

Kareena automatically covered her left hand with her right, embarrassed that she was wearing the ring again.

"Yeah. But I'm only wearing it because my parents still think he and I are engaged."

"Okay. Sure." Sheila put her drink down on the deck. "Can I see it closer?"

Kareena scooted toward her in her chair so her friend could get a better look.

"Well, that's just drop-dead gorgeous. And it's a family heirloom?"

"Yeah. It's really old. The stone was a gift from the newly minted king after the revolution from the Ottoman Empire in the 1800s."

"Wow. Too bad you have to give it back. The style suits you."

Kareena thought so, too. But it was going to return to its family when she could figure out a good excuse in the New Year, when she was starting fresh, going back to work, for why she and Zayn weren't engaged anymore. Unless he came looking for it before then.

"*Chalo yai* (let's go). Your mom is waving at us from the window."

They went in, leaving their jackets on the hooks by the back door.

"Girls, please take these into the dining room and set them on the buffet," her mother said to them, and to her daughter and sister. To her begging pup she admonished him and shooed him away.

Kareena shook her head, knowing there was no point in reprimanding her dog or removing him from their company. He'd whine the entire time wherever he was, wanting to know what he did wrong. And Kareena didn't have the heart to do that. It was like hearing a crying baby. Her motherly instincts always kicked in.

Instead, she did what she wasn't supposed to do, or at least what the puppy training school had discouraged. She pulled a little piece of potato from her mother's stir-fried curried vegetable dish and called her dog to her.

"Aloo, come Aloo. Here." She chucked the piece of potato far, through the dining room, and possibly into the front foyer. "Aloo, go find the *aloo* (potato)."

He dashed off happily.

That would keep him busy for about three minutes at least.

"Kara, please set the table." Her mother handed her the good China.

"There's seven here." She counted the stack in her hands.

"So?"

"We only need six."

Her mother sucked her teeth. "Go." She shooed her away from the kitchen.

Kareena passed the buffet filled with all of the Thanksgiving goodies from a mid-sized turkey and trimmings, to mashed potatoes, dinner rolls, and green beans. Interspersed amongst those were the Indian dishes her mother liked to complement the meal with, including goat biryani, curried vegetables, a tart cucumber salad, and mango *achar* (pickles). Thank goodness her *amma* had decided against making *pakoras*. There was always too much food, making the fried fritters unnecessary, and everyone left happy and full, with plenty of leftovers for the next few days.

Kareena finished setting the table as everyone gathered around to sit.

"*Shona*, you sit there," her father said, pointing at the seat that was beside the seventh extra place-setting.

Kareena shared a glance with her sister across the table. But she looked just as confused. She cast her gaze to Sheila, who shrugged and shook her head.

Was this going to be another … matchmaking set up?

Kareena had to gird her loins. There was no way, not after she and her father spoke, and even the few words she'd shared with her mother, who truly felt bad about causing everyone so much hysteria. But Kareena had only hugged her mom, telling her she understood. Her mother had gone from living in her father's house, to living in her husband's. Her ideals about independence were vastly different from Kareena's. Whereas her mother broke the mold from her well-off family by marrying her father and then coming to America to pursue continuing education and a career, she still held onto her husband as not only her partner, but her provider in many things. Her sense of independence came from getting an education and a job because she was never expected to in her household. So the thought of losing her husband, the man who'd taken care of her in many ways since she'd married him, had led her to spiral and she'd pushed that onto her eldest.

They all grabbed their plates and lined up at the buffet. Tamannah declared they should do dessert first so they could try everything before they got too stuffed.

"Next year, Tama," she said, winking at her daughter.

When they sat down, they all went around the table and shared what they were thankful for—something that Reyana had insisted they take on back when they were still in high school. Her father went first, saying he was thankful for his family, and everyone in that room, and his health. Her mother said she was thankful for modern medicine, and she held on to her father's hand tightly. Her sister's was about having the life she'd always dreamed, living in the hustle and bustle, but still getting to be close to her family. Sheila said something about yoga and the strength it gave her to carry on and heal. Tamannah said she was thankful for Aloo and for pumpkin pie. And when it came to Kareena's turn, she said a little vaguely that she was thankful for second chances and for being able to experience love again.

Her parents thought she was talking about finding Zayn for the second time. She was. But she was also thankful that even if things never worked out between them, she'd had that time with him in Greece. Had experienced a love so deep that now it took her entire heart. She was saddened at the idea of it not having a resolution, but life wasn't simple like that. She'd messed up, not once, but twice, and she needed to face the consequences. Right now, sitting around the table, she realized she had her family to help her get through that, at least for the day.

Kareena's phone buzzed with a text, and she ignored it.

"Aren't you going to see who that is?" Reyana asked, as they began to eat.

"Should I? It's a holiday."

"So? Maybe it's someone saying Happy Thanksgiving to you. I think I got over fifty texts this morning."

"Okay, Miss Social," Kareena teased, flipping the phone over.

The text was from Zayn. Her pulse picked up as she read:

"Do you still have my family's engagement ring? I need it for something important."

She felt like throwing up all of the pre-meal tasting she'd done.

She stared at her phone. Did she get back to him? What would she say?

Honesty. Remember, honesty is the best tactic.

"I do have it. I'm so sorry that I left with it. I grew used to having it on. How can I get it back to you safely?"

He didn't text back and after ten minutes, she realized he wasn't going to answer.

With a heavy heart, she picked up her fork, and took a bite of her mother's special *biryani*. She tasted dust. But she put on a brave face as her daughter happily chatted about how delicious the food was, but asked *Nani* directly if she'd ever had eggplant curried pizza.

"I don't think so, *Beta*. Why? Do you know of a good place to try it?"

"Actually, Zayn Uncle told me about it. It's one of his specialties. And *I* told him he had to try your eggplant curry and use that for his pizza, because no one, not even him, can top your banging barta. "

"*Baingan bharta* (mashed eggplant curry)," Kareena corrected at the same time her mother did. They both chuckled at each other.

"That's what I said, isn't it?" Tamannah asked, shoveling turkey and cranberry chutney into her mouth.

Kareena didn't have time to mull over Zayn and his eggplant curry pizza, his delicious cooking, and everything else she missed about him because the doorbell rang, making everyone look up from their plates. They exchanged curious glances.

"Are we expecting more guests?" Kareena asked, putting her fork down.

Her parents shared a look, before her father asked her to answer the door.

"I got it," Reyana said, brushing her hands off and jumping up. She left the room, warning Tama not to take her dinner roll and not to give her turkey to Aloo, before winking.

They heard her open the front door, and then boisterous conversation in the foyer. By this point, Aloo had run to see who it was and was happily barking.

Reyana came back into the dining room, her eyes, still green to match her hair, were huge, and she looked like she was holding in the biggest secret. She slid into her chair but remained silent.

"Who was it?" Kareena asked.

A deep voice from the dining room doorway suddenly spoke, "Sorry, I'm late. Happy Thanksgiving. Thank you for inviting me."

To Kareena's utter astonishment, it was Zayn ... here in Connecticut ... for Thanksgiving. He looked windswept, his thick auburn curls wayward around his head. His cheeks were ruddy from the cold, and he was still removing his scarf and had his jacket on.

He gazed at her; his cinnamon eyes masked for a moment as she stared at him, stunned.

What was he doing here?

Her father began to stand, and Zayn told him not to. He said he'd be right back and left, returning sans scarf and jacket, but carrying a tin. He was wearing a deep forest green, long-sleeve waffle knit polo. He seemed to love polos, and Kareena couldn't deny that polos loved him back. The material was like a second skin as it showed off his defined bulging biceps and accentuated his broad, wide shoulders. The thick gold necklace around his neck shone brightly as he stood there, a bit unsure. *Everyone* was a bit unsure, in fact, shocked to see him there, too. Everyone, that is, except Aloo, who was whining and grunting, all while trying to burrow into his long legs encased in black jeans.

Her daughter had jumped up, too, and ran around the table, hurtling herself at him.

"Zayn Uncle! You're back! I knew it. I knew you'd come back." She hugged him tight as Zayn looked down at her with a mixture of confusion and adoration. His free arm came around the girls' shoulders in a hug. "You missed us, Mommy especially, right?"

"I did. And I couldn't miss the holiday with some of my favorite people."

"Mommy said you had a lot to do with the restaurant. And that she wasn't sure you'd come back to take care of her in case her heart broke and she needed help fixing it."

And now he glanced up to her quickly, his eyes burning bright. "Is that right?"

She wasn't sure if he was asking her or asking her daughter, but Tamannah happily answered. "Yeah. Like *Nana*. His heart broke, and *Nani* was there to help him. But my Mommy doesn't have anyone like that, except you."

Oh jeez. This girl, Kareena, shook her head, smiling, rolling her eyes slightly at Zayn, her face as red as the cranberry chutney on her plate.

Zayn gave her a lopsided grin that made her belly tumble, before speaking to her father, "So, again, thank you, Sanjay Uncle and Leela Aunty for inviting me. And everything looks delicious." He paused. "I made my baklava." He brought it over to the dessert table next to the buffet before turning to address the group again. "But could I speak to Kareena alone for a minute?"

Wait, what? Her parents had invited him?

All eyes turned to her, and her mother was the one to say, "Of course, Zayn. And we're so happy to see you again. Please go, catch up." She smiled secretly, as though Kareena and Zayn were going off to canoodle, having been apart for almost two weeks now since she came back. "But hurry back. The food will get cold." She shooed them away with her hands. "And I made your favorite*, Gulab jamon.* Kareena helped!"

Ah, her last-minute *Gulab jamon* stubbornness made sense now..

Had her parents already known he would come? And her mother—had she really done a complete one-eighty regarding her feelings about Zayn? It seemed so. Her father's heart attack had really shifted everyone's thinking.

He nodded, his eyes only on her. "I wouldn't miss it for the world, Aunty."

Kareena shivered. Was that a promise about eating his favorite dessert, or something else?

She didn't know what to think. Maybe he was only here to ask for the ring back. He'd said he needed it for something important.

She got up and followed him out of the dining room. She aimlessly led him through to the back of the house, deciding on the TV room as a good place as any to speak in private.

CHAPTER 43

80

*S*he took him to the back den, pulling the double doors closed behind them.

He remembered this room, with the big, cushy L-shaped couch in tan corduroy, still there in the center. Everything looked the same, except there were more family photos, and there used to be an old school behemoth standalone flat screen TV. But now a sleek, thinner model, hung over the fireplace, where a cozy fire dwindled in the grate.

She turned around, with her hands clasped in front of her. In her pretty fuzzy mauve cardigan, over a sheer white button-down blouse and jeans, she looked absolutely stunning. It was always her chic simplicity that brought out her natural beauty. He'd missed her so much as he drank her in; it took everything in him not to reach for her and pull her to him.

She didn't meet his gaze. Her eyes were focused on her hands.

"So … thank you for inviting me," he started with, breaking the silence, wanting to hear what she had to say about him being there.

Her big almond-shaped eyes flew to him. "Zayn, I can't believe my parents invited you. I mean, I would have liked to, and I'm glad that you're here, but I know you must've had a lot going on back on the island. I didn't think you would have time —or that you would even want to see me…" She trailed off.

"Actually, I planned on coming to the New York area anyway. I had no plans to come *here* for Thanksgiving, except that your dad called me and wanted to make sure I was coming. I had no idea what he was talking about, but I played along. Seems like you were supposed to ask me?"

"*My* dad called *you*?"

He folded his arms across his chest. "He did."

"Zayn, after the way I left, I didn't think you would want to see me ever again. And I knew I had to face the consequences."

He didn't say anything, keeping his cool. He wanted to be understanding with this woman. She was going through a transformation and trying to figure out her own personal struggles. All he wanted to do was be there for her in that.

"What did my dad say?" She asked, her hands fidgeting.

"He said some really interesting things. He was nice; he apologized for being so prejudiced and judgmental toward me. But he couldn't quite come around to feeling apologetic about our high school romance. He thought we were too young to know anything about anything back then. But he definitely felt like life was giving him a second chance, and he understood why we wanted to pursue our relationship after finding each other again."

Kareena exhaled loudly. "Well, that's … something."

But Zayn wasn't finished. "He also said that he couldn't keep holding you back. That you weren't a child, and that you had to make your own choices. He realized that the point of having children was to teach them, let them learn and grow, and then let them go so they could begin their own lives."

Her eyes were enormous, and now her arms were folded across her chest too, as he relayed to her everything her father had said to him. And he wished she wouldn't stand like that. It made her full cleavage and the top curves of her breasts more apparent under her shirt's sheer material, and he had to keep himself from staring.

"Wow. He really said all that?"

He nodded. "He did. I have to admit that I was completely shocked."

He had been more than shocked. He'd received a text from an unknown number, and it said: **"This is Sanjay Uncle. Please call me."**

Zayn could only assume that his father had given Kareena's father his number.

Curious, he called him back immediately. Zayn knew the older man was still recuperating from major surgery, but he still had a few things he needed to get off his chest—namely, that it wasn't Kareena's fault that the older man had a heart attack. That he and Kareena were happy together, and why couldn't they understand that they truly loved and respected one another? They'd been kids the first time, but now they were full-grown adults. He had planned to tell the man that he was coming for her.

But he didn't have to. Instead, he'd listened to the heartfelt apology from her father, and the realization it wasn't in the older man's right to control his adult daughter.

Kareena pushed her hair behind her shoulders. He noticed the glint on her finger; she didn't just have his family's ring in her possession; she was actually still wearing it!

The clench in his heart made him wonder if he was having some sort of cardiac arrest, himself. He was overjoyed to still see her wearing it, even after everything.

"He's turning a new leaf," Kareena said. "When we talked, he said some of those things to me, too, especially when I told him once he was done recuperating, I was going back to you—I know that might not happen..." She said in a rush.

He let out a shaky breath at her words, and she went on. "I had to let him know that he couldn't determine my life anymore. I needed to be able to figure things out on my own, even if it's confusing, or he thinks I'm making the wrong choices."

She noticed him staring at her hand, and she covered it with her other one.

"I'll give this back to you. I promise. I would never hold on to this forever. I'm sorry that I took it when I left, and I'm wearing it to keep up with our charade for your inheritance—"

She sounded so flustered that he put a hand up, stopping her. "It's fine, Kareena. I understand."

"Okay. So, what do we do now?"

That was the million-dollar question, wasn't it? He wanted so badly to go to her and hold her. To kiss her and tell her everything would be okay. Because with him, she would be. But he wasn't sure if she realized that yet, remembering what his father had said to him—she needed to come to that conclusion herself.

He took a deep breath. "Well, I lost the restaurant and everything that went with it."

Her beautiful face, so unsure, completely fell. Her eyes welled up with tears, and they splashed onto her petal pink cheeks.

"What?" she whispered, her hands coming to cover her mouth. "Why?"

"Silas found out about our fake engagement. Someone heard us arguing and told him." He wasn't going to tell her it was Penelope. He'd let Pen tell her herself. The younger woman already felt horrible. He just hoped she could enjoy her honeymoon through all of this. Though, considering the events in the last week, specifically the day she'd left for her honeymoon, he had a pretty good feeling she was sitting on a beach slinging back Singapore Slings galore.

"But we were so close," she said, more to herself than to him. She still thought they were in this together. It made him feel light, and he smiled. She didn't notice, though. "Zayn, I am so, so sorry. I don't even know what to say. I don't even know how to make this up to you." Now the tears were falling unbidden, and she didn't even try to stop them. "Oh my God, I'm so sorry," she said, now apologizing for her anguish. She reached for the tissue box on the coffee table and pulled one out, dabbing at her eyes.

"We just … ran out of time," he said carefully. "When Silas found out it was all fake, he basically said I had lied to the Stavros family, to *Pappous'* honor, and the old man's final wishes."

Now she was angry, her forehead low over her thick brows. "And you believed him?" she asked almost shrilly, through her tears.

"I did at first. But after giving it a lot of thought, I'm not so sure I did any dishonoring. I don't know what the old man had in his head at the end. But when I met with the attorneys and asked them directly about it, they said he'd changed his will while on his deathbed. Maybe he was clearheaded, and most likely he wasn't, but he didn't want to follow the legal four-month waiting period to file claims, which is standard in Greece's inheritance law. He wanted it moved up, and he forced their hand to give me a shorter time frame."

"How did he do that?"

"He threw a bunch of money under the table at them." He shrugged. His grandfather might be honorable, but the man was wily and wielded the family fortune and name for the benefit of the next generation, whether they saw it or not.

"Okay," she said cautiously. "So, *now* what?" She clutched the crumpled tissue in her hand, sniffing.

This is when he felt right about going to her. He tugged at her hand and pulled her to sit next to him on the enormous, comfortable couch.

"Well, get this: I got a very angry call from Silas this morning, as I was landing at JFK."

"Now what does that cranky man want? I swear, he has a made-up bone to pick with everyone, especially you. I'm still trying to figure out what his problem is."

Zayn hid his smile, appreciating Kareena's support, but he knew Silas was salty for having undue pressure put on him as the eldest cousin. He hadn't had the opportunity to find himself. It wasn't so different from Kareena, except that Kareena had seen herself being pulled into a life she didn't want, and had attempted to halt it.

He went on, "Well, apparently, before midnight, a few hours before the claims period ended, my grandfather's attorney received a few claims to his will."

Her eyes slit as she pondered this. "What? How many?"

"Two to begin with, but then they kept coming in. In total, there's twenty-three."

He leaned back, forgetting how deep the couch was, but now recalling how he and Kareena would lie lengthwise and snuggle, sinking into the cushions—but only when her parents weren't there. Just nosy Reya, who wanted to hang out with them.

"People from all over the island, locals I've known my entire life, came forward, had paperwork filed, and made claims on my grandfather's will."

"*What*!?" Her face was a comically contorted blend of horrified fascination and an attempt to hold in her laughter.

"Somehow, these people found out that my inheritance was going away, so they rallied, got a lawyer—last-minute, mind you—and filed claims. It's all legit in terms of paperwork. I know the lawyer. But they're all fake in terms of the actual claims. I can show you the documents if you want. Silas screenshot them and sent them to me. Even old, Liannis filed one, saying he deserved as much percentage of the shares as my grandfather's other children because he was his illegitimate son."

"Mr. Liannis, you sneaky, loveable, old bastard," Kareena exclaimed, clapping her hands together and laughing, before snorting.

Zayn started laughing, too. The entire situation was so bizarre, he couldn't make it up. He thought it was all a joke until Silas called him and screamed at him, asking what his new game was. He knew then that Penelope must have rallied the locals. This was her way of making it up to him, especially when he found out who the lawyer was (a big-shot attorney who happened to be her new father-in-law). Somehow, the day she left for her honeymoon, she'd contacted many of the island folk, explaining the dire situation. No one had questioned what they should do, never blinked an eye when she said her new father-in-law would draw up the papers. They only needed to make a call to him at his hotel in Athens and find a way to sign the documents. It was shady as shit in more ways than one, but it bought him more time.

"And because so many claims came in, the attorney's office has had to do the proper paperwork to file motions. It's quite funny. Some have already been thrown out, and eventually they all will get tossed. But for the next few days, they'll be busy. Hopefully, they can get a good laugh out of it, too. I think there's one that claims a percentage of the olive oil mill proceeds because—let me see if I remember this correctly—the farmers who provide the grains and feed to the animals on the estate, claim they own the manure from those same animals. And because the manure fertilizes the olive grove every spring, technically, a portion of the olives and oil produced is theirs. Maybe they're correct but it's really all so convoluted. It'll take weeks to clear up."

Kareena continued laughing, deep belly laughs.

She wiped her eyes from tears that weren't of sadness anymore. "So what does this mean for you? How do we go back —" She huffed and started again. "The attorneys know our engagement was fake. Can they prove otherwise?"

Her cheeks reddened deeper.

"We?" he asked softly, his chest filling with unbridled hope. "What are you saying, Kareena?"

"I was—well." She cleared her throat. "Zayn, I'm so sorry for what I said back at the villa. I'm so, so proud of you, and I respect you, and I was brash and scared, and stupid—"

It was all he needed. He needed to hear her say she'd been wrong and that she didn't mean all of those hurtful words.

He tugged at her wrists and pulled her to him, onto his lap.

"You could never be stupid," he said, pushing her thick hair behind her ears. He rubbed his thumb over her plump bottom lip as he continued. "Brash, yes. A little mean, and well, I was hurt, but you were also scared about your dad. But I can tell you this, you do *not* need a strong man to help you get through life, supporting you. You've been doing it all by yourself these past few years. Why can't you see that?"

"But my father is there for me when I need his support."

"What father isn't, unless they're complete bastards." His own father was extremely supportive. When he was younger, he was so supportive that it became annoying as he tried to get Zayn into the world of corporate mergers and acquisitions. The point was, he'd always been there when he'd needed him.

She fingered his beard, scratching him softly with her nails. "Yeah, but I seem to rely on him for every big decision I need to make."

"*Used to.* You used to. I didn't see him approving of our fake engagement, nor waving you off as we took off for Greece. You have bravery and independence in there; you just need to channel it more. It's like swimming—"

"Oh my God. No," she said, placing a firm hand on his chest.

"Fine. I'll leave the swimming analogies out for now."

"Thank you. It was you, though. You coming back into my life is what made me braver and more independent, and not give a crap what everyone thought. A part of me worries that I'll revert to my old ways and rely on you the same way I did with my father, or Arjun, before he died."

"Honestly, I thought I would see more of that in you when we started this whole thing. I really did think the old Kareena, the one who did everything her family wanted her to, would still be front and center. But you kept surprising me. You're the one who started this whole fake fiancé charade in the first place. Would Kareena 1.0 be gutsy enough to do that?"

She laughed softly, shaking her head.

"You were already on your way to who you are right now, today."

"Kareena 2.0?" She asked, fingering his gold chain.

"Yeah. You're sexier, sassier, and *very* demanding. As I recall, *you* commanded me to use my chef's knife on you. To run it over your tits, down your belly, and to graze your pussy with it. I've never had the sheen of a woman's essence on my knife before. Please tell me that was only for my pleasure." Damn, the memory was sending blood rushing to his crotch, and he shifted under the weight of her.

"ZAYN!" she cried, mortified, her entire face and neck hot. She looked around, making sure no one was eavesdropping. She threw her hand over his mouth for good measure.

He pulled her hand from his mouth and held it, examining his family's ring, rubbing his thumb over it, making her warmer.

"Let me give this back to you." She began to pull it off, but he stopped her.

"Why?" he asked.

"You said you needed it for something important."

"Well, I don't anymore." Then he looked like he was thinking about something before he followed up with, "I actually do, but you're wearing it and you're the something, or rather, someone important."

His eyes gleamed brightly, his thick lips curved quirkily. He was so handsome, and she couldn't believe she was hearing what she thought he was saying. He still wanted her. His smile broadened as she realized he was waiting for her to say something.

"What?" she asked, breathless with the way he gazed at her.

"Kareena, I want to be with you, and not just in a fake engagement—not even a real engagement, though that will have to be part of it. I want to make it official. I love you so very much. I don't think I ever stopped loving you, from when we were kids. That time was brutal. We were so young. But it's so much better now. We can make our own dreams together. I truly feel like half myself without you. You *are* my entire destiny."

She looked at him with shock, adrenaline filling her veins. Her bottom lip trembled, and he reached out to smooth it with his thumb again.

"What are you saying?" She asked softly, still unclear, wanting to make sure she understood him completely. "You want me officially because you have a little more time before the claims period ends?"

He huffed gruffly, shaking his head.

"No. I mean, yes, the claims period is technically extended for a few more weeks. But I didn't know about that before I came to ask you a very important question."

She nodded, and when she didn't say anything further, he said tenderly, "Kareena, my sweet karma." He gathered her hands into his large, warm ones. "Will you marry me?"

Her eyes darted around his face, his beautiful eyes, his rugged beard, his sensual lips. Was this real? Was Zayn asking if she would marry him? There could only ever be one answer when it came to them. But he continued speaking, as if he needed to still convince her.

"Tamannah would be taken care of. Don't worry. Aloo, too. I'd care for them like my own—I *do* care for them like they're mine."

She saw the honesty written across his face; the warmth of emotion he had saying her daughter's name.

"And I want to be completely upfront and honest with you." He nodded. "My grandfather had added another clause to my inheritance."

She fingered his shirt collar and the hint of curly hair exposed. "I really think he may have hated you," she said flatly. She wasn't trying to be mean, but she couldn't understand why his grandfather had done what he'd done.

"Hah! No one can really understand it. I have to believe it's because he wanted me to find someone with whom I could share my life." He paused. "Let me explain. The second clause was that after I was engaged, and the property was mine, if I was married within the year, I'd get enough funding to use as start-up capital. Now, I had no intention of going after that last part. I had no intention of marrying, and I had my own start-up in the bank."

"*Sinful in the Kitchen*," she said softly.

"Right. He's my cash flow right now. So ... again, to be clear—I'd be marrying you for you, for us, for the fact that we are meant for each other and have been connected since the first day we met. I can refuse that money if we decide to. I have enough of my own to start the restaurant."

"You want me to help you make that decision?" she asked in wonder. Everything was happening so quickly, and she blurted out, "This is a lot to ask, Zayn."

"No more than what we've already pretended at. If we can get through the stresses of that, couldn't we get through the trials and tribulations of actual marriage?"

She thought about this, nodding. "True. You speak a pretty speech, Mr. Stavros. Where did this all come from?"

"I've been thinking about it for a while," he said honestly. "Probably since that day in Athens, when we visited the Parthenon."

She gasped, understanding. That day had been a turning point. "I think I knew then that we were headed somewhere more tangible. It's always been you, Zayn." She finally said the thought aloud that had taken up so much of her mind since the moment she'd run into him weeks ago. It hadn't been clear to her then; she'd been more than confused, but it slowly showed itself as they spent more time together, becoming crystal clear. "I'll never regret everything that happened—how we had to break it off as teens, how I married someone else, and even how we had to fake this whole thing initially. Because all of those things led me back to you, in some strange, uncertain path." She sighed happily. "I love you so much, Zayn. I'm fortunate we got our second chance, that fate threw us together again. I want to be with you, too." She breathed in deeply and exhaled. "Yes, Zayn. I want to marry you." She grinned from ear to ear. The words sounded more than right when saying them out loud. "I never want to be apart from you again." She hugged him tightly. "I missed you, and I'm so thankful you came today." She whispered in his neck, still feeling the remnants of shame from the way she'd treated him. "And that you can forgive me." She breathed in his familiar scent deeply, completely content.

"Me too, Karma," he whispered back, a little shakily. And she was floored by his honesty. A less self-assured man would walk away from what she'd said, how she'd behaved. But he came back and confronted her, completely certain in 'them,' though he knew it might not be easy.

They were lucky that fate was a stubborn entity and had never given up on them.

His lips met hers in a tender kiss, sealing their promise to each other ... all over again. This time it was real—realer than either of them could've imagined when they first started their charade.

He licked her lips, tasting her, coaxing her, and she wanted to get lost in him, reciprocating as she tangled her hands into the thick hair at the nape of his neck. She pressed herself further into his chest, feeling his heart thudding strongly in tandem with hers as they sank into the deep couch.

Their future was about to begin, and their excitement had no bounds. She was his karma—and he was hers—reclaiming each other once and for all. Now they would finally make their dreams come true together.

THE END...

NEW YEAR'S EVE
naxos island, greece

EPILOGUE

উপসংহার

*T*he night sky was a deep shade of violet-blue, blanketed with tiny twinkling starbursts. Waves crashed loudly against the hulking rocks that jutted out from the beach. Zayn had always thought those same rocks that he climbed and explored as a kid resembled mysterious beached ocean animals at night.

He stood under the glow of one of the recently installed heat lamps on the restaurant's refurbished outdoor seating area. The warmth kept the winter chill at bay, as he'd predicted, and along with lamps already in place, he intended to add firepits on each end of the deck that ran the length of the building. That way, it would be even more inviting with lounge seating for people to gather and socialize. He had a feeling people wouldn't want to leave the coziness he was about to create out here for patrons.

On the other side of the floor-to-ceiling windows behind him, the restaurant, Indoi-Yavanas Restaurant and Bar (he'd gone with one of Kareena's name recommendations), was abuzz with activity, as tables were set with white linen and gleaming

491

cutlery. Candles and twinkle lights were being placed and hung from every available surface.

The wedding cake had just been delivered, the one he'd worked on with a local pastry chef to get just right. The smallish three-tier cake stood on a pedestal, the pale green pistachio buttercream glossy and smooth. Brightly colored edible flowers, pistachio shavings, and pomegranate seeds were arranged in a waterfall cascading over and down the layers. It was cardamom-flavored, soaked lightly in saffron syrup with a hint of rosewater underneath the frosting. It was decadent to say the least, but perfect for the occasion, and one of the desserts he planned to have on his restaurant menu, though more simplified.

Thankfully, all of the indoor cacophony was dulled by the symphony of the ocean's tides outside, and Zayn was glad for the moment to himself. In just a few minutes, his life would change for good, and he couldn't wait.

He dug his hands into the pockets of his khaki pants and looked up at the stars, a grin permanently drawn on his face as he marveled at the turn of events since Thanksgiving. Not only had Kareena become his real fiancée, and he hers, but after discussing it very briefly and coming to the same conclusion, they announced over dessert that evening to everyone around the Sharmas' dining room table that they would be tying the knot on New Year's Eve. It just seemed appropriate to them, entering a brand-new year as a brand-new married couple. Kareena's mother had nodded, only piling Zayn's dessert plate with more sweets and bringing them to him with a squeeze to one of his broad shoulders. Her father had nodded approvingly, commenting on what a good omen this signaled. Funnily enough, when Zayn had told his parents the good news (the following morning, as Greece's time zone was ahead), his parents were just as happy that the two had reconciled and made similar comments about good omens.

His mother was the one who suggested they get married on Naxos. When he'd floated the idea to Kareena, Tamannah, who'd been on the floor sorting through boxes of Christmas ornaments at the Sharmas' home the day after Thanksgiving, had jumped up and concurred with excitement.

She clapped her hands together and practically bounced on her toes as she exclaimed, "Yes! Mommy, please?"

It'd only taken one more plea, from both him and her daughter, and even Aloo—who had no idea why he was hopping around the living room with Tamannah and Zayn—for her to break her placidity. She jumped up in glee, grabbing their hands as she agreed.

Everyone was excited and on board with this plan. Kareena's father even said he would be up for travel if given clearance by his cardiologist. Zayn offered the Stavros jet for all of them to take, as it would be faster and more comfortable, also ensuring that a trusted family physician would be at the Athens airport waiting to give Sanjay a once-over upon arrival.

In the meantime, they had a lot of organizing and planning to do. Questions arose that needed to be carefully thought through, but wouldn't necessarily need answers right away. Kareena pulled out her laptop and began typing notes, such as where their home base would be as a family, and whether this would impact Tamannah. For her, it felt better to have her daughter finish her year at her current school in New York City, and thus Kareena would stay there for the duration, too. Zayn liked this idea, as well. He only wanted to give Kareena space to ensure the security of Tamannah's mental health, and this sounded like it would give the girl time to adjust to any ideas of moving across the globe, which Kareena wasn't opposed to.

Zayn would fly back and forth between Greece and New York until the restaurant's official opening in the Spring. He could afford it, with the additional inheritance money coming in for tying the knot within the year, as stated in his grandfather's will. Kareena had wholeheartedly encouraged him to cash in on that portion of his inheritance. After all of the hoops he'd had to jump through to get his legacy, it was only right since he'd met all of the requirements. Which meant that *Sinful in the Kitchen* was on permanent hiatus. He didn't need that cash flow anymore. Currently, Sinful was only between him and Kareena when they wanted kinkier eroticism, which had already happened a few times since they reconciled.

Zayn hadn't received any arguments from his cousin. Silas only asked that the official marriage license be presented to the attorneys for legality's sake, and everything would officially be turned over to him. Zayn had a feeling that Silas had backed off, having been inundated with the shipping business as CEO of Stavros Titans. He didn't have time to worry about it anymore.

It was around Christmas time when Kareena solidified what she wanted moving forward, and the goals she wanted them both to work toward. He had just arrived back in New York. The snow fell in fat flakes that left a soft powdery layer on everything, making Kareena's brownstone and her entire block, in fact, appear like a festive gingerbread-house neighborhood.

"I'm going back to my psychiatry practice," she'd said, as classic carols played softly over the sound system in the background.

She hung stockings over the mantel, the fire burning low in the hearth. The smell of evergreens tickled Zayn's nose from the real tree she'd said Tamannah insisted on having this year, and she'd caved because she couldn't say 'no' to this request from her daughter. They never got a real tree, and she wasn't sure they would have a chance if they left New York for good.

She hummed along to Frank Sinatra as he sang "White Christmas." Zayn was wrapping presents he'd purchased abroad for everyone at her dining room table—the designated gift-wrapping station that Tamannah had proudly organized for the season (including scissors and tape connected with cooking twine, which was his contribution so they wouldn't lose either one in the holiday hubbub).

He asked her to elaborate as she fiddled with the stockings, each a thick white wool, with initials embroidered in red on the front. There was one for her, Tamannah, a small one for Aloo, and one even for him, with his initials, ZRS, on the front, making him feel all of the festive feels.

"I'm going to keep a handful of my long-standing patients and continue treating them in person if I can, or ... in Greece, over telehealth and video conferencing, when that happens."

"When?" he asked, pausing to look up at her, hope budding in his chest.

"I think that's where we're definitely headed, Zayn, don't you?" She turned to face him, her hair up in a messy bun. She wore a funny green and red Christmas sweatshirt that said, 'Be nice to the psychiatrist, Santa is watching' printed across the front.

He nodded and said, "I'm listening."

She explained that she had wanted to leave her practice, but that when she mentioned this to some of her long-standing patients, she was met with disappointment, and even tears. She'd been with some of them for almost a decade when she first began her career. She couldn't leave them hanging. So, she'd keep them and continue working part-time with her practice, so long as these patients were amenable to telehealth.

In her other time, she would continue to work with her sister on what she now considered 'their' podcast, fully owning that she wanted to be part of it. She could easily do this from any location. She'd already floated the idea to her sister, who'd been thrilled.

While they were in Greece for their wedding, this would allow Tamannah to see if she liked living on Naxos. The plan was to get her used to the idea, though no one could force her to love it. Deep down, something told Zayn that the little girl would, and he couldn't wait to share with her the places he'd played as a kid, or the treasures he'd found in hidden tidal pools. He got excited thinking about introducing her to some of his second cousins, who were closer to her age, and the local kids as well.

"I'm so proud of you, Kareena," he'd said in awe. She was coming into this newer version of herself—one who was taking the reins on her life and wasn't holding back anymore.

"Thank you," she said, her eyes shining brightly from the twinkle lights around the tree, and her hair gleaming a thick, glossy blue-black. "I know it's taken me a while to get here—to get to the final version of Kareena 2.0, but she's here, and I rather like her."

He'd stood and crossed the living room to her, gathering her in his arms, inhaling her bright, floral muskiness, as her soft, warm body relaxed into his. "Well, I love her, and all versions of her. But I can't deny that Kareena 2.0 is my favorite, by far."

He'd kissed her then, sweetly, taking his time, roving over her plush lips with his. A loud giggle broke them apart, and they looked up to see Tamannah peering down at them from the second-floor landing, her hands gripping the railing.

"Tama, be careful," Kareena warned. Tamannah's grin had only spread wider as she sprang down the stairs, Aloo hot on her heels.

"What are we talking about?" she asked, inspecting the presents slyly on the table. Zayn chuckled. He'd already wrapped everything that was hers, and they lay nestled safely under the tree.

He looked to Kareena for what to reveal to the girl. She shook her head, and he knew automatically that they would bring Tamannah into the plan slowly.

"We're wondering what you'll call me when your mom and I are officially married," he'd said off the cuff.

She looked at him thoughtfully. "You'll officially be my stepdad," she said in wonder.

"I will. But understand, Tama, I never intend to replace your real father, or the memory of him."

She nodded. "What do people in Greece call their dads?"

"I call my father Papa."

"Papa," she said thoughtfully. "How about Papa-Z?" she asked, her excitement beginning to show as her cheeks spread into a grin.

"I like the sound of that. It rolls off the tongue," Kareena said encouragingly.

"I like it, too," he'd said. Aloo barked, agreeing with them all.

KAREENA WAS in the back office of the restaurant, getting ready for the big day. Was she nervous like she'd been the first time she got married? Not in the least. She felt calm, her nerves placid as she looked at herself in the full-length mirror that had been brought in for her.

The dove-grey satin dress she wore reminded her of the one she'd worn to their fake engagement party. The material glided over her body, pooling at her feet. The sleeves were long, made of delicate lace in the same color, covering her arms, her chest, and her back. She might be a little chilly out on the deck when they had their brief ceremony, but she had a feeling she wouldn't even feel it, knowing that she would officially be Zayn's wife for the rest of her life.

"Here you go, Missy," her sister said, coming up behind her in a velvet burgundy floor-length dress. She held a simple floral crown made up of fluffy, blush-colored garden roses and local grasses, with bright crimson winter florals studded in between. It was exquisite and perfect for the occasion.

"You made this, Reya?" she asked in astonishment as her sister placed it on her thick waves and began to push bobby pins in to hold it in place. Her sister nodded, and Kareena was again floored by the different talents her sister held.

"I worked for that bridal company for a short stint after college, remember? I learned all sorts of wedding hacks, and more about floral creations than I ever wanted to."

She stepped back, and Kareena surveyed the final look. It was perfect, all of it, from the simple, gorgeous dress, molding to her curves, cut as if it were made just for her, to the fairy-like crown.

"I made one for Princess Tam-Tam, too, but simpler. You know she's going to want one."

Kareena nodded, feeling her anticipation rising, and the love for everyone there to share their special day.

"You look like a queen, Kara—not that you need a man to make you a queen, but ... damn. You look amazing, and so happy." Reyana clapped her hands in front of her chest in admiration.

"Thank you, Reya. I feel like a queen, and 'happy' can't even come close to how I feel right now."

Everything had seemed to fall into place as soon as she apologized to Zayn at her parents' home over Thanksgiving. He'd sought her out, come to her, even after everything she'd done to him. In essence, she was so grateful that he couldn't ever quit her, because he made her braver in accepting that they belonged together, and that what they had was one in a million. She needed a swift kick in the rear-end to figure it out, of course. She'd almost lost him for a second time, but he'd persisted.

"So, have you decided about moving here eventually? Because I could totally get behind that. I'd be a regular around here." Her sister leaned on the edge of the wooden desk.

Kareena laughed. "I wouldn't expect anything less from you."

She explained that she and Zayn would most likely move there for good, but they both decided to let Tamannah get used to the idea of being on Naxos for a good length of time.

So far, to say her daughter was like a fish thrown back into the ocean would be an understatement. Tamannah immediately took to the slower way of life, the proximity to the ocean, nature, and even the local kids in town who were around her age. There were mornings when some of the children came in a group to collect her daughter for an exploration playdate. And

Tama happily shoveled her breakfast into her mouth, threw on her galoshes and heavy raincoat, put Aloo's leash on him, and both of them sped out the door with barely a goodbye to either Kareena or Zayn.

Kareena was relieved. These were all positive signs, considering her daughter would eventually be attending the primary public school in town with some of these kids. She'd have an aide in class to assist with her high-functioning characteristics should they arise and need support, and would also have a home tutor to help her adjust. Her therapy sessions would need to continue on Naxos as well, and Kareena was all over that, finding leads through her professional network who would be a good fit for her daughter and their new family structure. She wanted to keep Ms. Lindsey, Tama's current therapist, but knew from a professional perspective that children did better with therapy when it was in person versus video calls.

Everything was all laid out. Her sister had been right; she could choose her own adventure. She had the means from the settlement sitting in a rainy-day fund to cover Tamannah's expenses, and to still live comfortably and contribute to her new situation.

In terms of her brownstone in New York, she wouldn't sell. It would be a place for them to go and stay while they were visiting the city and seeing family and friends in Connecticut. In the meantime, she was allowing Reyana to rent it for a very discounted price in exchange for taking care of the property. Reyana would take up residence on the garden floor, where there was a large bedroom and full bathroom to go with it. It was a perfect arrangement.

"Has Zayn started his therapy yet?" Reyana asked.

Kareena had been serious about helping Zayn with his

substance abuse problem, though she'd still only managed to learn very little swimming. Zayn would hold her to it when the weather turned warmer. She had absolutely no doubt about it, and he'd said as much.

"He's going to start in the new year. I'm helping him find a therapist who meets his needs and whose personality meshes. It's hard. He's so stubborn. He refuses to do group therapy."

"Well, maybe he's just really private."

Kareena nodded in agreement. "He is. I think he may need Cognitive Behavioral Therapy—you know, something to rewire his brain's initial impulse to reach for pills when he's stressed. But honestly, Reya, he hasn't shown any signs of wanting to reach for them. I know we're not together continuously, but he seems more relaxed, less wound up."

Her sister stood up, coming up behind her to straighten the crown on her head. "Hm, I wonder why that is," she said, with a gleam in her eye.

Just then, Tamannah burst into the room. She wore a burgundy velvet dress similar to Reya with a grey satin sash tied around her waist, and a matching little grey cropped jacket. The crown her aunt had made for her sat askew over her poufy hair.

"Mommy!" she exclaimed. "It's time—it's almost the new year!"

"Tam-Tam, let me fix this for you," her sister said, crouching down to fix Tamannah's crown.

"Aloo tried to eat it. I scolded him. I said, 'Bad, bad, Aloo,' but he only licked my face and tried to grab it again."

"Hmm, little mister is being a turd today, huh? No worries, I'll keep him on a tight leash during the ceremony." She stood up and turned to Kareena. "Are you ready, *Appa*?"

"More than ever. Let's do this!" Kareena said, her nerves—

good ones—making her heart bubble. She hugged her daughter tightly, and they shared a moment of encouragement. It was finally upon them: the time to go from it just being the two of them to a family of three.

She picked up the pretty bouquet with blush pink garden roses, white puffy peonies, and bright local blooms that still abounded along the countryside even in the chilly, 50-degree winter weather on Naxos.

When she came to the entryway of the partially finished and refurbished restaurant, her breath caught. The place was lit up with twinkle lights strung over the large potted ferns and threaded through the indoor wooden pergola overhead. It was romantic and magical, with all of the glass votives bouncing light everywhere. But her heart fluttered and almost stopped when she caught sight of Zayn standing outside with the officiant, beneath a heat lamp.

He wore a dark blue blazer over crisp khakis, and a white button-down underneath with a crimson tie that matched some of the bright local blooms in her bouquet. His boutonniere was a fluffy white peony, and in his simplicity, he looked elegant and manly, and a spark of complete ownership lit up her body in an all-encompassing love.

She followed her sister, who had Aloo on a tight leash, and then her daughter through the restaurant to the deck, decorated in simple florals and ivy, and more twinkle lights.

She saw chairs set up on one side, and her parents were there, as were Zayn's parents. Also seated were her best friend Sheila, Zayn's best friend Aariv, and his new fiancée.

It had been an uncomfortable conversation with Zayn when they discussed her being matched to Aariv last year. She'd completely forgotten about it with everything going on in her life since then. When Zayn curiously asked her about it, she sensed an anxiety in him, perhaps even a spark of jealousy. She'd told him it was at a time when she was completely out of it and numb. She'd have met any burp off the street if they were presented to her.

He'd chuckled, and she could tell he felt a little foolish. He ran a hand through his hair and said, "Yeah. I know. I'm sorry." Then he chuckled again.

"What?"

"I'm just imagining Aariv being called a burp off the street to his face."

They'd both had a good chuckle after that, but all was smoothed out now. Kareena had even spent time with Aariv and his fiancée, and even his cousin Mariam, over Christmas.

She also saw Penelope and Brutus sitting next to Sheila. Penelope waved spastically at her and mouthed, "You look amazing."

She smiled as tears sprang unbidden to her eyes. She was so happy to see her best friends and family there to share her and Zayn's special day.

When she stepped outside into the chilly night, the sound of the waves crashed as one of her and Zayn's favorite songs came on the sound system (a reggae ballad about love being the religion to live life by), and she stood corrected. She felt warm and tingly all over under Zayn's bright cinnamon gaze. The emotion in his eyes and on his handsome face took her breath away.

She dashed away her tears, wondering why she was so emotional all the time.

Zayn smiled encouragingly and mouthed, 'I love my Karma.'

When she was standing in front of him, he pulled her into an embrace and kissed her warmly, headily, though they hadn't exchanged vows yet. The audience hooted and whistled, and she distinctly heard Tamannah reprimand, "Papa-Z can't help himself. He always needs to kiss Mommy." She could practically see her daughter's eye roll and the shaking of her head.

When he released her, her cheeks were warmer, and she felt like she was floating on a cloud of love and security.

Somehow, they made it through their short vows. Tamannah had their rings and proudly handed them over at the right moment. As soon as the officiant announced them as man and wife, Zayn kissed her passionately again, murmuring that it was officially New Year's and he felt more than honored to be kissing his real wife on this special eve.

Her insides lit up as fireworks whistled into the sky, illuminating the night, the ocean below, and the guests' joyful faces in a myriad of sparkles. She felt Zayn's solid heart thudding against her breast, in tandem with hers. Around them, cheers, and congratulations as well as '*Opa's*' abounded, as did well-wishes for a happy and healthy new year. It was perfect, and as Kareena stared up into Zayn's dancing cinnamon gaze, she brimmed with anticipation to begin her life with the one man who'd always been her destiny, claiming their karma for good.

THE END

ACKNOWLEDGMENTS

ধন্যবাদ –
Dhanyabad –
Thank you

Thank you so much for reading Reclaiming Karma. If you loved it, please leave a review on Amazon and/or Goodreads. Indie authors like myself appreciate it, and appreciate readers like you!

If you would like to read His Karma, the high school romance novella that started it all for Kareena and Zayn, email me! Happy share to my readers before I get it up to sell on the ZON. (Limited time offer!).

I cannot tell you how hard this one was to write (goodness I think I said that about my last one, too). There are a lot elements to each character in Reclaiming Karma that I wanted to get right. But also, the state of what we are living in right now, today, has mentally stumped me from my creative juices (IYKYK). I hope I did Kareena and Zayn justice.

I want to thank my readers for being patient with me. I moved this release out three times and you still showed enthusiasm and trusted me to tell this story. My gift to you is the s*x scene with a chef's knife.

I want to thank my editor, Jess, for being patient with me, and for being my cheerleader and therapist through all of this.

I want to thank my street team (Paige, et al), PA (Cassie), and other promo teams, for holding my hand through pushing the release date out so many times. Your support means the world.

Lastly, I must thank my family for their patience and for letting me sit in front of my computer at the oddest hours while I toiled away at this one. And to those who took calls late at night to help me get this story right (the life of an indie author is far from normal—you are correct about that), I appreciate you.

Stay tuned for more interracial romances coming soon (I think you know who my next one is about—she's the complete opposite of her big sister, and there might be a love triangle in store for her!).

XOXO,
Khushi

ABOUT THE AUTHOR

I love romance, travel, exploring the South Asian identity, and personal transformation. As a South Asian American woman, I write about what I know, having grown up in the US and living coast to coast. When I'm not toiling away on my computer writing about love and self-discovery, I'm teaching crafting classes, hanging with my guys, and playing with my pup.

WANT TO STAY IN TOUCH?

Visit Kushi T. Saha at …
https://www.ktsromance.com/

Email:
ktsromance@gmail.com

Monthly newsletter sign-up: https://subscribepage.io/PG9p3a

https://www.facebook.com/KhushiT.S
https://www.instagram.com/ktsromanceauthor
Khushi T. Saha (Author of Desire's Unravelling) | Goodreads
Khushi T. Saha Books - BookBub
Amazon.com: Khushi T. Saha: books, biography, latest update